D0394628

The
FRAGILE
ORDINARY

Books by Samantha Young
available from Harlequin TEEN

The Impossible Vastness of Us
The Fragile Ordinary

THE FRAGILE ORDINARY

SAMANTHA YOUNG

HARLEQUIN®TEEN

ISBN-13: 978-1-335-01674-4

The Fragile Ordinary

www.HarlequinTEEN.com

Printed in U.S.A.

To the bestest friends a girl could ask for.

Here's to over twenty years of glorious friendship, and many more to come.

1

Edinburgh, Scotland

I am Comet Caldwell.

And I sort of, kind of, absolutely hate my name.

People expect something extraordinary of a girl called Comet. Someone effortlessly cool and magnetic. Someone who lights up a room and draws attention the way a comet does when it blazes light and fire across the sky.

But a comet, when you break it down, is the opposite.

It's an icy body that releases gas and dust.

Comets are basically great big dirty snowballs. Or, as some scientists have taken to calling them, snowy dirtballs.

Yup. A snowy dirtball. That makes more sense.

I was not a blaze of light and fire across the sky. I was just your average sixteen-year-old high school girl. An average sixteen-year-old who was spending the last day of summer uploading her latest attempt at poetry to her anonymous blog. The one with the comments turned off so I wouldn't be subjected to public opinion and ridicule. "The Day We Caught the Train" by Ocean Colour Scene blared out of my laptop as I worked. I had a thing for nineties and early noughties indie music.

My phone vibrated. I ignored it, making sure the typesetting on my latest post was just right. Because that's what I really cared about. The typesetting. Not the poem. Or that people would stumble across my blog and scorn the words torn from my beating heart.

The buzzing started up again and I sighed in irritation.

Vicki Calling.

As one of my two best friends, Vicki didn't deserve to be ignored. I put my music on mute and picked up. "I hope you know you're interrupting Liam and I, but keep it on the down low. Miley doesn't know about our secret love."

Vicki gave a huff of laughter. "Babe, I'll take it to the grave."

"So what's up?"

"What's up is Steph and I have been standing outside your house for the last ten minutes, ringing your doorbell. We can hear the music you dug out of a time capsule and Kyle has peered out the window at us and shooed us away twice."

Kyle was my dad. Although I thought of him as Dad in my head, I never actually called him Dad. My parents had taught me to call them Carrie and Kyle from the moment I could make vowel sounds.

Of course my dad had waved my friends away. Because answering the door for people who weren't there to see *him* would be too much like hard work.

I hopped off my bed, hurried out of my room and down the hall to the front door. As I swung it open, I was blasted by the familiar scent of the salty sea beyond our garden gate along with a rush of cool wind. I hung up my phone.

Vicki eyed my outfit carefully and then decided. "Nice."

To say I had a quirky taste in fashion was putting it mildly. I was currently wearing a white blouse with a Peter Pan collar underneath a preppy lilac cardigan. Very 1950s. I'd matched it with a turquoise multilayered silk petticoat, and a pair of Irregular Choice Victorian ankle boots. They were lilac and instead of laces they were adorned with turquoise satin ribbons tied into large bows.

Steph stared at Vicki as if to say, *Are you serious?* and then she gave me a pained smile. "Dude, surely Carrie notices you in *that* outfit?"

I chose not to be insulted.

Steph was petite with an enviable bra size and a butt that actually filled out her River Island jeans. She wore her long honey-blond hair in carefully arranged loose curls, and her makeup was always perfect. Fashion-wise she mostly wore on-trend clothes from the more expensive stores in the shopping center but dipped into high-end designer when her lawyer dad felt like spoiling her.

Right now she was wearing skinny jeans with purposely placed rips in them, knee-high brown leather boots with a low heel and a Ralph Lauren bomber jacket.

Unlike Steph, Vicki, the wannabe fashion designer, appreciated my attempt to be different. Although to be fair it wasn't really an attempt on my part. Or even an attempt to get Carrie to notice me—I didn't think it was anyway. I just wore whatever jumped out at me from my wardrobe that day.

Plus, 195 days out of the year, I had to wear a school uniform. The days when I didn't, you bet your ass I was going to have fun with my outfits.

Wearing an oversize thin cream sweater with an angled

hem, paired with bright green leggings with skulls on them, Vicki was more adventurous, like me. But she was naturally cool. This was a girl who could pull off the name Comet. She wore loosely laced black leather biker boots, large gold hoops in her ears and a bright green suede crossover body purse. Her tawny skin was flawless, so Vicki didn't wear as much makeup as Steph, whose pale white skin tended to blemish. At that moment, like usual, Vicki was wearing only a few coats of mascara on the thick lashes of her hazel eyes, and a touch of gloss on her full lips. Her dark brown afro danced above her shoulders in the wind as she turned to raise an eyebrow at Steph.

"What?" Steph shrugged.

"Filter," Vicki reminded her.

"It's fine." I waved off Steph's comment. We all knew Carrie wouldn't notice me if I ran through the house with my petticoat on fire.

"We didn't come here to pass judgment on your *cool as shit* outfit," Vicki emphasized for Steph's benefit, but our friend just rolled her eyes. "It's the last day of summer, Comet. We're going to a party. *You're* coming with us."

"A party?" I asked. The thought of going to a party to hang out with a bunch of our classmates who would either ignore me or make fun of me, when I could finish posting on my blog, then curl up with the book I was in the middle of reading, made me want to slam the door in their faces and pretend I'd never answered my phone in the first place.

As if she saw the thought on my face, Steph shook her head. "Uh. No. Dude, you have to come to the party."

"Steph, stop saying *dude*. You aren't American. And this isn't the 1990s." Although I wondered if I wouldn't have been better off as a sixteen-year-old in the 1990s. There was the music, of course. Oasis, hello! Need I go on? And then of course there was the lack of social media. I think there might have been instant chat back then. But if instant chat was a tiny school playground, social media was a city made up entirely of school playgrounds. There was plenty of laughter, games and messing around…but there was also that dark corner where the quiet kid got pushed around by the bully.

"Speaking of American—that's why you need to come to the party. Cute American boy is going to be there."

"And who's that when he's at home?"

"We so need to plug you in," Steph tutted as she tapped her phone screen, alluding to the fact that I avoided most social media platforms. After a few slides of her finger over the screen she held it up to me.

It was a blurry photo of some girl with her arm around some guy.

"What am I looking at?"

"Cute American boy," Steph replied in her *duh* voice.

I huffed, "You can tell he's cute from that picture?"

"Uh no. You miss everything. Everyone who has met him is talking about how cute he is on WhatsApp. When are you going to download it?"

A niggle of worry pierced at me but I just shrugged. "I'll get around to it."

"You say that all the time."

The truth was I didn't want to download WhatsApp and join our class group. The thought of my phone binging every second with a notification made my toes curl in my shoes with irritation. And yes. I was aware I was an anomaly among my kind.

"Anyway," Vicki said, taking pity on me. "You're coming, right?"

I really, really just wanted to get back to my book. The heroine had a crush on this boy at this new boarding school she'd been sent to, and I was at this part where it looked like he might like her back. "Whose party is it?"

My friends shared a look.

"Well?"

Steph sighed dramatically. "It's Heather McAlister's...but what she did was so long ago, Comet. You really need to get over it."

"Her words." Vicki pointed to Steph. "Not mine."

Hurt pierced me. While Heather no longer bothered me, having made the decision sometime ago to pretend I didn't exist, there was a time when she was my mortal enemy. She'd taken a dislike to me in our first year at high school for whatever reason and had tortured me for a year. Hid my uniform after P.E. class so I had no choice but to finish the rest of the school day in my gym clothes. Told Stevie Macdonald that I had a crush on him, prompting him to come up to me in the hall to let me down. He told me he was flattered but I wasn't really his type.

What he really meant was I was a geek and he was already having sex with girls older than he was.

Not that I'd had a crush on Stevie.

And let's not forget the time the teacher asked us in English what our favorite book was and Heather said, in front of everyone, that my favorite book must be *Matilda* because I could relate to having parents who hated me.

I'd suspected at the time that Steph had let something slip about my relationship with my parents when she'd attended

Heather's thirteenth birthday sleepover. Vicki, like a true friend, had turned down the invitation, but Steph had said she thought that would be rude.

She didn't think it would be rude. She was just afraid of not being popular.

I was mad at her but I hadn't said anything. Vicki said enough for the both of us, Steph stopped talking to us for a few weeks and then after a while we were all friends again. Like nothing had happened.

But Steph's attitude now brought it all flooding back. "If she'd called you STD Steph to your face and behind your back for an entire year, would you have forgiven her by now?"

My friend's cornflower blue eyes widened. "Did she call me that?"

"Probably," Vicki muttered.

"I'm making a point. The girl chanted 'Comet, Comet, she makes me want to vomit' at me every day for weeks."

Steph exhaled. "Look, Com, I didn't mean to be insensitive. I know she was mean to you. But she hasn't bothered you in years. Come to the party."

If it was Heather's party, that meant the guests would be every kid at our school who had no idea who I was. Meaning the ones who were involved in extracurricular stuff like… sports. Their social adeptness, their ability to walk into a room and just start chatting and laughing with complete strangers, was foreign to me. I was socially awkward and pretty certain no one was interested in hearing anything I had to say anyway.

Why would I put myself in an uncomfortable position, go to a party that would make me insecure and miserable, when I could be reading a book that made me feel giddy with anticipation?

"I can't." I shrugged, stepping back into my hallway. "I have to have a shower and get stuff ready for school tomorrow."

Vicki frowned at me while Steph threw up her hands. "What was the point?"

I flinched but shrugged, trying to appear as apologetic as possible.

"C'mon." Steph grabbed Vicki's hand. "It's freezing standing here. Let's go."

Vicki gave me a half-hearted wave and one last look I couldn't decipher, but hoped wasn't irritation. I watched my friends stride off down my garden path. They stepped outside, closed the gate and walked away along the esplanade.

The Studio, our house, sat right on Portobello Beach. Which meant I just had to walk out of my garden and across the esplanade, and I stepped right onto the beach. My bedroom, a guest bedroom, the kitchen, sitting room and a bathroom were situated on the ground floor of the white-painted brick midcentury building we called home. Upstairs, taking full advantage of the sea views, was Carrie's art studio and my dad's office. My mother was famous among the art crowd as a successful and generously compensated mixed media artist. My dad was a writer. He'd won a few literary awards for his second novel, *The Street*, a commercially successful book that had even been made into a British television mini-drama. The money from that novel paid for our house in this sought-after location. Although he did well with his books, my dad had never achieved the same heights with his subsequent novels, and I think he kind of enjoyed playing the part of the frustrated artist.

Most people thought it must be pretty cool to have semi-famous artist parents.

It wasn't.

At least not my parents.

The most thought my parents have ever given me was in choosing my name. For two weeks I was Baby Caldwell while they struggled to find something unique they could agree upon. Then they gave me a name I couldn't possibly live up to and proceeded to treat me with offhand kindness, disinterest and sometimes outright negligence. I was an accident, and not a happy one. My parents were too much in love with their art and each other to have any love left to spare for me.

That's why my friends were important to me. But so was self-preservation.

I shut the front door and locked it, then leaned back against it as a sudden headache flared behind my eyes. This wasn't the first time I'd refused to hang out with Vicki and Steph.

When we were kids we were all quiet, geeky, book-types, but when we got to high school they started to change. Steph decided she wanted to be an actress and even won a part in a local advert for a soft drink company. She came out of her shell, landing parts in the school plays, and as the years turned her from an average blonde girl into a stunning teenager, she got so much attention from boys that she became boy-crazy.

Vicki seemed happy to spread her wings, too, socially. And where Steph's bubbly loudness got her what she wanted, Vicki's laid-back, effortless cool made people flit to her. She was the kind of girl everyone wanted to be friends with. She was my BFF, and seeing her friendship circle grow was hard for me.

I would admit to being a little jealous.

Now I was worried, as well.

If I kept refusing to hang out with them if it involved hanging with other people, would Vicki and Steph one day give up on me?

The thought caused angry butterflies to take flight in my stomach and tears to prick my eyes. Some days I wished I could be more like my friends. But if it meant pretending to be something I wasn't, exhausting myself trying to please people who didn't really care about getting to know the real me, then I chose lonerhood. I chose books.

I slammed into my bedroom, not caring if the noise jerked my dad out of whatever sentence he was taking a painstaking amount of time over, and launched myself onto my bed. Lying flat on my stomach, I stared across my large bedroom at the shelves that lined two walls. Books, books and more books. Just the sight of all the shapes and sizes, all the colors, all the textures, stretching up on bookshelves that were fitted to the ceiling, made me content. No matter what was happening in my life, in my room, I had over eight hundred worlds to disappear into, and over a thousand others on the e-reader on my nightstand. Worlds that were better than this one. Worlds where there were people I understood, and who if they knew me would understand me. Worlds where the boys weren't like the boys in this one. They actually *cared*. They were brave and loyal and swoonworthy. They didn't burp your name in your ear as they passed you in the hall or bump into you a million times a day because they "didn't see you standing there."

I stretched across the bed, picked up the paperback I was reading and flipped it open.

No way was some cruddy party hosted by Heather Mc-Bitcherson better than the world I was holding in my hands.

2

If only you studied me
As hard as you study that canvas
It would set me free.
Instead bit by bit I vanish.
—CC

My dad wandered into the kitchen as I stood at the counter eating a bowl of cereal. As he strolled toward the coffee machine with his hair in disarray and his pajamas crumpled, he stared at me curiously.

He reached for a mug in the cupboard above the coffee machine. "You're in uniform."

I looked down at myself in misery. I loved clothes. I loved color and shape and throwing things together that other people might not think worked but that felt fun and adventurous to me.

I did not like the black blazer I was wearing over a scratchy white shirt, or the black pleated skirt with its frumpy knee-length hemline. I'd tucked in the waist, lifting the hem to just above my knees, so it didn't look as ridiculous. The blazer had gold piping and a gold crest over the left breast pocket. Matching it was the black tie with the small gold crest beneath its knot. My only concession to fun was my black Irregular Choice shoes. They had a midheel, closed just below my ankle and laced up. The fun was in the bright gold stars that made up the eyelets for the laces.

"When did you start back at school?" Dad turned to me once his coffee was brewing. He crossed his arms, then one ankle over the other, and peered at me over the top of his glasses.

"Today."

"Yeah, I didn't think I'd seen you in uniform before now. Jesus, that was a quick summer, eh?" He turned back to his coffee and scratched his neck. "Did you do anything fun with your friends?" I barely made the question out through his giant yawn.

"Yeah, I suppose."

"Aye?" He gave me a quick smile. "Good." Grabbing his coffee, he moved past me and patted me on the head. "When did you get so tall?" he asked as he stopped to pour himself out some cereal.

I held in an exasperated sigh. "I've been the same height for the last year."

"Really?" Dad seemed confused. "Are you sure?"

"Pretty sure." I was one of the tallest girls in my class.

"Well, you don't get that height from Carrie." He grinned.

I stared at my dad. All six foot three of him. My mum was five foot three. At five foot nine I certainly hadn't gotten my height from her. Or anything really. In fact, if I didn't already know my parents hadn't meant to have a child at all, I'd have suspected I was adopted.

To prove my point, Carrie shuffled into the kitchen, her lids lowered over her eyes so far that they were almost shut. Paint streaked one of her cheeks and her hair. While she was petite, compact, with olive skin, and had light brown hair and dark brown eyes, I was tall, slender, ivory-skinned with pale blond hair and light blue eyes. I'd inherited my dad's eyes, but otherwise we looked nothing alike. He was nowhere near as pale as I was and had dark brown hair. Apparently, I'd skipped back a generation, taking after my Swedish paternal grandmother in looks.

Carrie aimed for Dad, and he had just enough forethought to dump his bowl out of the way before she collapsed against his chest. "How long have I been in there?" she mumbled.

Dad chuckled and wrapped an arm around her, kissing her on the top of the head.

Painful envy stabbed my chest at the display of affection and I looked away so I didn't have to see it.

"A few days, love."

"Really?"

I sometimes wondered if Carrie really did get so lost in the art she was creating that the days just slipped away from her. Or if she only pretended to lose days because she thought it made her sound even more artistic. Dad was the only one of us allowed in her studio, and he'd creep in quietly to leave her food and beverages throughout the day.

"Wow." Carrie pulled out of his arms and went straight for the coffee machine. She didn't even look at me. "Diana better bloody love it, then. It's been a while since I did the hermit thing."

"Are you happy with it?" Dad asked.

Carrie gave him a sleepy grin over her shoulder. "You know I'm never a hundred percent happy with it. But it'll do."

Meaning she thought it was bloody fantastic. Her best work ever!

I grabbed up my book bag. "I better get to school."

"Oh, Comet." Carrie flicked a look at me as if she'd just realized I was there. "How is school going?"

The question was asked so she'd feel like she was attempting to care about her child's life. "It's the first day of term."

She shot an amused *oops* look at Dad. "Really?"

Dad nodded. "Comet's starting fifth year. Can you believe it?"

If it wasn't already apparent, Dad was the more involved parent of the two. If you could call his vague interest in my life involved.

"Fifth year?" She yawned. "What age is that again?"

In that moment I wanted to run upstairs to her studio, grab a paintbrush, and smear *I'M SIXTEEN, DIPSHIT!* all over her newly finished painting.

"It's sixteen, love," Dad said gently.

"No." Carrie frowned at me. "Did you have a sweet sixteenth?"

Wow. Okay. She was in fine form this morning. "Yeah." I grabbed my house keys and headed for the exit. "I spent it with a biker called Vicious and we made sweet sixteenth love all night."

I heard my dad's laughter and Carrie's confused murmurings as I wandered down the narrow hall to the front door. Outside, the cool morning breeze from the sea blew strands of hair free from my ponytail and I sauntered out of the garden gate onto the esplanade.

"Not saying hello this morning, Comet?" a familiar voice called out.

I stopped and looked over my shoulder into our neighbor's garden. Only a shallow wall separated our paved, no-fuss outside space from Mrs. Cruickshank's well-tended front garden with its rows of flowerbeds and tiny stretch of lawn.

Mrs. Cruickshank was on her knees by one of her flowerbeds, wearing her usual uniform of baggy jeans, holey knitted sweater and garden gloves. Her long gray hair was twisted up on top of her head in an old-fashioned bun that I was certain wasn't even in fashion when she was my age an unknown number of years ago. Thick, bright turquoise glasses were perched on her nose as she peered at me in amusement.

"Lost in your thoughts again, Comet?"

"Sorry, Mrs. Cruickshank. First day of school. I'm daydreaming," I gave her an apologetic smile.

"First day, eh? Ready for it? Those imbeciles you call parents feed you properly so you have brain energy for the classroom?" she asked, frowning.

I stifled a smile. Not much got past Mrs. Cruickshank. While she would speak to me all day if I had the time, she barely even managed a smile for Kyle and Carrie. Not that they really noticed.

Instead of answering her question, I deflected, "How are the daylilies coming along?" Over the years, despite my disinterest in gardening, I'd learned much from my neighbor about the plants that could survive in a coastal garden. Mrs. Cruickshank had been having trouble with her pink-and-yellow-gold daylilies the last we spoke. It puzzled her, because it was apparently a plant that thrived in most places, and she'd never had problems with them before.

"I replanted them. These new ones are coming along fine. But it's my lantanas that are looking well, don't you think?" She nodded to the bright orange, cheery flowers at the bottom of the garden with a smile akin to that of a proud parent.

"They look wonderful, Mrs. Cruickshank," I spoke truthfully.

She turned that smile on me. "Have a cracking day at school, Comet. I'm baking today. Be sure to nip around before tea and I'll give you some of whatever I cook up. Just for you, mind."

This time I did smile. My neighbor was a fantastic baker and generous, too. However, she wasn't that sold on me sharing her treats with my dad and Carrie. I reckoned it was to do with the fact that Mrs. Cruickshank and her husband hadn't been able to have children. She'd told me about it a few years ago, and it was the only time I'd seen her get emotional.

"Thanks." I waved. "See you later." I walked away, down the esplanade.

The beach always calmed me. The best thing my dad ever did was buy this house. Between the beach and my bedroom, I had a sanctuary here. I could spend longs hour on the sand, watching people pass by as I wrote my poetry. Houses, flats, bed-and-breakfasts, the Swim Centre, the Espy—a pub and my favorite place to get breakfast—sat along the sand-covered concrete esplanade.

I left early for school so I could stroll along it and enjoy the pleasant breeze of a mid-August morning. The sun was low in the sky, casting light over the sea so that it sparkled and danced as I walked along beside it in companionable silence. The salt air made me feel more at home than my own mother did.

What was new though, right?

There was no point in getting upset about it, because in five months I'd be seventeen, which meant in less than two years I'd leave for a university an ocean away. Upon which I had no intention of ever returning to my parents' home.

It was a twenty-minute walk to school, and the closer I got to it, the more I fell into step with pupils wearing the same uniform. It was here I became truly anonymous, the bright glitter of gold from my shoes the only spot of difference between me and the girls in front of me.

Suddenly I was at the school gates, staring beyond them at Blair Lochrie High School. It was built a year before my first year at the school, and there were strict rules and regulations about litter and maintenance to keep it looking its best. It was a modern building, all white and gray and glass.

As I stepped inside, I couldn't wait for the day I'd step out of it for the last time.

"I'm studying at yours after school," Vicki said without preamble as she sat down beside me in Spanish, our first class of the day.

"You are?"

She nodded vehemently, the tight corkscrews of hair several inches above her forehead swaying with the movement. "Otherwise, I'll get locked into watching Steph audition for the school show."

"They're auditioning already?" I frowned. "It's the first day back at school."

"Surprise auditions. They want raw performances or something. They're doing *Chicago* this year."

"Isn't some of that a little…I don't know…adult?"

She shrugged.

"So why are you studying with me and not giving Steph moral support?"

Vicki rolled her hazel eyes. "Babe, you know I love her, but after last night I need a little break."

This was not unusual for either of us. We did love Steph. Truly. But sometimes when she got lost in her own little world—which was a nice way of saying she became incredibly self-absorbed—it was hard to stay patient with her. The best thing to do, we'd discovered, was to discreetly take a break from her. "What happened at the party?"

Vicki glanced around to make sure no one was listening and then leaned into me. "The guy, the American guy, he wasn't into her. He was already snogging Heather when we got there. So Steph went after Scott Lister."

My eyes grew round. "Heather's ex-boyfriend."

"Ugh, aye," Vicki huffed. "Not only did she dump my ass the second we got to that party, but she got into a huge fight with Heather, and then blamed me for not stopping her snogging the face off Lister."

"I don't get it. Why was Heather mad at Steph for kissing Scott if she was kissing the new guy?"

"This is Heather we're talking about. Who knows what's going on in that twisted mind?"

"And Steph took the whole thing out on you?"

"Yup. She apologized, but I'm still kind of pissed off about it. Totally ruined the last night of summer." She nudged me with her elbow and grinned. "I bet you had a better night with whatever book you were reading."

I blushed. My friend knew me so well. Most of the time, like now, it felt as if Vicki just accepted who I was, but there were days that she seemed a little distant and annoyed, like last night, and I worried my hermit-like qualities irritated her.

"Hola, quinto año! Quién esta listo para comenzar español avan-

zado?" Our teacher Señora Cooper strolled into the room. She shot Vicki a smile my friend easily returned. Because Vicki's dad was a maths teacher at our school, a lot of the other teachers knew Vicki really well and liked her.

Although, I couldn't think of anyone who didn't like Vicki. Maybe Heather. But I didn't think Heather truly liked any other girl. They were either competition or beneath her notice. Nothing in between.

Señora Cooper's classroom door opened again, and my breath caught in my throat at the sight of the boy striding through it.

What the ever loving…

It was like he'd walked straight out of the pages of the book I had been reading last night!

Tall—very tall—with an athletic physique, the boy looked around the classroom and then at the teacher. "Spanish, right?"

I froze at his American accent.

This was cute American boy?

Okay.

Cute was entirely the wrong descriptor.

He had close-cropped dark blond hair, and his tan skin suggested he'd spent his life somewhere with lots of sun up until now. Light gray eyes scanned the room as we all looked at him, and he stood there seeming comfortable with the attention, like it didn't bother him at all. I'd be blushing and squirming if a room filled with strangers were staring at me.

"Como tu te llamas?" Señora Cooper asked with a raised eyebrow.

He gave her a lopsided smile, all white teeth and boyish charm, and this little unexpected thrill fluttered in my belly.

A feeling I got only when reading about swoonworthy book boyfriends.

I swallowed hard, not sure I was enjoying this new development.

"Tobias King. But you can just call me King."

Tobias King.

Crap.

He even had a book-boyfriend name.

I groaned inwardly as Señora Cooper told him to take a seat after checking her register to make sure he belonged in her class. As he passed me without noticing me, I took in his face and wondered how it was possible for a teenage boy to look like that. Sure we had cute guys at our school, but none of them looked like *that*. Like…a teen Viking!

He had a strong, chiseled jaw, a slightly too-wide nose—an imperfection that only added to his attractiveness—and a smile that could charm you out of your last Irn-Bru. It occurred to me, as he angled his long body into a seat beside Daniel Pilton, that he looked familiar. He shared more than a passing similarity to a certain star of a dystopian book-to-film franchise I had pinned to my bedroom wall.

I hunched over, hating this sudden awareness of the stranger.

"They don't grow them like that here," Vicki whispered, amusement in her words.

I smirked and shot her a look, but I must have been blushing because her eyes widened. Vicki being Vicki, she didn't push the subject, and Señora Cooper started teaching.

It was difficult to concentrate on that first class, because my imagination ran away from me. I could feel his presence, burning like a fire behind me, and suddenly he was the hero in a dystopian novel and I was the heroine. I was smart and sassy, he was brooding and taciturn. Whilst I didn't *need* help to take down a regime that subjugated women, he was my protector all the same. He taught me to fight harder and I taught him to live harder. After one particular battle we had to hide out alone, share sleeping quarters, and things got—

When Vicki nudged me hard, I jerked out of my daydream and was stunned to realize class was over and the bell was ringing for second period. Blushing, I fumbled to put my books in my bag.

"Are you okay?" she asked me, studying me too intently.

"I'm fine," I nodded.

"Hmm." She threaded her arm through my elbow and led me out of class. "You get weirder every day, Comet. You know I love that about you, right?"

3

I lost my focus today.
He was the cause.
No ordinary Monday.
'Til it turned out it was.
—CC

Quite without meaning to I found myself thinking about our new student for the rest of the morning and hoping to find him in my other classes. To my disappointment, I didn't see him in my next class, or during morning break, or in my third class.

Come fourth period I was sitting in Higher English at a desk by myself because Steph had gotten to class before me and bagged the seat beside Vicki. Vicki gave me an apologetic look as I surveyed the room. It was either take the empty desk at the front of the class or take a seat next to Heather. Even if she hadn't been glaring at me with a clear *piss off* expression, I would have taken the dreaded front table and sat without a partner.

The teacher, Mr. Stone, was my favorite. I'd had him in first year and again last year. When I saw his name on my curriculum this year, I was so happy. He was one of the few teachers invested in my work, and whatever I wrote, he seemed to get it. He was always encouraging me, and even though I was pretty sure I'd die of mortification if anyone else actually commented on my work, I didn't mind when he did. It never felt like a criticism, only an effort to make me a better writer. Still, I hadn't had the courage to show him my poetry. I didn't have the courage to show *anyone* my poetry.

He looked up from reading the register, probably counting to see if we were all there, and blinked in recognition when he saw me sitting up front. Mr. Stone smiled. "Comet, it's nice to have you back in my class."

I smiled in return and nodded—I hoped in a way that expressed I was glad to be there, too.

"It looks like we're missing one." Mr. Stone's gaze swept around the room. "Tobias King?"

"Oh, he's new, Mr. Stone," Heather piped up. "He's probably just trying to find us. I saved him a seat."

At that moment, Tobias sauntered casually into the room and my breath caught again.

Seriously. What was that?

That weird fluttering in my belly was back. I'd heard Vicki talk about how Jordan Hall, a college boy on her street, gave her butterflies every time she saw him. And Steph had butterflies over a new boy every three months.

Was this…was this that elusive crush?

Don't get me wrong; I'd had crushes before, but usually on actors and characters in books. They gave me a giddy, girlish ache in my chest. This was different.

This was nausea-inducing fluttering and an all-encompassing feeling of awareness.

Dammit.

This wasn't supposed to happen to me until college, where

I'd miraculously develop some social skills, or find a like-minded guy with an equal lack of social skills.

"Tobias King, I presume," Mr. Stone greeted him. "I'm Mr. Stone. You get a pass on being late today because you're new, Mr. King, but tomorrow I expect you to be here on time."

"Sure thing."

"Tobias, over here." Heather waved at him.

I suddenly remembered that Vicki said Tobias and Heather had snogged the faces off each other at her party the night before. Feeling deflated didn't stop me from studying his face when he saw her. Indecision and wariness seemed to flitter over his features before he cleared his expression and walked over to slide into the seat next to her.

"Right, now that we're all here, let's get started." Mr. Stone walked over to the pile of books on his desk. "This year we'll be covering one play, one novel and a number of pieces of poetry. First term—" he lifted up one of the books to face us "—we're studying *Hamlet* for the critical essay part of this year's exam."

There were several groans around the room, and I rolled my eyes. Who groaned at Shakespeare? Uncouth, uncultured, uncivilized barbarians, that's whom.

Mr. Stone started handing out a book each to us, and I took mine with a smile.

"Have you read it, Comet?"

I nodded. I'd painted the words *To Thine Own Self Be True* above my headboard in my bedroom.

He smiled back at me and then continued on, handing out the play to everyone.

I flipped open the copy, hoping the lure of Shakespeare would be enough to distract me from the beautiful boy behind me. This was English class. The only place at school I felt at home.

Tobias King wasn't going to fluster me or divert my attention from Mr. Stone and a class I loved.

Considering how disturbed I was by the thought of having a crush on a boy at this school, I was almost grateful for what happened next.

It was after lunch and I was heading to history. The wide corridors were filled with students milling around or walking to their next class. As usual I was slipping through the crowds anonymously when I saw him coming toward me.

My heart started racing in my chest.

He really had the most gorgeous smile.

And then I realized who he was smiling at.

Stevie Macdonald. And with Stevie were his crew of borderline delinquents.

Huh.

That surprised me. To be honest it surprised me Stevie was still in school. I'd have bet everything I owned that he would have dropped out as soon as he turned sixteen. His friends, too. But nope. There they were.

What surprised me about Tobias hanging out with Stevie was the fact that Tobias had to have achieved good grades at his old school to have been accepted into my Spanish and English classes. Stevie and his crowd weren't exactly high achievers.

But there they were, messing around like they'd known each other forever.

As Tobias neared me, my breath once again seized in my throat.

And then it was expelled with force when Stevie shoved Tobias and he clobbered me, nearly knocking me off my feet. Thankfully the new guy had fast reflexes. Almost as soon as he hit me, he turned and grabbed my arms to steady me.

"Sorry," he apologized, and for a moment our eyes met.

My skin burned beneath my shirt where his fingers gripped me, and I found myself entranced by the flecks of gold and blue in his eyes. They were more blue-gray than light gray like I'd thought.

The heat in my skin traveled all over me, and I knew my face was probably on fire.

Damn my pale skin!

Just like that, he let me go and turned to laugh at whatever Stevie had said. I stumbled a little, turning in shock to watch him stride away as if he'd never even touched me, talked to me.

Tobias King was *not* book boyfriend material! A book boyfriend did not knock the heroine quite literally off her feet and then walk away once they made eye contact.

"Nice," I muttered, infuriated.

It had been silly of me to think my intense reaction to Tobias King would be returned. He'd been here a day and was already the most popular boy in school.

This was the wake up I needed to shake me out of my stupid insta-crush.

After all I was just Comet Caldwell.

Great big bloody snowy dirtball.

"I was thinking we could 'study' at yours instead," I air-quoted as I fell into stride with Vicki.

The end of day bell had rung five minutes ago, and I'd

caught sight of my friend weaving through the crowds heading out of school.

For some weird reason, Vicki looked unsure. "Why?"

I knew the girls liked hanging out at my place because my parents never bothered us and because I was right on the beach. But I was feeling unexplainably prickly toward Carrie today and really didn't want to breathe the same air as her. "This morning Carrie either pretended to or genuinely forgot that I'm sixteen years old and have been for a while."

"What?" Vicki wrinkled her nose. "Babe, she gave you a birthday card. With money in it."

"No, apparently, Kyle gave me a card with money in it and signed Carrie's name."

"That's rubbish. I'm sorry." She wrapped an arm around my shoulder and gave me a squeeze. "Okay. Come to mine, then. I'm sure Mum won't mind, because today was her day off."

Vicki's mum was a general practitioner at the local doctor's surgery but ever since Vicki's younger brother, Ben, was born she'd worked part-time. Ben had been a surprise—a happy one—arriving nine years after his big sister.

"Well, if you're sure." I wasn't going to argue.

Vicki's house was on the way to mine, about a ten-minute walk from school and just a few blocks from the main street in Portobello.

Portobello, or Porty as it was known locally, sat on the east coast of Edinburgh, about a twenty-five-minute car journey from the city center. It used to be a beach resort with fun fairs and rides, but now it was more about volleyball, kayaking, sunbathing, swimming, dog walking and the arts. Years ago, as part of an art event, a steel tidal octopus sculpture had been installed on the beach. During low tide he was completely visible, but during high tide you could see only a tentacle or two.

We had independent stores, cafés and restaurants in Porty, and a Victorian swimming pool with an original Aerotone and Turkish baths. It was a village with identity and personality, and it had a laid-back vibe with a socioeconomic mix of low-to-mid income and mid-to-high income families. There were people who spoke with a more anglicized Scottish accent, like me and my friends, and those like Stevie who spoke in thick Scots. It was a mishmash, and for the most part I loved that.

But that came with problems. I knew some kids who were bullied for having less money than other kids, and kids like me who were bullied for being posh and a swot—a geek, a brainiac, a nerd. Our school had its "good" kids, its over-achievers, and then it had the "bad" kids, the disrespectful kids, the troublemakers and the underachievers. Overall, I didn't interact much with the "bad" kids, as I wasn't part of their circles, and I liked living in Porty.

That didn't mean I didn't have every intention of getting as far away from here as possible when I went to university. And I meant *far*. My dream university was in the US of A. The University of Virginia. It was really well-known for writing, for its literary magazines, poetry workshops and for its Pulitzer Prize–winning graduates. If that wasn't enough, the awesome Tina Fey graduated from there! Yes. If it took my blood, sweat and tears, I would become a proud alumna of UVA and no one, not *anyone*, was going to get in my way of seeing that dream come true.

"You're quiet," Vicki mused as we strolled in silence toward her parents' house.

I shrugged. "Just first day blues, I guess."

"Or…" She nudged me and grinned. "I saw you checking out the new guy."

I blushed crimson and shook my head frantically.

"Fine." She turned stone-faced. "Keep your secrets."

Frustration gnawed at me. Vicki took it personally when I kept things to myself, but it wasn't personal. I just wasn't a sharer. Not wanting to hurt her feelings, however, I sighed. "Fine. He's good-looking. That's a fact. Nothing more."

"Really?" She beamed at me. "Because I thought I saw your tongue roll out of your mouth when he walked into Spanish."

"Yeah, well, he ruined any illusions I might have had over his crush-worthiness when he nearly knocked me off my feet in the school corridor and then walked away."

"He didn't apologize?"

"Well, yeah, but it was like—" I grabbed her arms to demonstrate. "Sorry," I said indifferently, let her go and strode away quickly. Stopping I looked back at her. "I may as well have been a traffic cone."

She burst out laughing at my dry tone and hurried to thread her arm through my elbow. "I bet that's not true. You're really pretty, Comet. It's just this uniform does nothing for you. For any of us."

"Well *you* always look amazing."

"He needs to see you as the real Comet." She squeezed my arm, grinning at me. "He won't be able to take his eyes off you then."

It was sweet of her to try to reassure me, but I was over it. "It doesn't matter. Did you see who he's hanging out with?" I wrinkled my nose in disdain. "Stevie Macdonald and those idiots. Ugh. No thanks."

"Stevie's not so bad," Vicki disagreed.

"He's disrespectful to teachers," I argued.

"God forbid."

I frowned at her sarcasm. "Your dad is a teacher, Vicki. It should bug you, too."

"It would bug me if Stevie was disrespectful to my dad or to any of the teachers that give a crap, but I've only seen him wind up the ones that clearly are just there to pick up a payslip."

Realizing we disagreed entirely on the matter, I stayed silent.

She laughed. "Not all of us are afraid of authority figures, babe."

I wasn't afraid of authority figures. I just... I respected the adults in our lives who made time to talk to us, teach us things.

God... "I'm such a geek," I groaned.

Vicki started to shake with laughter, setting off my own, and we giggled all the way to her house.

When we stepped inside the whitewashed bungalow, Mrs. Brown kissed her daughter on the cheek in greeting and then turned to me. "It's lovely to see you, Comet." She engulfed me in a hug, one that I soaked up.

I could hear sounds of cartoons coming from the living room, and I could smell something amazing cooking in the kitchen.

Mrs. Brown let me go and smiled at me, taking me in. "You get prettier every day, Comet."

I blushed furiously, unused to such compliments, and she reminded me of Vicki as she laughed at my reaction. Vicki was a gorgeous blend of her mixed heritage. Where her mum was Caucasian with light hazel eyes and golden-brown hair, her dad was British Black Caribbean with dark umber skin, dark brown eyes and dark hair he always wore close-shaven in a fade.

"Can Comet stay for dinner, Mum?" Vicki asked, and I was surprised how tentative she sounded.

It had never been a problem before for me to stay over for dinner.

Frowning, I watched uneasiness flicker in Mrs. Brown's eyes before she nodded. "Of course."

"Will Dad be home?"

Again, Vicki's tone surprised me.

"He hasn't said otherwise."

They shared a look I didn't understand, and the sudden tension between them made me feel like an outsider. "I really should probably just go home."

"Nonsense." Mrs. Brown smiled brightly at me. Falsely. "But you girls must be hungry now. Let me make you a snack," Mrs. Brown said, striding down the hall toward the kitchen in the new extended part of the house. As she passed the living room, she raised her voice. "Ben, volume."

Almost immediately the noise from the television lowered.

I wouldn't want to disobey Mrs. Brown either. Although she was always kind to me, she had that matter-of-fact, authoritative personality that seemed so prevalent in GPs.

We followed her, not having to respond to her offer because she knew from experience that we weren't going to turn down a snack. I shot a questioning look at Vicki as we walked, but she didn't meet my gaze. Hmm.

I waved at Ben, who looked up from the couch as we passed and waved back so enthusiastically that I paused. Vicki's little brother was quite possibly the most adorable human being in the world, and the only child I'd met thus far in my short life to make me wish my parents had given me a sibling.

"Hey, Comet."

"Hey. How was school?"

He made a face. "It was okay." And I assumed my opener failed to pass muster because that was all the attention I was going to get. He returned to eating a banana and watching his cartoons.

I found Vicki and Mrs. Brown in their large, modern kitchen. Whereas our kitchen was the same ugly 1980s-looking disaster that had been in the house for decades, Mr. and Mrs. Brown had bothered to update theirs, and it was all clean lines, white and shiny.

The smell of pot roast made it the most inviting space despite its starkness.

Already in the middle of putting a banana, a sandwich and a cookie on a small plate each for us, Mrs. Brown smiled up at me. "Vicki said you had a particularly good day at school today. What happened?"

I shot a dirty look at my friend and then quickly covered it with a bland smile. "Mr. Stone is teaching us *Hamlet* in English. Vicki knows how much I love Shakespeare."

Vicki snorted. "*Right.* Shakespeare."

Her mother shook her head, smirking. "I know I'm missing something here, but from the look on Comet's face she doesn't want to talk about it so I'm going to let it go." She slid a plate over to me and then handed the other to her daughter, leaning in to cuddle her as she did so. "Stop teasing your friend about boys."

While I blushed again at her perceptiveness, Vicki huffed. "It could be about something else."

38

"Not at sixteen."

"Know-it-all." She rolled her eyes as she moved to the fridge and grabbed us each a bottle of water. "Thanks, Mum."

"Yeah, thanks, Mrs. Brown." I took my water from my friend so she could take hold of her own plate and then I let her lead the way to her bedroom at the front of the house. Ben's was just behind hers, and her parents' bedroom was in the new extension near the kitchen.

Vicki's room, much like my own, had barely any wall space left uncovered. Film posters, posters of her favorite rock bands and high fashion magazine spreads were pinned to every available space. She had two dresser mannequins, one wearing a half-finished corset-top, the other an almost completed steampunk-inspired dress. A bookshelf beside them held bolts of fabric, pins, scissors, papers and trays filled with beading, sequins and ribbons. Attached to the wall behind the mannequins was a corkboard and pinned to the corkboard were her designs.

My friend was wicked talented.

There were different-colored candles everywhere, and a bed with Moroccan-inspired jewel-tone, multicolored bedding with a ton of Indian silk cushions scattered over it. I kicked off my shoes and got comfy on her bed as she settled at her computer desk and immediately bit into her sandwich.

"Vicki?"

"Hmm?"

"Is everything okay?" My skin heated as I worried I was crossing a line by asking. "Between your mum and dad?"

Her gaze dropped to the floor and she swallowed. Hard. Expelling a weighted breath, she shrugged. "They argued all summer."

Not knowing what it must be like to have parents that argued since mine rarely did, I didn't know what to say. "I'm sorry."

Her gaze flew to mine, and I saw the anguish she'd been hiding. "A lot of it is about money. And about me."

"About you?"

"I'm costing them a lot." She gestured to the area of her bedroom dedicated to her design work. "None of that comes cheap. Plus, Dad doesn't think it's smart to just apply to London College of Fashion and the Rhode Island School of Design. And he thinks applying to Parsons is pointless."

It was true, Parsons School of Design in New York was one of the best design schools in the world and incredibly hard to get into, but if anyone could, it would be Vicki. I told her so.

She looked saddened rather than encouraged. "Dad wants me to apply for a business degree at St. Andrews."

I made a face, my stomach twisting with the thought. "No. No way. Vicki, you have to pursue fashion. You're amazing at it."

"Mum agrees." She gave me a tired smile. "Which is why she and Dad have been arguing a lot. Dad thinks it's all a waste of money."

"I don't get it. Your dad was always so supportive."

"Well, now reality is setting in and he realizes it's no longer a hobby." She shook her head. "Never mind. It'll work out. I'm sorry about Steph in English. I was hoping we'd sit together."

I moved with the abrupt change in subject, although I was concerned Vicki had been dealing with this all summer and hadn't told me. And probably wouldn't have told me if I hadn't felt the tension in the house. Did Steph know? It bothered me to think Vicki had confided in Steph and not me.

Forcing the worry away I just nodded. "You seemed cool with her at lunch." Even though she'd made our ears bleed talking about the upcoming impromptu audition and complaining that it was unfair for the teachers to have them give unpolished, unpracticed performances. It was only the first round of auditions, however, and she'd get a chance to practice for the second round if she made it.

Neither Vicki nor I had gotten a word in edgewise, but Vicki hadn't seemed that concerned. Not that she was really a drama-llama anyway.

"Life is too short to get annoyed at Steph when she gets like that." She shrugged. "Still, I could have used the break from her in class. Plus, I hate that you're sitting on your own."

"You know that if I couldn't sit with you or Steph, I'd prefer to be on my own anyway."

She nodded but stared in an assessing way.

"What?"

"I just… It would be great if you'd come out of your shell this year. People have no idea how cool you are."

I chuckled. "Because I'm not. I can barely string two words together around new people and none around boys. Once upon a time you used to be the same."

My friend gave me a sympathetic look. "I grew up, Comet," she replied gently.

I flinched. "And I haven't?"

"Just…just try harder. I think you still think you're that little kid who couldn't speak to her parents, much less anyone else. You're not her anymore. Try. Please. For me?"

I nodded, the ham and cheese sandwich Mrs. Brown had made me suddenly tasting like dust in my mouth. The thought of trying to be more social made me uneasy. I didn't want to be put in situations that made me sweat under my arms and flush strawberry red like a loser.

I wanted to feel safe and comfortable.

And I didn't see what was so terrible about that.

4

How do you conquer each moment,
When you have no one on your side?
Make peace with the idea that life,
Is just one continuous high tide?
—CC

Walking toward form class for daily registration that morning, I saw Steph coming toward me and braced myself. I worried for a second that she knew Vicki and I had been avoiding her last night, but the nearer she got to me the bigger her smile grew. When we met outside the classroom door she threw her arms around me and hugged me.

Used to Steph's impromptu displays of affection I laughed and hugged her back.

"That was for yesterday." She pulled out of the hug but huddled against me as we walked into our form room together. "I know I just went on and on about myself. I got so worked up about the audition. Anyway, everything okay with you?"

And this was why it was difficult to stay mad at Steph. I smiled at her as we sat down at a table together. "Everything is fine with me. How did the audition go?"

"Wait, wait." Vicki suddenly appeared, sliding into a seat at the table. "I want to hear."

"I already apologized to Vicki on Snapchat last night," Steph said, which explained Vicki's renewed enthusiasm for supporting her.

"The audition?" Vicki said.

Steph beamed. "It went great. All those hours spent singing 'All That Jazz' in the shower paid off. They asked me back for another audition next week."

I squeezed her arm. "Steph, that's great. Well done."

"Thanks. Ahh! I so want to play Roxie."

"You'd be the perfect Roxie," Vicki insisted.

"Not if I have anything to do with it."

In unison, we turned toward the new voice, and residual anger from long ago burned in my throat. Heather. It was hard for me not to resent her, and I wasn't sure I cared if that made me unforgiving.

Vicki leaned back in her seat, one eyebrow raised. As cool and laid-back as my friend was, she could also emanate serious pissed-off vibes. Like now. "And what does that mean?"

Heather smirked. "I made it to the second round auditions, too." Her gaze zeroed in on Steph, who was staring up at her with a mixture of guilt and irritation in her eyes. "And I'm going after the part of Roxie."

This was a surprise, because Heather had been director's assistant on the school shows for the past few years. She loved bossing people around. She had not, however, played a part before.

Why now?

Perhaps because Steph had snogged Heather's ex-boyfriend at her party and she was evil and vindictive?

We were all thinking it.

Vicki snorted. "Good luck with that, but I wouldn't hold your breath."

"Why?" Heather's gaze locked with Steph's. "Because you're so special? Aye, right."

"Take a walk, McAlister," Vicki huffed. "No one likes a drama-llama."

My onetime nemesis gave Vicki a narrow-eyed gaze but strutted across the room, hips swaying, hair swinging, and took a seat with her friends.

"I hate the way she walks." Steph glowered. "Where does she think she is? At a bloody runway show?"

There was a tiny, tiny part of me that was a little gleeful about all this. It was wrong. It was small. I knew that. But Steph had been disloyal once in order to play nice with Heather McAlister, and now she was getting a taste of why it was futile to suck up to a girl like Heather. She enjoyed causing problems and misery for people.

"What a cow." Steph turned to look at us, her blue eyes round with shock. "Was she always such a cow?"

Vicki and I exchanged a look. "Yes."

"God. You kiss someone's ex-boyfriend and you might as well have murdered him, the way she's acting."

I caught sight of movement in my peripheral and turned as Andy Walsh, a video-game-and-rugby-obsessed boy in our class who somehow managed to cross social cliques with admirable proficiency, leaned his chair on its back legs toward us. He balanced it perfectly as he whispered to us, "It's not about Lister. She's just pissed off because King messed around with her at her party but doesn't want to date her."

Tobias.

"So she's taking it out on me?" Steph whined.

Andy shrugged. "She's taking it out on everyone. And it's not like King made her any promises."

I noted the hero worship in Andy's eyes and *just* stopped myself from rolling mine.

Vicki grinned at him. "Seriously? That would make him the first guy to *not* run around panting at Heather's arse."

Andy grinned back. "The guy is a god among men."

I groaned but Vicki chuckled. "I don't know about that, but I'm definitely starting to like him more."

Once Andy had turned his attention from us, Steph leaned toward me. "I know why she's being a bitch to me, but now I also know why she was a bitch to you, Comet. At the party I asked her friend Liza why Heather has such a problem with you."

Not really sure I wanted to know why Heather had a problem with me, I stiffened.

Vicki, however, demanded, "Tell us, then."

"Well…" Steph's eyes lit with the power of knowing gossip we didn't. "Apparently, Heather's life isn't as perfect as she wants people to think. Her parents are on her constantly to be the best. At everything. And she was. She was top of her class at her primary school. Then first year hits and you, Comet, scored top marks in our English and history projects in the first term. Liza said her parents gave her such a hard time about it, and that's why she came after you. That's why she can't stand you. Because you showed her up to her parents."

Despite Heather's cruelty, I felt more than a flicker of compassion. While my parents didn't show me enough attention, Heather's sounded overbearing. It didn't soothe the humiliation I'd felt when she was bullying me, but at least now I understood that her lashing out had nothing to do with me personally.

It would appear to be a pattern of Heather McAlister: taking her crap out on the wrong people.

After registration, we dispersed for our classes, Heather throwing Steph another sneering, challenging look before she left. I shook my head, patting my friend's shoulder in comfort. "Ignore her. She can't even play the part of the villain originally."

"Eh?"

"Well…" I gestured to where Heather had disappeared down the corridor. "It's like she's watched every American mean-girl movie and combined and adopted the roles as her own."

"It doesn't matter. She's still trying to mess with me." Steph worried her lip.

Vicki threw an arm around Steph's neck. "Like we'd ever let that happen."

Our friend gave us a grateful but still tremulous smile, and we parted ways for our different classes.

Every day in English Mr. Stone told us he would assign a part from *Hamlet* to a student and we'd read through a scene. The thought made me nervous, because I was soft-spoken and hated having to try to project my voice to be heard in the room. As I waited for everyone to filter in to class at seventh period, the nervousness I felt dissipated as Tobias walked into the room with Andy. Andy murmured something to him, and they both looked at Heather. Andy punched Tobias playfully on the arm, almost in a *good luck, man* kind of way, and Tobias walked toward Heather wearing a blank expression on his face.

Mr. Stone had told us yesterday that the seats we had chosen were now our assigned seats for the rest of the year. Tobias was stuck.

I tried to appear inconspicuous as I followed his movement, peeking at him from behind strands of my hair. Heather glared at him as he approached, and then shifted her seat and her stuff away from him like he had a disease.

He didn't acknowledge her, instead taking his seat and leaning back in his chair with his hands behind his head like he hadn't a care in the world.

Soon class was in full progress and I was happy to escape unscathed as Mr. Stone asked Steph to read the queen's part.

There was a moment of awkwardness when he asked Tobias King to read for Hamlet.

"No thanks," Tobias replied, creating a hush of shock in the room.

Mr. Stone crossed his arms and stared impassively at the newcomer. "No thanks?"

"Yeah."

I looked over my shoulder, because everyone was looking at him and it was nice to be able to stare without anyone watching me. Tobias had his chair tipped on its hind legs with his arms over the back of it, all casual insolence.

"I wasn't really giving you an option, Mr. King. Participation is a part of the grade in this class."

Tobias shrugged, staring at my favorite teacher. "Then I guess you'll need to mark me down because I'm not reading the part of some pansy-assed Danish dude that wants to screw his mom and can't get over the fact dear old daddy is dead."

There was sniggering around the room but not from me. I turned away from the boy I'd thought was beautiful when I'd first seen him. Funny how the more I heard from him, the less attractive he became to me.

Mr. Stone scowled at Tobias. "You don't have to read, Tobias, but you do have to show me some respect. Watch your language and get your chair on the ground. Now."

Mr. Stone's authority rang around the room, and I peeked back over my shoulder to see Tobias do as he was bid. However, he didn't wipe that annoyingly bored look off his face.

It was almost comical how quickly Michael Gates, a guy in the year above us, agreed to read the part of Hamlet after that.

Mr. Stone relaxed, clearly refusing to allow one kid to ruin the class, and we continued.

"'Good Hamlet, cast thy nighted color off, and let thine eye…'" I wanted to look over my shoulder and grin at Steph as she read, because she was reading the queen's part in a fake English accent that was causing a buildup of giggles in the back of my throat.

Michael read as Hamlet with absolutely no inflection or enthusiasm. Poor William must have been rolling in his grave to hear it.

"Stop there, Michael, thank you," Mr. Stone said. "What do you think is being said here between the queen and Hamlet? Comet?"

I raised my head from the words on the page, feeling everyone stare at me.

Mr. Stone gazed at me encouragingly. "What do you think, Comet?"

It wasn't that I wasn't used to answering questions in class. We'd had to do class talks, where we either did a presentation to a group of peers or to the entire class. I'd hated every minute of those, but I'd gotten through them. I guess I was nervous because there was a person in our class who had never heard me talk, and I was passionate about this stuff, while he seemed to think it was all a joke.

Come on, Comet. Like you should care what that Neanderthal thinks of you?

"I think," I started, "the queen is questioning Hamlet's continued grief over losing his father. When she says, 'cast thy nighted color off' she means his mourning clothes *and* his mood. And then she asks why, when everyone knows of the inevitability of death, should Hamlet's father's death be so unique. It's almost like she's questioning whether Hamlet's grief is real or for show, and Hamlet replies that yes, from his outward behavior it might be easy to think he's just acting a part, but he insists that his grief is deeper than mere appearance."

Mr. Stone stared at me a moment and the class seemed to wait with bated breath along with me. A slow smile curled his mouth and he nodded. "Excellent, Comet."

I flushed, relaxing in my chair, as he asked Michael, who was reading the king's part, to continue.

Pleased with myself, relieved I really did understand the flowery, beautifully overcomplicated prose of Shakespeare, I settled back in my seat to follow the rest of the scene. But that burning sensation I had on my neck when the class was staring at me, waiting for me to answer, hadn't gone away. In fact, it felt like my neck was burning hotter.

Giving in to temptation, I glanced over my shoulder, searching for the cause, and froze, breath and all, when I did.

Tobias King was looking at me.

Really looking at me.

Our gazes held for a moment, and my cheeks grew warm as my heart picked up pace.

Tobias frowned and jerked his gaze away.

Flushing harder, I turned back fully in my seat and willed my heart rate to slow.

So what if Tobias King had finally noticed me. He was a bad boy. He was arrogant, cocky, hanging out with guys who were going nowhere in life, and he definitely shouldn't be in my Higher classes with me. I was not attracted to this boy, and I should not feel a thrill of anticipation, a flutter of butterflies, just because we'd made eye contact.

No.

Nope.

Definitely NOT.

I was Comet Caldwell. I might be many things, and not many other things, but I was above having a crush on a boy who disdained Shakespeare.

"Uh, Comet." Mr. Stone approached me after the bell rang.

I looked up from putting my books and jotter away. "Yes?"

My teacher leaned a hand on the desk and lowered his voice as the rest of the class filtered out for their last class of the day. "I was wondering if perhaps your dad might be interested in coming in next term to talk with the class about writing skills."

An instant flush of irritation rushed through me and then worse…

Self-doubt.

Had Mr. Stone paid attention to me only because of who my dad was?

"I just found out." He smiled, looking sheepish. "I never put K. L. Caldwell and your dad together. It was Mrs. Bennett that told me yesterday."

Mrs. Bennett was my third-year English teacher. She'd also tried to get me to ask dad to come speak with the class.

"Um…" I stood up, pulling the strap of my heavy bag onto my shoulder. "Did Mrs. Bennett tell you my dad doesn't do school talks?"

The light of anticipation died in his eyes as he straightened. "She mentioned it. I was just hoping he might have changed his mind."

I shook my head. "I'm sorry, Mr. Stone. I really am. But it's not his thing. He asked me not to ask him again. He doesn't like being put in the position of having to say no to me," I lied.

"Oh, then don't, please," Mr. Stone reassured me. "It was just a thought. You better get to your next class."

As I was leaving he called my name again. I looked back and he gave me an encouraging smile. "You did well today."

"Thanks, Mr. Stone." I smiled back and left his classroom feeling reassured that my favorite teacher liked me as a pupil and not as K. L. Caldwell's kid. But the lie I'd told him, and not the thing about my dad not enjoying saying no to me, sat heavy on my chest, refusing to shift.

I hated lying.

Yet, I hated the idea of my dad coming into our class and talking about writing and books with us. There was no way I'd let the rest of the world see the strange dynamic between me and my father. Plus, he'd love the whole thing. Educating young minds. Passing on literary wisdom. I didn't want him to have that.

I didn't want him to have any part of the one place in my life right now, outside of my beach and bedroom, that fit me.

"Comet!"

Startled by the interruption, I pulled out my earphones and twisted my neck to find my dad standing behind the bench I was sitting on. The sea wind blew his hair off his forehead and his T-shirt batted around his body like a flag.

I looked out at the sea and frowned to see how rough it was getting out there. The clouds above us were growing steadily dark.

"Carrie made her celebratory chicken curry. Thought you might want some."

Although when I'd gotten home from school I'd eaten two muffins that Mrs. Cruickshank had baked, I wasn't going to say no to Carrie's chicken curry. Grabbing my stuff, I hopped off the bench and followed my dad over the esplanade and into the garden.

He glanced over his shoulder at me. "You're not even wearing a jacket. It's cold out here, Comet."

Goose bumps prickled my skin, but I hadn't even noticed, I'd been so lost in writing. "Yeah."

After dumping my notebooks and pens in my bedroom I found my parents sitting at the island in the kitchen eating the only thing Carrie knew how to cook.

A bowl of curry had been left out for me, and I grabbed a water from the fridge before sitting down with them. Every time Carrie finished a commission, she made enough chicken curry to last us days. However, usually it was left to either Dad or me to feed us. I had to give my parents props for that. They had never forgotten to feed me. As far as I was aware.

"Kyle said you were writing. Again," Carrie commented as I dug into my curry.

I froze and looked at them both through lowered lids.

"Finally going to admit we've got another writer in the family?" Dad teased.

"I'm not," I lied. "It's homework assignments for English."

They seemed to accept that. Or at least they pretended to.

"I wish I was writing a bloody homework assignment." Dad frowned at his dinner. "I wrote fifty words today. *Fifty.*"

"Honey, it will come." Carrie wrapped her small hand around the nape of his neck and squeezed him in comfort. "It always does."

He gave her a pained smile. "I think maybe I need a change of scenery."

I covered my snort with a cough, but neither of them were looking at me. We lived on a beach! Hello! He had the best view of any writer, ever.

"Well, we could go away." Carrie flicked a look at me. "Comet's old enough to stay home alone for a few days."

Again with the covering of more snorts.

I'd been old enough to stay home alone while they went on a mini-break together since I was thirteen years old. It was just another reason Mrs. Cruickshank didn't like my parents. They'd left me to take a mini-break to Vienna, and our neighbor hadn't realized I was home alone until my parents' return. She'd told me to tell her next time so I could stay with her. I hadn't ever actually stayed there, but the few times my parents did leave me at home while they traveled, she'd kept an eye on me and cooked dinner for me. To be fair Dad hadn't seemed all that keen on the idea of leaving me, but Carrie had insisted she'd been left home alone far younger than that and it had never bothered her.

Except, I knew from my confounded curiosity and eavesdropping that the last part wasn't true. As I'd grown older, stumbling—sometimes deliberately—upon their private conversations, I'd learned there were reasons that Carrie treated me like I was more of a housemate than her daughter. And although I was angry on her behalf, I was still furious on my own behalf, too.

"Why don't we go to Montpellier for a long weekend? You love it there."

Montpellier was my dad's favorite city in southern France. I waited, dreading him saying yes. We might not spend huge amounts of time together when we were at home, but it was comforting to know they were there when I went to sleep. I hated being alone in the house at night. Whenever they left me, I slept with a baseball bat I'd borrowed from Steph beside my bed. Pride stopped me from slipping over to my neighbor's house to stay in her guest bed. I didn't want her to know it bothered me when my parents left me.

Dad turned to me, a plea in his eyes. "How would you feel about it, Comet? I just... I really need a break. Help with the writer's block."

I shrugged, like it was no big deal to me. "You guys do what you want."

"There!" Carrie beamed at me. "We can go."

He grinned back at her. "When should we leave?"

"I'll see if I can book us in somewhere this Thursday to Monday." She tilted her head. "Maybe we should consider making this a monthly thing. Why don't we look at property while we're there, get an idea of house prices?"

"I love the idea." He glanced back at me. "As long as Comet's okay with that?"

I swallowed a piece of chicken, the food I'd consumed suddenly sloshing around in my stomach. "Sure. Buy a holiday home in the south of France. I'll just assume I'm not invited to these monthly weekend breaks."

He gave me a pained look but Carrie scowled. "Comet, we've come this far without you turning into a sullen teenager. Don't start now."

"That would be a 'Yes, Comet, you assume correctly.'" I pushed my bowl away, no longer hungry. "Don't worry about it. I prefer when you're not here anyway."

After locking myself in my room, I slumped back on my bed and stared at my ceiling. When we first moved into the house I'd wanted glow in the dark stars all over my ceiling. The problem was the ceiling in my bedroom was higher than one in the average house. Before my bed was moved into the room, my dad had borrowed tall ladders and stuck the stars on the ceiling under my direction.

He and Carrie had argued that night, because she'd been left to unpack so much herself while he "arsed around with bloody stickers on the ceiling."

A year later, when I asked if I could get fitted bookshelves, Dad hired a guy, didn't even inspect the work as it was happening, or notice that I'd asked for the added expense of a ladder and rail so I could reach the highest shelves and move across them like Belle in the bookshop scene in *Beauty and the Beast*. When it was finished, my dad just paid the guy without commentary, without caring.

That was my dad. One minute he cared. The next he didn't.

Mercurial.

That was one of my favorite words in the English language.

However, I doubted any kid wanted their parent to be mercurial.

I grabbed a pen and opened my notebook to write it all down.

A ball of frustration tightened in my chest. Why did I need that constant reminder? I should just *get* it by now. I was on my own. I always had been.

Enough of the woe!

I slammed my notebook closed and crossed the room to my bookshelves. It was time for a mood changer. My eyes lit on the first book in a bestselling teen vampire series. The heroine was sassy, kick-ass and she was all those things despite being neglected by her parents. I pulled out the book and curled up with it on the armchair in the corner of my room.

As I fell into my heroine's adventure, my parents, the house…it all just melted away.

5

Much to my disturbance, I discovered that just because you tell yourself you can't possibly be attracted to a Neanderthal, doesn't mean you suddenly stop being attracted to a Neanderthal.

It was the only explanation for how hyperaware I seemed to be of Tobias King's whereabouts. As it turned out we had three classes together. He was in my maths class as well as Spanish and English. All Higher classes, and from the little I'd gleaned over the week—because my ears were hyperaware of him, too, and pricked up anytime I heard someone discussing him—Tobias was in only Higher classes.

If his first week was anything to go by, however, he wouldn't be there long.

Thursday, we were in maths, and I was sitting next to a girl I didn't know well, Felicity Dodd. If it was possible, she was even quieter than I was. We hadn't spoken a word to one another.

We hadn't gotten that far into class when I became aware of

a low hum of noise, and it struck me quite quickly that it was the sound of music blasting out of earphones. Our teacher, Ms. Baker, heard it, too, and stopped to scan the room. I turned to look behind me, my eyes automatically zeroing in on Tobias.

And sure enough…

He was the cause of the noise.

He had his head buried in his arms on the desk, and the white wires of earphones could be seen coming out of his ears.

Frustration boiled inside of me. What was this kid's problem? Jesus! Did Mummy and Daddy drag him away from America and he was trying to punish them by being a total dipshit at school?

Boo-hoo!

At least they hadn't left him there. I'm pretty sure my parents would have left me if they flitted countries. And hey, let's not rule the possibility out. There was still time for total and complete abandonment.

Scowling, I looked up at Ms. Baker to find she was doing the same. Her hands flew to her hips. "Mr. King."

Nothing.

Of course not.

His music was too loud.

Our teacher turned her attention to Tobias's neighbor, Becky Ford. "Miss Ford, could you please nudge Mr. King?"

Becky looked like she was wishing she'd sat anywhere else as she gently nudged him. He didn't budge.

"Harder, Becky."

She shoved him.

Tobias's head flew up, whipping around to glare at her.

Becky glared back and pointed to the front of the room.

Confused, he followed her direction. Upon realizing he'd

been caught, he stared blandly at Ms. Baker, who mimicked taking earphones out of her ears. Rolling his eyes, Tobias did her bidding.

"What's up?" he said.

I thought Ms. Baker's head was going to explode. Instead she held out her hand. "Give me that."

"Give you what?"

"Whatever device you're using to listen to music while you're in my class."

"It's my phone." Tobias shook his head. "No way am I giving you my phone."

I swallowed a gasp. His attitude was the kind I'd expected to put up with in years one to three. But in fifth year, I was in classes with other driven people who needed good grades to achieve whatever their future ambitions were. I did not expect to have to put up with this crap from someone in my class, and I was sure Ms. Baker was thinking the same thing.

"I don't know how things are done in the US of A, Tobias, but here, when a teacher confiscates something from a pupil for good reason, that pupil does not refuse."

"This one is."

The class shifted collectively in their seats.

"If you don't hand over your phone, you can just get up out of that seat and walk yourself to Mr. Jenkins's office."

"And who the hell is that?"

Really?

Attracted to that? I thought to myself.

"Mr. Jenkins is an assistant rector here, and watch your language."

"Assistant rectum? That's an unfortunate job title."

Someone snickered at the back of the room.

"I'm sure you've already been made aware of this, Tobias, but *rector* is our term for principal. An assistant rector is a vice principal. Perhaps you understand how much trouble you're in now."

"Whatever." Tobias stood up abruptly, his chair scraping against the wooden floor. "Just point the way."

Ms. Baker marched toward the classroom door to open it for him, and the door happened to be in front of my desk. She stopped him at the door and gave him directions to Mr. Jenkins's office.

"And Tobias," she said quietly, but I was right there, so I heard every word, "despite your grades and test scores, you will not last in my class with this attitude. If you'd like to remain in Higher Mathematics, you better rethink your behavior. Do you understand?"

His answer was to salute her and stride out the door.

Ms. Baker stared after him, looking concerned and peeved at the same time.

Finally, she slammed the door closed and continued with class as if nothing had happened.

"What are the plans for the weekend, then?" Steph said as she sat down at our table in the cafeteria. Despite the fact Vicki and Steph both had friends outside of our circle, only the three of us ate together at lunch. I had a feeling this was deliberate on their part and for my socially awkward benefit. Either that or I embarrassed them. Neither reason made me feel great about myself.

The cafeteria was the hub of the school. Glass doors ran along either side of it, but could only be accessed from inside. A massive staircase spiraled into the center of the cafeteria and led to the upper floor classrooms like English. Ground-floor classrooms were dedicated to subjects like Home Economics, Graphic Communication, Engineering, Chemistry, Biology and Physics.

At one end of the cafeteria was the lunch counter, where our lunch ladies and gentlemen provided *okay* meals. A new health program had been instituted in the school so, along with burgers and chips, we had fresh salads and soups.

There were never any burgers left, but there was always plenty of salad.

At the opposite end of the room were vending machines—soft drinks, water, chocolate bars, packets of crisps. And along from them, pool tables. I didn't know who'd had the bright idea to give us the luxury of pool tables in the cafeteria but I wasn't sure how long that luxury would last.

Tobias, Stevie and their crew were playing on one table while their dinner plates were scattered over the other.

"Earth to Comet?" Steph waved a hand in front of my face.

I jerked my gaze away from Tobias and tried not to blush.

I failed.

"What were you staring at?" she frowned and glanced over her shoulder.

Vicki saved me. "The idiots at the pool table."

There was a loud hoot from the boys, and Stevie playfully shoved Tobias as they all laughed.

Steph rolled her eyes. "I'm surprised they've even lasted the week. Stevie got kicked out of two of my classes."

"The new guy got kicked out of one of mine," I offered.

"Why even bother coming to school?" Vicki wondered.

"To wind up the teachers and piss the rest of us off." Steph shrugged. "Anyway, this weekend?"

"My parents left yesterday for a long weekend in Montpellier."

Both my friends' heads jerked up from their plates. "Seriously?" Steph said, sounding excited about it in a way I didn't understand.

I nodded cautiously.

They looked at each other and grinned.

"Okay, what's with the evil mastermind smiles?"

"Party at Caldwell's," Steph explained.

My stomach dropped at the thought. "No."

Their expressions fell.

"No way." I shook my head. "My parents would kill me."

"It's not like you owe them anything, Comet," Steph grumbled. "They practically ignore you."

That stung but I didn't let it show. "Actually, I'm pretty certain I owe them my existence. An existence they would snuff out if I let strange teenagers into the home where they work. You know…expensive artwork and unfinished manuscripts lying around."

Vicki slumped. "She's right."

"Oh come on," Steph huffed. "That house is perfect for a party. It's a mess, stuck in some time warp. The only reason it's even clean is because Kyle is obsessive about cleaning it."

Irritation flexed its muscles within me, curling my fingers tight around the bottle of water in my left hand. "Are you trying to say *I'm* filthy? Unclean?"

Steph's eyes widened at my unfamiliar tone. I rarely got pissed off with my friends. Correction: I rarely revealed when I was pissed off with my friends. "No, I didn't mean that. God, Comet, I'm sorry. You know I say stuff without thinking."

"No, you say mean stuff when you don't get your way."

Vicki's jaw dropped and I couldn't work out if that was horror, amusement or respect in her eyes or even a mixture of all three. Steph flushed.

An awful silence fell over our table.

We stared at anything but each other as the noise of the cafeteria faded into the background. The impulse to apologize, to make things all right, clambered up my throat, and the determined stubbornness within me tried to stop it. However, the truth was my friend had apologized, and it just made me an ungracious arsehole to not accept it.

"I'm sorry." My gaze flitted to Steph, who looked ready to cry. "You apologized. It was mean of me not to accept it."

My friend looked up at me in relief and gave me a tremulous smile.

"Phew!" Vicki relaxed back in her chair. "Okay, now that's done with, back to this weekend. Before you say anything, Comet, I get it. We can't have a party while your parents are away. But we could have a sleepover and not tell *our* parents your parents are away. Instead we could go hang out with Jordan and his friends."

Jordan as in Jordan Hall? The nineteen-year-old almost boy next door Vicki had been crushing on for two years? I raised an eyebrow and she laughed. "We ran into each other this morning, and he mentioned his friend was having a party on Saturday and I should come."

Steph's eyes almost bugged out of her head. "Oh my God. Oh my God!" She squealed and reached across to squeeze Vicki's arm in excitement. And then she swung her gaze back to me. "Comet, come on! We have to do this for Vicki."

I didn't want to hang out with a bunch of college boys.

I didn't want to go to a party where no one knew me and wouldn't care to know me.

I wanted my friends to just sleep over at my house so I wouldn't be alone the entire weekend.

No doubt seeing the thought in my eyes, Vicki's expression fell, disappointment clouding her features. She gazed at me in reproach, as if to say, *You promised you'd try.* And I had promised, hadn't I?

Feeling angry butterflies at the thought, I nodded. "Sure. Let's do it."

While Steph practically bounced in her seat with excitement, Vicki's disappointment melted into gratitude. "Thank you."

I smiled in return, but inside I was already dreading this weekend more than I dreaded end-of-term exams.

When the girls asked me if I wanted to hang out with them after school the plan had always been to lie and tell them I had a dentist appointment. Before lunch I would have felt bad about the lie, but after stewing over our conversation in the cafeteria I didn't feel guilty about heading into the city without them. Being corralled into doing something I didn't want to—being made to feel guilty for not wanting to go to some party with strangers—made me feel resentful. It also made me feel even more insecure than normal. While most days I could argue that wanting to live inside the world of books more than I wanted to live in the real world was perfectly rational considering how boring and sad my life was, there were days like today when I couldn't. Because Vicki and Steph made it seem like it wasn't normal. And maybe they were right.

Maybe there was something wrong with me.

Maybe I really was a weirdo.

Good thing I was going to the one place I didn't feel that way.

After school I hurried home and changed out of my uniform, and then I caught the bus from Portobello High Street in the center of town. It took me into the city, to Edinburgh University, and from there I walked to Tollcross where my favorite café was. Pan was this almost ludicrously hipster café for poets and artists. There was a mishmash of murals painted on the walls, and a gallimaufry of furniture, including tables and chairs, sofas, armchairs and beanbags. Rugs of all sizes and colors had been thrown across the scuffed hardwood floors, and the café counter was discernible as such only because of the coffee machine behind it and the cake stands on it. At the far end of the room a small stage with a mic awaited poets and musicians. While I ordered my usual—a hot chocolate with whipped cream on top—a young guy, around college age, was onstage reading a poem from the crumpled piece of paper in his hand.

Taking a seat at the back of the room, loving how no one here paid attention to me or my ruby-red Dorothy shoes, I took a sip of my hot chocolate and listened. The guy's voice trembled and his hands shook, but it was hard to tell if it was from nerves or because of the subject of his poem.

"It was like a knife of white heat
Plunged into my chest
Exploding in a myriad of pain and anger.
Like a long lost letter unopened,
Its pages waiting to bring

A sudden dawning;
To complete a puzzle that once
Had been so difficult
For a little boy to understand.

The realization is consuming in its accompanied rage.

Does he know what he did?

A little boy suffers as another
Parades his falsities
To an audience of jesters.
His teardrops fall
Among the court of
Villains and victims,
Whilst another's falls silently
Behind his eyes and down
Over his broken heart."

As much as I loved being at Pan, soaking in the good and the bad poetry and the fact that you could be a purple elephant in this room and no one would care, I could never dream of getting up on that stage and reading my own poetry aloud. It was only upon visiting the café that I'd discovered something depressing. Apparently, I belonged to a group of poets that had fallen out of fashion.

A poet whose poetry rhymed.

The only poets here who rhymed were the spoken word artists—those who wrote slam poetry.

I wasn't a spoken word artist.

And the only other kind of poet I'd come across in Pan

were the free verse poets. Maybe rhyming wasn't cool anymore. I was a lover of Robert Burns, William Blake and John Donne. I loved rhyming. I loved the challenge of it. But I knew that a lot of people thought rhyme felt forced and that poets shouldn't be constrained by it.

Being in the minority didn't give me a lot of confidence in my work. Pan was the one place where no one made me feel abnormal. I did not want to put myself in the position of being judged by a crowd of people I admired.

Shoving my worries aside, I lost myself in other people's thoughts, emotions and imaginations. The poetry café was another escape. The surrealism of the venue, with its murals and tie-dyed fabric billowing across the ceiling like a canopy, made it feel as if I had walked into a dream. Here, I was in a bubble in the same way I was when I cracked open a book. Yet, it was different because I was alone without really being alone. I was surrounded by real live people who liked the bubble just as much as I did.

"Comet?"

The familiar voice made me tense.

No.

This wasn't happening.

Not here, where I was perfectly anonymous.

My inability to be disrespectful to the owner of the voice made me look over my shoulder and up. Sure enough, Mr. Stone stood behind me with a cup of coffee in hand and the leather satchel he wore that was always bursting with papers slung over his shoulder. His smile was curious as he stepped toward me. "Do you come here a lot, Comet?"

I nodded. *And since when did you start coming here?*

As if he'd heard my unspoken thought he said, "A friend

recommended this place. I usually do my marking at school but I fancied a change of scenery. Do you perform?" He gestured to the stage.

I shook my head.

"Do you have material you could perform?"

My heart rate increased at the inquisition. I knew Mr. Stone didn't mean it as an inquisition, but the intrusion upon a part of my life I kept private unsettled me. "Maybe."

He gave me a knowing nod. "You should think about performing. Your poetry assignments are stellar. You're talented. You intend to go to university, yes?"

I nodded again.

"Well, universities look at your outside interests and passions. Lots of kids have good grades. You'll need something that stands out. Performing here regularly would be a start." He smiled at me again, clearly waiting for a response.

I didn't know how to respond. My palms were sweating and I was feeling cornered. Thankfully, someone else stepped onstage and Mr. Stone leaned over to whisper, "I'll leave you to it. But think about it, Comet."

"Thanks, Mr. Stone," I whispered.

But inside I was yelling at my favorite teacher for pointing out something I'd been doing my best to ignore. That my excellent grades weren't a guarantee of admission into the University of Virginia, and that a university such as it was would be looking for students who stood out among the crowd. Mr. Stone was right. Being a part of Pan, gathering the courage to tread the stage here, was just an example of what it would take to make it into UVA and flourish there if I got in.

I couldn't just sit passively by in the audience.

Yet I wanted to.

For the first time, I couldn't just enjoy myself at Pan. Instead I imagined myself finally being brave enough to get up there and perform. Of being brave enough to remove the anonymity from my blog and use it as part of my application process for university.

Yet, I didn't make a move to do anything. I was stuck. Courage wasn't something you found at the bottom of a hot chocolate or in a few words of encouragement from your favorite teacher. Courage was clearly something I needed to find, but how was I supposed to when there was a big part of me that didn't mind the fact I hadn't discovered it?

Going to UVA was the biggest goal I had in my life. If I wanted it that badly…surely something would have to give?

6

Shakespeare said it best,
To thine own self be true.
To his wisdom, I attest,
So I'll be me, you be you.
—CC

How the hell did I end up here?

I had asked myself that question maybe thirty times from the moment we'd arrived at Jordan Hall's friend's party. The party was in a flat less than a minute from my house and from what I could tell was rented out by four students. The flat's windows looked out over the sea and from the noise blaring from the speakers in the sitting room I was surprised it hadn't been shut down by the neighbors downstairs yet. Everyone here was college age or older, and I felt like a kid as I stood in the corner of the room, nursing a can of soda.

I wasn't oblivious to the looks being thrown my way, and it was making me nervous.

It was a rare occasion when I was uncertain of my wardrobe choices, but tonight I was. I stood out from this art crowd, who all wore a surprising amount of black for supposedly creative people. Tonight, I was wearing above-the-knee-length bright yellow socks, an oversize blue tartan shirt dress with a large slouchy black belt around my hips, a black boyfriend cardigan with a brooch shaped like a yellow teacup pinned to it and a pair of patent blue-and-white striped Irregular Choice ankle boots. They had an oversize blue bow on the side, but what made them *really* different, was the fact that the heel wasn't conventional—it was a mini-sculpture of Alice from Disney's *Alice in Wonderland*.

My parents might not pay me a lot of attention but they gave me a generous monthly allowance and, while I did save some of it every month, I spent a lot of it on books and clothes. Nearly every pair of shoes I owned were Irregular Choice. I could probably open my own shop with how many pairs I had in my closet.

Vicki, who had disappeared with Jordan almost the moment we'd arrived, suddenly reappeared. She strode over to me, grinning happily. I gave her a fond smile even though I secretly blamed her for putting me in the position I was in. Loving people was complicated, right? "You look happy."

She nodded. "Jordan is so cool...and—" she stepped into me, her back to the room, and gave me this look I didn't understand "—his friends are fascinated by you."

I blushed. "They think I'm a weirdo, right?"

Vicki laughed. "No. The opposite. They don't realize you're shy. They just think you're mysterious and unusual—but in a good way. These are art students, Comet. They like different." She gestured to my clothes. "A few of the guys have asked who you are."

This time I blushed for a whole other reason. "Funny. Steph bolted from me as soon as we got here." She didn't have to tell me she was embarrassed by how I was dressed.

"Steph wouldn't know individuality if it bit her on the backside." Vicki threaded her arm through mine. "These aren't high school students, Com. They appreciate someone that knows who they are and isn't afraid of it. Talk to one of them."

The thought of talking to one of these strangers made me want to run in the opposite direction. What if I said something stupid? Or couldn't speak at all and just stood there gaping at them like a guppy? I suddenly found myself irrationally angry with Vicki for trying to push me. It may have been residual irritation from Mr. Stone's surprise appearance at Pan this week and his unwanted but sensible words of advice. He hadn't meant to be pushy and neither had Vicki, but I felt pushed all the same.

"Jordan's friend Ethan told us he thinks you're gorgeous." She subtly nodded her head to the opposite side of the living room. "He's the one in the black Biffy Clyro shirt, standing near the television with the redhead."

My gaze flew in that direction, curious despite myself about a guy who would call me gorgeous. No one, as far as I was aware, beyond Vicki, had called me gorgeous before. To my surprise the guy in the Biffy Clyro shirt was cute. Really cute. In that disheveled "lead singer of a rock band" kind of way.

Our eyes met and he smiled at me.

Stunned, I looked back at Vicki and she laughed. "Told you."

I wanted to run. Run right out of the party, down the beach and lock myself inside my empty house. I didn't know how to speak to boys my age; how the hell was I supposed to speak to an older, more experienced boy? And I didn't *want* to speak to him. I didn't know him. He was just a random at a party, and speaking to him meant a racing heart, sweaty palms and most assuredly boring him until I was mortified by his discomfort.

I wanted to kill my friend.

"He's coming over. See you later." And just like that Vicki was gone.

Yes.

Definitely going to kill her.

"Hi, how's it goin'?"

My gaze flew to the guy who was now standing in front of me. Ethan, wasn't it?

Our eyes were on level with one another, and I realized Ethan was the same height as me. He had a rangy, sinewy physique, however, that gave the illusion of greater height. The dimple that popped in his cheek with his lopsided grin was all kinds of charming.

He brushed his dark hair off his forehead. "I'm Ethan."

"Comet," I said quietly. *And I'd like to leave now.*

"That is such a cool name." Ethan grinned harder. "Really suits you."

It really didn't. "Thanks."

We stared at each other and I blushed. Again.

Ethan's eyes brightened. "So…you go to Blair Lochrie with Vicki?"

I nodded. Words! My head was filled with bloody words, and yet I was taking so long to come up with ones that sounded okay that the silence just stretched between us.

A gaping, yawning chasm of silence.

Mortified, I looked anywhere but at the boy in front of me.

"So, uh, is that a cartoon character on your shoe?"

Stunned he was still standing there, I shrugged. "Kind of. It's Alice from *Alice in Wonderland*. She's really a book character more than a cartoon, because Lewis Carroll published the novel in 1865 and the Disney version came out eighty-six years later, although technically my heels are the Disney version of her…" *Shut up! Someone shut me up!*

To my wary surprise, Ethan nodded like I'd said the most fascinating thing ever. "Cool."

Sensing it was my turn to ask a question I blurted out, "Are you an art student?"

He shoved his hair out of his face again, and I had to curb the urge to advise him he should just cut it if it was annoying him. "Aye. Photography. But I'm more focused on my band, right now. We're called Lonely Boy, inspired by the song from the Black Keys. We're kind of The Black Keys meets the Arctic Monkeys meets Babyshambles. Our musical aesthetic is alternative punk-dance-rock wrapped up in a social conscience. We've been playing a lot of gigs in…"

As it turned out, there were some boys you didn't have to say anything to. You just had to pretend to be interested in what *they* were saying.

After an hour of listening to Ethan, lead singer of Lonely Boy, wax poetical about his life in the band, I excused myself to use the bathroom. I had a headache and needed the reprieve. On my way out, Steph cornered me.

"What does *biomorphic* mean?" Her pupils were large, her skin was flushed, and she was swaying a little.

"How much have you had to drink?" I nodded to her beer.

"Just a few." She waved me off. "Comet, hurry, what does it mean?"

"Biomorphic? Why?"

She stamped her foot like a petulant child. "Because the

cute art guy I'm talking to keeps calling his work biomorphic, and I'm just smiling at him like an idiot because I don't know what it means."

I took her beer. "You've had enough. And it means taking living things, like plants, the human body, and making abstract images from them."

"You are so smart!" She kissed my cheek and hurried toward the kitchen at the end of the hallway, not even aware I'd taken her beer. I ducked back into the bathroom and poured the rest of the bottle down the sink.

Yes, I was *that* girl at the party.

Buzzkill girl.

This time when I stepped out of the bathroom I was stopped by Ethan.

He grinned and touched my arm. "There you are. I thought someone else stole you away."

My cheeks grew hot again as I shook my head.

And then he was kissing me!

My first kiss, and it just happened!

No warning. Nothing!

And it was awful.

It was like he was trying to eat my mouth and wriggle his tongue in it at the same time!

Thankfully it didn't last long, and he pulled back to smirk at me. "Let me get you a beer. Don't go anywhere."

The skin above my top lip and below my bottom was wet with his saliva.

Get the hell out of here, Comet! And I listened to myself. Without thinking of Vicki or Steph, I hurried past the bodies in the crowded hallway and darted outside. Running down the steps, I didn't even care if my Alice heels broke from my manic escape. I just wanted out. I threw open the main door to the building, and it banged against the wall. Loudly.

"Whoa!"

I skidded to a stop at the shout, noting to my horror the crowd of kids standing near our local pub, the Espy. Embarrassment flooded me when I realized it wasn't just anybody standing there. It was Stevie and his gang of miscreants.

And Tobias King.

Tobias had his arm around a girl I didn't recognize, a beer bottle dangling from his hand. He stared at me, frowning.

"Ye awright, Comet?" Stevie called. Alana Miller, a scary, would probably take my head off if I looked at her the wrong way, girl in the year below me had her arms around his waist.

I managed a nod at Stevie and then threw a reluctant glance at Tobias, who had dropped his arm from the unknown girl and was staring at me intently. Flushing harder, I turned from them and started to walk down the esplanade.

"What the fuck is she wearing?" I heard a girl cackle, and there was more laughter.

I hunched into myself and picked up speed.

That speed turned to full-out running once I knew I was out of sight, and I didn't stop until I was at my front door. It was only once I was inside my bedroom that I managed to relax somewhat.

And then I slumped onto my bed and fought the urge to cry as I wiped at my mouth and shuddered.

That was kissing? That horrible, wet, slug-like act was kissing?

Every time I got to a scene in the book where the hero and heroine finally kissed, it made me flush hot in a good way, and my chest filled with this delight, this giddiness that was hard to describe.

I had yet to read a book where the heroine got her face munched on!

"Ugh." I shuddered again.

Of course my first kiss would suck. Literally. I don't know why I ever expected anything else. And this was exactly the reason I should have stayed home tonight—so my illusions wouldn't be shattered by a presumptuous nineteen-year-old boy who had *not* received permission to put his mouth any-where near mine!

I yanked off my clothes, only slowing to take care with my expensive boots. Just as I was slipping into my pajamas, my phone made a little jingle of a noise, alerting me to a text.

Vicki : WRU@

I sighed and quickly replied. I went home. Tired. I'll put a key under the mat for you. xx.

Two seconds later it pinged: RUOK xx.

Yeah xx

Although I didn't like the idea of putting the key under the mat, there was really no other way for my friends to get in the house other than for me to stay awake all night. And I didn't want to. I wanted to sleep so I could forget the fact that my mouth had just been attacked.

On that note I flossed and brushed my teeth. Thoroughly. And then I rinsed it multiple times with mouthwash. Staring into the mirror, I got a flashback of the feeling of Ethan's kiss and shuddered again. "Ugh!" I made a face at myself.

Tomorrow I was going to do a reread of my favorite romance just to get this awful real-life imagery out of my head.

I awoke with a start, my heart in my throat, the blood whooshing in my ears.

"It's just me, babe," Vicki's voice whispered in the dark, but it sounded thick and cracked.

"Vicki?"

Down the hall I heard water running from a tap while Vicki's silhouette solidified out of shadow as my eyes adjusted to the dark.

She pushed the covers back and climbed into the bed. The denim of her jeans rubbed against the light fabric of my pajama bottoms, the floral perfume she wore mixed with the scent of beer enveloped me, and the soft, tight curls of her hair tickled my chin as she wrapped her arms around my waist and pressed her face to my collarbone.

I felt her body shake.

I felt something wet drip onto my skin.

Sleep deserted me at the realization that my best friend, who rarely cried, was sobbing quietly against me.

Concern kicked my heart into speed and something ugly twisted in my gut as I closed my arms around her and held her tight. "Vicki?" I was afraid. Afraid to ask what happened, all manner of dark suspicions lurking in my mind.

She held on tighter but didn't say anything, didn't relieve me of my fears.

The flush of the toilet brought my thoughts back to Steph as I heard the bathroom door open and her stumbling steps down the hall. My bedroom door swung open and shut, and Steph's dark figure rounded the bed and got in at the other side of me.

Not even a minute later her drunken snores filled the room.

"Vicki…what happened?" I dared to ask.

I wasn't sure she'd answer.

But then…

"Jordan," she whispered tearfully. "He wanted to have sex. I said I didn't want to, and then he said I was too young for him and…he went off with some girl from his class."

Dipshit.

Arsehole.

Wanker!

I tightened my grip on my friend. "I'm sorry he did that."

She cried a little harder, and I tried to soothe and hush her. After a while I felt her body relax. I was sad for her. I hated that a boy had treated her so poorly when he was lucky Vicki Brown had even noticed he existed.

Yet, there was a part of me that wasn't surprised.

In fact, it just drove home to me why my book boyfriends were a million times better than the real thing. Tonight I'd gone to a party for someone else because I'd made a promise to try harder. However, years ago I'd made a promise to myself, and that promise was painted above my headboard.

To thine own self be true.

Be true to yourself.

Standing in the corner of a party, talking to a boy who bored me and pretending that he didn't, allowing him close enough to violate my lips… I hadn't wanted to do any of those things. I hadn't wanted to go to the party in the first place! And look where it got me.

Worst night in a long time.

From now on, I did what *I* wanted to do.

I would remain true to myself.

Stay at home reading a lot of books and writing my poetry.

Even if everyone, including my best friends, thought it made me the biggest antisocial weirdo in Porty.

7

They all want to solve you and your mystery,
But I don't.
They want to unravel your secrets, your history,
But I won't.

I keep lying to myself, safe from your jagged edge,
All the while my curiosity tries to lure me off the ledge.
—CC

September first was the day I decided to push the boundaries of the school uniform. Our dress code was pretty strict but over the last few weeks I'd gotten away with adding cute, kitschy brooches and pins to the lapels of my blazer. So a week ago I'd asked Vicki if she had time to make me a few pairs of knee-high socks. In black. With gold stripes. They matched the uniform! They just jazzed it up a bit. Vicki whipped them up in a week and today was the first day I was wearing them.

I thought they looked cute, but I had to admit I was a little afraid of a teacher pulling me up for them.

Being worried about wearing outlandish knee socks was the least of my concerns. But I didn't know that when I walked into the school building that day.

I didn't know that until English class.

After a few weeks we'd made fast progress with *Hamlet*. We were on Act Two Scene Two, and Penny Shaw in the year above me was reading the part of the First Player when I became aware of someone hissing something at someone behind me.

The hissing grew more frantic, followed by the sound of stuff thumping to the floor.

We all whipped around to look as Tobias King got out of his chair to pick up his books and jotter from the carpet wearing a beleaguered look on his face. I glanced at Heather to find her opting for an angry, smug expression.

"What is going on over there?" Mr. Stone snapped.

Heather and Tobias seemed to cause some kind of kerfuffle in every lesson, so I could understand why Mr. Stone's patience was growing thin.

"Nothing, Mr. Stone," Heather answered sweetly.

"Nothing?" Tobias huffed, still standing as he stared down at her incredulously. He turned to Mr. Stone. "You do realize I'm sitting next to someone in need of a mental health professional?"

"GFY, Tobias!" Heather yelled.

"I have a teenage sister, Heather." Mr. Stone looked so harassed that I felt sorry for him. "I pretty much understand every text abbreviation under the sun. You can wait outside the room until the end of class and stay there until I come see you."

"But—"

"No buts, Heather. And when you return to my class, Tobias will no longer be sitting next to you. I'm tired of the two of you causing disruptions. Tobias, grab your things and take the seat next to Comet."

The blood suddenly whooshed in my ears as my heart rate shot up. I stared in horror at Mr. Stone, and he gave me a reassuring look.

How had this happened?

How was it possible that one little sentence had completely ruined my day? No...wait. My entire year in English class.

The seat next to mine made a rough scraping sound against the hardwearing carpet, and I stared determinedly ahead as Tobias King's large body settled beside me. I could feel the sprawl of him, the warmth, and smell his faint spicy citrus scent.

My cheeks burned and my muscles tensed as I held myself away from him. As good-looking as this boy was, his indifference, his delinquent behavior, had taken a toll on my crush. I'd thrown him over in favor of a fictional immortal boy warrior called Noah.

However, it was hard to remind myself of that when he was so close—so terrifyingly close—that my body hummed with awareness. I couldn't concentrate on what was being taught. All I could focus on was the shift of his legs under our desk, the way his arm almost brushed mine as he lifted a hand to drag his fingers through his hair and the irritated sigh that escaped him.

I wasn't the only one who heard that sigh.

"You disagree, Mr. King?" Our teacher stared at him.

Disagree about what? What had I missed?

Dammit!

"I didn't say anything."

I almost jumped at hearing Tobias's voice so close to me. It had a deep, husky quality that I found pleasant despite myself.

It was the accent, I tried to reassure myself. It was different, and I liked different, that was all.

Really.

"You didn't have to say anything. The sigh was enough. If you disagree with Penny's understanding of the scene, there are politer ways to respond, Mr. King. Why do you disagree?"

What had Penny's understanding of the scene been? Oh my goodness, I never daydreamed in English! Damn Tobias King.

He answered with bite, "I think it's pretty clear Hamlet isn't referring to his mental state as the devil."

What? I searched the text in front of me and read it, trying to understand.

"Read the passage again, Tobias. And then tell me what you think it means."

"I don't want to read it."

"Do you want to fail?"

Tobias shifted in his seat, and I risked a glance at him. As soon as my gaze landed on his face, he looked at me.

Crap.

I whipped my gaze back to my text, my cheeks furnace-hot with embarrassment. Then, to my surprise—to all our surprise—Tobias began to read.

And read well.

"Play something like the murder of my father
before mine uncle; I'll observe his looks,
I'll tent him to the quick; if 'a do blench,
I know my course. The spirit I have seen
May be a devil, and the devil hath power
T' assume a pleasing shape; yeah, and perhaps,
Out of my weakness and my melancholy,

As he is very potent with such spirits,
Abuses me to damn me. I'll have grounds
More relative than this—the play's the thing
Wherein I'll catch the conscience of the king."

My breath stuck in my throat as silence reigned over the classroom. It would appear that the magical something Tobias King had—that magnetism—could be used against me.

Because the boy made Shakespeare hot.

It didn't seem possible that a teenage boy with the wrong accent could make Shakespeare hot.

I gulped.

"Very good, Tobias," Mr. Stone said, sounding as astonished as I felt. "Now tell me what you think Hamlet is saying."

"He's saying that the ghost may be using his grief against him to manipulate him to take action against Claudius. So Hamlet has decided he needs to be sure and wants to use the play to get some kind of proof of his uncle's betrayal."

"Yes," Mr. Stone nodded, his gaze softening ever so slightly. "That's exactly right. Well done."

As class continued, I struggled to stay focused. It was hard to after discovering there really was a reason Tobias King had been placed in my English class. The boy was smart. So why was he hanging out with Stevie Macdonald and his crew of miscreants?

And why oh why did he have to be the one boy whose voice made the hair on my arms stand up?

Just before the bell rang, Mr. Stone announced something that took my day from bad to worse. "Team assignment. We're going to get your talking outcomes out of the way this year, since I know how much you love those."

We all groaned. Well, I didn't groan. I blanched.

"To make things somewhat easier on you, you will be working in teams of two. Look at the person sitting next to you, because they just became your talking outcome partner."

No.

No. Way.

I looked at Mr. Stone like he'd just betrayed me, and he gave me a small smile before addressing the rest of the class. "Each of you will be given sections of the play to present on. A few of you will be sharing the same assignment, so it'll be interesting to see what you come up with. You'll have roughly a month to put your presentations together. I'll provide you with your talk date and time next class. I'm coming around with your assignments now."

Mr. Stone stopped at Tobias and me first, and I still hadn't gotten over my shock so it was a miracle I even processed what he said to us. "Tobias, Comet, I want you to present on Hamlet's character development through his soliloquies. Remember to pick quotes from the soliloquies to present to the class to highlight your analysis of his character evolution." He placed a copy of the assignment on our desk.

We were silent a moment, an awkward, terrible silence, as Mr. Stone moved on to the rest of the class. I couldn't be the one to speak. It seemed impossible. Even though I was panicking at the thought of messing up an English assignment, I was unable to turn to Tobias to arrange time to work together. That would bring reality crashing down around me.

Tobias did it for me. "So I guess you'll want to get together to do this?" He flicked his piece of paper with the assignment on it. He couldn't have sounded less enthusiastic if he tried.

For some reason my irritation with his tone helped clear my throat. "Yes. I don't want to fail."

I still hadn't looked at him, but I could feel his gaze on my face. The burn of it was too much, and I finally caved and returned his stare. Tobias seemed to study me for a moment and then he sighed heavily. "Fine. My house after school."

Wonderful.

Not only, I guessed, was I going to be lumbered with most of the work, I was going to have to drag my butt out of my comfort zone and visit a boy. At his house. "Where do you live?"

"Do you know where Stevie lives?"

"Stevie Macdonald?"

"Yeah."

"No, I don't." Why on earth would he think I would?

"He's my cousin. My mom and I are staying with him and his mom for a while." He flipped his copy of the assignment over and began to scrawl on the blank side. Finished, he shoved it toward me. "Tonight. Seven o'clock. Be there. If you don't show, I'm not waiting around."

I was shocked to hear that Tobias and Stevie were related, but suddenly their attachment to each other made more sense to me. Perhaps it was merely familial obligation that had brought such different boys together in friendship?

As much as I hated to say it, considering I was already anxious about the fact that I had to go over to Stevie Macdonald's house that evening, I said, "One night won't be enough."

Tobias's lips curled into an arrogant smile. "I've heard that before."

It was so cocky that even I couldn't stop my eye roll. Nor

could I stop the pink blooming on my cheeks, which only made him chuckle.

Flustered, I stared studiously at the address he'd written down.

After another moment's silence, Tobias said, in a surprisingly gentle tone, "Okay, don't get all worried-looking. We'll work out other times to do the assignment when you come over tonight."

Before I had a chance to think up a reply, the bell rang for the end of class. I shoved my stuff into my bag in one sweep and shot out of my chair. A minute later—because I'd moved that quickly—I was halfway to the cafeteria.

I needed distance from the American, and I needed a few moments to gather myself before Steph and Vicki teased me about my presentation buddy.

"So tell me, does Tobias King smell as good as he looks?" Steph said without preamble as she and Vicki sat at my table in the cafeteria.

I shot her a droll look and she giggled.

"Don't, Comet." Vicki shook her head adamantly. "Don't let her encourage you. Tobias King is the last boy you want to crush on. Guys like him are users."

Hearing the bitterness in her words, I felt a pang of sadness for her. And more than a pang of anger toward Jordan Hall. Ever since he'd made Vicki cry, she'd had moments of ragey bitterness. It had been only a few weeks since the incident, and I was hoping time would heal her wounds.

"Boys can be dipshits." She stabbed her straw into her carton of orange juice. "I'm giving them up."

Steph looked horrified. "No way."

Determination blazed in Vicki's eyes. "Yes way. I need time to forget he who shall not be named, and then I'll be cool. But I'm not falling for just anyone."

"So…" Steph frowned, obviously not sure how to process the idea of a world without boys. "What are you going to do with yourself?"

Vicki burst out laughing while I struggled not to roll my eyes. "I'm just concentrating on me and design school. Parsons may be a long shot but the London College of Fashion is not and I'm going there if it takes all my blood and sweat. But no tears!" Vicki shook her head vehemently. "Tears just hold you back."

Frowning at her, I really, *really* hoped time would heal the wound Jordan had cut into her. Until she'd cried in my arms, and the subsequent moody days since, I'd had no idea how much Vicki had liked Jordan. If he were in front of me right now, I might have kicked him in the nuts. And I wasn't a violent person by nature.

"Well, just because you've given up boys, doesn't mean the rest of us have." Steph huffed. "We're allowed to talk boys."

Vicki just shrugged.

Steph turned to me and grinned. "You guys are meeting up, right? To do the presentation?"

The thought of going to Stevie's house that evening to work with Tobias made my skin prickle with a cold sweat. Tobias King inhabited an entirely different planet from the one I lived on. It would be like trying to talk to someone who didn't speak a language known to man.

"He's Stevie's cousin. I'm going there after dinner—"

"Second cousin," Steph interrupted.

"What?"

"Tobias is Stevie's second cousin. Their mums are first cousins."

"How do you know that?" Vicki said.

Steph threw her a mysterious smile. "I know everything."

"Well cousin, second cousin, whatever. The point is that I'm not crushing on Tobias," I semi-lied. "We're working on this presentation and that is it. Sorry. No boy talk from me."

Her lips parted at my announcement but then they pinched together for a few seconds before she let out an exasperated, "You two are no fun."

"There are other things to talk about," I reminded her. "Like the school play." Only last week, Steph had landed the part of Roxie Hart opposite Lindsay Wright, the sixth year playing Velma Kelly. And thankfully, Heather was in the chorus.

Steph's face lit up, and Vicki shot me a grateful smile. For the rest of our lunch we sat and listened patiently to our friend as she divulged the trials and tribulations of putting on a grand show.

Although all the while angry butterflies fluttered wildly in my stomach.

All I could do was stare at the building. I willed my feet to move but it was proving difficult. Stevie lived on a street that bordered Portobello and Niddrie. It was a good thirty-five-minute walk from my house on the beach, and our situations couldn't have been more different. While I lived in a midcentury seafront home, Stevie and Tobias lived in a drab building that housed six flats. Stevie's flat was on the ground floor. The gray pebble-dash render on the building, along with the overlong front lawns and toppled rubbish bins, gave the place a depressing feel.

It bugged me that Tobias lived here, and I couldn't explain to myself why that was. I wondered why he and his mum had to live with Stevie. What happened to them back in the US?

And suddenly Tobias was there, standing in the open entrance to the building. His face was in shadow, but I knew it was him by his height and the way he held himself. He wore only a T-shirt and joggers, no shoes, just socks, and he had his hands stuck in his pockets. "You plan on coming inside anytime soon?"

I jolted at his question, and to my everlasting mortification I blushed again, before finally making my feet move toward him. "I wasn't sure I had the right house," I lied.

He smirked. "Right. You're one of the smartest girls in school but you don't know how to read a street sign."

I ignored his sarcasm. "How do you know I'm one of the smartest girls in school?"

"Stevie told me. Plus, you can't exactly get into the classes you're in if you're stupid."

"True. So why do *you* pretend to be?" The question was out of my mouth before I could even think about it.

Tobias looked as surprised as I felt. He also did not deign to answer me. Instead he led me inside the ground-floor flat, and the lingering smell of Chinese food hit me as I stepped into the narrow hallway. I followed him, dodging the several pairs of shoes that were strewn in the hall near the entrance.

As we passed an open doorway, I glanced in and saw two women lounging on a couch. There were empty Chinese takeaway containers on the coffee table in front of them. One of the women was thin with wispy fair hair. Her neck was bent at an awkward angle, and it appeared she'd fallen asleep. The other woman met my gaze as I passed. I got an impression of pale skin and dark hair, but we were moving too quickly down the hall for me to observe anything else.

"Tobias, where are you going?" The woman's voice rang out just as he put his hand on the knob of a door around the left-hand corner at the end of the hall.

"Room," he called back. "I told you I have an assignment to work on."

"Well, I'd like to meet your friend. Where are your manners?"

He shot me an exasperated look like it was my fault. If only he knew I was even less inclined to meet the person I was guessing was his mother. The less I knew about Tobias King, the better. He gestured for me to go back the way we'd just come, and I drew to a halt at the sudden appearance of the tall brunette from the couch. She had big, sad, dark eyes and chin-length dark hair, pale skin and freckles across her nose that, along with her trim, slender physique, made her look too young to be the mother of an almost seventeen-year-old boy. Appearance-wise there was very little of her in Tobias. I wondered if he took after his dad. And then I wondered where his dad was.

She looked at Tobias and raised an eyebrow.

He sighed heavily, as if she were forcing him to do something unpleasant. "Mom, this is my English presentation partner, Comet Caldwell. Comet, my mom."

"Hi, Mrs. King," I said. "It's nice to meet you."

"Call me Lena, please." She spoke with a Scottish accent muddled by an American one.

"Okay." I smiled, but it faltered as her gaze drifted over me in an assessing manner and I suddenly realized I should have perhaps dressed more conservatively for coming to Tobias and Stevie's flat. I was wearing a dark green velvet skirt with a black-and-green striped top with arms that were tight at the wrist and then puffed out in balloon sleeves. On my feet were green flats with an oversize yellow bow on the front.

Not giving away her thoughts, Lena turned to her son. "Carole is worn-out. Try to keep it down."

"Where's Kieran?" Tobias asked.

If I remembered correctly, Kieran was Stevie's little brother. He was around six or seven years old.

"In Carole's room reading. I'll keep an eye on him. You just get your homework done like you promised."

"That's what Comet's for," he said.

Ass.

His mum seemed to think it was a crappy comment, too. "Don't you leave all the work to Comet. Promise."

"I could make that promise, Mom, not keep it and you still wouldn't do jack about it. That's what you're good at, right? Being a liar and doormat." He didn't wait for her to answer, just turned and bulldozed his way into the room behind us.

Lena stared after him wearing an expression of embarrassment and hurt.

Me? I was in shock and wondering what the hell I'd walked into.

"Are we doing this or what?" Tobias called, presumably to me.

His mother slid me a wary look and I gave her a shy, pinched smile before I darted into the room.

"Leave your bedroom door open a little," Lena called.

Tobias got up off his bed and immediately shut the door.

Okay.

I was guessing he and his mother didn't have the best relationship. Or Tobias was just a dick.

I was suddenly very much aware of the smell of too much teenage boy in one room, and I realized why when I saw the two beds and the floor around the bed nearest the window littered with clothes and football stuff.

"I share a room with Stevie," Tobias explained as I unwillingly stepped farther into the boy pit. The walls were a dark gray and covered in posters of football players around the messy bed. The walls behind and opposite the bed that was made and had no crap around it were covered in Lego and Minecraft posters. I raised an eyebrow, and Tobias smirked at me. "This is Kieran's bed. Until Mom and I find a place, I'm in here with Stevie." He gestured to the pit side of the room, "Kieran's in with his mom, and my mom's on the couch. It's a little crowded." He sat down on his bed, picked up his copy of *Hamlet* and his notepad from his bedside table and shuffled back against his pillows and the wall.

"Where is Stevie?" I asked instead, gingerly placing my bag on Tobias's borrowed bed.

"You can sit, too." He smirked at me, like he knew I was uncomfortable being this close to him.

I sat on the bed. I could feel Tobias watching me, and all I kept thinking was that this was probably the first time he had a girl in his room to do *homework*. I wondered if he could guess that this was the first time I'd been alone with a boy, or furthermore alone with a boy in his room.

I squirmed, wishing I was at home with the book I was currently reading instead.

"Stevie's out," Tobias finally replied, drawing my gaze to his. He narrowed his eyes at me. "Disappointed?"

Disappointed? That Stevie was out? Why would I be disappointed? "Excuse me?"

He seemed to assess me and then finally shook his head. "Never mind. Let's get started."

It was difficult to concentrate on anything but the fact that I was on Tobias King's bed, sitting across from him, feeling his gaze on me as I took out the notes I'd already started making. To my surprise, as we worked, Tobias gave a lot more input than he'd suggested he would.

After about an hour of study we'd pulled a number of quotes from Hamlet's soliloquies to back up our analysis of his character development. We worked easily with each other—another surprise—seeming to grasp *Hamlet* with a similar understanding.

"I'm going to grab a soda. You want one?" Tobias asked.

It was the first thing either of us had said that didn't relate to Shakespeare, and I noted, to my further shock, that I'd lost the restless, squirmy feeling I'd had earlier. The easy way we collaborated had distracted me from my discomfort. "Um…sure."

He got off the bed and left the room, and I took the opportunity to look around again. Tobias's side of the room wasn't neat as a pin—there were clothes strewn across a chair in the corner and piles of schoolbooks on the floor. But compared to Stevie's side, it was tidy and clean. My room could get messy, too, especially when I was caught up in schoolwork or a series of books. Unlike Vicki and Steph, I had no one on my back telling me to clean my room. I wondered if it was the same for Tobias and Stevie, or if their mothers' requests for them to tidy the room were continually ignored.

My curiosity over the boys' situation annoyed me. Stevie was just a step up from a thug, and Tobias was not only his second cousin but apparently his friend. That really said it all.

But why then was Tobias here, doing his homework with me, when he could be out with Stevie causing mayhem or whatever it was Stevie got up to?

Tobias strode back into the room holding two glasses of Coke. "Here."

"Thanks," I said, taking one.

My eyebrow nearly hit my hairline when he sat down on the bed, this time so close that our knees were almost touching. I could feel the heat of his body, and I desperately tried not to blush yet again due to my stupid awareness of him.

"So why are you here?" I blurted out in an attempt to steer my wayward thoughts back on a decent course.

Tobias smirked. "Is that a philosophical question?"

See! Much more intelligent than he'd have other people believe. But why? "You're obviously smart but you don't seem to care about class. So why are you doing this presentation with me when you could be out with Stevie?"

He shrugged. "My mom has been giving me a hard time lately. I thought if she saw me pretending to put a little effort in at school, she might lay off. That's why I asked you to come here instead of going to your house or meeting somewhere. If we studied somewhere else she probably wouldn't have believed me about meeting up with you to do homework."

I wasn't totally buying it.

Reaching across the bed, I picked up the copious notes he'd made. "This is pretending, is it?"

He glared and took the notes back from me. "As long as we get it done, why do you care?"

"I don't." I looked down at my own notes. "I just think maybe you like this stuff more than you let on."

"No one likes Shakespeare, Comet."

My head jerked up, my eyes flashing in indignation. "I do."

Tobias chuckled. "I stand corrected."

There was a knock at the bedroom door and it opened. The top half of Lena's body appeared around the door. "One, I told you to keep this open," she said to her son. "Two, it's getting dark outside and time to wrap this up." She looked at me. "How are you getting home, Comet?"

"I'm walking so, yeah, I better go." I said, gathering my notes and sliding them into my bag. I wasn't exactly looking forward to walking home in the dark.

"I'll walk you," Tobias said.

The thought of having to endure a thirty-odd-minute walk with the American sent me into a fluster. "No, that's okay."

"Tobias will walk you, Comet, no arguments," Lena said before turning to her son again. "Where's Stevie? I'm going to help Carole to her bed and she hasn't seen him all day."

I glanced from one to the other, curious over the strange look that passed between them. Why was Lena helping Carole to her bed? Was she sick?

"Out, I guess. I'm not his keeper."

Lena sighed. "Fine. Good night, Comet." She disappeared before I could return the sentiment.

"So…" Tobias dragged a pair of trainers out from under the bed. "When are we doing this again?"

"When are you free?" I asked, watching him shove his feet into the trainers and not do up the laces correctly. I'd noticed it was the fashion among Stevie and his friends to not tie their laces. I didn't get it. Who wanted their shoes to be flopping off their feet all the time?

"You're frowning."

"I'm not," I denied.

His lips curled up. "Okay, whatever you say." And then he further surprised me by holding the door open for me and gesturing for me to walk out ahead of him.

Very gentlemanly.

When we passed the sitting room I saw that it was empty, and once again I wondered about the situation here. Why was everyone crammed into this tiny flat? What was wrong with Carole? Where was Stevie? And where was Tobias's dad?

"So I want to get this presentation out of the way," Tobias said as he closed the front door of the flat behind us. Although I was dreading the walk home with a cute boy who flustered me, I was suddenly very glad for his presence. Outside, there was a group of boys I didn't recognize, one on a bike, the others sitting on the wall of the building next to Stevie's. They looked at us as we approached, their loud conversation halting, and I noticed two of them were holding bottles of cheap wine. They couldn't have been much older than us, perhaps even our age.

"Awright, King?" The one on the bike gave Tobias a chin lift.

Tobias merely nodded, but I felt him shift closer to me.

"Who's the bird?" The blond with one of the bottles in his hand called out, and my gaze flew to the ground as I found myself center of their attention. "Gie us a look at ye, then. Nice legs." He whistled loudly.

I tensed as we passed, listening to their laughter.

"Keep walking," Tobias said under his breath, like I needed to be told that.

"No' in the mood for sharing the night, King?"

"Not tonight. Later."

It was only when their laughter was a distant noise that I let myself relax marginally.

"Like I said, I want this assignment over with. Think we can get it finished up if you come here after school tomorrow?"

The thought of traversing his neighborhood again made me anxious, but I wanted the presentation finished, too. "Possibly. We'll need more than an hour. But if we get the work done I can type it up, and then we could get together to practice it before our talk date."

"Fine. Can you come here straight after school? That way I can walk you here. Then get one of your parents to pick you up?"

Right. Like that would happen. "They're busy. I can walk."

He was silent a moment. "I'll walk you."

"You don't—"

"You want to be alone, passing guys like that?" he interrupted me, sounding snarky.

I shot him a look of annoyance. "Fine, you can walk me."

For some reason that made him smile.

8

Those are my words, my thoughts, my soul,
You took them from me without apology.
So why do I want to forgive what you stole,
And hope that you like my ideology?
—*CC*

It took me a while to fall asleep that night. The walk with Tobias had been mostly silent, the quiet between us broken only by passing traffic and my murmurings of "It's this way" and "We need to cross here."

He'd insisted on walking me right to my door, and he'd stared at my town house for so long that I wished I knew him better so I could work out what his expression meant. Eventually, he'd looked at me and shrugged. "I'll see you tomorrow." Then he'd started to walk down my garden path.

"Uh…can you find your way back okay?"

Tobias glanced over his shoulder. "I'm good." He pushed open the garden gate.

"Uh…well…"

He looked back at me again, and this time I did recognize his expression. Impatience.

"Thank you for walking me home."

The impatience melted out of his features and his gaze dropped to my feet before it moved up my body to my face in a way that made my skin prickle. Something softened in his expression.

"You're welcome, Comet."

I hadn't been able to get the sound of his voice saying *You're welcome, Comet* out of my head as I lay in my bed. It seemed totally unfair that the first boy in real life to make my cheeks warm and my belly fizzle would have to be Tobias King.

Someone so totally opposite me it wasn't even funny.

And now I had to spend even more time with him.

I became so preoccupied with the thought of meeting Tobias after school and walking to Stevie's and his flat with him, and then working in close proximity in their bedroom again, I was utterly useless as a friend. I barely had any recollection of anything Vicki or Steph said to me all day, and it became clear to them why when we walked out of school at the end of the day and I told them I had to wait for Tobias.

"So that's why you've been so distracted all day," Steph said, sounding put out. "You get to spend the afternoon in Tobias King's bedroom."

My God, was she jealous?

It sounded like she might be a little envious.

"Oh, Comet, please don't tell me you like him," Vicki said, not sounding jealous at all, but very concerned.

"I don't," I lied.

"Good. Because he's a bad boy. And you're…"

"Comet," Steph supplied, like that explained everything.

Ugh. It did explain everything.

Total opposites.

"Well, I don't. Now go, before he thinks we're standing here gossiping about him."

Steph laughed and threaded her arm through Vicki's to lead

her away. I gave Vicki a reassuring smile and a wave when she looked over her shoulder at me, still plainly concerned.

"Ready?"

I almost jumped out of my shoes as I spun around to find Tobias towering over me. He was alone.

Hmm.

I'd been partly nervous about meeting him to walk him to his flat because I'd suspected Stevie would be joining us. Relief moved through me. "No Stevie?"

Tobias's brows drew together. "No. Why would there be?"

I shrugged, confused by his somewhat belligerent response. "You live together."

"He skipped out after lunch."

Of course he had. I turned away so Tobias wouldn't see me roll my eyes. "I suppose we better go then."

If I'd thought last night's walk was quiet, this one was positively dead. We said not a word to one another. I was going to start up conversation, attempt to *not* be socially awkward, but Tobias seemed lost in his thoughts and his silence made me lose my nerve.

"You're not afraid of me, are you?" He spoke up suddenly, only a street away from the flat.

The question surprised me so much my tongue loosened. "What? Why would you think that?"

"The way you reacted when Mr. Stone made me sit next to you. Your hands were shaking yesterday. You were nervous at Stevie's flat. The way you're acting now."

"It's not that I'm afraid of you."

"So you're just shy as shit?"

What a charming adjective. I wrinkled my nose. "Maybe."

Tobias chuckled. "You don't have to be shy around me. Contrary to popular belief, I'm not actually Satan."

"No one thinks you're Satan." I shook my head. "Just… maybe not the kind of boy who would talk to a girl like me. I get that." I wanted to assure him that I knew we were just presentation partners and not actually friends. "So let's just get to your place and get our work done."

"First…go back. The part about me being a guy who wouldn't talk to a girl like you. Explain."

I frowned at the demand. "I'm academic. I like school. You…you may be smart, but clearly you don't like school."

"I can see where you might think that." He nodded and then flashed me that boyish grin. "But maybe you're wrong."

"Possibly." I nodded. "I don't really know anything about you."

"I don't know anything about you either. Most girls are pretty talkative about themselves. You're not. You're kind of a mystery."

Tobias King thought *I* was a mystery.

That made me laugh, and his eyes widened as he watched me, his mouth curling up at the corners in that way it was wont to do in lieu of an actual smile. "I've never seen you laugh before."

Did he think I was some emo, miserable teenager incapable of it? "It's been known to happen once in a while."

This time he full-out grinned at my dry tone. "Apparently."

We turned onto his street and I watched the smile on his face drop as he took in the sight of the building he lived in. "You don't like it here?" I guessed.

He shrugged. "It's somewhere to lay our heads, I guess. Mom is looking for a place."

104

I wanted to ask all the questions that had built up inside of me since yesterday, but a slight warmth had grown between us and I didn't want it to dissipate because I was being nosy.

When I followed Tobias into the flat, the first thing that assaulted my ears was the sound of cartoons, reminding me of Vicki's house after school with Ben. As soon as the door slammed shut behind us we heard, "King, is that you?" just before a little boy threw himself out of the living room and hurried down the short hall to grin up at Tobias. He was about six or seven, as I'd suspected, a mini-me of Stevie, and he was hopping from one foot to the other like he had ants in his pants. "Yer home early. Where's Stevie? Come play the Xbox with me!"

"Kieran." The blonde from the couch yesterday appeared in the doorway of the living room. She had dark circles under her eyes and a weary expression on her pretty face. "I told ye, yer cousin is working on a project with his friend from school." Her gaze moved to Tobias and she gave him a fond smile. "Hi, darlin'."

"Carole." Tobias gave her his lip curl. "This is Comet. Comet, this Stevie's mom, Carole."

"Nice to meet you."

She smiled. "You, too."

"Comet," Kieran suddenly said. "Cool name! Can I come sit with you and Comet?" he asked Tobias.

"Sorry, buddy." Tobias mussed his little cousin's hair in affection. "We've got work to do. I'll come find you after."

Kieran's face crumpled with frustration. "But—"

"Kieran, come watch yer cartoons and give Tobias and Comet some peace."

To my surprise Kieran, although pouting comically, did as

he was told and disappeared into the living room with one last soulful look at us. Carole gave us another tired smile. "I'll keep him occupied. Yer mum called. She's working overtime."

Tobias barely acknowledged this. Instead he gave her a scowl along with a nod of his chin and turned to me. "You know where you're going, right?" He gestured up the hall. "I'll be there in a sec."

Realizing he wanted privacy with his cousin, I walked down the hall, giving her a shy smile before I disappeared around the corner. However, I hadn't quite made it to the bedroom Tobias shared with Stevie when I heard him ask, "Did you see the doctor?"

I froze, curiosity and, let's face it, nosiness, getting the better of me.

"I was working until two. I didnae have time before picking up Kieran from school."

"You told Mom you'd go." He sounded frustrated.

"As I told Lena, I'm fine. I'm just fighting off this flu."

"Mom said—"

"While yer mum is at work, I'm the adult in charge of ye here. So stop worrying about me and go be a kid. Worry about yer schoolwork. Lena says yer grades are suffering, and if I find out it's because Stevie is leading ye astray, I won't be happy."

"I do what I want, not what anyone else wants."

"Then ye'll only have yer own stupidity to blame when ye end up living in a flat like this, working at a job with crap pay and no future. Yer so smart, Tobias, smart enough to listen to me when my son won't. Lena says ye enjoyed school back in the States. Pretending to not like it because my kid doesn't like it is the opposite of smart."

"I don't need a lecture, Carole."

"Don't ye? Life is short, kid. Don't waste it pretending to be something yer not."

I hurried into Stevie and Tobias's room before I could hear Tobias's response. I didn't want to get caught eavesdropping. But I was intrigued about Tobias's life even more than I had been the night before.

When Tobias came into the room I was already settled on the bed with my notes spread out on his duvet. He kicked off his shoes and got on the bed, swiping his notes off his bed-side table. He was quiet and broody again.

"Kieran is cute," I said, attempting to break the silence.

His expression softened a little. "Yeah, he's a funny kid."

"He seems to like you."

"What's not to like?"

I rolled my eyes, and this time Tobias chuckled. "Not so shy anymore, huh?"

And just like that I blushed, making him laugh harder. Pretending to scowl, I stared ferociously at my notes, trying to remember where we'd left off the night before.

"You're cute when you blush."

My gaze flew up at that comment, my heart suddenly pounding. Tobias was staring intently at his notes, like he hadn't just given me a compliment. A compliment that had the blood whooshing in my ears and flooding my cheeks. When he refused to meet my stare, I looked back down at the papers in front of me.

"I think we're on the fifth soliloquy, right?" he said, as if he hadn't called me cute.

Deciding it was best for my mental state to go along with the pretense, I cleared my throat. "Right."

As we worked, the easiness fled and it wasn't because of Tobias's offhand compliment. It was because of my reaction to it. Steph or Vicki would have said something coy or flirty back, and the compliment would have been forgotten as the conversation continued. But not me. I didn't know how to react, and I overanalyzed and wondered if he really meant it or if he was messing with me. Then I started to think he really was messing with me and how mean that was!

I exhausted myself trying to focus on our presentation and mentally berate Tobias at the same time.

Almost two hours later my belly was growling in hunger when the bedroom door suddenly flew open and Stevie was there with an annoying smirk on his face. "I thought Mum was havin' a laugh when she said ye were in here with Comet Caldwell."

Tobias scowled. "We're working on stuff for English."

"Aye, very good." Stevie sauntered over to me and smiled in his cocky, cheeky way. "Awright, Comet?"

"Stevie," I mumbled, looking down at my notes.

"I thought you were out with Jimmy and the guys?" Tobias said.

"Aye, I was. I got bored without ye, mate."

"That's sweet," Tobias teased. "But…kinda working here."

"I can see that."

I glanced up at the suggestive tone in Stevie's words. But he was frowning, looking down at our notebooks and copies of *Hamlet*. "Maybe I can help? Anything is better than listening tae Forrester go on aboot that bird he tagged at the weekend."

Tobias chuckled. "Why not? But if you're helping, you're bringing us snacks."

"Munchie patrol." Stevie rubbed his hands together glee-fully. "On it."

The thought of having to hang out with Tobias *and* Ste-vie freaked me out. "Actually…we're uh…we're almost done here. I can type up what we have and then we can finish the rest at school." Earlier, while Tobias was talking to Carole, I'd emptied my bag on the bed. Now I began shoving every-thing I thought was mine back into it.

There was silence at my abrupt announcement, and al-though I was looking at them, I was pretty sure they were throwing each other bemused looks. Ignoring that suspicion, I stood up, still avoiding their gaze.

"I'll walk you home," Tobias said, getting up quickly.

"Oh no, I can walk it alone. It's still light out."

"I'll come with ye," Stevie said.

"No-no, it's really okay."

When neither answered, I glanced up to find Tobias look-ing between Stevie and me with a crease between his brows. I glanced at Stevie. He was eyeing me, like he was trying to work out something about me.

"Okay. See you."

I was almost at the front door when I heard the heavy foot-falls behind me, and looked over my shoulder to see Tobias following me. He wore a no-nonsense expression.

"I'm walking you at least to the High Street. No argu-ments."

Since I had a feeling he might stalk me all the way to Porty High Street, which was minutes from my house, I gave in.

This time our walk was even quieter than the night before. And instead of hearing him say *You're welcome, Comet* over and over in my head as I tried to fall asleep that night, I heard his voice on repeat telling me I was cute when I blushed.

I was nervous about going to school the next day for a different reason. Whereas yesterday I hadn't wanted to spend more time with Tobias, now I was worried he was going to avoid me. He'd been really weird and distant while walking me home.

What had I done?

And why did I care?

It turned out I had worse things to worry about than Tobias ignoring me. First, Assistant Rector Mr. Jenkins saw me in the halls and quietly asked me to return home at lunchtime to change out of my gold striped socks—the fascist. Second… well…the second thing was a doozy.

Three days out of the week we had a seventh period. Thursday and Friday were everyone's favorite days because we had only six periods and school ended fifty minutes earlier. Those fifty minutes were supposed to be filled with extracurricular activities and homework sessions. Can you guess how many pupils used it as such?

Wednesday was already kind of rubbish for the mere fact that it was a Wednesday. Plus, I had two free periods after lunch but then English seventh period, so I couldn't just go home. Instead I did all my homework in the library during my free periods. I didn't mind it too much, because seventh period *was* English.

That was…until the second thing hit.

Tobias King.

Not avoiding me.

And it was so much more than just not avoiding me. It was the total opposite of not avoiding me.

There were butterflies in my belly as I took my seat in English, ignoring Steph's giggle and Vicki's pointed look. Tobias wasn't there yet, thank goodness. Steph would have teased me even more if she'd known his voice had kept me awake for a good part of the night.

I was attempting to study *Hamlet*, waiting for everyone to filter into class, and pretending not to be aware when a shadow fell over me and the chair beside me scraped backward. This pretense would have continued if Tobias hadn't settled into his seat and slapped a familiar notebook on top of the open pages of my copy of *Hamlet*.

Confusion was my foremost emotion.

"You left this at my place last night. I found it under the bed."

And then understanding dawned and with it…ultimate mortification. It must have fallen off the bed after I'd emptied my bag.

The notebook was no ordinary notebook. It was by Paperblanks, made of sewn leather and dyed a gorgeous shade of teal. All my notebooks were Paperblanks. They were expensive but looked so beautiful together on my bookshelves that I didn't mind the dent in my allowance.

However, this notebook contained the ramblings of my teenage mind. My poetry.

Apparently Tobias King had been in possession of my private, innermost thoughts in rhyme since yesterday. I felt so shaken and vulnerable that I might as well have been sitting in class naked.

There were thoughts in that book that no one knew I had.

No one. My thoughts. My own. And this boy who was practically a stranger...

I shuddered, fighting the desire to burst into tears. Instead I curled my fingers tight around the book and reached for my bag. Without looking at Tobias, I shuffled the notebook into my bag out of sight, as if the action would erase the book from his memory.

Maybe he hadn't read it...

I winced at the naive wishful thinking.

Of course he'd read it.

Oh God, what if Stevie had read it, too? They shared a room, after all!

"I—"

"Act Three Scene One, today." Mr. Stone strode into the room, cutting off whatever Tobias was going to say to me.

My cheeks felt like they were on fire and as I moved to pull *Hamlet* closer to me, my fingers trembled. I thought I heard Tobias release an aggravated sigh. In an effort to block out everything about him, I hunched around my copy of the play and thanked my decision to leave my hair down today. It acted as a curtain, falling across my face, hiding my burning cheeks from him and everyone else.

For the rest of class, I was lost in manic thoughts and fears. If Tobias had shown my poetry to Stevie Macdonald and his group of idiots, my life was over. They'd never let me live it down. Worse—what if they'd taken photos of the pages? What if I walked into school tomorrow to find snapshots of my poems plastered all over the walls?

Or even worse, all over the internet without the shield of anonymity my words were currently protected by?

My stomach roiled.

My knee bounced under the desk in agitation as I imagined my life at Blair Lochrie if my friends and classmates ever got their hands on those poems. They'd decimate me. Some were so personal.

I flinched, remembering I'd written a poem about my first kiss the other week. *No.* No bloody way! I'd written it down to get it out of my head, like I did most of my worries or concerns. It was supposed to be funny, to cheer me up, but in the wrong hands it was embarrassing, and it would be cruel if Ethan ever got word of it. The fact that Tobias might know I'd compared my first kiss to a slug mistaking my tongue for a mate was beyond mortifying.

And that was the least of what I'd written.

I didn't hear a word in class.

Not a word.

When the bell rang I just grabbed up my books and bag and darted out of the room before anyone could speak. As I hurried along the corridor, I tried to shove my books into my backpack but the action stupidly slowed me down.

"Comet, wait!"

I was going to throw up.

His hand clamped down on my shoulder, and suddenly Tobias was right in front of me in an increasingly crowded corridor. I stared up at him in reproach, waiting for him to bring the guillotine down on life as I knew it.

Instead he stared at me, searching my face for what felt like forever.

Then he did something that surprised the hell out of me. "I, uh…" He scrubbed a hand over his hair and glanced at his feet. "I really liked your poems."

I was a mass of conflicted emotions in that moment, but overruling them all were confusion and distrust. "What?"

His gaze flew to my face again. "I know I shouldn't have read them… I'm a nosy asshole… But they were really good."

I couldn't detect an ounce of remorse in his tone, despite his words. Was he making fun of me? Was this all a big joke to him?

The anger I'd been feeling burned into bitterness, melting the shyness I usually felt around boys into ash. "Did you show them to anyone?"

Tobias flinched—at my accusing tone or just at the question, I couldn't be certain. "I wouldn't do that."

Really? And how the hell was I supposed to know what *King* would or wouldn't do to get a laugh out of his friends? As far as I knew, he didn't take anything in life seriously, and I was just supposed to believe that he'd found the poetry of a boy-shy, introverted bookworm "good" and that he had no intention of turning me into an afterschool special?

"Comet, are you okay?" Suddenly Vicki and Steph were at my side, Vicki looking from me to Tobias with suspicion. Whatever she saw in my face made her cross her arms and glare at the American.

I tensed, silently begging him not to say a word.

"I was just asking Comet a question about our presentation." He shrugged, and my tension eased. As if he knew, he smirked at me. "See you later."

I watched him walk away, hope and fear now fighting with one another equally. Was he telling the truth about liking my poems? Had he really kept my notebook to himself and not shown it to Stevie? Only time would tell, and until then I'd have to walk around with giant butterflies in my stomach, waiting for that guillotine to fall or not fall.

"What was that all about?" Vicki said. "You looked angry at him."

"No." I shook my head. "He was just asking when we were meeting up to finish the presentation. I said we'd already discussed it and he should probably start concentrating if we want to pass our talking outcome."

"You did not!" Steph looked wide-eyed at the thought. "Comet, you're going to blow your chance with him."

I stared at her like she'd lost the plot. "Since when did I have a chance with him? Since when did we want me to have a chance with him?"

"Since you still have virgin lips."

I flushed at the way she smirked as she said it, as though she enjoyed the fact that I had less experience with boys than she did. She probably did enjoy that fact. For Steph, life was one big competition. Even with her friends. "Actually I don't," I said, pleased when her eyes rounded in shock.

"What? Since when?"

"Since you were too drunk at Jordan's party to see me kissing his friend Ethan."

"No way!"

"Yes way." Vicki nodded, surprising me. She shrugged as I gave her a questioning look. "Ethan told us that night. He said you two had been snogging and then you just disappeared. At the time I was...well... I was a bit drunk and into Jordan Ass Hall. Then you never mentioned it so..." Irritation shone in my best friend's eyes.

I could only assume she was mad at me for not confiding in her.

Again.

Any other day I'd stew over it and try to think of ways to make it up to her. However, I had bigger problems today.

"It wasn't a big deal." I started to walk away, the corridor emptying as everyone else hurried to get home or to extracurricular activities.

"It was your first kiss, Comet. How is that not a big deal?" Steph frowned.

"Because it wasn't." And sadly, it really hadn't been.

As we strode outside I glanced around, preparing myself for Tobias and his friends to jump out and start mocking me. Instead there were just pupils strolling with friends like I was.

No one paid attention to me.

The tightness in my chest, however, didn't ease.

"Comet, you're not even listening. Earth to Comet!"

I threw Steph an exasperated look, surprising both of them when I said, "I have to go, okay. Talk later."

For once I didn't care if my behavior would have them talking about me behind my back. All I cared about was getting home in one piece.

Yet, when I did cross the threshold of my home, my anxiety didn't lessen.

Instead I thought of the personal social media pages I used infrequently. What if Tobias had posted something on there?

I threw my bag on the floor of my bedroom and dived for my laptop. Heart pounding in my chest, I started scouring every social media site I could think of. Finally, after discovering Tobias hadn't even been on his own social media pages for months, despite being tagged on Instagram and Facebook by a lot of my classmates in photos from parties, I relaxed marginally.

But only marginally.

Because even if Tobias didn't share my poetry with anyone else, *he* had still seen it. This boy I'd spent some time with but knew little of had seen deep into my soul. And he didn't seem to care or understand how big of a deal that was.

Tears pricked my eyes at the injustice of it. I rummaged through my backpack for the offending notebook, then flopped down on my bed and cracked it open, preparing myself for the torment of rereading words I'd written, now knowing someone else had read them, too.

As I read poems that ranged from silly, inconsequential meanderings to ones of longing and loneliness, the tears began to spill over. These were my thoughts. Mine. No one else's.

How dare he steal into my thoughts and take them from me!

And what an idiot I was for giving him the opportunity! I was so mad at myself for not realizing my notebook was missing, for leaving it for him to find. I was probably angrier at me than at him!

Frustration burned through my tears, and as the wet blur cleared from my vision I was stopped in my ragey inner protests at the sight of a Post-it note on one of the poems. Scrawled in messy, boyish writing were the words, "This is my favorite. TK."

It deflated me entirely.

Confused me.

Bewildered me.

And worse…softened me.

I peeled the Post-it note off the poem and reread it.

For the longest, loneliest time,
I thought it was me, not you.

So I tried to see it in rhyme,
Work out what was real and true.

For years there have been secrets,
Hidden in those distant eyes.
Truths that are your weakness
Because you want to keep them lies.

It doesn't make me feel better,
Knowing you're so messed up.
I thought it would free me of your fetters,
But here I am still locked up.

Some would say I need empathy,
For the pain you've had to endure.
But for you I've run out of sympathy,
You're my villain…and there is no cure.

If Tobias was telling the truth, and this poem really did speak to him in some way, I was curious. Curiouser than curious. This was one of my most revealing poems about the state of my relationship with my mum. Did he understand that? It was possible, considering his less than warm interaction with his mum the other night at Stevie's. Or did he relate to the poem because of his mysterious, apparently-not-in-the-picture dad? Or did the idea of the poem have relevance to another aspect of his life?

Just knowing my words had touched him changed my perspective of Tobias and made me wish I'd had the courage to ask him all my nosy questions, after all.

That was, if he was being honest with me.

But why was he being honest with me?

He'd admitted himself that he didn't know me.

Had my poetry, plus our short time together, made him feel like he could trust me?

A new breed of butterflies awoke inside at the thought of Tobias and me becoming friendly enough that we trusted one another. Until now he'd been a mix of fantasy-book boyfriend come to life and a confusing troublemaker who could make me feel at ease one minute and then a nervous wreck the next. Now I was almost desperate for classes tomorrow, to see what he would say or do.

I wanted more than anything for him to be telling the truth, not only about keeping my poems to himself, but about liking them. The former was out of self-preservation. The latter, however, was about something else entirely. The idea of being friends with Tobias filled me with what felt like electricity. My heart beat harder, faster, and my fingers and toes tingled with restless energy.

It was like I'd been sleepwalking for the last sixteen years, and now I was awake.

Really, truly, awake for the first time.

9

Yesterday there was nothing but gray sky,
Now there are sunbeams where once there were clouds.
Yesterday I felt as though I had no ally,
Now I have someone who sees me among the crowds.

—*CC*

There were no weird looks or whispers behind my back as I walked into the school the next morning. No one said a word to me in form class, so I concluded that Tobias had been telling the truth. He hadn't shown anyone else the poetry.

I relaxed at the thought, although not completely, because I was still anticipating seeing him in English for first period. We saw each other for the first three periods on a Thursday because we had English, Spanish and then maths together.

Vicki and Steph barely said a word to me in form class. Now that I wasn't anxious over everyone finding out about my poetry, I found myself concerned over alienating my friends even more than usual.

"Do you guys want to study at mine after school?"

"I can't. Rehearsal," Steph said.

I looked at Vicki expectantly.

She gave me an apologetic smile. "I said I'd help out with the costumes for the show. I'm going over some sketches with Ms. Scott and taking cast measurements."

"Oh. Okay. Do you need help? I could keep you company and it would look good on my university applications."

"There would be nothing for you to do."

My belly roiled as I tried to convince myself they weren't deliberately avoiding me. Which was hard to do when they walked ahead of me toward English class.

Staring forlornly at their backs, I was distracted, which was why it took me a second to realize someone had fallen into step beside me. I startled and glanced up into Tobias's gorgeous face.

He grinned down at me. "You were somewhere else there."

I nodded, still struck by his size *and* the fact that he was walking with me to class.

"Are you mad at me?"

I tensed, feeling more vulnerable than I ever wanted to feel as we walked into class together. Should I be honest with him or not?

Ignoring Steph's and Vicki's pointed stares, I settled into my seat and said to Tobias, as he sat next to me, "I should be mad at you."

Tobias leaned in, his breath caressing my cheek as he whispered, "Don't be mad. Your secrets are safe with me, Comet."

I turned to look at him, our noses inches from one another as I stared into his bright eyes. "I admit it was my fault for leaving the notebook at yours...but still...I never willingly gave you those secrets."

Finally, remorse clouded his gaze. "I know. I'm sorry. They're all good secrets, though. They say good things about you. Trust me with them."

A part of me—a huge part—wanted to sway into his words, be wrapped up in the spell of his deep voice and magnetic charisma. But my confusion over why someone like Tobias could possibly understand someone like me, and *like* me, won. I felt a shutter come down over my eyes, blocking him out, and he must have noticed it. His smile turned into a scowl seconds before I unlocked my gaze from his.

Unfortunately, as silent as I was with him, I couldn't escape Tobias. We had Spanish next, though thankfully, he sat at the back of the room. I didn't even have the support or distraction of Vicki in Spanish anymore as she'd dropped the subject after week one and was taking Modern Studies with Steph instead.

I didn't know if it was my imagination or not, but I honestly thought I could feel Tobias's gaze on the back of my neck.

And then I couldn't even escape him in conversation during our morning break.

Steph and Vicki found me in our common room, which happened to be a music room on the second floor. Other classmates were there, too, hanging out with their friends, but Steph and Vicki zoomed in on me.

"What was that?" Vicki said.

"What was what?"

"Don't play dumb." Steph slid onto the tabletop beside me and put her feet on a chair. "I thought King was going to snog you in front of everyone."

I felt my cheeks flush. "Wh-what?"

"What were you talking about?" Vicki stood in front of me, arms crossed. Was I under interrogation?

"Class," I lied.

She scowled at me. "It looked more than that."

"It wasn't." I looked between my friends. "What's the big deal?"

"The big deal is that it looked intense between you and Tobias King this morning. Your faces were, like, right here." Steph placed her palm inward to just short of the tip of her nose. Her features seemed pinched. "He looked really into you."

I blushed harder and, to my chagrin, squirmed in delight, remembering him calling me cute. "He's not. He just likes to wind me up about class." That was half the truth, at least.

Steph looked more than ready to believe that over the idea that he fancied me, and I wondered if she even knew what she really wanted. Tobias to like me, or for him—no correction, *every* boy—to like her instead.

Vicki did not look convinced. But instead of pursuing it further, she challenged me in another way. "It's my cousin Sadie's eighteenth this weekend. We're all invited. Her parents are on holiday."

I knew Sadie and liked her. Her parents were extremely successful in buying and selling property and had a lovely Georgian town house in Stockbridge. But a party was still a party after all. And even though I knew this was a test, I couldn't bring myself to do something just to make Vicki happy with me again.

"I don't like parties, Vicki. You know that."

Steph huffed. "You're seriously the most boring teenager on the planet."

Hurt, I looked down at my feet. I was wearing black-and-metallic-gold brogues today. At least my clothes weren't boring.

"Steph," Vicki reprimanded softly.

"Hey." Steph wrapped an arm around my shoulders, drawing my gaze to her face. "You are who you are, Com. Doesn't mean we don't love you."

I gave her a tremulous smile instead of scowling at her like I was mentally. Satisfied with my response, she dropped her arm and turned to Vicki. For the rest of break, whether they realized it or not, my friends spoke to one another like I wasn't there. My chest ached as I watched Vicki laugh with Steph, and I realized that somehow over the last few weeks my best friend and I had grown apart. A wall had slowly risen between us, and I didn't know how to stop it from becoming too epic to climb.

I saw Tobias in maths but didn't speak to him.

I never saw him for the rest of the day. He and Stevie and their annoying crew weren't in the cafeteria at lunch. The reprieve might have made me happy, until I realized Steph and Vicki were also nowhere to be seen. When I texted them, Vicki replied: We both had free period b4 lunch. Munchin' @ Nana's. C U l8er. xx.

More hurt and irritation ripped through me. Nana's was this great little café off Porty High Street that we all loved. Nice of them to tell me they were eating out of school. I could have joined them. Huffing, I yanked out a battered copy of Angela Carter's *The Magic Toyshop*. I'd discovered Carter over the weekend when I'd read a review of one of her short story collections, written by a blogger I followed. I'd hit the library, determined to make my way through all her weird and wonderful work.

As amazing as her writing was, however, I couldn't concentrate.

I hated this distance between my friends and me, and I felt

solely to blame. But what could I do? Change who I was to keep them?

Every great book, play or poem in the world told you to be yourself, and I wanted to. I did. But clearly the authors of those works didn't know what it was like to be a teenage girl in the twenty-first century.

My mood hadn't lifted any by the time dinner rolled around. It was a typical day in our household. Carrie was locked in her studio working on another commissioned piece, and Dad had ordered Chinese food because he was actually making some progress with his book and couldn't spare the thirty minutes it would take to cook something, apparently. My offer to make something was rejected.

"You know pork chow mein is my brain food," he'd said.

Weird, weird choice of brain food, in my opinion.

Despite his excuse for not making dinner, he didn't seem all that keen to get back to his office as he sat down at the kitchen island with me to eat.

"So, I saw you're reading *Hamlet* for English," Dad said, as he finished off his meal.

"Yeah."

"I know you've probably read it a few times already." No, really? Was it the big painted quote above my bed that gave it away? "But I wanted you to know I did a paper on it at uni. Just...well, if you ever need help."

It was such a small thing, but the offer, the act of taking some interest in my life, lifted me from my melancholy. I sat up straighter in my stool. "Really?" I said.

My dad frowned at whatever he heard in my tone. "Of course."

"I know you're busy but…I have a presentation to write. I worked on it with a classmate and we're almost finished. Would you…" I suddenly felt vulnerable all over again. Not quite as vulnerable as I'd felt knowing Tobias had read my notebook, but still… I never let my dad read my work. Maybe I'd lowered my guard because I was feeling especially alone in that moment. "Would you read through it for me?"

Dad beamed at me, seeming thrilled that I'd asked. "Of course, Com. Let me just run upstairs with food for your mum and then I'll be down to read it."

Just a few weeks ago, I would have resented the idea of Dad sticking his nose into my writing. It was amazing what a bad day could do to a person's attitude.

While he carried a tray of food upstairs for Carrie, I hurried to my bedroom to print out what I'd written so far based on my and Tobias's notes. Back in the kitchen with the essay, I waited.

And waited.

And waited some more.

After twenty minutes, I went into the hall and quietly climbed a few stairs, straining to hear.

Carrie's giggles and the low rumble of my dad's voice met my ears. I climbed a few steps more. The sounds of kissing and soft moans filtered down from above and just like that, melancholy crashed back over me.

Resentment filled my chest until it was so tight that it hurt.

I strode back down the stairs and threw the essay into my room, the papers flying up and floating down to land all over. I grabbed my jacket from the coat hook by the door and shoved my feet into wellies while I zipped it up.

After wrenching open the front door, I stormed outside

then slammed it shut, hoping the sound interrupted my parents' amorous pursuits.

Selfish arseholes.

All of them.

Every one of them.

Or maybe I was the problem.

After all...out of everyone who had hurt me today, I was the only one who was alone.

Blinking back tears, I strode out of my garden and was almost out the gate when I heard Mrs. Cruickshank's voice. "You all right, Comet?"

I turned to find her sitting on the bench that abutted the wall of her house, wearing a thick cardigan and cupping a mug of something that steamed in the chilled air. I was pretty sure it was peppermint tea, her favorite. "Hi, Mrs. Cruickshank." I almost winced at the croaky sound my voice made in the air between us. I hoped she didn't see the sheen of tears in my eyes.

I knew from the way she leaned forward, frowning, that she did. "Do you want to join me for a cup of tea and tell me your woes, sweetheart?"

On any other night I would. But tonight I just needed solitude. "Thanks, but I'm just going to take a walk."

She nodded, seeming to understand. "Well, you know I'm always here. A cup of tea goes a long way to fixing a problem."

I gave her a small smile. "Thanks, Mrs. Cruickshank."

"Happy walking, Comet." She sat back against the bench and raised her mug to me.

Giving her a small wave, I darted out of my garden and began to walk along the esplanade. The tide was high in the evenings this time of year, so I couldn't walk along the beach. Instead I watched the water rush the sand, like finger-tips stretching toward something that was just out of reach. It persevered, slowly but surely growing closer and closer to the wall of the esplanade.

"Comet?"

The familiar voice jerked me out of my isolated thoughts.

Somehow—and I didn't know how—Tobias King was standing on the quiet, sand-speckled esplanade, staring at me. He wore only a thin sweater over a T-shirt, the fabric fluttering in the coastal wind. His hands were jammed into his jean pockets, and he was staring at me almost as if he were willing me not to run away.

"I was hoping I'd see you," he said, taking a few steps toward me.

I hugged myself, wondering why this boy kept seeing me at my most vulnerable. "Why?"

Instead of answering me he asked, "May I walk with you a little?"

I didn't know if it was his correct use of grammar or the gentlemanly way he asked…or if my reason for nodding yes was bigger than an appreciation of good manners. He'd caught me in a moment of absolute loneliness, and I was so desperate for company that I let myself believe he was sincere. Tobias's interest in me was too tempting to ignore.

Falling into step beside him was surreal. Here was the most popular boy in our year walking beside me, casting me surreptitious looks as I tried to find something to say to him. Strangely, my struggle to find words wasn't borne from shyness like it usually was. I was beyond that with Tobias now that he knew so much of me. In a weird way, knowing that

he seemed drawn to me even after he'd read my poetry obliterated my insecurities with him.

My inability to make conversation was borne of having too
much to ask. I was no longer afraid of being nosy. He knew
so much about me; it felt only fair that he reciprocate.

I didn't know what to question him about first: his life before Scotland; his parents; why he was friends with Stevie and
Co. Was it familial obligation? Still, I'd seen them interact at
school and at home. The two cousins might seem like night
and day, but they were clearly close.

Above all, I wanted to ask what was it about my poetry
that drew Tobias to talk to me.

"Are you sure you're not scared of me? Or shy, or whatever?
Because you're not talking." Tobias gave me a small smile,
but he looked uncertain.

The idea that this too cool, too popular, too good-looking
boy was worried I was afraid of him or unnerved by him made
me feel all warm and fuzzy inside. I grinned at him, and his
eyes widened ever so slightly.

"I just don't know what to ask first."

"Meaning?"

"Well, you know so much about me already, I think you
should allow me to ask some questions so we're more even."

Tobias considered this and then smirked at me. "Okay. Hit
me with it."

"Okay. Where in America are you from?"

It could have been my imagination, but he seemed to relax
at the question as if he'd been expecting me to ask something that would make him uncomfortable. "I'm from North
Carolina."

"I thought people spoke with a Southern twang in North Carolina?"

"Some do. I'm from Raleigh, though." He threw me a rueful look. "Plus, you know my mom is Scottish."

"I take it that's why you moved to Scotland? Your mum wanted to come home?"

Tobias's shoulders hunched around his ears and he shuddered. "It's cold. I should have brought a jacket."

When no answer to my question was forthcoming, I frowned and stared out at the darkening sky and water. Hurt bloomed in my chest, and I tried to tell myself it was ridiculous to be hurt that Tobias wouldn't share his story with me, but it didn't work.

"My dad died."

The words brought my head whipping around so fast that I felt a burn lash up my neck. Ignoring it, I stared up into Tobias's pained expression, and the ache in my chest transformed. The pain was for him now.

He looked down at me and winced at whatever he saw in my face. "I don't want pity, Comet."

"It's not pity. I'm just sorry, Tobias."

His lips parted on an exhalation as he scrutinized me— my face, my words, everything. After a moment he nodded. "I believe you."

"How did he…"

"Car crash."

The words were bitten out, stolen not given, and I realized that I didn't want Tobias to tell me all the meaningful things about his life if he was only doing it because he felt obligated to balance us out. It felt cruel, somehow. So I changed the subject. "Was school different in Raleigh?"

Tobias's shoulders dropped from his ears and his features smoothed out. A light reentered his eyes, and I knew I'd made the right decision not to push him. He gave me a small, boyish smile that made my belly flutter. "A little different. I was different."

"How so?"

"I was a straight-A student, youngest starting quarterback in my school in a decade, dating the head of the dance team, on the school paper, sophomore class president. You name it, I was it."

Stunned, I tried to process what all that meant. It sounded to me like Tobias King had been a king at high school back in the States. I tried not to think about the kind of girl who would have been head of a dance team. Beautiful and athletic, no doubt.

My opposite.

I flinched, throwing the thought away. Tobias and I weren't like that. Now that I knew he was hiding the pain of losing his father, his drastic shift in behavior here made total sense. Even his attitude toward *Hamlet* became clear—which, if you stripped away plot threads and themes, was at its core about a young man who loses his father. Maybe that was why Tobias liked my poems—because I admitted to loneliness in them. Maybe Tobias was lonely, too. It certainly seemed like there was disharmony between him and his mum. And although he had his cousin, Stevie didn't cross me as someone Tobias could actually talk to.

Maybe he'd come to me because he wanted a friend. A real one. It wasn't ideal considering the way butterflies raged to life in my belly anytime he smiled at me, but I liked the idea of being Tobias's confidante. I liked the idea of him being mine.

A thought occurred to me as we strolled. Tobias's life back in Raleigh sounded exhausting. "It sounds like a lot of pressure."

He shot me a surprised look.

We stared at one another, slowly coming to a stop in silent mutual agreement.

"I guess," he agreed.

"Is that why you're friends with Stevie? I mean, I know he's your cousin. But maybe it's because he messes around and doesn't put pressure on you to be responsible."

Tobias's eyebrows pinched together. "Stevie's my friend because he's my friend, not because he's my cousin."

"But you seem so different from one another." I was trying to understand.

"Stevie is a good guy."

I was concerned Stevie *wasn't* a good guy and that he was more than likely going to lead Tobias down a dodgy path in life. Tobias was smart. Really smart. And I thought maybe buried beneath his rubbish attitude toward teachers and his mum was a good guy whose whole life had been upended. For all I knew Stevie was smart, too, but he wasn't acting smart. He stood by while his friends bullied my classmates. He'd strolled into school with a black eye and a burst lip more than once from having fought with rival schoolkids from neighboring towns.

Worst still, rumor had it that he and his friends liked to shoplift in the city center. That was all crappy behavior that could lead to more dangerous behavior.

"Wait…" Tobias shook his head, as if he was confused about something. "I thought… Don't you have a crush on Stevie?"

"A crush…on Stevie?"

132

He nodded, his gaze boring into me like he wanted to unearth all my secrets. "Stevie told me you have a crush on him."

Bloody Heather!

My cheeks burned with embarrassment. "He still thinks that? That's a rumor Heather McAlister made up years ago when she was intent on making my life miserable. Stevie? No!"

His expression cleared, and his shoulders seemed to relax. "No crush on Stevie?"

"You thought I liked Stevie this whole time?"

"Yeah." He grinned suddenly. "Now I know you don't."

Unsure how to interpret his reaction, and wanting the conversation off me and any possibility of me having a crush on Stevie Macdonald, I opted for changing the subject. "Do you miss it? North Carolina? The high school, football, your girlfriend?" I almost winced at that last part.

"Not now." He shrugged. "Maybe one day. But it's kind of good to be free of all of it. My dad wanted a lot from me. I didn't really have much time to be... I don't know. I just didn't have a lot of free time."

"Your friends must miss you, though?"

He smirked but it was somewhat bitter. "My best friend, Jack, he's a year older. A senior now. He's starting quarterback on the team and he's dating Ashley. My ex." He threw me a dark look. "No one misses me, Comet. They moved on as soon as I left."

"Have you?"

"Yeah. It's high school. One day it'll be a distant memory."

I wasn't sure that was an honest answer, but I thought Tobias believed it was, so I let it go. We walked along in companionable silence as I tried to find the courage to ask the question that had plagued me from the moment he'd returned my notebook to me.

"Tobias?"

"Yeah?"

I liked the smile in his voice when he answered. It was a much nicer sound than the tight way he'd answered my questions about his old life. "Did you…" My stomach flipped so hard I had to suck in a breath against it.

"Comet?"

"Did you really like my poems?" The words rushed out of my mouth.

Quite abruptly Tobias stopped walking and turned to face me. The pull of his gaze was so strong I had no option but to stare up into his eyes. "Yes, Comet. I really liked your poems."

Something warm and sweet flooded me but before it even had time to settle, he continued, "Reading them…well…it was the first time in a long time that I didn't feel so alone."

My breath stuttered at his confession and, standing there on the esplanade with this boy who had once been a stranger, I felt something within me shift. I suddenly felt this fierce protectiveness toward him. His kindness, his understanding and his connection to my poems created a bond that flared in the dusk between us.

For the first time in a long time, I didn't feel so alone either.

10

Hope,
They say it dies last.
There's a cruelty in its stubbornness.
Hope,
I hope it dies fast.
Or it could be the end of us.
—CC

I was filled with apprehension the next morning as I made my way to school. Last night had felt like a dream, like a scene from a book. Talking with Tobias had been surprisingly easy in a way conversation hadn't been since I'd been about twelve.

When we were kids, Vicki, Steph and I had chatted with the same ease that we breathed in and out. Something had changed over the last few years, and talking with them had become more of a struggle. I was afraid of disappointing them the way I disappointed my parents.

For the first time in years, I'd talked without worrying about what the person listening might think. That the person I'd been talking to was *Tobias King* had been surreal. At first. Until he'd opened up to me and become just…Tobias.

More than anything I did not want to walk into school only to discover Tobias was going to ignore me.

I didn't see him before form class or on my way to biology,

and I was stupidly disappointed he hadn't searched me out before classes started. Dread filled me as I sat in the library during my free second period. Tobias and I had three classes together next. The possibility of being ignored by him hurt. A lot. Too much.

Feeling like my ankles had been weighted, I walked with such a slow trudge toward Spanish class.

"Didn't get much sleep last night?"

I startled as Tobias suddenly appeared beside me, grinning down at me quizzically.

All the tension melted out of me and I suddenly felt like a balloon let loose from its weight. I gave him a confused smile. "Excuse me?"

"You're walking like a zombie."

"Oh." I blushed and shook my head. "Just daydreaming."

"You're embarrassed." His smile widened, his eyes sparkling with mischief. "What the hell were you daydreaming about?"

To my chagrin my cheeks grew even hotter. "Nothing. School. Spanish."

"A likely story." He nudged me with his elbow. "But I'll give you a free pass."

"Magnanimous of you." I rolled my eyes, pretending not to be mortified that Tobias obviously thought I was day-dreaming about him.

I mean, I was, but I didn't want him to know that. It would crush me if the thought of me fancying him made him un-comfortable. I needed him to know—even if it was only a half-truth—that I wanted to be his friend above all else.

He chuckled as we walked into class together. "Anyway… *Yo conozco todos tus secretos.*"

136

I already know all your secrets. I made a face. "That's what you think."

This time he laughed outright, winked at me and strolled to his chair. Ignoring the curious looks from some of my classmates, I slid into my seat, feeling like butter about to slide off hot toast. Somehow, I stopped myself from melting into a puddle under my desk.

But my heart was beating outrageously fast.

Laughter and a wink from him, and I was as giddy as a five-year-old at Disney World.

It was difficult to concentrate in class. And if it was hard to stay focused in Spanish, it was even more so in maths, because Tobias walked to class with me. That wasn't the part that threw me—although we were getting some curious stares from people in our year who were clearly wondering why we were strolling along like friends.

No, the part that threw me was when Tobias stopped us just outside of maths class.

"Any plans for tonight?"

My heart rate sped up. "Not really."

He nodded and then looked around the corridor casually. "I'm going to take a walk down the beach again." He turned back to me. "Around seven."

My belly was now fluttering all over the place. "Good to know."

We shared a last, secret look before walking into class to take seats on opposite sides of the room.

"So what exactly does a quarterback do?"

We sat, Tobias and me, shoulder to shoulder on a bench facing the water. The sun was still out, although low in the sky, and every now and then someone would appear walking down the esplanade, often with a dog or two. Other than that, it was peaceful, quiet, and we'd had no distractions from each other for the last hour.

"Uh…well the QB is like the leader of the offensive team. He's the guy that usually calls the plays in the huddle. A lot of responsibility falls on him, because he's the one guy who has his hand on the ball for almost every offensive play."

I still had no idea what a quarterback was. I laughed. "Maybe one day you should explain American football to me first before we start talking players."

"We'll watch a game. It's easier to explain that way."

"Do you miss it?"

He was quiet for a moment, suddenly seeming sullen as he stared at the water, and I regretted my question. Until this point we'd talked easily about everything and nothing at all.

"Yeah," he finally said. "I miss being part of a team."

Hating the despondency in his voice, I found I wanted to fix it. "Have you ever considered rugby? There's a regional team in Porty."

"I dunno." He shrugged.

"Think about it."

Tobias looked at me as if searching my face for something. "Okay. I'll think about it."

I smiled, and his gaze dropped to my mouth before traveling lower. I flushed at his perusal and even more so when he grinned and looked back out at the water. "I like the way you dress."

Tonight I was wearing a short flared navy skirt with white polka dots. The contrasting waistband featured three mismatched buttons down the front and was a pink-and-blue

138

tartan. To keep warm I was wearing thick navy tights with magenta patent leather Doc Martens. I wore a plain navy jumper, and over it a navy fitted jacket with an old-fashioned tailcoat detail in the hem. The coat had pink-and-blue tartan elbow patches, epaulettes and large buttons.

"Some people would say it's weird."

Tobias shook his head. "Just different. It makes you stand out from the crowd." He tilted his head, studying me intently again.

I squirmed. "What?"

"I just… Well for someone who is apparently shy, you don't dress like you don't want to be seen."

"Being shy doesn't mean not wanting to be seen," I responded, vehemently even. His eyebrows rose at my tone and I hurried to explain. "Sometimes I find it difficult to talk with people I don't know very well because… I don't know. I guess I'm worried what they'll think of me. That I'm boring or silly. I don't want to think like that, Tobias. It isn't a choice to worry what other people think of me. I wish I was like Steph and Vicki, who can talk to anyone, talk to boys like it's the most natural thing in the world. Talk to teachers like they're people and not authority figures to be feared.

"I had this teacher once." I shivered just remembering her. "In primary six. I was ten," I explained. "For some reason she took a dislike to me, and I always found it confusing since I barely said a word in class. Every morning she'd walk in with this pinched look on her face, thunder in her eyes and make us recite the Lord's Prayer. If we so much as stumbled over the words, she made us repeat it on our own. She started to pick on me a few months into the year. She was like my very own Professor Umbridge from *Harry Potter*. If I got a solution wrong she'd make me get up in front of the whole class to answer it correctly at the board. That only made me more nervous, made me blank, and she would stand there huffing and sighing and bullying me to get to the right answer. I was usually in tears by the end of it.

"She even accused me of cheating once, even though the girl I apparently cheated from did poorly in all subjects compared to me. But, no, I was the culprit. I was terrified of her.

"Worse, though, was when she mocked a poem I wrote for class. She made me read it aloud in front of everyone, even though I didn't want to. She sneered at me the entire time. And then later, when we got our work back from marking, mine was covered in notes that basically told me to start again. She did that to me with every writing challenge.

"I think she eventually lost her job a few years later. Something about shoving a boy out of her classroom. He smacked into the wall opposite the door and got a bloody nose."

"Jesus." I felt Tobias's stare, but I couldn't look at him. I didn't want to see his pity. "Did you tell your parents?"

I shook my head, embarrassed that confiding in my parents hadn't been an option even then.

"You can't let one teacher affect who you are, Comet."

My gaze jerked up to meet his. "I'm not," I said indignantly. "I'm… I know all teachers aren't like her. Mr. Stone is a brilliant teacher."

"Yeah? So has he seen your poetry?"

I squirmed a little, reminded of my conversation with Mr. Stone at Pan and how I'd been avoiding thinking about his words of wisdom. "Well, not my personal poetry, no."

"Does anyone know about your poetry?"

"I have a blog," I announced triumphantly. "All of my poems are on there."

"Is it anonymous?"

I glared at him and he laughed. "I bet you even have the comments turned off."

"What's your point, Mr. King?"

Tobias nudged me with his shoulder. "My point is that you let one teacher steal away your confidence. That's ridiculous. Your poems are great, Comet. You should share them with the world. If you can walk around in yellow tights and pink boots, surely you can share some poems."

As lovely as his confidence in me was, I wasn't quite ready for that. "What yellow tights?" I evaded.

"You were wearing yellow tights the night you ran out of that party."

"Oh."

"Comet?"

At his questioning tone, I looked up and sighed. "Don't you get it, Tobias? This—" I gestured to what I was wearing "—it's my way of fighting the girl who doesn't want to share her poems with anyone. This is the part of me that could give a crap what anyone thinks of me. I'm proud of myself when I walk down the street wearing the clothes I want to wear, because it means I'm standing up for who I am. I wish… You have no idea how much I wish I could care less what anyone thinks about me at all, whether it's my clothes or the words coming out of my mouth or the words I put on paper.

"But I do care. Too much. And I don't think I'm strong enough to handle anyone reading my work yet. Okay?" I held my breath, fearing that Tobias would be disappointed in me.

To my utter shock and delight, however, the boy at my side

took my right hand, turned it palm up and slid his over it. Tingles shot up my arm as his long fingers tickled my palm and then intertwined with mine. He squeezed, holding tight, and looking out over the sea he said softly, "Okay."

Okay.

Just that one word. That one word and the way he held my hand made me fall.

And I fell hard.

My crush on Tobias only worsened over time.

For the next few weeks we met up as much as possible at the esplanade, the only thing changing between us the layers of clothing as autumn overpowered late summer. But despite talking to me during classes, Tobias never hung out with me at school. In fact, he made a concerted effort to not even look at me during lunch in the cafeteria. It was like I didn't exist.

Not only did that hurt, but watching him mess around with Stevie and his friends pissed me off. Tobias wasn't like them. He wasn't a bully or disrespectful to teachers or a thief, and I could not understand how the boy who was so sweet to me could be so rude to our teachers and even some of our classmates when he was with his friends.

This lack of contact between us outside of class reinforced that Tobias just wanted a friendship with me. And a secret one at that.

It would be foolish to hope for anything more. Yet, anyone who's ever had a crush on someone always has hope. Foolish or otherwise.

My hope was crushed on a Wednesday.

It was fourth period and I'd asked my history teacher if I could use the bathroom. Since I was a good student, she gave me a bathroom pass without hesitation. Knowing Tobias was in chemistry fourth period, however, I decided to take the long route to the bathroom, i.e. the one that was completely out of the way but would take me past Tobias's class.

That was my state of mind now. Complete and utter awareness of Tobias King. Every morning was better because I woke up knowing I'd get to see *him*. I was always on Tobias alert, waiting to catch a glimpse of him, to hear his voice, brush his arm with mine.

It was on that ridiculously girlish thought that I spotted Tobias in his chemistry class. The sight of him brought me crashing down to Earth with a bang. Instead of breaking an arm or a leg on impact, I broke my naive little heart.

Jess Reed, a sixth year *everyone* knew, was sitting next to Tobias. The table pod they sat at covered their bottom half so the teacher couldn't see Jess's hand on Tobias's thigh as they murmured with one another, heads bent close. Tobias smirked flirtatiously at whatever she said, making no move to remove her hand from his leg.

Jess Reed.

I was such an idiot.

Spinning back around, I blinked back the sting of tears and attempted to fight off the gnawing ache that pulsated in my chest. Jess was a year older than us. She was small and curvy, with tons of shining dark brown hair, perfect bronze skin and huge tip-tilted dark eyes with eyelashes that seemed to go on forever. Every boy in school fancied the pants off Jess Reed.

She was head of the events committee and a karate champion. Hot and a total badass.

How the hell could I think Tobias would see me—pale,

gangly, bookish me!—as girlfriend material when he had the likes of Jess Reed flirting with him?

I crashed into the nearest girls' bathroom, thanking God it was empty, and locked myself in a stall. Tears spilled down my cheeks and I swiped at them angrily.

Fighting for calm, I took deep, slow breaths. Eventually the tears stopped, my breathing returned to normal and with it my sense returned. My overreaction to seeing him flirt with another girl was a wake-up call!

I didn't want to be one of those girls who became so obsessed with a boy that nothing else mattered. That wasn't me before Tobias and I'd burn my entire collection off Irregular Choice shoes before I let it happen to me now. There was more for me to worry about than if Tobias King fancied someone else. And what did it matter anyway? Come graduation, I was gone! I would hopefully be on my way to Virginia, and nothing and no one was getting in the way of that dream. Which brought me back to the things I needed to be focused on—like finding extracurricular activities to become involved in for college applications. To stop ignoring Mr. Stone's advice to be brave with my writing and poetry. And to find a way to mend the breach in my friendship with Vicki who had been there for me long before Tobias ever was.

Tobias King was a problem and not just because of my unrequited crush.

Maybe it was time to reevaluate our friendship.

The shame I'd felt earlier that day in the girls' restroom returned as I sat listening to Vicki and Steph talk about the school show during lunch in the cafeteria.

Tobias liked me for me.

But did he?

He wasn't the one sitting with me at lunch every day. Vicki and Steph were. They hadn't abandoned me. Well, sometimes they went to Nana's without me, but most of the time they ate in the cafeteria with me.

I was mortified by my behavior. Ashamed that I'd let us drift apart. Especially Vicki, when I knew she needed my friendship more than ever. I waited until Steph left the table to grab another soda to ask Vicki, "How are things with your mum and dad?"

Vicki blinked at the seemingly random question. I knew it sounded like it came out of nowhere, but I didn't want my friend to think I didn't care about her life anymore. She shrugged, giving me a sad little smile. "They still disagree about my future."

"I'm sorry."

"I just hate being the reason for them arguing, you know?"

"I know." I reached across the table and squeezed her hand. "You know I'm here if you ever need to talk."

"Yeah?" She cocked her head and studied me. "Why don't we talk about why every day for the last few weeks you haven't been able to keep your eyes off Stevie's crew? Anything to do with a certain American?"

The thought of anyone knowing how much I liked Tobias—even if it was Vicki—made my body lock with tension. I removed my hand from hers, withdrawing into myself. "Of course not. I didn't realize I was looking at Stevie all the time. They bug me. You know that."

Anger flashed in Vicki's eyes. "Right. Sure."

I flinched at her sarcasm.

Thankfully, Steph returned and I could pretend there wasn't

this awful distance between me and Vicki. I struggled to find something to say to my friends that they'd want to hear or talk about, and then I remembered they were going to another party at the weekend.

"Are you guys looking forward to Ryan's birthday party?" I said, hopeful that my interest would ease the tension between us.

Steph grinned and opened her mouth to answer but Vicki beat her to it.

"Why do you care?" she practically snarled. "It's not like you're going."

She might as well have slapped me.

Even Steph shot her a horrified, confused look.

As for me, I just stared at her, stunned, wondering when our friendship had gone so terribly wrong. As tears stung my eyes for the second time that day, I scraped back my chair, letting my hair fall over my face. "I just remembered I need to get something from the library. I'll see you later."

But I didn't see them later, and the next day I was deliberately late to school, missing form class. I opted to walk home for lunch, and in English I refused to lift my head out of my copy of *The Cone Gatherers* by Robin Jenkins. We'd moved on from *Hamlet* this week, and I loved Mr. Stone's choice of literature this semester because I hadn't read it.

In that moment, however, the book was the last thing on my mind. I wanted to be anywhere but there.

"Hey," Tobias said as he settled into his chair next to me. His arm brushed mine as he pressed in close. "Why did you cancel last night? You okay?"

Yesterday I'd texted Tobias to tell him I couldn't meet up

with him, but I hadn't given him an explanation. I'd been hoping—

The truth was I didn't know what I was hoping. I was conflicted. Part of me wanted Tobias to just forget about me so I could forget about him, but the other half of me hated the idea of losing his friendship.

"I'm fine," I mumbled. "Just tired."

"Com, look at me."

Not wanting to, but knowing enough of Tobias now to know he was dogged when he wanted something, I unwillingly lifted my gaze to meet his. He frowned at whatever he saw in my expression. "What happened?"

"Nothing happened. I told you. I'm tired." I looked down at my book and didn't utter another word for the rest of class. Not even when Tobias tried to crack jokes under his breath that would normally have had me repressing giggles and kicking his shin beneath our desk.

When the bell rang, I quickly gathered up my stuff and hurried to leave for my next class. Tobias caught up with me and dropped his head to ask, voice low, sounding worried, "Did I do something?"

Guilt suffused me at the bright concern in his eyes. "No," I assured him. "No…it's just…girl stuff, okay. Vicki and Steph…"

"Vicki and Steph what?"

"It sounds immature."

"Comet."

"I don't think they like me very much anymore." My lower lip trembled as I fought back tears and I laughed hollowly at my ridiculousness. "Sorry."

"Don't apologize." He looked around, shifting, and I wondered if he was worried about people finding out we were friends. The thought was supremely depressing. "Look, we can't talk here. Meet me tonight?"

"I can't," I said, the refusal immediate and instinctual. As guilty as it made me feel, I went with it, because clearly I wasn't ready to hang out with him alone again just yet. "I promised my parents we'd have a proper family evening."

He frowned so deeply I wondered if the lie was that obvious.

"Okay." He shrugged. "Well…you know…call me if you need me or whatever."

And then he was gone.

Frustration tore through me and I felt like screaming.

This week sucked. It beyond sucked. It was a cesspit of everything shitty and screwed up.

This week could go to hell along with any remnants of the little social life I had.

11

I am your safe harbor when the waves lose their blue,
Just tie yourself to me and hold on tight.
And when I need you to be my safe harbor too,
Your hand in mine will make everything right.

—*CC*

As much as I resented my parents' attitude toward me, I resented their close friends Jo-Jo's and Mishka's even more. They were an artist couple—she was Scottish and beautiful and he was Russian and passionate. While Dad and Carrie at least acknowledged my existence, Jo-Jo and Mishka actually went so far as to pretend I wasn't in the room.

I'd disturbed their perfect little foursome, you see. My parents used to host these big parties and go traveling all the time with their friends. They'd stifled a lot of that because of me.

Damn me and my need for food, water and protection. I was such a needy child.

Anyway, I knew when Carrie and Dad went off to a Jo-Jo/Mishka party not to expect them home until late in the evening...the following day.

That meant I was alone in the house on a Saturday night. I had the baseball bat at the side of my bed, most of the house lights blazing and I was curled up in my room reading *Circle of Friends* by Maeve Binchy. I found Benny so relatable but

my heart hurt reading about her friendship with Eve. It reminded me of what I currently did not have with Vicki. So
when my phone buzzed with a text and Vicki's name flashed
on screen, relief and trepidation mingled.

Vicki: I'm sorry. Miss u. u ok? Xxx

My eyes blurred with tears of relief.

Me: Miss u too. Glad to hear from u. u ok? Xxx

Vicki: I'm gd. @ Ryan's prty. wywh. Tobias is here. Steph md
play for him bt Jess Reed all over him. xx

My stomach dropped just imagining it. And what the hell,
Steph? Ugh, that girl needed attention more than a day-old
baby.

Feeling sad but at least glad Vicki was talking to me I texted
back: Steph must be pissed xx

Vicki: She'll goi. Night, babe xx

I texted good-night back, thinking maybe Steph would
get over it, but would I?

After that it was increasingly difficult not to become way
too involved in my book when beautiful Nan sabotaged Benny
and Jack. "What a bitch!" I yelled, throwing my e-reader on
my bed.

That was it. I needed a calming cup of Earl Grey before
I could continue. Glaring at the offending reading device, I
marched out of my bedroom and tried to talk myself down.

Muttering under my breath about losing my mind, I'd had an in-depth discussion with myself about becoming overly involved in fictional worlds by the time I returned to my bedroom with my cup of tea.

However, just as I entered the room, my phone buzzed again.

Tobias's name flashed on the screen and my heart leaped into my throat as I lunged for the phone.

Okay, so I wasn't cool or unaffected like I might prefer. Instead I fumbled to unlock the screen.

Tobias: Thot u'd b @ Ryans. Ur friends r.

I grinned like a fool. I'd missed him. Two nights we'd spent apart. That was all. Two nights. And I missed him desperately.

I didn't care if he was making out with Jess Reed—

Okay, I cared.

But I cared more about my friendship with him than my jealousy and disappointment, or my worry that he made me lose focus. I decided then and there I could be friends with Tobias without losing myself in our friendship again. I could care about him and still care about my other friends and my passions and goals. I could still be me.

Me: I don't really do parties.

Tobias: Yeah? I'm nt feeln it either. U hme?

YES, I AM HOME. I AM HOME RIGHT NOW!

My fingers shook as I typed: yeah…

Tobias: Cn I cme ovr?

"YES!" I yelled into the room and then giggled at my nut-
tiness.

Me: Sure.

There. How was that for cool?

I was a nervous bag of energy as I waited for him to arrive.
Tobias was giving up a night with Jess Reed to hang out with
me? What did that mean?

Unless…

An ugly thought prodded past all my hopeful ones.

Maybe he and Jess had already hooked up.

Was he using each of us for different things?

I couldn't bring myself to really think of Tobias as a user. It
didn't feel like he was using me when we hung out together,
because we both got something out of it.

I didn't have long to work myself into a nervous stupor,
because Tobias showed up at the house only fifteen minutes
later. He must have hurried his cute little arse off.

Don't think about his arse, Comet, I said to myself as I swung
the door wide-open to let him in.

"Your parents don't mind me hanging out?" he said, stepping into the hall beside me.

He towered over me.

I kept forgetting how much bigger he was than me despite
my long legs. A whiff of yummy aftershave almost made my
eyelids flutter in rapture and I mentally cursed myself again
for being *that* girl. The one whose intelligent brain melted

out of her ears around a beautiful boy. I shook off my attraction, determined *not* to be that girl.

"They're not here." I closed the door behind him and locked it, and then walked down the hall to my bedroom. "This way."

I was standing in the middle of the room, waiting for him in nervous anticipation, and was pleased at the surprise on his face when he walked in and realized we were in my bedroom.

"And your parents won't mind that they're not here and I'm in your bedroom?" His gaze swept over the room, lingering over the bookshelves and the quote I had painted above my bed. I'd already made sure the room was clear of anything embarrassing, like underwear.

Then Tobias's eyes fell on the poster I had on my wall. It was of a certain gorgeous Hollywood actor who played one of the heroes in a heroine-led book-to-film franchise.

He and Tobias shared a striking resemblance.

Tobias cocked an eyebrow, threw me a pleased smirk as I blushed from head to foot, and then he shrugged out of his jacket. As he settled into my armchair I cursed myself for not taking the damn poster down before he got here.

"So…" I sat down on the edge of my bed and scrambled to think of anything that would make him forget about the poster. "The party was boring?"

"Yeah." He was still staring around at the room, drinking in every little thing. I wondered what he found so fascinating. "People are fake. I wasn't in the mood for fake tonight."

Meaning he thought I was real?

I flushed at the compliment. "Do you want something to drink?"

"Soda if you've got it?"

When I returned with a glass of Coke for him, his fingers brushed mine as I passed the tumbler to him. A frisson of awareness shot through me and I felt *things* in my body— tingles in places I only ever got tingles when I was reading a romance.

Knowing I was probably glowing tomato red, I turned around and willed myself to calm down, before I slumped back on the bed to face him.

"What's with the banner?" He pointed to the wall adjacent to my bedroom door where I had a University of Virginia pennant I'd bought online pinned to the wall.

"One day that pennant will be pinned to my dorm room wall."

He seemed surprised. "You want to apply to the University of Virginia?"

"They have a great writing program."

"I'm sure colleges here have great writing programs, too."

I shrugged. "They aren't thousands of miles away across a massive ocean."

His eyes were filled with questions and, to my surprise, I realized I trusted him enough to provide him with answers. "You asked about my parents. If they would mind you being alone in my bedroom with me. They won't care, Tobias. They *don't* care."

His brows hitched toward one another as he leaned forward, elbows on his knees. "What does that mean?"

Even though my heart was beating hard in my chest at the very idea of anyone knowing just how empty things were between me and my parents, I found that I wanted Tobias to know why I wrote the kinds of poems that I did. Why I wrote his favorite one in the notebook he'd read.

"They didn't want me. I was an accident." I shuffled back against my pillows, getting comfortable. "They've always been distant with me, even when I was little. I didn't know any better then. And to be fair, Carrie—my mum—was more hands-on then than she is now. Marginally. She had to be, I suppose. Dad was always a little more enthusiastic. But as I got older, more independent, Carrie lost all interest and with her disinterest came my dad's. I didn't understand what I'd done wrong." I rolled my eyes, the bitterness rising up inside of me. "I still don't. I think they tell themselves that it's okay, that they're artists and artists are a little self-obsessed. But not all artists who are parents are self-obsessed. Men and women can write books and paint pictures and still be good parents.

"But not Kyle and Carrie Caldwell." I huffed. "I always used to wonder why Dad would show interest in me and then suddenly just stop. But one day, a few years ago, I overheard a conversation I wasn't supposed to."

I was silent so long, remembering that day, that Tobias prodded. "Comet?"

I blinked and looked across the room at the boy who was staring at me with such concern and tenderness that I wanted to launch myself into his arms.

No one ever just hugged me anymore.

Never my parents.

Vicki and Steph had stopped.

I pushed the thought away. "I think something happened to my mum. Dad's parents died before I was born but Carrie's parents are alive. And she has a sister. I've never met any of them. I think they hurt her growing up."

"Hurt her? You mean…like abused?"

I nodded. "I think so. Whatever happened, I think it

messed her up good. And I think my dad saved her. All she cares about is Dad and art. And she's not good at sharing. I think... I think she feels threatened by me. Afraid that somehow by loving me, Dad would love her less. They argued about him helping me with a project at school—that she needed his attention now more than I did. So I started to wonder if maybe that's why my dad would suddenly stop helping me with homework or change his mind about going to a museum with me.

"Is it her, to appease her? I don't know." I shrugged, the action belying my depths of feeling on the matter. "It doesn't matter what the truth is. The results are the same. They have no time for me. They don't give a crap. Which is why I'm applying to the University of Virginia and getting as far away from them as possible when I graduate."

I wasn't looking at Tobias when I finished. I was ashamed. A child should have changed Carrie—should have given her someone to love and trust beyond my dad. But somehow I wasn't lovable enough.

"Comet. Look at me."

His voice, the kindness in it when he spoke to me, had become addictive. And I think that's why I'd told him the truth about my family. I wanted him to absolve me of the part I played in not being who Carrie needed me to be, and not being the kind of kid my dad would choose over her.

I looked at him and found what I was searching for. Concern, anger, tenderness, all blazed from his beautiful eyes. For me.

"Now your poems make total sense," he said.

I nodded.

"Your parents are assholes, Comet."

Succinct. To the point. And I was afraid very, very true. I smiled at him gratefully even though I held a sadness inside of me I didn't think anyone would ever be able to relieve me of. "Thank you."

"My dad was an asshole," he said. "He pushed me all the time to be the best. I had to make straight As for him because he'd never gotten anything lower than a B. I had to play football and campaign for class president. I had to be perfect. Because he was perfect." He scoffed, and I winced at the rage I saw in the darkest depths of Tobias's eyes. "He wasn't perfect, Comet. He was a hypocrite. He died in a car crash with the woman he'd been screwing behind my mom's back for years. Worst part? My mom knew. She knew, and she let him do that to us all the while he preached at me the whole time. And I worked my ass off!" He flinched when he realized he was yelling. Sighing, he settled down and I fought the urge to walk across the room and hug him. "I wanted so badly to make him proud, because he did so much for us. He was this big shot lawyer and because of him I was going to be a legacy pledge at his fraternity house at Northwestern. I'd be pre-law just like my old man.

"I drove around in my GMC Sierra, wearing the best clothes money could buy, plenty of cash in my wallet, thinking even if I wasn't living *my* life, I was living a damn good one, you know? How could I complain about feeling pressured when my dad had done all this before me? He was perfect. The perfect lawyer, perfect dad and the perfect husband.

"I bought into the bullshit. But I'm done. I was done the moment my mom told me the affair had been going on for years. Some woman in his firm. She had a family, too. Fucked us all up when they died together. A nightmarish cliché." He swiped angrily at the tears in his eyes and glared at my ceiling. "And then my mom told me she was moving us here. I didn't want to at first, but then I realized it was good. Because here I can be anything I want to be. I can be me without being the me my dad wanted me to be."

Hurt squeezed my chest tight as I stared at this boy who was so kind to me when he himself was in so much pain. I found myself desperate to save him from losing who he really was. Even if it made him lash out at me. "Is that what you're doing?" I said it gently, trying not to antagonize him. "Hanging out with Stevie and his friends who don't seem to care about anything. Not handing in homework on time. Mouthing off to teachers. Taking mean verbal swipes at kids who probably have their own crap going on. Is that what you're doing, Tobias? Are you being yourself now? Because I don't think you are."

He stared at me and I braced myself. I hoped he saw my question for what it was, and not an attack. Finally, after what felt like forever, he said, "When I first got here, I didn't want to care about anything. I *didn't* care about anything."

His use of the past tense made my breath falter. "And now?"

"Now…" His gaze burned into me. "Maybe you reminded me that I didn't just care because my dad wanted me to care. Maybe…I just care."

12

If our friendship means being your dirty little secret,
You can keep it.
—CC

Without having to say the words out loud, Tobias and I agreed that something changed in our relationship that night. Some deeper connection was formed out of the already thriving friendship between us.

Which was probably why I got pissed off enough to cause our first argument.

It was just after we returned to school from the October break. We'd had two weeks off and I was tired of dodging Vicki's and Steph's questions about what I'd been up to on the days I wasn't with them. Maybe I was a terrible liar, I don't know, I just knew they were suspicious I wasn't being honest and hadn't been for a while.

I didn't want to keep my friendship with Tobias from them. Or from anyone. I was proud that he was my friend and I wanted him to be proud to be my friend, too. Yet, somehow I had silently agreed that we would keep our friendship just between us, even though I didn't know why. Since he talked happily with me in class, I'd assumed that Tobias wouldn't have a problem with me talking to him in the lunch line.

Vicki and Steph were already seated when I entered the cafeteria, and I was giddy to note that Tobias was at the back of the food counter line with Stevie. Anytime I saw Tobias I was giddy, addicted to his presence.

"Trying to decide between the 'dinner ladies may have urinated in it' pea soup and the 'they went one process too far on this leathery beef patty' burger?" I joked, as I came up behind him.

Both he and Stevie turned around. Stevie was somewhat confused by my sudden chattiness but he chuckled, "Aye, I know, right?"

Tobias, however, seemed startled by me making conversation. So startled that he just gave me a vague nod and turned his back on me again. Thankfully, Stevie had already turned away, because I think I must have turned fifty shades of red.

Hurt and mortification swirled inside me and I found myself glaring at the back of Tobias's head. As though he felt my heated stare, he rubbed the back of his neck. By the time he was being served, I'd imagined our interaction happening over again with many different endings. Half of them involved Tobias declaring his undying love for me in some fashion, and the other half involved me taking epic verbal retribution for his public snub.

Once they'd paid for their dinners, he and Stevie began to walk away, but as his cousin wandered in front of him, weaving through the tables, Tobias looked over his shoulder at me. His expression was remorseful.

I turned away, snubbing him right back.

By the time lunch was over and I was sitting in English class, I'd worked myself into a fiery mass of anger. How dare he—the boy who knew more than anyone how much I didn't need any more rejection in my life—snub me.

As he strode into class, head and shoulders above most every other person, his gaze flew directly to me and he seemed to pick up stride. He slid gracefully into the seat, shifting it closer to mine. "Comet."

I stared straight ahead at the whiteboard, ignoring him and the urgency in his voice.

"Comet, don't," he snapped.

Snapped? At me? *He* was mad at *me*?

I glared at him, outraged to find him glowering back at me. "*You* gave me the cold shoulder."

"I was surprised," he hissed back, flicking a look over his shoulder as if to see if anyone was paying attention.

"Afraid people will find out you've been spending your nights with a loser?"

"Don't say that about yourself," he bit out.

"Why not? That's how you made me feel."

"Afternoon, everyone." Mr. Stone strolled into class and placed a cup of coffee on his desk so he could pick up a pile of papers. "We're taking a break from the book today to work on your poetry assignments for this term." He handed me a work-sheet, and just like that my argument with Tobias was put on pause.

It wasn't until halfway through class, when Mr. Stone left the room to deal with a query from another teacher and the noise level rose, that Tobias continued where we'd left off. "I'm sorry I made you feel that way. But I thought we were just keeping... us...on the down low."

I narrowed my eyes, still hurt. "Because you're ashamed of me?"

"God, no." He leaned toward me, and my gaze dropped to his mouth. "Look, you're right about Stevie's friends. Some of them aren't great guys. Stevie's been friends with them a long time and he doesn't really want to hear it. So while I've got Stevie's back, I'm stuck hanging around not-so-good guys. Just because I have to doesn't mean *you* have to. And I don't think you should." He rubbed a hand over his head, looking uncertain as he stared at our desk instead of at me.

How was it possible that Tobias could make me feel so hurt and dejected one minute and then make me feel like I finally had someone watching over me?

Was this love?

Was this how it felt?

This whirlwind of emotions—of certainties and uncertainties, of hopes and fears?

Was this me? In love? With Tobias?

My breath faltered at the thought and I found I could not speak.

Tobias's gaze flew to mine. "Comet? You still mad at me?"

I shook my head. *No! I'm in love with you, you big idiot.*

Of course I didn't say that. Instead I swallowed past the massive lump of realization that was lodged in my throat, "No. But I don't think you should be hanging around people you're not comfortable with. You should try harder with Stevie, make him see he deserves better friends. Then maybe *we* can all be friends?"

If Tobias was surprised by my offer to be friends with Stevie, I was even more so. But Tobias saw something good in his cousin and I trusted Tobias.

He visibly relaxed. "Believe me, I'm working on it."

I nodded, worried that Tobias was martyring himself for his cousin and hopeful that Stevie was worth the trouble.

Although things between Vicki, Steph and I were a little better, they weren't anywhere close to perfect. My friends were still working hard together on the school show, growing closer to one another every day. I felt like an outsider in our little threesome, but I guessed it was karma because I'd never bothered to think how Steph must have felt when Vicki and I left her out of things.

Their preoccupation with the school show, however, was good in that I could hang out with Tobias as much as I wanted to without lying to them. I'd noticed that Tobias hadn't really recommitted to school like I'd hoped he would. He was still spending a lot of his free time with Stevie doing who knew what.

So when he offered to try to make it up to me for being cold to me that day in the cafeteria I came up with a plan that would benefit us both. I made Tobias agree to come over to my place after dinner to work on his poetry assignment. Of course, my assignment was already done since I'd written a poem a while ago that fit the assignment perfectly. Our presentation on *Hamlet* went really well; we'd both gotten As, and I used this, along with his guilt, as leverage to get Tobias to agree to let me help with his poem.

That meant I got to enjoy his company while reading a book as he did his homework, only stopping to answer his questions when he had them.

To me that was the equivalent of being offered a free ticket to The Wizarding World of Harry Potter at Universal in Orlando.

Ah-mazing!

And it kicked off superbly.

I'd just let Tobias into the house when my dad happened to come out of the kitchen with a mug of coffee in his hand.

He stopped abruptly at the sight of the tall, handsome boy standing next to me in the hallway.

"Comet?" he queried softly before taking a casual sip of his coffee.

"Kyle, this is Tobias, a friend from school."

"Nice to meet you, Tobias." Dad offered his hand.

Tobias stiffened beside me, his gaze dropping to the proffered hand, and I could almost hear him cursing out my father in his head for being a dipshit to me. He reluctantly shook my dad's hand, but he didn't return the platitude.

I loved him for being mad at my dad on my behalf.

"We're going to study for English." I pointed to my bedroom door.

Dad's brows drew together. "Alone? In your room?"

Annoyed at the accusatory, concerned tone, I grabbed Tobias's hand and led him toward my room. "Yes."

Tobias followed me, squeezing my hand in solidarity as we disappeared into my bedroom and closed the door behind us. I dropped his hand to put both mine on my hips in irritation.

My friend grinned. "You showed him, huh."

"It's just hypocrisy," I grumbled. "Pretending to care."

"Maybe he does care." Tobias kicked off his trainers and lay down on my bed as if he did it every day. "He seemed to care."

"About me getting pregnant maybe. God forbid I add another unwanted mouth to feed into the household."

Tension suddenly filled the air, most of it emanating from Tobias, and I understood by the flush high on his cheeks and the uncomfortable way he cleared his throat as he pulled his English homework out of his backpack that I'd said the wrong thing. I'd just suggested Tobias and I might be in here having sex.

Embarrassed, tingling in places I shouldn't be, my lips feeling weirdly swollen considering no one had been near them, I turned away under the pretense of looking for a book to read.

As I scoured my bookshelves I changed the subject, hoping I hadn't made Tobias too uncomfortable. "Do you have any idea what you want to write about?"

"Not a clue."

I grabbed a book that caught my fancy and headed over to lie down beside him. We'd lain like this before on my bed and I didn't want to not to do it, because that would just draw attention to the weirdness between us.

"Let me see." I held out my hands to see what notes he'd written down in class today.

He handed them over, trusting me with them.

For the next ten minutes we talked about his poem, the style he could use, and then I left him to it to read my book. For a while I was perfectly content with Tobias's warm body next to mine, slowly losing myself in an epic fantasy world about a female assassin.

In fact, I was so lost in my book that I didn't hear Tobias say my name the first time. Not until he took the book right out of my hands.

"Hey!"

He grinned at me. "You were gone. I've been trying to get your attention for the last thirty seconds."

I blushed. "Sorry. What were you saying?"

"I was saying, are you really going to lie there and read while I work?"

"I believe I was." I gestured to my book, clutched in his hands. "It's more fun than what you're doing."

He looked at the book and then at me. There was something surprisingly solemn in his expression. "You're always reading, Comet."

The way he said it made me tense, and I tried to laugh it off, teasing, "Books tend to be more interesting and fun than reality, Tobias."

But Tobias didn't laugh. "Anytime I ask you what you've been up to, you've either been writing poetry for your anonymous blog, visiting that poetry café you won't take me to or reading a book. When everyone else is at a party, where is Comet? Alone in her room, reading a book."

Hurt that he would say that, that he would think it, when I'd thought he was the one person I didn't have to worry about disappointing, I sat up to reach for my book, but he deliberately held it out of reach. "I'm not boring. Fictional worlds are just better. Give me the book, Tobias." I reached for it again, and he held it above his head. "Tobias."

"Fictional worlds are better?"

"Tobias!" I lunged for it but he jerked back and I swayed into him, my hands coming down on his chest for balance.

We froze.

Our heads close, our eyes locked.

I didn't know if it was my imagination or not, but Tobias's chest seemed to rise and fall a little faster, his breathing shallow.

"Better than reality?" he whispered, staring at my lips. "Than what's right in front of you?"

Heat suffused me and this overwhelming restless feeling enveloped me, making my fingers curl into his T-shirt as I watched his head move slowly toward mine. My lips seemed to swell, as if inviting his to touch them.

Please, I whimpered inwardly. *Please, kiss me.*

His warm breath caressed my lips and my eyes fluttered closed as my heart thudded in anticipation.

Rock music suddenly blared into the room, startling me, and I pushed up off Tobias's chest.

Tobias frowned and reached for his phone. "It's Stevie." He pressed the hang up button. "I'll just text him." He held my book out toward me, watching me carefully. I didn't know how to read him. Was he disappointed we'd been interrupted, or was he glad? I reached for the book, and he snapped it away from me momentarily. "Stop hiding in these." He shook the book. "Be in the moment. You never know when it might disappear."

What the hell did that mean?

I took the book back, watching him text Stevie and receive a reply. "What does *he* want?"

"Why do you always use that snarky tone when talking about Stevie?" he huffed.

I frowned, wondering why we were arguing. "What tone?"

"Like he's scum. He's not scum."

"He's not exactly Mr. Wonderful either."

Tobias sat up, glowering at me. "What happened to wanting us all to be friends? You can't be friends with someone you think is scum. You don't even know him."

"You're right, I don't. And I want to trust you about him because your friends say a lot about you. But the way that whole crowd acts make it hard."

"Oh, so because you're friends with Steph I'm to assume you're a vapid, narcissistic princess?"

"Tobias!"

"What? You can trash my friend but I can't trash yours?"

"I'm not trashing, Stevie… I just… I'm worried about you. I'm worried that you're trying so hard to protect Stevie from making mistakes with those idiots he calls friends that you're forgetting about yourself and the way you want to live your life."

"I told you I've got Stevie's back because he's a good guy. I don't need to explain that further." He rolled off the bed, giving me a look of reproach. "He doesn't talk crap about you because you're shy as shit. He doesn't judge you. Not like you judge him, and you of all people should know better. And I'll remind you that he's not just my friend, he's my family."

"I'm sorry." I scrambled off the bed, hating that he was mad at me. "I—"

"Just because Stevie's dad is in prison doesn't make him like his dad. He hates his dad for putting his family through that, and now his mom's health isn't great and he's got his little brother, Kieran, to look out for. It's a lot. Cut him some slack."

Remorse flooded me. "You're right." I hurried over to him, needing to touch him, needing him to know I wasn't a judgmental bitch, even though I had been. I gripped his wrist and squeezed it in reassurance. "I'm sorry. I don't know anything about Stevie and the truth is, he has never been mean to me. Ever. Even when Heather lied and told him I had a crush on him, he was nice to me about not liking me in return. It was mortifying, but he didn't mean it to be mortifying. I promised myself I'd give him a chance because you see the good in him and from now on I'm going to live up to that promise."

Tobias frowned and then turned away from me. I hurried to follow him out of the room. "Where are you going?"

"I need air."

Wondering if *I need air* was code for *I need to get away from you*, I stood by my bedroom door, watching him stride down the hall. I crossed my arms over my chest. "I said I was sorry. If I'm big enough to apologize, you should be big enough to accept the apology."

He glanced over his shoulder and frowned at me. "Who said I didn't? Are you coming or what?"

I made a face at him for being deliberately hard to read, but walked down the hall toward him. "I don't hate Stevie." I grabbed my coat off the peg and followed Tobias out of the house. "And I didn't know his dad was in prison. And I didn't know Carole was so unwell."

"I thought everyone knew about his dad."

Guiltily I shrugged. "I guess I probably didn't want to hear anything about him since..."

"Since?"

"You're right," I admitted hollowly. "I wrote him off. I'm sorry."

My apology produced an appreciative, almost tender, smile as we walked out my garden gate and turned down the esplanade. I tightened my scarf around my neck as Tobias shrugged his hat down lower over his head.

"Were the autumns like this in North Carolina?" I teased, hoping to get us back to a sense of normalcy.

"At night it was cold. But it's cold here all the time. Plus... harsh wind. I don't know how you guys can trick-or-treat in this crap."

I laughed. "We're hardy. And are you trick-or-treating this year, Mr. King?" Halloween was right around the corner, but all anyone my age seemed excited about was the school Halloween dance. Vicki and Steph had been talking about it for the last few weeks.

"No. Are you?"

But before I could answer in the negative we were interrupted by a deep voice shouting, "Yo, King!"

We both froze and looked up ahead to see a figure hurrying toward us down the esplanade.

13

I judged you and that's the awful truth.
You didn't pass my test, so I labeled you a thug.
I judged you when I had no proof;
Lumped you in with the rest, swept you under the rug.

—CC

Nervous butterflies erupted in my belly as Stevie appeared in front of us. He waved us down, heading toward us with his familiar boyish, loping stride. Wearing only a light jacket over his jumper, no hat, no scarf, with his hands jammed into his jean pockets and his shoulders hunched at his ears, he made me feel cold just looking at him.

It distracted me from the fact that he was here. In front of us. For some reason.

"Awright?" Stevie drew to a stop, his green eyes bouncing from me to Tobias. "Whit's happnin'? This where ye've been sneakin' off tae all the time?"

Tobias scowled at his cousin. "What are you doing here?"

"I've seen ye dodgin' doon this way loads. Ye dodged me again." He waved his phone at us, shivering. "Wondered why?"

"Don't worry. I'm not cheating on you."

Stevie laughed at Tobias's teasing. "Yer doin' somethin'

tho'. Or some*one*." His gaze shifted to me in speculation. "Just surprised by who it is."

"Watch it," Tobias warned. "It's not like that."

I didn't know whether to be happy that Tobias was putting Stevie in his place or irritated that he so vehemently denied there was anything romantic between us. Apparently that earlier almost kiss I couldn't get out of my head had been completely accidental. Tobias must have been relieved after all when Stevie's call interrupted us.

Tobias seemed displeased that Stevie had found us out. He'd argued that he wasn't ashamed of me, but was it really that terrible if Stevie knew we were friends? He had just spent the last ten minutes telling me I was wrong about Stevie. That he was a good guy. So why couldn't he be trusted to know about our friendship?

As if coming to a decision, Tobias nudged Stevie playfully with his shoulder. "Walk with us."

I eyed Stevie's attire. Or lack thereof. "I want some fries. They'll let us into the pub if I order something to eat."

"Aye, sounds gid," Stevie agreed immediately.

He needed warmer clothes but I just stopped myself from telling him so.

It was a quiet walk to the pub and we were pleased to discover it was quiet inside for once. The bar itself, the tables and chairs, the wooden floors, the steps and hand-carved banisters that separated the bar area from the restaurant area were mahogany in the traditional pub style. Down a narrow passageway by the bar there was a smaller room at the back of the building, with a roaring fire and couches, armchairs and tables for a more relaxed dining experience. People could even bring their dogs into this part of the pub.

To my delight we got a table by the fire, and when I ordered the fries I gave the boys free reign over them. Stevie's face flushed bright as he dived in. I frowned, watching him eat hungrily, wondering why I hadn't noticed that his cheekbones looked sharper these days. In fact, he looked lankier all over.

I shot Tobias a look of concern and he returned it with a grim one of his own.

What was happening with Stevie?

"So whit is wi' aw the secrecy?" Stevie asked with a mouth full of fries. "You two, I mean."

"People can be dicks." Tobias shrugged like it was no big deal. "I didn't want Comet getting shit for being my friend."

Stevie grinned. "Ye mean shit from aw the lassies that fancy ye?"

I blushed while Tobias rolled his eyes. "I mean shit from people. Specific people. The guys can be tools. Especially Jimmy and Forrester."

Jimmy and Peter Forrester were two of Stevie's crew and one of the reasons I'd been so judgmental of Stevie. They were dipshits. No other word for them. They were bullies who mocked and teased anyone that liked school or was smart, or was different from them in any way.

"True." Stevie nodded. "They dinnae have tae know. Why no' tell me, though?"

"Comet wasn't sure about you," Tobias said truthfully, embarrassing the hell out of me.

Stevie just laughed when I turned beet red. "Think I'm an arsehole, Comet?"

I shook my head vehemently. "I don't even know you."

"So...ye've decided to let me be part of yer wee group?" Stevie teased Tobias, but there was a hint of ugliness in his tone—anger, maybe. "Dae I have tae prove myself tae yer wee girlfriend?"

From the darkening of Tobias's expression I sensed an argument brewing so, quite surprising myself, I jumped in to diffuse it. "You don't have to prove yourself to anyone, Stevie."

He smirked. "Well, that's whit they tell us, ay."

Surprised by his rueful observation I realized quite quickly that Tobias was right. I knew nothing about Stevie Macdonald.

"Whit dae ye two talk aboot, then? When yer hangin' oot?" Something in his tone suggested he didn't quite believe us when we said we were just friends. While I squirmed uncomfortably, Tobias just brushed his tone away.

"Stuff."

"Descriptive."

I laughed at his sarcasm and he grinned at me.

Tobias huffed. "I don't know. What do we talk about?"

I shrugged, not wanting to be the focus of attention between the two of them. I'd much rather sit and listen while they chatted.

"Right pair o' conversationalists you two are, eh." Stevie snorted. "Yer no daen anythin' tae convince me that ye are'nae hookin' up."

"Life, music, books, TV, movies, random stuff," Tobias supplied.

"Speakin' of, Comet, did ye watch that new Netflix horror show? Jimmy wouldnae shut up aboot it and made me watch it. Scared the crap oot o' me."

Once again I was taken aback. It seemed incongruous to his reputation that Stevie would admit to being scared of a horror TV show. "I don't like horror."

"Aye, me neither," Stevie agreed, pinching more fries. "Gimme a jailbreak movie or heist flick or porn any day o' the week. But horror? Nah. Ick."

Ick?

Tobias's gaze flew to mine in concern, as if I might be affronted that Stevie said the word *porn* in front of me. But he had nothing to be worried about. I thought Stevie was funny. To my shock and chagrin.

I giggled, making Stevie grin harder. "Whit kind o' movies dae ye like, Comet?"

"Stuff you wouldn't like probably."

"Like that Mr. Darcy crap?" He wrinkled his nose.

A few weeks ago I might have been offended, but there was actually something kind of charming about the fact that he even knew who Mr. Darcy was. "Yes, actually. You've heard of Mr. Darcy?"

"Aye," he grumbled. "Ma mum has watched that stupid show like a million times."

I assumed he meant the BBC miniseries. A young Colin Firth as Mr. Darcy.

Yes, please.

"So have I."

Stevie's eyes flew to Tobias's in mock concern. "She's no' made ye watch it, has she?"

Tobias reached for a fry, seeming far more relaxed than he'd been just a few minutes ago. He shot his cousin that boyish grin that made my insides turn to mush. "How do you know I don't want to watch it?"

"You? Watchin' ponces ponce aroond talking aw posh? Mr. Let's No' Go Find Us Some Lassies to Shag but Watch the Football Instead?"

"Stevie," Tobias warned lightly.

"Sorry, Comet," Stevie said immediately. "But still…" He turned to me fully. "Does he talk aboot American football as much wi' you? Because it's aw he talks aboot wi' me."

I shook my head because Tobias rarely talked about it, unless he was telling me a story about his life back in Raleigh.

"Help me oot then. I've tried and tried tae get him interested in real football. Help."

I wrinkled my nose. "I don't like football."

Stevie stared at me for a second, just blinking. "Yer lucky yer pretty, Comet, or I'd no be talkin' tae ye after that. Doesnae like football." He tutted and shot Tobias a look. "Ye dinnae know whit yer missin'."

"I've played soccer, Stevie. I really do." Tobias took a swig of his Coke and leaned back, smirking. "It's got nothing on football. Real football."

"Ye barely touch the ball wi' yer feet," he argued. "Why the fuck dae ye call it football? *We* actually kick the damn thing. Wi' these." He pointed to his feet.

Laughing, I sat back, surprised to find I was enjoying myself listening to Tobias and Stevie tease one another. As the evening wore on I discovered they did it with everything. But it was all good-natured. They seemed to enjoy ribbing each other and trying to get me to take sides with them in every new debate.

Stevie and I had little in common and he was definitely rough around the edges. But he was funny, and he seemed as good-natured as Tobias said he was. My whole life I'd grown up in school with Stevie Macdonald and I'd never once thought to look beneath the surface. Instead I'd stuck my nose in the air where he was concerned, telling myself

I was better than him because I didn't hang around with a group of delinquents, mocking people, shoplifting and taking the piss at school.

When I searched my brain, I'd never actually seen Stevie openly bully anyone. It was always Jimmy and Forrester and the idiots that trailed after them. Yet I'd blamed Stevie anyway. I still didn't think it was right that he stood by and let them treat people that way, but who was I to judge? It was hard to stand up to your friends when they were the only thing you had.

I knew that better than anyone.

So I made the decision right there and then to give Stevie the chance Tobias wanted me to. For Tobias I would have done it anyway. But getting to know Stevie, seeing that beneath the bravado and cheekiness was a nice guy with a crappy home life, I did it for me and Stevie, too.

Because maybe Tobias was right. Maybe if you took a chance on people, rather than writing them off before getting to know them, reality could be fun.

That night in the pub was fun. It was easy. It's how I imagined friendship should be.

The Halloween dance came and went, and was just one more reason for distance between Steph and Vicki. They didn't even talk about it in front of me, assuming I'd been locked in my bedroom reading. Alone.

The truth was I had been in my bedroom, but I hadn't been alone. I'd been hanging out with Tobias and Stevie.

Since his discovery of our friendship, Stevie had kept our secret. He and Tobias acted the same around me at school—meaning they pretty much ignored me outside of class. However, since his discovery, Tobias and I had seen less of each other, too. He was hanging around with the boys more again, and when I did spend time with him Stevie usually tagged along.

The timing was suspect.

After all, the last time Tobias and I had been alone, we'd almost kissed.

I tried to reassure myself that it didn't have to do with our almost kiss. That it most probably had to do with the fact that Tobias and his mum had moved into their own place a few weeks ago. Tobias said Lena had been waiting on the settlement money from his dad's estate. Once they had it she'd moved them into a much nicer neighborhood. Which meant Stevie and Tobias were merely hanging out all the time because they no longer lived together.

And despite that sounding completely rational, I couldn't help but fear it was more about the almost kiss and an attempt to avoid another mouth-to-mouth incident happening.

Dejected, but attempting not to be, I tried to move on from the moment, but every time I got to a scene in a book where the main characters gave in to their attraction to one another, I'd close my eyes and imagine what it might have been like if Stevie hadn't interrupted us.

Would Tobias have given me the kind of kiss I'd been waiting on my whole life…or would kissing just turn out to be a disappointing fiasco?

Part of me wasn't sure I even wanted Tobias and me to become a reality, because I loved daydreaming about him. I loved longing for him. It made every day more exciting. I'd sit during biology and imagine getting a bathroom pass and on my way to the toilet someone would haul me into a broom closet. That someone would turn out to be Tobias, and he'd tell me he just couldn't go on another minute without confessing how he felt about me. And then he'd pull me into his arms and kiss the life out of me.

Sometimes in the daydreams we were already dating and he'd get jealous I was spending time with someone else or I'd get jealous he was flirting with Jess Reed and he'd have to beg and plead with me to forgive him. I basically made up little novellas about us as a couple in my head.

The truth was I worried that Tobias and me, the reality of us, couldn't live up to the fictional us I'd created.

Maybe he was right to put some distance between us.

I was thinking all this as he wandered off to the bathroom, leaving me and Stevie alone in my room. Although I was more comfortable with Stevie, I wasn't anywhere near as relaxed around him as I was with Tobias. I stared around my room, trying to think of something to say.

"It's a bit weird yer parents havnae come tae check on us," he suddenly said from his position slouched on my armchair.

I shrugged. "They're a bit self-involved."

"Aye?" He made a face. "I get that. Ma da is a selfish bastard."

Not knowing if it was polite to ask about his criminal father or not, my expression turned sympathetic.

"He's in prison," Stevie offered. "For nickin' cars."

"I'm sorry."

"Aye, well." He blew out a breath, suddenly looking exhausted. "Stupid fuckwit. Should be at hame, helpin' us. Especially with ma mum…"

My earlier concern for Stevie came flooding back. He still hadn't put on the weight he'd lost and he didn't have warmer clothes. With Carole distracted by some unknown illness and Kieran, and Lena and Tobias no longer there, who was taking time to look after Stevie? On that thought, I sprang off my bed and opened my closet. After a visit to the poetry café the other day, while Tobias and Stevie were off doing who knew what with their friends, I'd spotted something for Stevie in a sports shop on my way home.

"These are for you."

Stevie gave me a speculative look as he cautiously took the carrier bag from me. His eyebrows hit his hairline as he pulled out the plain black scarf, gloves and the black Nike beanie hat. "What…"

The way he just stared blankly at the accessories made me question my impulsive decision to buy him them. I felt my cheeks grow hot with embarrassment. The boy probably thought I was an idiot. A mummying, boring idiot.

Oh God.

I was!

"I can afford tae buy my own clothes," he said tightly.

Not wanting to offend his pride I hurried to assure him. "I know. But you won't. I get cold just looking at you, Stevie. It's for me more than for you."

"Com…" He looked up at me and then bestowed on me such a sweet smile that if I hadn't already been head over heels for Tobias King I might have swooned. "Ye didnae have tae dae that. Thanks."

At his sincere gratitude I relaxed, smiling as I sat on the edge of my bed. "You're welcome."

He started taking the tags off everything and putting it all on, making me laugh. His next words, however, put a halt to my amusement. "Mum's sick, Comet. Really fuckin' sick."

The words were choked, desperate and pleading.

And I felt utterly helpless. "Stevie…"

Tears shimmered in his eyes as he looked at me. "She's got cancer."

Oh no. "I'm so sorry."

"I've got Kieran and I've got ma mum…and I just…"

My heart pounded in my chest, disbelieving that this boy, whom I'd barely known just a short while ago, was confessing his secrets to me. His trust in me made me want to protect it, to make sure I didn't do anything to harm it. "Just?"

"I just want tae disappear. Forget everything. Ye ever want tae just disappear, Comet?"

Knowing there wasn't a lot I could do to help him, and hating it, I offered him the only thing I could. Solidarity. Gesturing to the bookshelves around my room, I said softly, "I disappear all the time."

Stevie's sad eyes danced along the bookshelves. "Aye. S'pose ye dae."

We shared a melancholy smile just as Tobias came back into the room. He stopped at the sight of Stevie in his beanie hat, scarf and gloves. "Going somewhere?"

"Comet bought me presents." Stevie grinned, and I marveled at how effortlessly he wiped away the grim pain, burying it beneath layers of cheeky boy charm and mischief.

Tobias raised an eyebrow, taking in the accessories, and then he gave me a questioning look.

"Well, he obviously wasn't going to buy himself those things. This way he feels obligated to wear them and I know he's keeping warm."

Stevie laughed. "Dae ye think she might buy me a car next?"

"Oy, don't push it." I threw a pillow at him, feeling more myself with him now that he'd been real with me.

Tobias didn't laugh. Instead he flopped down on the bed and started playing with his phone.

I frowned at Stevie but he just grinned. "He's feelin' left oot, Com. Poor baby didnae get a scarf."

"Fuck off." Tobias rolled his eyes but he didn't look up from his phone.

I wanted to rip the phone out of his hand and tell him he didn't need a scarf when he had my love. But I was neither brave nor cheesy enough to do it. Instead I shoved his leg playfully. "What's up?"

"Nothing. Just texting." He stuck his phone in his pocket and gave me a smile that didn't quite reach his eyes. "What do you guys want to do tonight?"

I shrugged, feeling uneasy about the lack of affection in his gaze. Who had he been texting? According to rumor, he and Jess had snogged at Ryan's party. But that was it. There had been nothing else said about Jess Reed, as far as I was aware, but maybe I was out of the loop. "Who were you texting?"

"What are you, our mother?" he teased but there was an edge to his tone. "Scarves, now nosy questions?"

Hurt pulsated in my chest and I blushed. "Sorry."

"Dinnae apologize." Stevie threw the cushion I'd thrown at him at Tobias. "Wanker."

"I was joking," Tobias lied. But I saw the remorse in his eyes as he reached out to tug gently on my hair. "I'm sorry."

"It's fine." I gave him a smile I didn't mean, because I didn't want any weirdness between us. Jumping off the bed to put distance between us, I wandered casually over to my window and sat on the window seat. "What *are* the plans?"

Tobias scowled at me, and I wondered what the heck I'd done now.

"I like this room. Let's stay here," Stevie said, slouching even farther in my chair. "Watch a movie or somethin'."

"Yeah, sure, whatever." Tobias kicked off his shoes and swung his long legs up on the bed. He patted the space beside him. "Comet?"

Annoyed at him and I wasn't even sure why, I gave him a brittle nod. First, however, I opened the closet door that hid my TV, grabbed the remote and then lay down beside Tobias. I left quite a bit of space between us.

As we flicked through Netflix, trying to decide what to watch, I was aware of him shuffling closer. By the time the action movie the boys had voted on was finished, the left side of Tobias's body was pressed along my right and Stevie was asleep on the armchair, still wearing the winter accessories I'd bought him.

14

You're kind but the mask you wear makes you mean,
You're sweet but your silence can be so cruel.
You're all that, more, and everything in between
You're the king but I won't live under your rule.

—*CC*

"I think it's bullshit this no talkin' tae ye at school," Stevie had said in the first week of November, and that was before I gave him the gift of winter accessories.

I'd quietly agreed but Tobias's response was, "You really want her on Jimmy's radar?"

They'd shared this grim look that made me sigh in exasperation. "Why are you friends with him if he's so bad?"

"*He's* friends with him." Tobias pointed to Stevie.

Stevie just shrugged. "He's been ma mate forever. And the only reason he's a wee shit sometimes is because of his big brother. Treats him like crap. Winds Jimmy up and sets him off on someone else."

"That's what siblings do though, right? That's not really an excuse for the terrible things Jimmy says and does to people," I said.

"I'm no' talking about normal sibling fighting, Com." Stevie gave me a sad look. "His brother...well, it's no' ma business to say anything but believe me, things are crap at home for him."

And that had been the end of the discussion, because I suppose I didn't know anything about Jimmy. But still, I didn't think it was an excuse for bullying people.

By the middle of November I was growing increasingly tired of being ignored by the two boys who were my friends. It was bad enough that Tobias and I rarely saw each other alone anymore, but he and Stevie had started ditching me for the wondrous conversations of Jimmy and Co. If they were so awful, why had I been ditched for them? Despite my hurt, I made the decision to focus my energy elsewhere. So far I still had not taken Mr. Stone's advice to get up on the stage at Pan, or take any steps toward pushing myself outside my comfort zone regarding my writing. And Mr. Stone was right. If I wanted to impress colleges, then I needed to become proactive. For weeks, I'd been working myself up to do just that. I still wasn't quite brave enough to recite my poetry at Pan, but finally, I found the courage to share my poetry with someone other than Tobias.

Palms sweaty throughout my English lesson as I prepared to make myself vulnerable, I ignored Tobias's quizzical stare as I sat, tense, beside him.

The bell finally rang for the end of class and as everyone packed their books away my friend turned to me. "You okay?"

"Yeah. I just need to talk to Mr. Stone. I'll catch you later."

"What's going on?"

"I just need to talk to him about classwork."

"You're acting weird."

I wasn't the only one. But I wasn't going to go there. Today wasn't about Tobias ignoring me at school. Today was about my future. "I'll see you later."

Not looking particularly happy about being dismissed, Tobias reluctantly left.

"You coming?" Steph and Vicki stopped by my table as I got out of the seat, waiting for the class to empty.

"I'll catch up with you. I need to talk to Mr. Stone."

The girls didn't question it, and soon everyone had emptied out of the classroom. Mr. Stone looked up from packing his overstuffed satchel with more papers. "Comet? Everything okay?"

There was no turning back now.

My mouth was so dry that I felt my teeth stick to my upper lip as I tried to open it to speak. Wetting my lips, fingers trembling, I dug into my bag and pulled out the folder I'd brought with me to school. "I…uh…well I know you're busy but um…well, I brought some of my poetry. I think it's poetry anyway. I mean it is poetry. Uh…" *Oh God, floor open up and swallow me whole!* "Well…I was just wondering if you… You told me to think about doing something with it and I just wondered if you'd…" I held the folder out toward him, feeling like I might burst into tears any second now.

As if sensing my panic, Mr. Stone quickly took the folder from me. "I'd be happy to read your work, Comet."

I gave him a brittle smile. "You don't have to if you're busy."

He smiled reassuringly. "I'm looking forward to it. Thank you for allowing me to. I'm truly honored."

Now I wanted to cry, because he was being so kind. "Thank you, Mr. Stone." I exhaled, willing the nervous fluttering in my stomach to quit it. "And I, uh…well I was thinking…if you think my work is good enough maybe I could do something more with it. I've looked into what other schools in Central Scotland are doing and a few have founded their own lit mags. I thought maybe we could create a school literary magazine, too. Online. Maybe even in print, too, if the school budget would allow it. And…I thought perhaps I could take a stab at being the editor." It was bold. I knew that. One, asking for a lit magazine and two, suggesting I run it. But if I wanted the University of Virginia to take me seriously, I needed to be bold. "If you think my writing is good enough I could maybe even use the magazine to show-case my poetry."

Mr. Stone stared at me with wide eyes. Almost like he'd never seen me before. His silence caused the blood beneath my cheeks to burn.

"Or maybe not. I'm sorry, it—"

"No," Mr. Stone hurried to say. "Don't be sorry. I'm just surprised. But in a good way. It's great to see you showing initiative like this, Comet. And I think the magazine is a wonderful idea."

"Yeah?" I grinned, relief flooding me that not only he wasn't laughing at me, he liked the idea!

"Definitely. Leave it with me."

"Great. Okay. Great." I nodded, backing away toward the door.

"And I'll read your work as quickly as possible. I wouldn't want to leave you in suspense for too long."

Reminded that he'd be reading my private thoughts, I gave him a tremulous smile before hurrying out of the room.

"I'm going to be sick," I whispered to myself. But along

with the nausea, I felt…proud. I was proud of myself and energized by it.

Virginia, here I come.

As it turned out, a few days later, Tobias was still avoiding me outside of class so he had no idea about the brave step I'd taken for my future. I felt like I had no one to talk about it with, no one to calm my nerves. I'd been there for Tobias. I'd been a good friend to him. And now that something important was happening in my life, he wasn't anywhere to be found.

That pissed me off.

Perhaps it was the hurt or frustration, but one Thursday as I sat in the cafeteria while Steph and Vicki talked about the school show rehearsals incessantly I decided to make a change.

I'd been staring at Tobias the entire lunch period, willing him to look at me. My longing for him had gotten painful, the giddiness of daydreams and imagination buckling under the weight of missing him. Of being disappointed in him. I needed him to prove he was worth my hurt and the only way he could do that was by being around me again. He needed a second chance to be a good friend. *I* needed him to have a second chance.

It wasn't that I was ignoring his fears about putting me on Jimmy and Forrester's radar. But our friendship was suffering because of his refusal to acknowledge me and I was done with pretending.

Tobias always said he was tired of fake.

I was tired of it, too.

I got up from the table, vaguely aware that Steph and Vicki had stopped midconversation to stare at me. I was on a mission, however, and left them behind as I began to weave my way through the tables of students toward Tobias.

As if he sensed me coming, he looked up from the conversation with the lads and his eyes narrowed at whatever he saw in my expression. As abruptly as I'd left my table, Tobias got up, ignoring Forrester shouting after him, "Oy, where ye goin'?"

Tobias's answer was to plonk himself down beside Jess Reed and begin flirting with her.

Jess Reed.

It was like I'd been dropped out of the window in Carrie's art studio and upon landing the breath had been knocked right out of me. It hurt so bloody much.

Aghast my gaze swung back to Stevie, who was staring at me in anger. Angry at me or at Tobias?

Tears flooded my eyes and I could feel people staring at me, probably wondering why I was just standing in the middle of the cafeteria looking like I was about to cry. I turned on my heel and strode out of there, nearly knocking a younger student off her feet in my hurry to disappear.

As soon as I slammed out of the double doors I began to speed walk down the corridor, trying to think, through all the chaos inside my head, where the nearest bathroom was.

"Comet, wait!" Swift feet thudded on the tiled floors behind me.

A strong hand gripped my arm and I found myself being hauled to a stop by Stevie. We were the same height, our eyes on level. His were clouded with sympathy and annoyance.

"That was really shitty o' him, Com. I'm sorry. I'll have a word wi' him."

"Don't." I shook off Stevie's hand. "Jesus, I only wanted

to come over and say hello to you both. Am I that much of a loser, Stevie? Because this rubbish about protecting me is… it's nonsense! It feels made up, and I'm the idiot that actually believed it."

Stevie studied me thoughtfully. "Ye like him, don't ye?"

Fear thickened my throat, made my mouth dry. I licked my lips nervously. "Of course. He's my friend. *Was*."

"*Is*. But I mean, fancy him. Ye fancy him."

"No, I don't," I vehemently disagreed.

"If ye say so." And then Stevie hugged me.

I stood, shocked, as he held me tight in his strong arms, my nose pressed to his shoulder. And the warmth and solidness of him felt so good I wrapped my arms around him, too, and pressed my entire face to his shoulder.

We stood like that for what felt like forever until I mumbled, "Why are you hugging me?"

I felt him shake with laughter. "Why no'? Ye feel better, right?"

"Everything okay?" The sound of Tobias's voice drew Stevie and me apart. I brushed a strand of hair nervously behind my ear, wishing I'd left my hair down so I could hide behind it. "What's going on?"

The hard accusation in his voice flipped a switch inside of me. I went from hurt to angry in a millisecond. My gaze flashed to his to see him looking at me and Stevie with suspicion, as though two people couldn't hug without it meaning something romantic. "This is what friends do, Tobias," I snapped, gesturing to Stevie. "They acknowledge you exist and comfort you when you're upset." The last word broke as tears spilled down my cheeks without my permission. I hadn't meant them to! It seemed lately I was unable to control my feelings. And everything felt too much, too big, too overwhelming.

It was mortifying!

Tobias looked as horrified as I felt.

"Comet!" Vicki suddenly appeared, shoving Tobias aside to get to me, with Steph on her trail. Her expression flared in outrage at the sight of me in tears. "What did you do?" she demanded of Stevie and Tobias.

"Nothing," I mumbled, swiping angrily at my tears. "Let's go."

Tobias took a step toward me. "Comet—"

"Leave her alone," Steph threw out as Vicki hustled me down the corridor toward the bathroom.

As soon as we got inside they locked the door and Vicki handed me my backpack. I must have left it at the table and didn't even realize. Dropping it, I slumped against the cold tiled wall. "Oh God…please tell me I didn't just burst into tears in front of Tobias and Stevie?"

"Sorry, babe," Vicki winced. "You kind of did."

"On that note—and it's not that I'm not concerned or anything that you were crying—what the hell, Comet?" Steph's hands flew to her hips. "You *know* those guys? They know you? And I don't mean from class—have you been hanging out with them behind our backs?"

I blushed furiously, giving myself away. "It started a while ago…"

And so with a rapt audience in front of me, I told the story of my burgeoning friendship with Tobias King, and how I stupidly fell for him and kept getting hurt by his indifference in public.

"I'm so sorry I didn't tell you," I pleaded with them to understand. "I'm just an idiot for listening to him."

"Oh, Com." Vicki hugged me tight, and it was such a relief to be held by her I almost squeezed her to death in return. "We're all idiots when it comes to boys."

Steph put her arms around both of us.

It was a lovely moment.

Then Steph said, "Anyone else just excited that Comet likes someone? For a while there I couldn't work you out, Com. Straight, gay, something else? Who knew!"

Confiding in my friends felt so good that Steph's ridiculousness didn't even bother me. In fact, I'd missed it. And I told her so by laughing so hard I almost cried again.

Like the biggest cliché, I waited for Tobias to apologize.

I thought at first it would happen in English next period but he never showed for class. My thumping heart and sweaty palms had been for nothing.

My phone was glued to my hip for the rest of the day and evening.

But nothing.

And he didn't show up for English the next day either.

The weekend passed slowly with no word from him or Stevie. I was preoccupied. Not just with thoughts of the boys, but worrying about Mr. Stone's reception of my poetry. After deciding to confide in Vicki about my poems, and how Mr. Stone was reading them, my best friend roped Steph and me into going to Glasgow to shop in order to take my mind off the boys and my poems. Yet I was still distracted. Again. Instead of being angry with my distance, however, they were sympathetic. Finally, Steph could relate to a daydreaming

Comet, because now she was daydreaming about a boy, and Vicki knew it was about more than just the boys. It was about me putting myself out there with my work for my future.

"I'm proud of you," Vicki had whispered to me while Steph was in a changing room trying on a dress so short there was no way she could allow her dad to ever see it. "Maybe when you're ready, you'll let me read your poems, too."

I'd squeezed her hand, grateful for her support. Just grateful I had her back.

My worry over losing Tobias's friendship transformed into annoyance when he first blanked me as he walked into Spanish the following week, and then when he ignored me entirely in English class. Between that and the fact that Mr. Stone walked into class with my folder under his arm, I was distracted from our lesson completely by my apprehension over his opinion, and over Tobias's coldness. Trying to focus on what should be the priority rather than on the boy next to me, I watched as Mr. Stone slipped the folder under a pile of papers on his desk and then welcomed the class.

I tried to listen as he talked about classwork, but it was incredibly difficult, and when he asked me to stay after class I felt a strong wave of nausea.

Tobias sat as far from me as possible, flinching when my foot accidentally brushed his under the table. At the first ring of the dismissal bell he shot out of his chair with the precision of the one o'clock gun at Edinburgh Castle. He was gone before I could even draw breath.

I tried to pretend I wasn't angry at him. That his behavior didn't matter as much as what Mr. Stone had to say to me about my poems. But as much as I wanted it to be true, it wasn't. Plus, it felt better to be angry than to think about how much Tobias ignoring me hurt. My days were suddenly gray again, and I almost hated him for having that kind of power over my mood.

Shaking the melancholy off, I waited in my seat as everyone else filtered out. Vicki, probably having guessed what our teacher wanted to talk to me about, threw me a bolstering smile before she walked out of the classroom.

When we were alone, Mr. Stone took my folder off his desk and came to perch on mine. He handed it back to me wearing a small smile. "These are wonderful, Comet. Thank you so much for allowing me to read them."

All the air I'd been holding in seemed to deflate out of me, and my teacher chuckled at my obvious relief.

"Your perspective is refreshing and honest. May I ask what university you're thinking of applying to?"

"The University of Virginia. They have great writing and poetry programs," I said automatically, reeling from his praise.

He looked surprised but in a good way. "That's a wonderful goal, Comet. And I think the literary magazine would help you achieve it."

Hope suffused me. "Are you saying we can start the magazine?"

"I've spoken with Ms. Fergus, our department head, and she's happy to let us give it try. With you leading the helm as editor."

My belly roiled with a mixture of excited and nervous flutters. It was a lot of responsibility and I didn't know if I could do it, but I was willing to try.

"That's brilliant." I gave him a tremulous smile.

Mr. Stone grinned. "Great. Okay. Well, I think with your exams coming just after Christmas break, it might be best to launch it next term. That will give us time to get the site and our team organized. I'm going to advertise that we're recruiting a lit mag team but if you know anyone who might like to join please let me know."

Amazed that I'd made this happen, I gathered my stuff, bidding my favorite teacher a good afternoon. I couldn't wait to tell Vicki and I wanted to tell Tobias.

But over the next week I rarely saw him, Stevie and their crew around school and despite not wanting to be, I was concerned. I was anxious about what they could be up to. And I was worried that Tobias was going to get himself kicked out of Higher classes.

"Okay, I've had enough." Vicki dropped her tray down beside me in the cafeteria with a bang, drawing my gaze from Tobias and Stevie's empty table. "No more moping over Tobias."

"Agreed." Steph made a face. "All that frowning is going to give you wrinkles, Com."

Yes, because that was what I was most worried about in life. "What do you suggest?"

She ignored my dry tone. "Antiwrinkle cream. I've already started using it."

"You're weird," I replied.

"Forget Steph's premature antiaging regime." Vicki waved the subject off. "You, Comet Caldwell, are done moping after Tobias King. Don't you think he knows you're just sitting around waiting for him to show you a little bit of attention? That's where all their power lies. But you have to take the power back."

"And how do I do that?"

"Look, I know you're not a party person, but word has

it Tobias will be at this party some guys who used to go to school here are throwing."

"It's Dean Angus," Steph grimaced. "He's dodgy as hell."

"Dodgy how?"

Vicki shrugged. "He runs with a dodgy lot. Possibly criminals. But Tobias will be at this party. We can just show up, we don't have to stay long. We're just sending the message that your life doesn't begin and end with Tobias King."

The angry part of me wanted to go to the party to show Tobias that very thing. Yet the concerned part of me was wondering why Tobias and Stevie were hanging around some guy who was possibly a criminal. My protectiveness toward them flared despite their ill treatment of me lately.

"You're right. Let's do it."

15

Bye to all those lonesome detours,
For you are mine and I am yours.

—CC

This was a bad idea.

I'd known it was a bad idea before we'd even stepped foot into the flat where the party was being held, but the feeling of trepidation I'd felt only worsened as we made our way through the crowded, narrow hall.

Head-pounding dance music flooded from the center of the flat, the deep bass vibrating in my chest, making my heart rate speed up. The smell of cigarette smoke, stale beer and musty air surrounded me, as I took in the mix of age groups with uneasiness. There were people my age, but there were also girls a little older, perhaps eighteen onward into their early twenties, and there were men much older than that.

As I passed an older girl eyeballing Vicki, Steph and me, she blew smoke from her rolled-up cigarette at me and I wrinkled my nose at the pungent, awful, herby smell. That lady was *not* smoking a normal cigarette.

"This was a bad idea." I turned to the girls at the opening to the living room. "Maybe we should leave."

"It's just a little weed, Comet," Steph said. "Relax."

I huffed and turned back to the crowded room. Searching

the faces of the people milling around, drinking, smoking, talking, some snogging each other's mouths off, I couldn't find Tobias. This was a mistake.

And then three people moved, revealing a sofa and coffee table in the middle of the room. Surrounded by older boys I didn't recognize was Stevie. As if in slow motion, like some horrid scene in a movie, I watched as Stevie leaned over the coffee table with a rolled-up bit of paper, placed it against his nose and inhaled a line of white powder from the coffee table.

"Holy crap." I thought I heard Vicki say over the excruciatingly loud music. "Did Stevie just snort cocaine?" she yelled in my ear.

Yes.

My friend Stevie just did a line of cocaine in some stranger's dodgy flat.

Betrayal stabbed me in the gut as I watched him wipe his nose and settle back on the couch to laugh at something one of his companions said. It was then I noticed Jimmy was there, too. Where was Tobias?

I couldn't see him in the room…but was this why he and Stevie had stopped hanging out with me? Was Tobias in on this, too? Throwing his life away? Rage rushed through me as I spun on my friends. "Where's Tobias?"

"Who cares?" Steph yelled. "Let's get out of here. This was definitely a bad idea."

"What happened to 'it's just weed'?" I snapped.

"That was…" She gestured behind us and then pointed her hand toward the coffee table. "That's a much longer jail sentence!"

"I'm not leaving!" I shook my head. Not until I found Tobias so he, Stevie and I could get out of there.

Steph looked at me like I was crazy.

Vicki scowled at me. "I'm not leaving without you!"

"Then you're not leaving yet either!"

Steph raised her hands in the air. "Idiots! My parents catch me here and I'm dead! Sorry, I'm out!" She pushed her way back through the gathering crowds in the hallway.

"You should go after her!"

Vicki shook her head. "Not leaving without you!"

Sighing, I spun back around to do another search of the room. Definitely no Tobias. When I looked back at Vicki she was pulling her jacket closed over the V-neck sweater she was wearing, staring warily across the room. Following her gaze I saw a man who might be in his thirties leering at her. I hated the idea of Vicki being in this hellhole just for me. "Go wait outside," I said loudly. "If I'm not out in fifteen minutes, come find me."

"Comet—"

"Go!" I shooed her. "I'll be fine."

Reluctantly my friend left, shooting one last wary look at the leering creeper.

I pushed my way back into the hallway but this time I turned left into the small kitchen. It was crowded, too. I stood on tiptoes and ducked down low, attempting to see past bodies to the people sitting at the small breakfast table.

Not Tobias.

Feeling overwhelmingly warm in my jacket, the same tailcoat hem one that Tobias had said he liked so much, I tried to open the buttons on it and realized I was trembling like crazy. Forcing back tears that would be of absolutely no use, I leaned against the wall by the kitchen door and closed my eyes.

I think I was in shock.

Why would Stevie take cocaine? Cocaine! My God. I gritted my teeth in outrage. And my goodness, if I discovered that Tobias was doing drugs, too, I was going to tear him limb from limb!

I just want tae disappear. Forget everything. Ye ever want tae just disappear, Comet?

Fresh tears stung my nose and I shuddered, holding them back. *Oh, Stevie, there are better ways to disappear.*

Feeling hollow, I opened my eyes and jerked back against the wall. An unfamiliar guy was standing in front of me, smiling quizzically.

He was just a little taller than me with dark eyes and close-shaven hair. There was a wiry hardness about his build that reminded me of Stevie. He was dressed similarly, too, in a sports T-shirt and tracksuit bottoms. My study of him made him smile, revealing crooked teeth that gave him a friendly snarl.

He might have been cute if I didn't feel so alone, shocked and intimidated by this entire place.

"Dean," he said loudly, holding out his free hand. He held a bottle of beer in his other.

Realizing this was Dean Angus and thus it was his party, and frightened of bringing trouble on myself, I decided the best thing to do was shake his hand politely. "Comet."

"Sorry?" He leaned in, turning his ear toward me so he could hear.

"Comet."

He shook his head and grinned at me. "I didn't get that."

And he probably never would with this dance racket thudding through the entire building. "Corrine!" I lied on a shout.

Dean nodded. "Nice to meet you. Who are you here with?"

Lie, Comet, lie. "Iain," I said confidently, hoping there were so many people here Dean would think nothing of it.

I was right. He just nodded again. "Where do you work, then?"

"I'm still at school."

"College?"

Damn my height. I shook my head and his brows furrowed. "High school? What age?"

"Sixteen," I answered honestly, hoping that would send him on his way.

To my distaste he smirked and stepped closer, completely invading my personal space. The smell of aftershave was almost obliterated by the stale smell of beer on his breath. "Let's go into my bedroom."

That was it? That was how fast these things happened? Really? He just expected me to go into his bedroom…and to what? Have sex with him? I shuddered at the thought.

"I better find my friends." I moved to the side, hoping to slip away, but he grabbed my arm and I felt his hot breath on my ear.

"Stay. Find them later." His hand left my arm to settle on my hip, and he squeezed, making me jump back against the wall. The dipshit didn't even give me a moment to breathe, pressing his body up against mine to whisper in my ear, "I've been eyeing yer legs since ye walked in." His hand was back on my hip again, "Please tell me ye've not got a boyfri—"

Suddenly he was stumbling back from me, his beer splashing over his T-shirt.

My eyes flew to the reason and relief crashed over me.

Tobias.

He glowered down at Dean, looking ready to…well, kill him.

"What the fuck?" Dean threw the bottle in the corner and stood up to Tobias, not even caring that Tobias had at least four inches and many pounds of muscle on him. "Ye playing at, King?"

"You leave her alone." Tobias stepped in front of me, blocking me from Dean's gaze.

"This is my place. I'll talk to who I want. Take who I want. Don't see yer name written on her."

"She's sixteen."

"And?"

"She's walking out of here without you hassling her, Dean."

I peered around Dean to see his face had darkened with fury. He stepped into Tobias, shoulders thrown back, his chest puffed out and his fists clenched, ready for a fight. "Do ye realize who yer talking to, wee boy? I'm not just some pissy wee wanker at yer high school ye can boss around because yer a big guy. Ye mess with me and I can end ye, right."

There was something about the malicious gleam in his eyes, the air of invincibility he gave off, that made me believe him. What the hell had I walked into? What were Stevie and Tobias involved in?

Nausea swam over me, and I clutched Tobias's shoulder to stop myself from vomiting my anxiety all over Dean's peeling linoleum floor.

Tobias tensed. "Just let her go, Dean," he said more softly now.

Dean shook his head. "I'm king here, not you. Ye want her, ye get the fuck out of here with her...and I swear, *Tobias*, if I ever see yer ugly face around me again, I'll give you a kicking in ye won't wake up from. Understood?"

To my disbelief, Tobias hesitated.

But only for a second.

He gave a short, jerky nod, turned around and, without looking at me, gripped my biceps in his arm and forcefully led me out of the flat.

"What about Stevie?" I yelled over the music.

Tobias ignored me.

"Tobias!"

"He doesn't want to leave. Come on!"

"You don't need to drag me! I'm coming willingly!"

Yet Tobias didn't let me go. Even when we met Vicki halfway down the stairs and she let out a huge exhale of relief, he didn't let go.

"I thought I was going to have to call the police or something," Vicki chattered nervously as we all hurried down the graffiti-covered stairwell. "What happened in there?"

"I…" *actually don't really know.* "Tobias?"

He didn't say anything. Not until we were outside and he finally let me go. "What the hell, Comet?"

I flinched under the force of his anger. "What?"

"What were you doing here?"

"It was my fault." Vicki grabbed my hand in support. "I heard about the party and dragged her here."

"You didn't drag me here." I shook my head, not willing to let her take the blame. "I came because I heard you'd be here. Is that why you've been avoiding me?" My own anger overwhelmed me now that we were safe from the clutches of Dean. "Because you and Stevie are taking drugs? Cocaine, Tobias!"

"Jesus Christ, keep your voice down," he hissed, glancing around the darkened streets. There were a number of streetlights out in this neighborhood. I had to wonder what kind of place it was if none of the neighbors would complain about the awful noise coming from Dean's flat.

Or maybe…they were just afraid of him.

"What is Dean involved in? What are *you* involved in?"

"I'm not taking drugs," he said forcefully. "Now let's go. I'll walk you both home."

"Tobias."

"Comet, move!"

I glared at him but began to stride forward. "You're not the boss of me, Tobias King."

"Now you get sassy? Shit," he muttered, his long legs eating up the ground ahead of us.

Vicki clung to me as we hurried to keep up with him. "Thank you." I gripped her hand tightly. "For staying."

She gave me a small, sad smile. "I know things have been weird between us until recently but I still love you."

"I love you, too. I'm sorry. About everything."

"Me, too."

Tobias threw us an exasperated look over his shoulder, and we kept quiet the rest of the long walk home. When I tried to ask questions he ignored them until I was wound so tight with worry and anger I thought I might just explode.

Vicki led us to her house from Main Street. She hugged me before going inside and said, "Come around mine tomorrow. Please?"

I nodded. "Definitely." We had a lot to talk about. A lot to put right in our friendship. Despite the horrendousness of our evening, something positive had come of it. It could lead to Vicki and I being closer than ever.

Once she was safely inside, Tobias fell into step with me

while we walked toward my house. Too angry to speak, I stewed in silence.

As we approached the esplanade, Tobias touched my elbow and drew me to a stop. I stared up at him, a million questions in my eyes. Yet instead of answering any of them, he did the one thing I didn't expect. He lifted a hand and pressed his cold fingers to my cheek, brushing the tips across my cheekbone. That light, tender touch and the stirring emotion in his gaze sent a shiver down my spine.

"Tobias?"

He blinked and dropped his hand, shoving it back in the pocket of his jacket. "You scared me tonight, Comet."

Disbelief cascaded over me. "*I* did? Me? *I* scared you? Tobias, I saw Stevie snort a line of cocaine! And when I tried to find you, I was accosted by some idiot who threatened to kill you and made it sound like he could actually do it!"

"He probably could." He scrubbed a hand over his hair and bit out a curse.

"What is going on? Please, tell me."

He studied me a moment and eventually sighed. "Can we go back to yours?"

Like Kyle and Carrie would even notice. "Of course."

By the time we got to the house and I let us into my bedroom, I was a jittering wreck. Massive waves of nervous energy were emanating from Tobias, making me worse. He was rarely nervous about anything. Once inside my room, I waited impatiently as Tobias slumped down on my bed, elbows on knees, head in hands.

I shrugged out of my jacket and unwound my scarf. Still waiting.

"Comet," he huffed, not looking up. "Sit down, okay, you're making me nervous."

"You're making *me* nervous." I sat on the armchair across from him. "You and Stevie didn't kill someone, did you? Did Dean dispose of the body for you and now he's blackmailing you?"

Tobias's broad shoulders shook and he lifted his head to stare at me with amusement tinged with sadness. "You've got to stop reading so many books."

"Never."

He smiled at me, his look so tender that I squirmed with the need to shoot across the room and throw my arms around him. Instead I met his gaze and asked directly, "What happened back there?"

"I just chose you over Stevie," he said.

I swear my eyebrows must have hit my hairline at this pronouncement. "What?"

"Stevie and some of the guys have been hanging around Dean more and more. Dean is a dealer. And he's part of something bigger—we're talking an adult-sized, criminal gang who deal drugs and steal cars for a living. Dean deals cocaine to kids. Blair Lochrie High School is one of his grounds. He sells to quite a few kids there."

At our high school?

Class A drugs at our high school?

"Bloody hell," I whispered. "Where have I been?"

"Where I prefer you—safe with your nose stuck in a book."

"Tobias… Stevie?"

Hearing the worry in my voice, he winced. "I tried, Com. I tried to keep him out of it, but he's so messed up and I couldn't stop him. I hung around to make sure he was okay."

206

"Is that why you've been avoiding me?" God, please let that be why he was avoiding me.

"Yes." A million apologies swirled in his gorgeous eyes. "I didn't mean for Stevie to find out about you, because I didn't want you anywhere near the stuff he was getting involved in. But then you two got along, so well I thought you might…have feelings for each other, so I told him that he either stopped hanging around Dean or he stopped hanging around you. He agreed keeping you out of that stuff, away from the boys, was better for you. So we stopped coming around as much and then stopped coming around at all. Tonight was his initiation into Dean's crew. It was supposed to be both our initiations, I guess, because Dean was sending Stevie to some other party with drugs, and I was following Stevie as backup. Now I'm not."

There was so much to process in what he'd just said.

My brain blurted out the first thing it wanted to deal with. "Stevie and I don't have feelings for each other. I don't like *Stevie*, Tobias."

His eyes widened as my tone implied that I liked someone else. "No?"

"No."

"Good. Because I just left him to that hell." He stood up and started pacing back and forth. "I tried to help him even if it meant hurting you, and he just let himself get pulled further down into that crap."

I stood up, reached out to touch him, to slow him down. He stilled, looking at my hand on his arm. "What did you mean? You chose me over Stevie?"

"Comet, Dean made it clear that if I left with you, I couldn't go around there or anywhere near him again. So I either had to stay and go with Stevie as his backup on a drug deal and leave you to handle Dean on your own, or I could walk out of there with you and leave Stevie to do it alone. For good." His gaze moved over my face, as if he were committing each feature to memory.

My heart started thudding so hard the blood rushed through my ears. "So you chose me."

"Of course," he choked out. "I'd never let anything happen to you. And seeing you there... I never want to see that crap touch you again. It was a wake-up call for me. I don't want to be a part of that shit either. That's not me."

Seeing something in his expression made me brave in a way I never thought I could be. Knees trembling, I stepped up to him and placed a hand on his chest, over his heart. His chest was strong and hard beneath my hand, his body heat surrounding me and that woodsy, spicy, citrusy scent he wore teasing my senses. I wanted to sway into him, hold him tight, and never let go, but I had something important to say first now that I had his absolute attention. "Being a good student, working for something, achieving something, playing hard at football...it wasn't all for your dad, Tobias. There is no maybe about it. Deep down you want those things for yourself, too. You're smart and good and such a special person." I gave him a tremulous smile, wondering if how I felt for him was as obvious to him as it was to apparently everyone else. "You deserve the life you really want."

His chest rose and fell faster beneath my hand as we stared into one another's eyes. Tobias licked his lips, as if he was nervous. "What if I want to get my grades back up?"

"Then I'll help."

"And join the rugby team?"

"Then you'll try out."

He nodded and slowly lifted his hand to cover mine. He took a step closer to me, his breathing sounding a little shaky. The thud of his heart racing beneath my palm made mine accelerate. My legs shook and my fingers curled into Tobias's shirt. "And...what if what I really want...is you?"

Joy flooded me. I can't truly describe the feeling. The euphoria. The excitement and thrill and fear and worry that cascaded through me at the thought of being with Tobias King.

No matter the plethora of emotions that came with his question, my answer was instant and absolute. "Then you have me."

16

Once there was a cold man in a dark hole,
And he offered a boy a choice.
"I'll destroy your pain in exchange for your soul,
Or live your days down here with no voice."
—*CC*

Hearing and feeling Tobias's heart beat beneath my cheek was the most wonderful feeling in the world. Despite my worry for him and for Stevie, I couldn't help but feel happy as the boy I loved slept in my bed with his arm around me.

The morning sun woke him around nine in the morning. He groaned and then grew still, maybe realizing I was curled up against him. For a moment I tensed, fearing he was going to regret everything he'd said last night.

Instead he trailed his fingers down my arm. "You awake?" his voice rumbled above me.

I smiled, liking the tingles that bubbled and fizzed in certain parts of my body at the mere sound of his voice. "Yeah."

"What time is it?"

I told him.

"Crap."

"What?" I asked, sitting up as he reached across the bed to where his phone lay on the bedside table.

"Stevie and my mom." He cursed again as he flicked the

screen. "They've texted and called a bunch of times. I better call my mom back first before she calls the police or something." He pressed the screen and held the phone to his ear. "Mom," he said almost immediately. "I'm fine." Tobias scowled. "I'm a big boy...no...no, I didn't...I'm with Comet..." Streaks of color appeared high on his cheeks, surprising me. Tobias rarely got embarrassed. "No, we just fell asleep...yeah...I'm on my way." He hung up and gave me an apologetic look. "I have to go."

At his beleaguered tone, I placed a reassuring hand on his arm. "She's your mum. It would be weird if she wasn't worried you didn't come home."

"Yeah, whatever." He shook his head and got off the bed, leaving me to frown at him.

Tobias seemed to be in a continually bad mood with his mother. I wish I had the guts to tell him to talk to her about why he was so mad, but I didn't want to push too hard too soon on such a delicate subject.

"I'll go appease her," he said, slipping his trainers on. "Then come back?"

I opened my mouth to agree and then remembered my promise from the night before. "I'm going over to Vicki's this morning."

"Right. How about I meet you outside the Espy around three o' clock?"

Relieved and delighted that he not only didn't regret saying what he had last night but that he wanted to see me again so soon, I grinned and got off the bed. Tobias gave me that boyish smile of his and I reached for his hand, needing to touch him.

He squeezed mine, a solemnity entering his gaze. "I want

to invite Stevie to meet us. I'm hoping that together we can talk him out of this bullshit. When it was just me I wasn't getting anywhere, but he cares about you. Maybe he'll listen."

I nodded, loving him even more for wanting to help his cousin. "Definitely. If we let him know we're here to help him through everything with his mum but that we can only do that if he walks away from Dean and the drugs…maybe he'll see sense."

I hoped.

Tobias hoped, too. I could see the turmoil in his eyes and I wanted desperately to be able to take it away.

It was as I was leading him from my bedroom to the front door that I heard the hallway floor creak behind us. I turned ever so slightly, catching sight of my dad in my peripheral. Ignoring him I hugged Tobias goodbye and waved him off down the garden path. I closed the door and turned to face my father. He stood frowning at me in his pajamas, a cup of coffee in one hand, a piece of toast in the other.

"Did that boy stay over?" he asked, sounding incredulous.

His tone suggested I'd done something wrong. I stiffened. "Yes."

Dad took a step toward me, glowering now. "Don't you think that's something you should run past us first? You're only sixteen, Comet."

"Almost seventeen." I bristled. How dare he suddenly play the parental card! Just when I was happy and didn't need him, he wanted to stick his nose in where it was not wanted! A fire lit inside me and swept out of me before I could control it. "And let's not play the concerned parent act, Kyle." I strode toward my bedroom and shoved open the door. "You don't get to decide which parts of my life you want to take

an interest in. Having a kid? Kind of an all-or-nothing deal."
I stepped inside, gripping the door in my hand as I sneered
at him. "You decided long ago it was nothing for you. No
changing your mind now." And with that I slammed the
door in his shocked face.

Walking to Vicki's not too much later, I felt a lightness
in my step. Having the courage to put my dad in his place
and bring the truth into the open had lifted this weight off
my shoulders I hadn't even known I'd been carrying around.
Before Tobias, I could be snarky to my parents, but I never
would have had the courage to call them out for being atro-
cious parental units.

I was changing. It seemed as if I'd started to change from
the moment Tobias and I became friends.

I could only hope I was changing for the better.

Because the truth was I still had so many insecurities regarding Tobias. Maybe it was because I felt so much for him
that I worried so much more about how he felt about *me*. I'd
barely slept the night before, listening to him breathe slow
and easy, sleeping like a baby in my arms. The truth was I'd
been caught in this place of absolute glee and absolute fear.
Although we had admitted we wanted to be with each other,
neither of us had said how we felt about the other. And Tobias...

Well, he hadn't kissed me.

Yes, he held me while he slept, but there was nothing sex-
ual about it. He didn't even wake up with morning wood
and, according to all the books I'd read, that was supposed
to happen. Although...he *had* been exhausted, falling asleep

almost immediately when we'd lain down on my bed last night. I'd read that exhaustion could affect a boy in *that* area.

Or maybe I'd just read the entire situation wrong?

No.

I couldn't have.

There had been definite eye smoldering, and I knew from my extensive reading that eye smoldering was an important part of the mating ritual.

Then why hadn't he kissed me?

Was he trying not to push me because he thought I was fragile? Was he worried about my reaction to his kiss after reading my poem about my first kiss with Ethan?

Oh God.

Well…to be fair I was a little worried about that, but I *wanted* to like Tobias's kisses! And even if I didn't, I'd already decided I'd put up with them just to be with him. I was totally willing to make that sacrifice.

Then there was the fact that as much as I wanted *everything* with Tobias, I was worried about our possible future together. When I was thirteen years old, I'd made the decision that I was going to university somewhere far away from my parents. After reading an online article about colleges best known for writing that were located in the States, I'd discovered the University of Virginia. I'd Googled what I could about it and fallen in love with the idea of studying there, and I'd become stubbornly focused on UVA. It was my dream college and I wasn't ready to give up on that dream for anyone. Not even Tobias.

But if Tobias was here and I was there…where would that leave us?

I was seriously overthinking this, considering the boy hadn't even kissed me yet!

This was all on my mind as Vicki invited me into her house. Even so I noticed her dad's car wasn't parked in the driveway, and it occurred to me that it was weird Vicki had been allowed to invite me over. It was a Sunday. Sundays were Family-Only Day at the Browns'.

Before I could question her about it, Vicki grabbed my wrist and hauled me into her room, then closed the door quickly behind us. "What happened?" she asked me all wide-eyed.

Chuckling at her eagerness I sat down on her bed, taking in the fact that her room was a colossal mess. The school had given her some funds to put together the costumes for the school play and it had clearly taken over her life. Thankfully, it got to go on her application for design school. Bolts of fabric were scattered over the floor, completed and half-finished costumes were hanging on doors, chairs, sprawled over blanket boxes. An almost completed 1920s flapper dress was on one of her mannequins with boxes of sequins and beading on the floor around it. I marveled at her artistry, wondering how she managed to create such wonderful pieces.

Her talent was out of this world. "That looks amazing."

"Yeah, yeah, tell me what happened." She shooed off my compliment.

I laughed at her eagerness and promptly told her what Tobias had explained to me once we'd dropped her off at home the night before. "So you see, he's not into drugs. We're going to meet up later with Stevie and try to talk some sense into him."

"And if you can't?" Vicki frowned in concern.

"I like Stevie. I'm worried for him, obviously. But I can't get involved with someone who is involved with drugs. If I can't talk him out of it, then I just have to make peace with the idea of leaving him to it. I can't tell anyone at school, because Stevie could get put away in Young Offenders. I can't tell his mum because she…is really ill at the moment and shouldn't have to deal with it. Stevie's seventeen. He's nearly an adult. What else can I do but try to persuade him? Tobias told me he would walk away from Stevie, too, if he doesn't stop. I didn't get the impression this morning that he'd changed his mind about that."

"Wait. What?" Vicki jumped down on the bed beside me, eyes round with excitement. "This morning?"

I laughed, enjoying being the one with something juicy to tell for once. "He slept over."

"You slept together?" she squeaked.

I shushed her, afraid her mum would overhear us. "Just sleeping. He didn't even kiss me."

Confusion wrinkled her forehead. "He didn't?"

Her reaction brought all my insecurities to the forefront. "I should be worried, shouldn't I?"

"I'm not sure. Did he actually say out loud that he wanted to go out with you?"

Had he? "Well…no." I shook my head, completely confused myself now. "But…it was implied. You had to be there."

"Hmm." My friend did not look convinced, and suddenly my heart was racing madly in my chest. "But you're seeing him today?"

"With Stevie, yes."

"When Stevie leaves, you have to ask Tobias straight out

whether or not you're dating. No way I'll have him playing you, Com."

Her protectiveness was sweet but I was not reassured. She seemed too easily ready to believe that I'd gotten Tobias wrong somehow. His reputation didn't exactly lend itself to the idea of him being a good boyfriend, but I knew Tobias. I did.

A little annoyed with Vicki for making me doubt everything, and even more annoyed with myself for being so easily doubtful, I changed the subject to the one that didn't make me annoyed with my friend. Only concerned. "Where's your dad? His car isn't in the driveway."

For a moment Vicki just stared at me.

And then she burst into tears.

No buildup.

Just bawling.

I immediately wrapped my arms around her and drew her head to my shoulder, holding her tight as her body shook with her tears. "Vicki?" I eventually asked when her tears slowed.

She pulled away from me to wipe at her cheeks, blobs of mascara now congregating around the corners of her eyes. "He moved out, Comet." She choked on the words, her lips trembling. "Weeks ago."

Guilt slammed into me.

"That's why I've been so mad at you. My dad's gone, and I couldn't even talk to you about it."

"Oh God, Vick." Tears filled my eyes now, "I'm so sorry. I'm such a horrible friend."

"No." She shook her head vigorously, her afro bouncing around her shoulders as if incongruous to her emotions, "We've both been crap friends. I could have just talked to you, told you, and I know that you would have made time and been there for me. I just… I needed someone to be mad at. I don't want to be mad at them, because I don't want to make things worse. They said it's just a break, but I'm really worried that they're never getting back together." She reached for my hand and covered it with both of hers. "I'm sorry for taking it out on you."

I hugged her again, my pulse beating fast for her. I wished I could take away her worries or carry them for her instead. The truth was I couldn't really understand what it must feel like to worry about parents splitting up and a family being torn apart. However, I had always envied Vicki her life with her family. It hurt me that she might not have that special unity in her life anymore.

"They promise it's not about me," she sniffled, resting her head on my shoulder again. "They said they were frustrated with each other and taking it out on us. They said they didn't want that, so they were taking some time apart. But I don't know if I believe them—I think I might have caused this."

I squeezed her waist. "Vick, it can't possibly just be about their differences over what you should do with your life. There has to be more to it than that. I'm positive."

"You think?"

"Of course. Don't blame yourself. Maybe they really do just need a break. They've been together a long time—they're bound to need some space from each other."

She sat up. "Your parents don't."

I snorted at the comparison. "My parents are the most dysfunctional codependent couple on the planet. Please do not use them as an example of a good relationship."

"You don't think they have a good relationship? They're so in love."

Bitterness and resentment, feelings I kept buried deep down most of the time in order to function, rose up inside of me. "To the detriment of all others. You can be in love and not be selfish dipshits, Vicki. If your parents need a break to be better people for you and your brother, then that's a hell of a lot more love and consideration than my parents ever gave me."

Something shifted in Vicki's expression, lightened maybe. "I guess. I never thought about it that way."

"Just give them time."

Vick nodded and then she smirked at me. "Do your parents know Tobias stayed the night?"

I grinned and recounted the conversation between me and my dad.

Her mouth fell open in half shock, half laughter. She studied me, almost as if she'd never seen me before. And then she just flat-out grinned. "I think I like Tobias's influence on you."

As much as I was desperate to see Tobias and afraid to at the same time, I'd like to think I'm not *that* self-absorbed. I did offer to spend the rest of the day with Vicki, not wanting to leave her alone when she was feeling so down about her parents' separation, but she insisted she had a ton of work to do for the show.

I knew the show meant a lot to her and Steph but I was kind of glad it would be over soon. It had stolen all their time, and yes, as petty as it may seem, I was jealous it had brought the two of them closer together.

Nerves returned with a vengeance as I made my way to the esplanade. Not only was I jittery over my confusing conversation with Vicki about what it was Tobias wanted from me, but I was tense over meeting up with Stevie. We were basically about to hand him an ultimatum, and ultimatums usually didn't turn out well.

As soon as I saw Tobias standing outside the Espy my heart started to pound, my pulse thrumming hard in my neck. He turned and caught sight of me and began to stride up the street toward me. His pace quickened and he seemed so determined my knees quavered a little.

When he reached me I opened my mouth to say hello, but the greeting died on my lips as he cupped my face in his warm hands and bowed his head to kiss me.

Shock, thrill, fear, want, all mixed inside of me as I closed my eyes and clung to his arms. His lips were soft, coaxing, brushing against mine, teasing me. Heat flashed through my body from the tips of my toes to my cheeks, and I leaned in, looking for something beyond even this. This felt nothing like Ethan's kiss.

It was lovely…and yet… I wanted more.

Tobias drew his lips from mine ever so slightly and murmured against them, "Open your mouth."

I flushed even hotter at the command but did so without hesitation. When his mouth returned to my mouth he touched his tongue to mine, just a flick, a torment that made me whimper in confusion. Everything within me seemed to tighten, coiling into an increasing tension as his tongue danced more forcefully with mine. It was a dance I easily followed, kissing him back with more fervor, my fingers digging into his arms.

This was the more I'd been waiting for.

This was everything.

He broke the kiss, gasping my name against my lips.

I blinked, discombobulated. My whole body hummed with an urgency I'd never felt before.

Tobias leaned his forehead against mine as we sought to catch our breaths and equilibrium. "I should have done that last night," he finally whispered.

Relieved laughter bubbled out of me in giggles that made him smile with such affection that I wondered how I could have possibly doubted his feelings for me. Tobias King liked me. Me. Comet Caldwell. If someone as special as Tobias could like me so well, maybe I was a little bit special, too? At least…that's how he made me feel.

"Finally got together then, have ye?" Stevie's voice interrupted our moment.

Tobias stepped away from me but slid his arm along my shoulder, drawing me into his side as we turned to face Stevie. I felt Tobias tense against me as I let out an involuntary gasp. It wasn't because of how skinny and underfed Stevie looked, or because of the black circles under his eyes, stark against the paleness of his skin, all of which made sense now that I knew about the drugs. What made me gasp, and what likely made Tobias bite out a curse, was the fact that Stevie's left eye was almost swollen completely shut, and there was a nasty cut on his upper lip.

"What the hell happened?" Tobias snapped.

"You and Comet together?" Stevie sneered.

"Yeah, Comet and I are together," Tobias said, and I would have squirmed in delight to hear the words out loud if I wasn't so worried about Stevie. "Now what happened to you?"

"I didnae have ma backup with me that's what happened." Anger flashed at us from his good eye.

I looked up at Tobias and saw him grow pale. "What did they do?"

"They didnae want tae pay what they'd arranged tae pay Dean. Took the drugs and gave me a beating. Jimmy tried tae help keep them off, but one of them was a big guy. As big as you."

I flinched at the accusation in his voice and burrowed into Tobias's side. This wasn't his fault!

"Dinnae worry, though. Dean's taking care of the arse-holes. But he doesnae trust me anymare. He's no' payin' me whit he was supposed tae, and willnae be until I've proved maself. I needed that fuckin' money, King. Now I'm up shit creek. Aw because my fud o' a best pal didnae have ma back."

Tobias appeared stricken. "I'm sorry. Did you have some-one look at it?"

"Aye, Mum put some salve and shit on ma lip and I iced ma eye."

"Let me explain what happened."

"I've no' got a lot o' time. Mum's no' doin' so gid the day, and I need tae watch Kieran for her."

"We'll be quick. Let's walk," Tobias said, keeping his arm around me as he turned about and started walking toward the esplanade. I glanced over my shoulder to see Stevie's face cloud over in a way that made my stomach churn. It almost looked like he hated us. When he caught me watching, his expression cleared and he hurried to catch up with us.

"So whit is this all aboot?" He kicked sand ahead of us as he fell into step beside us.

"This way," Tobias said instead.

We followed where he led, no one saying a word until he stopped us down by the shore away from prying ears. He faced Stevie, expression grim, and I tightened my arm around his waist to remind him he had my support. The winter wind pushed at us but we stood strong against the way it pinched our cheeks and rocked our feet.

"Last night was it, man," Tobias said. "Do you even know that Comet came looking for us and got cornered by Dean?"

Stevie shrugged, looking anywhere but at us. "Something was mentioned."

"So you know I can't show my face around Dean or those guys anymore? It was either let him do what he wanted to Com or get out of there and stay gone. That's why I couldn't come with you."

Stevie cut me a look of irritation. "Whit were ye thinkin' turnin' up there?"

Concern and anger flared out at once from me. "What are *you* thinking, snorting cocaine? I can't believe I even asked that question out loud. I feel like I'm in a bloody Irvine Welsh novel."

Shame darkened his face but only for seconds before his expression turned defiant and mulish. "It's nothin'. Just a bit o' a laugh."

"A laugh? A joke? Dean isn't giving you that shit for free, Stevie," Tobias snapped. "You got the crap kicked out of you dealing for him. You're seriously going to keep going with this?"

"He's ma mate," Stevie argued. "And I wouldnae have had the crap kicked out of me if you'd been a better mate!"

"Tobias is trying to help you. We both are. Stevie, you're better than this."

"Oh get off it, Comet," he huffed, eyeing me angrily. "Ye wouldnae have given me the time o' day if it werenae for his say-so." He pointed to Tobias. "This is me. Like it or leave it."

Tobias shook his head, openly seething with frustration. "That's what I'm telling you. I told you before I didn't want Comet near this crap, and I'm telling you now *I* don't want near it."

Realization fell over Stevie's expression, and with it came pain that he quickly covered with disgust as his gaze bounced between us. "So whit? We're no mates anymore? Ye havenae got ma back? Is that whit yer sayin'?"

"Stevie." I let go of Tobias to reach for our friend but he stumbled away from me, holding his hands up to ward me off.

"Screw this," Stevie bit out. "I dinnae need this. I dinnae need you! First you and yer maw fuck off just when ma mum needs ye—"

"Mom asked Carole if she wanted us to stay and your mom said no and wouldn't be talked out of it, so don't put that on us."

"Whit the hell does ma mum know? She's no' the one havin' tae deal with this. I am! And tae look after her and look after Kieran am gonna need money, and pals at ma back I can count on tae help me get it. Which means I dinnae need *you*." He pointed at Tobias and then cut me a killing look. "And I definitely dinnae need yer pity. Go fuck yerselves." He spat in the sand at our feet and stormed off.

For a moment all I could do was watch him retreat, his body hunched with cold and rage. And pain. The waves pushed forcefully against the shore, the sound soothing and calming, and completely out of sync with all of our feelings.

I shivered at the chill, wondering what I could have said or done differently. Wondering if I should go after him.

Heat enveloped me as Tobias pressed his chest to my back and wrapped his arms around me. His cold cheek pressed against my temple. "That went well."

I grimaced, holding on to his arms. "I'm sorry."

"We'll give him some time. Hopefully he'll think about it and come around."

Hearing the sadness in his voice, I pulled out of his embrace, but only so I could face him and bury myself against him. Our arms tightened around each other. "It's horrible to even think this…" I sighed heavily. "This is one of the crappiest days ever, but…it's also one of the best."

Tobias kissed my forehead. "I know what you mean. If I didn't have you…I would have gone down that road with Stevie, and that scares the hell out of me."

Worry pricked me at his words as I thought about what I'd only just said to Vicki that morning about my parents. It would do Tobias and me no good to become too dependent on each other. And yet, I wondered how it was possible to stop that from happening when all I wanted was to be with him. The thought of our inevitable separation in the future was already trying to niggle at me. I firmly shoved it away. "No, Tobias." I pulled out of his grasp and stared at him sternly. "You wouldn't have. I know you, and you would have found your way back to yourself with or without me."

He gave me this sympathetic smile I didn't quite understand. "No need to panic, Com. It's okay for us to need each other. We won't be like your mom and dad."

Surprise rooted me to the spot at his eerie perceptiveness. "How…"

"I know you." He shrugged. "I've read your poems. I know that their obsession with each other makes you angry. Worries you. But they're assholes." He grinned at me. "We're not assholes. At least, I think we're not."

I laughed and leaned into him. "Sorry. I didn't mean to put that on us." I cuddled him closer, loving that I could touch him anytime I wanted now. "You're very wise, Tobias King."

"Nah. I just pay attention to Comet-related stuff."

His words caused a flutter in my chest, one that only worsened delightfully as we began to stroll along the beach.

"Hey, I'm definitely trying out for the rugby team. I've decided."

"You should!"

Tobias grinned at my excitement. "Okay."

I decided to share my own news. "I let Mr. Stone read my poetry and asked him if I could start a school lit mag. He said yes."

His eyes widened. "Comet…that's amazing. I know that couldn't have been easy for you."

"I guess we're both making changes."

He smiled. "In the spirit of that… I was wondering if you're still okay to help me get my grades to where they need to be? I don't know if you know this, but you're dating kind of a slacker."

I laughed, not sure if I was laughing at the joke or laughing because he said we were dating. "Yes!"

Chuckling at my enthusiasm, he somehow managed to pull me closer. "You are adorable, do you know that?"

Adorable wasn't beautiful or sexy or mysterious...but the way Tobias said it, it might as well have been. "I'll take it."

A few minutes later the warmth, the joy between us, seeped slowly away, drowned by reality and concern. "He'll be okay, Tobias," I promised quietly, knowing instinctively where his thoughts had wandered.

"Yeah." He nodded, but there was doubt in his eyes.

17

What's with all the speculation?
It's only boy meets girl.
Get over this sad fixation,
It makes me want to hurl.
—CC

It was my first day attending school knowing I'd see my boyfriend there.

My boyfriend!

Vicki had cackled in delight when I'd used the term on the phone before school that morning. I'd called her to get her up to speed on all the kissing that had happened yesterday. Lotsa kissing!

Kissing was yummy.

With the right boy.

With my boyfriend.

My boyfriend! Ah! I never saw that coming.

It was as I walking to school to meet *my boyfriend* at the school gates that I realized something: I hadn't picked up anything to read in forty-eight hours. That was so un-Comet-like! Moreover, I only sort of missed it.

Okay, if I was being honest with myself I was a little antsy to get back to the book I was in the middle of reading, but I'd just been so busy. Tobias and I had spent the rest of Sunday together and by the time he'd gone home I had to catch up on my homework. I was just too tired to pick up a book after that. I might have missed it, but I didn't really mind.

Biting my lip in giddiness, I picked up my pace, eager to see Tobias even though I'd seen him less than twelve hours ago. He was waiting for me at the school gate, just like he'd said he would, and I swear my knees wobbled at the sight of him. Leaning his back against the gate, one knee bent with his foot flat to the wrought iron, he watched me approach with this low-lidded look and this small smile on his gorgeous lips.

Drinking him in, I noted he was wearing a very smart new herringbone coat over his uniform. He had his scarf tucked into it. Very stylish.

Very HOT.

And I wasn't the only one who noticed. A group of girls, possibly third years, shot him longing looks and burst into giggles as they passed him. Tobias was completely unaware of his effect on the younger girls, staring at me as he was.

I almost wanted to look over my shoulder to make sure there wasn't some supermodel walking behind me. Nope. Just me. At least I felt stylish enough to stand next to him, wearing my current favorite item of clothing—a knee-length fitted turquoise coat that had this amazing full, pleated skirt. I'd matched it with a bright pink scarf and fuzzy earmuffs.

I slid the earmuffs off, grinning at him as I approached. Tobias pushed off the gate to meet me. Instinctively I reached out to touch him, running my hand down his lapel. "New coat?"

He shrugged before taking hold of my hand. "Mom bought it for me a few weeks ago. Thought I'd throw it on."

"It looks good." I felt my cheeks heat up as my gaze devoured him.

Tobias laughed. "Okay, I'm glad I wore it now."

For a moment he dazzled me so much that I was unaware of anyone else. But awareness returned pretty quickly. Glancing around the school grounds, I checked nervously to see if anyone had noticed Tobias holding my hand. So many of the kids around us were younger and thus could give a rat's arse.

Then I caught sight of one of Heather's minions, staring at us with her mouth open wide enough to shoot peanuts into it. Tobias must have noticed, too, because he gripped my hand tighter. "Ready for this?"

I looked up at him and nodded. "A little nervous but ready."

He held the door open for me and we strode into the school, then came to a stop at the stairwell. "I'll see you in Spanish."

I smiled and moved to walk away but he didn't let go of my hand. Instead he tugged me to him and pressed a soft kiss to my lips. The kiss made me blush to the roots of my hair and Tobias chuckled. Rolling my eyes, I playfully shoved him away. "See you later, you egomaniac."

His laughter followed me down the corridor, filling me with confidence. We could do this. We could get through this first day no matter what it brought. And I was saying this as someone who hated attention as much as Steph needed it.

For the first time in a long while I was eager to see my friends in form class, hurrying over to the table where they were already waiting for me. Vicki smiled brightly at the sight of me just like she used to, and I gave thanks that for once the pieces of my life were fitting *somewhat* well together. It could be better, obviously, i.e. my parents and Stevie, but who needed perfect when I had a boyfriend and best friends?

It was still so weird to say that word. *Boyfriend.*

Boy. Friend.

Boyfriend.

Boyfriend!

Okay, I needed to stop.

"So I hear you have a boyfriend, Comet," Steph teased as soon as I sat down.

I snorted. "You sound like my great aunt Mildred, if I had a great aunt Mildred."

Steph eyed me in confusion. "What do you mean?"

"You're relieved. That I'm off the shelf. Spinster no more."

More confusion.

I sighed. "You thought I'd never get a boyfriend."

"Not true," she argued immediately. "I thought you were perfectly capable of getting a boyfriend. I just didn't think you *wanted* one."

"Not just one." Vicki nudged me, grinning from ear to ear. "*The* one. Tobias King."

"Well, just be careful, Comet," Steph said with all the wisdom of someone three months younger than me. "King is a little bit of a player."

Annoyed and trying not to be, I shrugged. "You don't know him."

"Uh, he's in my P.E. class."

Vicki and I shared a look, and I pinched my lips together to stop myself from bursting into laughter.

The giddiness and laughter was somewhat squished when the bell rang for second period that morning. Tobias had made it to Spanish before me so all we could do was make eye contact across the room and smile at each other. I decided I'd never get tired of his smile.

Or the butterflies it let loose in my belly.

After class Tobias threaded his fingers through mine and

he walked me to biology. That was when the giddiness was taken over by the nervousness as our classmates started to take notice of us. I squirmed, hating that feeling of being under a microscope. For most of my life I'd gotten by under the radar. The only time I'd been caught like a bug under a glass had been when Heather set out to make my life miserable. Thankfully, it hadn't lasted long, but for those few months I'd dreaded school.

I received another sweet kiss on the lips before he left me in the doorway to biology and I almost walked into the doorjamb as I dreamily turned from watching him stride off. Hoping my cheeks weren't blazing, I hurried to my pod and got out my jotters.

"Psst."

"Psst!"

I frowned and glanced over my shoulder in the direction of the noise.

Jayla Hancock, a girl in the year above me, was staring at me incredulously. "Are you and Tobias King…like…dating? For real?"

Jayla Hancock had never paid me one whit of attention until now. She was best friends with Jess Reed.

Oh dear.

I nodded stiffly, returning my gaze to my books, but not before I caught her stunned expression and the gasp of surprise from the girls at her pod.

Their scandalized whispering made me want to dive under the counter and hide.

"Really?"

I looked up at my neighbor, Wendy Shen. Wendy and I

were perfect pod buddies. We both talked very little and we took our schooling very seriously. "Excuse me?"

"You're going out with King?"

I was shocked she even knew who he was, let alone seemed delighted at the prospect of my dating him. "Yes."

Wendy grinned, her dark eyes bright. "Nice one. He's hot."

Her comment was so unexpected that I burst into laughter. Holy crap. You would have thought I'd just started dating a famous person!

The battle with myself to see the funny side of everyone gossiping about me and Tobias lost ground as I walked to the library for my free period. I'd dawdled a little in the girls' bathroom before it, so by the time I'd started making my way there the halls had emptied out again.

When I saw Stevie turn the corner at the bottom of the corridor I was walking down, my steps faltered. It was different seeing him now, for many reasons, one of which was not having Tobias at my side.

Stevie froze for a second when he saw me and then he started to stride with determination toward me. For some reason a flash of warning heat scored up the back of my neck and I gasped as suddenly Stevie put his bruised face inches from mine.

Angry green eyes burned. "Ye tell anyone whit I said aboot ma mum or dad or any o' the shit I spewed when I thought ye were ma pal, ye'll regret it. Alana and the lasses want tae gun for ye. Dinnae give them a reason."

I was so in shock by the sudden threat I just stared at him.

He pushed me back into the wall and slammed the space

above my head with the palm of his hand, making me flinch in fear. "Understood?"

I nodded quickly, my breathing becoming rapid, wondering how things had escalated so badly in the wrong direction between us. "Stevie—"

"Just keep yer mouth shut. Ye've done enough. Ever since King started being friends with ye everything got screwed. They moved oot. Mum got sick. And now ma best pal has deserted me. Aw fur *you*." He gave me a look of disgust and then pushed away from me. My body shuddered as I struggled to get my breathing back to normal.

Stevie's eyes flickered over me, the anger in them seeming to waver for a moment. He screwed up his face and scrubbed a hand over his head. "Fuck!" he bit out as he hurried away from me.

I glanced either way down the hall but there was no one there to witness what had happened. Trembling, jittery, feeling sick to my stomach, I hurried toward the library and to the safety of others. Stevie was… That hadn't been my friend back there. My friend would never have frightened me like that.

He needed help.

But if I told anyone, an adult, Stevie would end up in so much trouble and with his mother being sick, it was the last thing that family needed. I didn't know what to do.

There was no way I was telling Tobias.

Tobias would more than likely punch him for frightening me like that.

Plus there was the fact that Alana Miller would come after me if I told on Stevie. She and Stevie had something casual but long-term going on between them. She was a scrappy girl, always on the defensive about something. I knew two of her brothers were in prison, and the entire family had a reputation in town for being aggressive and dangerous. They were constantly in fights with other families. She was raised rough and tough and didn't seem to know any other way. Since the school year had begun, I knew of at least two physical fights she'd gotten into. One of them was with a boy.

So even though I stewed over Stevie and fought with myself on what to do, I didn't mention our encounter to Tobias in English class. It was easy to let it slide to the back of my mind, because by fourth period everyone was buzzing about us dating.

Tobias held my hand under the table as people shouted harmless, teasing taunts across the classroom. My neck was on fire under the heated stares in the room. Tobias rolled his eyes when someone shouted, "We hope you're treating her right fine and good, Mr. King," in a fake Southern accent.

"You okay?" he asked.

"I'm fine."

"You sure?" His eyes were bright with mirth. "Because you're stopping the flow of blood in my hand."

I immediately released my tight hold on him and gave him a sheepish, apologetic look.

"What is all the excitement about?" Mr. Stone said loudly as he walked into the class. "I could hear you from the other end of the corridor."

Tension glued me to my chair like a tongue to an overfrosted ice lolly. *Please, no one say anything, please, please.*

As if they heard my inner prayer, my classmates did me the courtesy of not embarrassing me in front of my favorite teacher. It might have seemed silly, considering how proud I really was to be holding Tobias's hand, but I wanted Mr.

Stone to always see me as the girl who was dedicated to his class. If he found out everyone was gossiping about me and Tobias, I'd seem like just another silly teenager.

I thought we were home free when the bell rang for the end of English but after I'd put all my stuff into my bag, Tobias took my hand. It turned out making sure he knew I was proud to be his girl trumped impressing my favorite teacher, because at that instant, standing in front of Mr. Stone, I made the decision to clasp Tobias's hand tight.

Sneaking a peek at Mr. Stone as we walked away, I saw him frowning at our hands.

I sighed inwardly.

Over time he'd come to realize Tobias was smart, and that there was so much more to him than a mouthy, angry teenager. I suspected Mr. Stone was getting there already, but he didn't know that Tobias was grieving. If he thought I was a fool for dating "bad boy" King then…well, truthfully, that would suck, but I'd deal with it.

We were almost out of the door when Heather McAlister suddenly blocked our way. She curled her lip in disgust at me before turning to Tobias. "Her? Really?"

I felt my boyfriend tense but before he could even say a word, Vicki shoved her way between us. "Comet isn't to blame for everything that goes wrong in your life, Heather. So…shoo." She gestured for her to leave, like she was an unwanted bug at our friendship picnic.

I smiled gratefully at the back of my best friend's head.

She was my favorite.

Clearly stumped for a comeback, Heather stormed away.

"Nice." Steph threw her arm around Vicki.

"Agreed." Tobias nodded in approval.

I smiled at her. "Thank you."

Vicki glowed under our praise. "No one messes with my Comet."

"Heather's just jealous." Steph threw Tobias a look over her shoulder. There was a look of longing in her eyes that bothered me. Steph wasn't interested in Tobias for who he was— she loved how much attention he got. She wanted a piece of it.

A streak of possessiveness coursed through me, surprising me. I tightened my hold on Tobias's hand and glared at the back of my other friend's head.

Two seconds later I was berating myself for it.

Steph loved being center of attention, but she would eventually be happy for me. It would just take her a little longer than Vicki. Once people stopped speculating and putting Tobias and me under the spotlight, Steph would think nothing of us.

However, it was too early for that, which I realized as soon as we walked into the school cafeteria. It was a place where people usually paid little attention to anything that was going on beyond their own group of friends.

Today they noticed.

It would appear that students of all ages had heard the news that King was going out with Comet Caldwell, of all people. Most had probably had no idea 'til now who I was. The staring made me feel paranoid, the noise level seeming to rise when Tobias sat with me and my girls instead of heading over to Stevie and his crew.

And that was when everything took a turn for the worse.

"Oy, too good for us now, King!" Forrester shouted, drawing everyone's attention.

"Ignore him," I said.

"I'm going to." Tobias bit into his burger, staring straight ahead.

I exchanged worried looks with Vicki and Steph.

"Tapping virgin arse doesnae make ye God, King!" Jimmy shouted and the group of them laughed.

Wanting to die I ducked my head against Tobias's shoulder, to hide, but also to murmur, "Don't," when I saw him shift in his seat. The muscle in his jaw popped but he nodded reluctantly.

But the mocking continued as one of them affected a posh feminine voice, "Ooh, Tobias, you'll need to brush the cobwebs from my vagina before you stick anything in there!"

My hand clamped down hard on Tobias's thigh as stifled laughter muffled in ripples across the room. His muscle was hard underneath my hand, and I could feel the heat of anger emanating off him. I was angry, too. Mortified. Seething! However, I refused to give anyone the satisfaction of seeing me walk out of that cafeteria.

"Oy, Comet! When yer done wi' him, give me a call and I'll show ye whit a real man can do between yer legs!"

I shot a glare over my shoulder, searching out Stevie.

Our eyes met as more degrading comments were thrown our way by his friends.

Finally, after what felt like forever, he looked away and said something to the group that made them laugh at us. I tensed, waiting for more barbs to come, but their eyes flew over my head and I turned to see assistant rector Mrs. Penman striding through the cafeteria. She stopped, staring at Stevie and his boys. "Word has reached me that verbal filth is being thrown around the cafeteria," her voice boomed around the room with authority. "This is your one and only warning. I hear of it again and it's a three-day suspension for all those involved."

Quiet descended on the room and then she turned on her heel and left. Not a minute later a disgruntled-looking soci-ology teacher entered the cafeteria and began to patrol.

Tobias finally turned to look at me. Guilt shone out of his eyes. "I'm sorry."

Horrified that he should blame himself, I slid my arm around his shoulders and crowded into him, not caring what anyone thought. "Don't. Stevie's just acting out."

"Why is Stevie acting out?" Steph asked curiously. "And what happened to his face?"

"Well..." I didn't feel it was my place to explain all of the crap going on in Stevie's life and why he now saw us as trai-tors, but she knew about the cocaine so... "I think he got in a fight. And after what we saw at Dean's party... Tobias and I are keeping our distance from him. He won't stop hang-ing out with those guys so we can't be involved with him."

"Good." Steph nodded. "I was really worried you were getting in with the wrong crowd, there, Com. No offense," she said to Tobias.

He barely acknowledged her. Instead he stared into my eyes, anger pushing through the guilt. "It doesn't give him the right to set those guys on us. On you."

"It's just the first day since the bust up. He'll get bored and leave us alone," I reassured him, hoping against hope that I was right.

18

If only there was a button she could push,
And suddenly she'd be covered in armor.
Her skin protected from your ambush,
Your bullet-shaped words couldn't harm her.
—*CC*

It was a particularly cold late November morning. The trees were nearly bare and glittered with frost. The sea was a dull gray, choppy and uninviting today, making me shiver as I passed by then strode away from the quiet beach through town. I'd sacrificed my head in the name of fashion, wearing a purple woolen headband that just covered the tips of my ears. A woolen flower shot through with silver was attached to the right side of the headband near my temple. I wore matching purple gloves, my turquoise coat and purple ankle boots. I was thinking about Stevie, warring between guilt for taking Tobias from him and fear that he and his friends would continue to make our lives miserable. The boy I knew wouldn't do that to us, but I hadn't recognized him in the one who'd confronted me in the hall the day before. Still I held on to my hope.

It turned out hoping Stevie and his crew would grow bored was wishful thinking.

"Oy! Slut!" I heard someone behind me yell.

Of course, I was the farthest thing from a slut so I ignored it, assuming some girl was calling after her friend in that insulting fashion that had become so popular lately. Like for instance the time Steph greeted Vicki and me in the cafeteria with, "Hey, bitches," and I got up and left the table in protest.

"Dinnae ignore us, slut!"

Well, that didn't sound friendly at all.

I glanced over my shoulder and almost tripped at the sight of Alana Miller and three of her friends hurrying along the pavement behind me.

"Aye, you!" She pointed at me, her pretty face scrunched up in aggression. "Think yer something 'cause King's goin' oot wi' ye? Yer just the sad wee geek ye were yesterday."

Whipping back around, I picked up pace.

"Dinnae ignore us, bitch!" one of the other girls shouted.

And yet, despite trembling from head to foot at their intentions, I was going to ignore them, hoping they wouldn't make it impossible. In other words, hoping to God they weren't going to make this physical. I wouldn't put the possibility past Alana.

Adrenaline pumping, I marched toward the school.

Why had Stevie set her on me? I hadn't said a word!

"Aw look at her, running off tae her wee boyfriend. Dae ye no' embarrass him wearin' those dodgy charity shop clothes?"

Other students glanced at us in speculation, stepping out of my way when I passed, clearly not wanting anything to do with Alana Miller. I didn't blame them. She was scary as hell! Fear clogged my throat at the thought of Alana getting her hands on me. I turned the corner and relief flooded me at the sight of Tobias at the gates.

"Enjoy him while ye can." Alana's harsh laughter made

me shiver. "He's gonna get bored wi' a wee geeky bitch like ye in nae time!"

She sounded closer so I moved faster.

Tobias suddenly pushed off the gates and although I couldn't see his expression clearly from here, I could tell by the way he started striding quickly, his movements jerky with tension, that he knew Alana was having a go at me.

Suddenly he was jogging toward me, his gaze narrowed over my shoulder in anger. "Problem here?" he called out as he came to a stop beside me.

I sagged against him in relief and his arm instantly came around me. Don't get me wrong; I'm not proud of being relieved to be rescued by a boy. However, I'd lived most of my life with my head buried in the pages of a book. Alana Miller had kicked and bit and eye-gouged her way through life since she was at nursery. This girl would annihilate me if she got her hands on me. Whether it was Tobias coming to my rescue, or Vicki and Steph, I would have been relieved for the backup.

"Piss off, King," Alana sneered as she and her girls passed us. She shot me one last threatening look and I shivered, acid flooding my stomach.

"What happened?" Tobias asked, concern etched all over his face.

I placed a trembling hand to my forehead, wondering how on earth I'd become a target for the worst bully in school within twenty-four hours. For doing nothing! For dating a boy! And refusing to be around someone who was using coke. That didn't sound unreasonable to me.

"They just appeared," I told him breathlessly. "Started calling me a slut, making fun of me for dating you. Stupid stuff…

but…" I met his anger-filled gaze "…it's Alana Miller, Tobias. I've known her my whole life. She's itching for a fight and she…she's vicious."

"I won't let her hurt you." He put his arm around my shoulder and drew me tight to his side. I relaxed marginally at the feel of his warm lips on my temple below my headband. "The guys gave me shit yesterday. I was walking home from rugby tryouts and bumped into them. They taunted me all the way home."

I clung to his waist, hoping my nearness would comfort him. "I'm sorry."

"Yeah, me, too. I really didn't think Stevie would be this kind of a problem."

However, it turned out our former friend was going to be a massive problem. By the time we sat down in the cafeteria for lunch, we understood Stevie and his friends had no intention of letting us get on quietly with our lives without them.

"Oy, oy!" Jimmy shouted across the room, drawing our gazes as we sat down at a table with Steph and Vicki. "The lovebirds are back!"

Some of the people around us snickered while Steph muttered under her breath, "Not again."

Tobias and I shared a stoic look. We'd already decided not to engage with any of them, in the hopes that they would grow bored more quickly if we gave them no reaction. It sounded like we had a plan, that we were strong and ready to face Stevie's order to his crew to bully us. The truth was, however, at least for me, that it was only day two and I already felt unsettled and ill at school. Dread filled me every time I had to leave the safety of a classroom and venture down the hallways. I anticipated bumping into one of them and having to endure their nastiness, and the embarrassment of knowing my peers might think some of the things Stevie's crew were saying were true.

I pushed the food on my plate around, nauseated at the thought of putting any of it near my stomach.

"I bet when ye bang her, King, she's still got a book in her hand!"

That was from Stevie, and not only did it make me want to curl up in a corner somewhere to hide my mortification, it really hurt, because it meant Stevie was using what he knew about me against me. He'd been in my bedroom, my private space, seen my private things and heard my personal thoughts on all different subjects. And while I'd been threatened to keep my mouth shut about what I knew, he apparently had no compunction about doing to me what he didn't want done to him.

"She wouldnae have a book in her hand if I banged her," Forrester boasted.

Tobias's knuckles turned white as he gripped his fork.

"Remember, ignore them," Vicki advised, the only one of us who looked unaffected and in control.

The obscenities kept flying our way, a constant stream, and Jimmy and Forrester illustrated some of what they were shouting with lewd playacting at their table. Some people looked annoyed and uncomfortable for us, most probably because Tobias was well liked. But a lot of people snickered and laughed at what Stevie and his crew were shouting and doing.

"Let's no' forget his other wee pals er there," Jimmy yelled, smirking villainously. "They two are tasty. Gettin' a shot at them two tae, eh, King? Got yerself a kinky wee foursome, eh?"

"Oh God." Steph looked like she was going to be sick.

"Have they got nothing better to do than shout about sex?" Vicki scowled at them. "Probably because they're not getting any."

"Oy, blondie, how are ye on yer knees?"

"That's it." Steph stood up, her cheeks blazing. "I'm gone."

"Steph!" Vicki shouted after her but Steph was already hurrying out of the cafeteria, making Stevie and his lads crow with laughter. "She just gave them what they wanted."

"We can't blame her." I sighed. "If they don't stop soon I'm going to vomit all over this table."

Tobias reached for my hand. "They'll get bored," he repeated, but he himself looked like he was hanging on by a thread.

And then our savior stormed into the cafeteria in the form of Mrs. Penman. At her side was an older dinner lady I hadn't seen leave the room. She pointed at Stevie's table, and Mrs. Penman nodded at her before marching toward them. We watched as she said something to them. They clearly gave her lip back because she stiffened and said something else. And then suddenly she roared, "Move!"

The entire cafeteria hushed as Stevie and the boys scowled at her but did as she asked, swaggering ahead of her out of the cafeteria. They flashed wicked grins at us, Jimmy winking at me, and I jerked my gaze away.

In that moment I hated them.

Even Stevie.

Once they were gone, Tobias slid his arm around my shoulder and pulled me against him. "You did good."

"You both did," Vicki agreed.

I smiled at her. "You did better than any of us."

"Well, I was barely their target. It's easier for me to tell you to just ignore them." Her expression was sympathetic, concerned. "I'm sorry they're doing this to you. And—" she glanced down at her phone and winced "—just an FYI…if I were you I'd continue to avoid all social media. They just sent out a filthy post about you on Messenger to a whole bunch of us."

Tobias and I shared a weary look. "This is one of those moments when being an anti-social-media introvert actually works in my favor."

He grinned but it didn't quite reach his eyes. "Guess so."

It was English last period but as soon as the bell rang Tobias had to hurry to the rugby park to see if he'd made the local boys' rugby team. The lit mag wasn't up and running yet so I had no extracurricular activities to stay at school for. Vicki had encouraged me to tag along with her to the school show rehearsals and Tobias had seemed relieved that I wouldn't be walking out of school alone, so I'd agreed.

I should have kept to the agreement but frustration and anger clouded my judgment. I attempted to tell myself that the fear Stevie's friends were making me feel was nowhere near as bad as the cowardice I'd feel if I allowed them to make me change my routine.

"Comet…" Vicki shook her head in concern as we stood outside English. I'd just told her I was going home instead of accompanying her to the school auditorium. "No."

"I can't wait around for you to make a decision, sorry." Steph backed away, looking anything but apologetic.

I felt like shouting *surprise, surprise* after her. "I'll be fine," I promised Vicki instead. "I'll text you when I get home."

There was little she could do to change my mind, but as

I stepped out the front entrance of the school and saw them waiting at the gate I almost turned back around. I'd considered sneaking out the back entrance through the teacher's car park, but it would mean a detour down a street Forrester lived on. His parents weren't around a lot so I knew from Stevie that Forrester's was the most common hangout for them. There was a possibility of running into them all no matter which entrance I left through. Trepidation moved through me in waves of nausea and quivering tremors. Knees shaky, I tried to look as casual as possible as I walked down the stairs and made my way toward the gates.

Jimmy saw me first and hit Stevie on the shoulder. They all turned. All of them were together, including Alana and one of her friends.

"Aw aye, here she comes," Jimmy called out as I approached. I stared straight ahead, not giving them the satisfaction of meeting their eyes so they could see my fear. My body was in revolt against my stubbornness, desperate to take off into a sprint away from them. "Dinnae worry, Com Com, we never got suspended. Just a gentle warnin'." They all cackled like hyenas.

I strode through the gates, praying they wouldn't follow.

My prayers fell on deaf ears.

"Such a stuck-up bitch," Alana said as I heard their footsteps fall into rhythm behind me. "What the hell does he see in her?"

Jimmy's answer was so unbelievably crude I wanted to disappear. My shoulders hunched around my ears as if I could block out their comments.

Then Stevie's voice joined the herd, "Nah, she's no' givin'

it up. Thinks hers is made o' solid 24-carat gold. She'll just tease him til his gonads drop aff."

His words hurt most of all. The frightened tears I'd been holding back spilled down my cheeks, and I hurried my steps so they wouldn't catch up and see. Everything and everyone became a blur as they cackled at my back through town, shouting obscenities.

Their insults crashed over me, battering me with humiliation. People passed, throwing me concerned looks, but it was only as the sea came into view ahead of me that a familiar voice jerked me back into my immediate surroundings. "Oy, leave her alone!"

I looked up to see Mrs. Cruickshank storming across the street toward me with her shopping bag in hand, yelling at my bullies.

"Get lost!" Alana yelled back.

"You filthy little buggers, leave her alone or I'll call the police." Mrs. Cruickshank waved her mobile phone at them.

"Aw screw this," Stevie huffed.

And I glanced over my shoulder to see him giving them all a jerk of his head. They muttered insults at my neighbor but turned on their heels and began to stroll casually away. Not once did Stevie look back at me.

My face crumpled as sobs just exploded out of me.

"Oh dear, Comet, come here." Mrs. Cruickshank reached my side and put her free arm around my shoulders.

I swiped at my tears, embarrassed that I'd had to be rescued by my elderly neighbor. "Thank you," I managed to say.

She nodded, face etched with concern. "What was that all about?"

I sucked back more tears.

"Okay." She led me onto the esplanade. "Well, you should

tell someone. And by someone I mean *someones*. And by *someones* I mean your parents."

The thought of my parents made me cry harder, because they were the last people I could turn to with this. Instead I took Mrs. Cruickshank's shopping bag from her. "I can't tell them."

"Then in exchange for you carrying my shopping, I'll make you a cup of tea."

Still shaking with adrenaline, I found the idea of taking comfort in my neighbor—a grown-up I trusted more than most—appealing, and I walked with her down the esplanade toward home. The shopping bag jerked in my hand as we were hit by a rush of cold wind.

"Ooh, a cup of tea sounds grand right now." Mrs. Cruickshank raised her voice to be heard over the wind.

Anything sounded grand to me as long as it meant being away from Stevie and his crew.

My neighbor hurried to let us into her house, and we passed through the familiar narrow hallway with its Persian-style carpet and walls cluttered with photos and artwork. Mrs. Cruickshank's house smelled like beeswax, lavender oil and turpentine. When I was younger and lacking in diplomacy, I'd asked why it smelled the way it did and what it was. She told me it was her homemade furniture polish.

The smell waned in the kitchen, a lovely light room that overlooked a small courtyard, much like ours. Except whereas our courtyard was overgrown and dirty from lack of use, Mrs. Cruickshank's courtyard was bordered with flowers in the summer and had a little table and chairs where I knew she enjoyed drinking her peppermint tea and reading the newspaper.

The courtyard looked a little bare and lonesome in the

winter, but the kitchen—a far more modern kitchen than our own—was warm and inviting because of the wood-burning stove at one end near a small couch and coffee table. I put Mrs. Cruickshank's shopping on her kitchen countertop, offered to help and was promptly told to sit down on the couch. I watched, feeling my shakes fade as my neighbor bustled around putting away her shopping. When she was done, she moved on to lighting the fire, and the kitchen became all the cozier for it.

Finally, she settled down beside me on the couch and handed me a mug of peppermint tea, then shoved a plate of biscuits at me.

I took a biscuit while she sat patiently, staring at me.

Finally, I said, "One of them used to be a friend. He's my boyfriend's cousin."

Mrs. Cruickshank gave me a slow, small smile. "Boyfriend?"

"Tobias."

"Is that that the handsome tall Yank you've been walking with?"

I chuckled at her old-fashioned words. "Yes."

She nodded, seeming pleased for me. And then she sobered. "So why is this other boy now following you home with his friends, shouting rude comments at you?"

Sadness overwhelmed me. "He's a good person, really. He's just..." And I found myself telling her the gist of the story, without mentioning anything to do with Stevie's involvement with drugs.

"So he's angry that Tobias has moved out just when he needs him, angry that his mum is sick and also angry that Tobias wasn't there to help him out of a fight? And he has decided to blame you for this because it's easier than feeling powerless?"

I nodded at her grown-up perspective, thinking that was probably true. I'd become Stevie's emotional punching bag. "Yes. But I suppose some of it is my fault. Tobias didn't want to hang around with the people Stevie was hanging around. They're not a good crowd. And when he thought I might get dragged into it, he made the choice to be with me and cut out Stevie. But we asked Stevie to come with us. To stop hanging out with those bad people, too."

"Bad people?"

I shook my head, unwilling to divulge more.

Mrs. Cruickshank sighed. "Well, all I can say is that I think you did the right thing. You and Tobias. As much as Stevie might be hurting over losing his cousin's friendship, he had other choices in front of him. Bullying you is not going to solve his problems."

"So what do I do?"

My neighbor settled her empty mug on her coffee table and turned to face me fully. "I know most adults would tell you to report it, and I do think you should. But I also know that reporting it doesn't always make it stop. My advice is to do what you think is right for everyone, Comet. Trust yourself. And keep in mind that this moment in time is just a blip on the radar of your life. Don't twist yourself up in knots over it, when in a few years' time it will be a distant memory." She clasped my hand in hers. "Don't waste your emotions on this, my dear. Give them all to the things that make you happy, here and now."

Like Tobias. And my poetry. And books.

I heard her words, and I knew there was wisdom in them,

but I didn't know how easy it was going to be to follow that advice when I still felt shaky inside after what had just occurred.

Not long later I left Mrs. Cruickshank and as I walked down my garden path, staring up at the large picture window to my mother's studio, I found myself growing resentful that I was unable to turn to my parents for the kind of advice and comfort our neighbor had given me. With those feelings churning along with my residual fear I walked into the house and slammed the door behind me without really meaning to.

Well, maybe subconsciously I meant to.

It took me a moment to realize Carrie was coming out of the kitchen with a half-eaten chocolate bar and a bottle of water in her hand. I'd hardly seen her for the past week, because she was working on another private commission. She wore charcoal smudges on her temple, chin and the white artist's smock that she had in every color. My mother. A cliché.

An explosive anger toward her suddenly fought to be free and I shuddered to hold it in.

Carrie cocked her head to the side, studying me. "Are you okay?"

I'd thought, when I was hurrying down the street with taunts and sexually aggressive insults slamming into my back, that I'd never felt more alone. Yet, staring at this woman, this stranger I'd lived with my whole life, the loneliness, the fear, quadrupled. And it rushed out of me toward her. "When have you ever actually given a fuck?" I shrieked.

Her face slackened in shock and I sped down the hall, tripping over a pair of boots in my hurry and colliding with my door. I growled in outrage and pushed it open, then threw it shut with so much rage that the doorframe shuddered as it crashed shut.

"Oy!" Carrie banged on it.

I immediately slid the lock into place.

"You don't talk to me like that, Comet!"

I rolled my eyes, wiping my tears and snot from my nose. "Go away!"

"Ugh!" Carrie screeched, sounding like a petulant child.

"What on earth is going on?" I heard Dad's voice. It sounded like he was at the bottom of the staircase.

"We're living with a bloody teenager, that's what's going on!" Carrie's footsteps stomped away, and I heard them clobbering up the stairs.

A minute later I heard a gentle tap on my door. "Comet?"

The concern in his voice caused fresh tears to spill down my cheeks, because I needed him to worry, I needed him to care, but I also knew it was only ever temporary. I'd rather have nothing from him than have him give it only to take it away again. White-hot pain lashed across my chest and I hugged myself tight, trying to stop my insides from splitting apart.

"Comet?"

I stifled my sobs, silently pleading with him to go away.

"Comet...I just want to know that you're okay."

Realizing he wouldn't leave until I spoke I struggled to pull myself together.

"Comet?"

"I'm fine," I croaked.

"You don't sound fine."

I fought for more composure and succeeded. Marginally. "I'm fine, Kyle," I said, and this time my voice sounded stronger.

He was silent a moment and then I heard him sigh. "All right. I'm…well… I'll be upstairs if you need me."

I do need you, I wanted to scream as I heard his footsteps fade away from my door. *I always need you! But you're never there! They're just words! They're not real! You don't mean them!*

In the history of worst timing ever, Tobias called me not too long after that. I'd cried some more, my face swollen and puffy, my nose bunged up with snot, and my voice hoarse from the constriction of trying to keep my sobs locked inside my throat.

If I didn't answer, it would worry him after everything that had happened in the cafeteria.

"Hey, how'd it go?" I attempted to sound normal as I answered.

"The coach thinks I've got a lot of potential." His deep, familiar voice soothed me. "He's letting me train with them. Whether I get to play remains to be seen until we know what I can do on the field. But there are a lot of guys from our school on the team. They seem cool." He sounded happy. I was glad for him. I was. There was nothing I wanted more than for Tobias to be happy. But his hopefulness made me feel more isolated. More vulnerable. More like the victim Stevie wanted me to be. And I knew right there and then that Mrs. Cruickshank's advice was going to be too difficult to follow.

Because how could Stevie be so cruel? He wasn't cruel. I knew him. He wasn't cruel!

"Comet?"

"That's wonderful. I'm so happy for you."

Silence met my response. And then, voice tight, Tobias demanded, "What happened?"

I winced, wishing he didn't know me so well. "Nothing happened."

"Something happened. Are you with Vicki and Steph? I don't hear any noise in the background."

Feeling guilty, I admitted, "I went home instead."

"Comet." He sighed. "Who was it? Who gave you crap?"

"It was nothing, okay. Just let it go."

"What did they do? Who?"

"It was all of them. Stevie, Alana, their friends. They just..." I squeezed my eyes closed, fear and indignation coalescing inside of me. "They just were doing what they did at lunch."

"Except you were on your own." He bit out a curse.

"It's fine."

"It's not fine," he snapped. "I'm going to kill Stevie."

The idea of him and Stevie getting physical made the fear overthrow my indignation. "No. Leave it. I mean it, Tobias. They *will* get bored. We just need to wait it out."

And I needed to remember that this moment in our lives wouldn't last forever.

Easier said than done.

19

How easy it would be to just disappear again,
But not without you.
For you I'll stay here and endure all of them,
Just. Please. Stay. True.
—CC

The person I should have been most wary of was Stevie, I guess, because it was clear none of this would be happening to us without his say-so. But as much as I tried to hold on to my hate for him, I still remembered the tears in his eyes when he talked about how sick his mum was, and the fierce way he'd held on to me when he'd hugged me in comfort.

Stevie was in a lot of pain, and I still felt sorry for him. That didn't mean I wasn't furious at him. Because he'd set Alana and Jimmy on us, and those two were the ones I was most afraid of. They had aggressive impulse control problems and one of these days they were going to slip Stevie's leash. I was sure of it.

The verbal abuse continued for the next few weeks, and both Tobias and I had to change our phone numbers because Stevie clearly had shared them with his delinquent friends. I'd gotten one-word texts calling me every insult under the sun, and they'd tried to taunt Tobias into a fight by saying ugly things about me, his mum and even his dad.

It was awful.

Vicki wanted us to report it, but Tobias and I had both agreed to just give it a little more time. Despite everything, we didn't want to get Stevie in trouble, holding on to hope that our friend was still buried under all that callousness. Plus, neither of us had much faith in the adults in our lives, and I knew that made us reluctant to speak up, too.

Tobias and Vicki refused to let me out of their sight. If I wasn't with one of them I was with the other. I dreaded school.

I dreaded it in a way I couldn't believe I dreaded it. It was even worse than the days of primary six and my teacher from hell, even worse than Heather's petty stunts. What I hated most was not knowing what was going to happen when I got to school. Would it be words meant to shame and humiliate me? Or would it finally progress and become physical? I had to hope Stevie would never allow that to happen, but I had to wonder if he was just too far gone to care anymore.

The sick feeling in the pit of my stomach never left me as I waited apprehensively for their next move.

Our bullies were taking a toll on my and Tobias's burgeoning relationship. Some might say he was just handling me with care, but it felt like he'd put this wall up between us when it came to being romantic with each other. His kisses were never more than quick pecks on the lips, and when he held me he could have been a brother hugging his sister. I was starting to seriously worry that he'd decided he didn't *want* me anymore. It would be understandably difficult for him to broach the subject, considering what we'd put ourselves through to be together.

I wanted to talk with him about it.

But I was scared of what he might say.

The words were on the tip of my tongue as Tobias lay sprawled on my bed with our Spanish homework scattered in front of us. In true Scottish winter fashion, it was stormy outside with the wind lashing rain against my window. I was lying next to Tobias, with my elbow bent and my head supported in the palm of my hand. I chewed on a pen, studying his handsome face as he frowned at the essay he was working on.

His phone buzzed between us, jolting me out of my anxious musings. He flicked it open and the corners of his mouth turned up a little. "Who is it?" I blurted out, envious of anyone who could make him smile.

"Luke Macintyre."

I nodded. Luke was in the year above us and he was on the rugby team. "What does he want?"

Tobias shrugged, putting his phone back down. "He was just inviting me to go hang out with him and some of the team."

Never wanting to be the kind of girl who would stop him from seeing his friends, I insisted he should go. He shook his head.

"Tobias, I'm fine."

His gaze met mine, his filled with way more worry than a teenage boy's should be. "You say that but I know it's not true."

Frustrated by his belief that I couldn't handle myself I sat up. "Look, are things great right now? No. They are not. But—and I really appreciate it, I do—I don't need twenty-four-hour surveillance and protection. I'm in my room, safe and sound."

He grinned at my exasperation. "Have you ever considered that I might just prefer hanging out with you?"

I rolled my eyes at his teasing and shoved him playfully, but Tobias grabbed my hand before I could pull back, and he tugged on it. When I fell against him with a startled laugh, surprise and heat flashed through me when his lips came down on mine and he kissed me.

Really kissed me this time.

When I touched my tongue against his, his groan vibrated deliciously into my mouth and I whimpered a little, needing him closer. Our papers crinkled beneath us as Tobias rolled into me, his strong body pressing mine to my mattress. My hands curled in his hair as I willed his hands to move from my waist. Anywhere. Everywhere. I just wanted him to touch me. Trying to encourage some wickedness, I shifted my leg over his hip so he shifted deeper against me.

Even though I felt him react, the next second he was off me, sitting up on the bed, trying to catch his breath.

I lay there, my arms suspended in the air where his head had been, wondering what on earth had happened.

He'd stopped.

"Why?" I huffed, sitting up and smoothing my sweater down.

"What?" He wouldn't look at me.

It was bad enough not knowing what I was walking into at school every day, but not knowing whether my boyfriend really wanted to be with me was the last straw. "Do you not fancy me?"

Tobias whipped around to look at me, incredulity written all over his face. "What? Comet, why would you say that?"

I blushed, mortified by my insecurities. "Well… I just…"

He grabbed my hand, pressing it against his chest where I could feel his heart's speedy thud. "Of course I do. Believe me—" his eyes smoldered as they wandered lazily over my face and body "—I do. You're beautiful."

I blushed again, this time from the compliment. He'd never called me beautiful before.

He groaned, touching my hot cheek. "And even more so when you do that. Why would you think otherwise?"

Still confused I explained, "You never seem to want to kiss me, never mind do anything else."

"I kiss you all the time," he argued.

"Without tongue," I boldly and indignantly snapped.

The idiot looked ready to burst into laughter. *"Okay…"*

"I'm being serious, Tobias. You peck me on the lips now and then but you never seem to want to do more. I'm not made of glass. I'm not…" I bit my lip and looked away, hearing the taunts again. "I'm not *frigid* like they say I am."

Tobias shifted closer to me, eyebrows drawn together. "I know. What they're saying…it is getting to me, just not like you think. I try to ignore them even though I want to teach them a lesson they won't forget. But I want everything to be good for us here, and I want that more than I want to pummel Jimmy's face in. I hate the way they talk about us, about you. I worry about how it makes you feel…and I didn't want to make the wrong move or seem like I was pushing for all the stuff that those guys are talking about. I want you to be ready, and I don't want anyone's crap messing up how we feel when we're together like that."

His explanation was the loveliest, most thoughtful explanation I could have hoped for. And it also made me realize I'd been kind of a self-absorbed brat. I wasn't the only one affected by the bullying. I sometimes forgot to look past the big, tall, strong guy who had seemed invulnerable that first day I ever saw him. I knew better. And I was guilty of being a bad girlfriend.

"I'm sorry they made you feel like that." I inched closer to him, leaning my chin on his shoulder. He was staring at a spot on my wall, the muscle in his jaw popping. That alone should have told me how bothered he was by the guys and their stupid comments. The sweep of his jawline was sharp, masculine and angular and just one of a few reasons Tobias looked older than sixteen. His handsomeness never ceased to affect me, and every day that he showed me how gorgeous he was on the inside, he grew more beautiful to me on the outside, too. Something I'd been longing to ask him prodded at me until I couldn't contain it any longer. "Can I ask you something?"

He turned to look at me, our noses inches apart. "You can ask me anything."

"Have you... I mean...rumor has it you and Heather... well...slept together." The words tasted bitter leaving my mouth.

Shaking his head before pressing a sweet kiss to the tip of my nose, he said, "Never."

Relief flooded me. I think I could bear the thought of him having had sex with anyone but Heather. Although her bullying seemed like small change compared to Stevie's crew, I'd still never forgive her for picking on me all those years ago, no matter her reasons.

"Have you...had sex, though? With the girl you used to date back in Raleigh?"

"Ashley?" He frowned. "Nah. She comes from a very Christian family. She doesn't believe in sex before marriage."

More relief began creeping over, hope even, "So does that mean you're a virgin, too?"

Tobias's expression turned apologetic and I felt myself stiffen without meaning to. "No."

"Then who?" My stomach churned at the thought of him with another girl, but I wanted to know.

He pulled away, rubbing the back of his neck, something he only ever did when he was uncomfortable. "Why is it important?"

Now I really needed to know. "I thought you and I could talk about anything?"

"Well, you sound annoyed and I don't want to end up arguing over something that doesn't affect how I feel about you."

Suspicion began to creep over me. "If it meant nothing, then just tell me who she is."

Exhaling heavily, he shot me a baleful look. "I barely remember it, Comet."

"Tobias."

"Fine. It was a couple of weeks after I just got here. I was still pretty messed up about everything and Stevie took me to a party over the summer. At Jess Reed's house."

I think my heart stopped.

"I was so wasted," he hurried to explain at the sight of my unmasked hurt. "Comet. Come on. So was Jess. I can hardly remember it. My first time. It was just a drunken fumble in her bedroom."

It was more than a fumble. He lost his virginity to Jess Reed. My first selfish thought was, why couldn't it have been anyone else? Jess was gorgeous, and I already felt hugely insecure about how I fared in comparison.

Yet, as I looked into my boyfriend's eyes I started to think how I would feel if I could barely remember the first time I had sex. It was a sad state of affairs. All of it. Losing his dad, his anger with his dad, his refusal to admit he was still angry with his mum. And because of it all he'd lost something he'd never get back. "That doesn't sound very special."

"I didn't need it to be," he said bluntly. "I just wanted to get lost for a while."

I nodded, understanding, but also wondering how many times he'd gotten lost. And with Jess?

"It was one time." He seemed to read my thoughts. Shifting closer to me again, he took my arms in his and tugged me to him. His arms banded tight around me as I hugged mine around his shoulders. Lips inches from lips, his gaze filled with so much tenderness I finally felt like I could breathe for the first time since *her* name came up, Tobias whispered, "When you're ready it'll be like my real first time, too. Because I know that when it's you and me, I'm going to remember every second for the rest of my life."

Love for this boy filled me so completely in that moment I couldn't hold it in anymore. "Who says I'm not ready? I love you," I whispered, brushing my mouth softly against his. "I love you, Tobias."

His answer was to kiss me with such ferocity I'm surprised our bodies didn't combust. Passion blazed between us, the kind I'd only ever read about in books, and as he pushed me to my back and began to touch me the way I dreamed of, I heard him murmur over and over, "I love you, too. I love you, too."

My virginity wasn't lost that night, although we came pretty close, but our worries were lost. Our cares and anxieties floated off to hover in some empty space outside the bubble we created in my bedroom as we learned to love each other in new ways.

It was the first time in weeks I was free of everything but love, and finally I could say I took my neighbor's advice and channeled all my emotions into something good.

20

Push, push, push until you push too far.
All that pushing pushed you out,
And you don't know who you are.
—CC

Admitting I loved him and having Tobias reciprocate eased most of my insecurities about our relationship. Although walking through the halls at school wasn't easy, I felt less alone than I had in the previous weeks. I also realized our relationship was heading somewhere serious. Physically. And that I not only wanted that but I wanted to be smart about it.

So I'd confided in Vicki that I wanted to go on the pill.

"You want to go on the *pill*?" She'd started to freak out when I told her in the girls' restroom at school.

"Shh," I'd said, even though we were alone. "Yes. Just in case. Will you come with me to the pharmacy? A nurse or consultant, or whatever, takes you into a room and asks you all these questions before they'll give you it. I don't want to do that alone." I'd blushed just thinking about it.

Vicki had stared at me in shock but nodded. "Okay."

And so she'd been my support when I went to the pharmacy to get my birth control. And it was every bit as mortifying as I'd imagined. But in a weird way it was a distraction from school.

I was tired of dreading school, exhausted because these last few weeks I'd become almost paranoid in my awareness of what was going on around me there. That hyperawareness was draining. Or it could have been that I'd become more confident in myself. Or I'd just reached the end of my tether. Whatever it was, it burst out of me one morning as I walked to school.

Alana and her crew had followed me to school a few times, so for the most part I tried to leave for school earlier than they would. That morning, however, I was running late. As such it wasn't long before I heard behind me, "Oy, geek! Did ye dress in the dark this mornin'?"

My first instinct was to hunch into myself and hurry but as the insults rained down on me, growing closer and closer, I found my feet slowing down while my heart rate took off.

"One of these days I'm goin' tae knock that smug, ugly look off yer face!" Alana shouted.

And suddenly I was spinning around in reaction.

Alana and her girls skidded to a halt, while I fought to control my breathing, wanting to come across bored and indifferent even though every nerve inside me was trembling. A bead of sweat rolled down my back as I stared blandly at her.

"That threat is getting boring," I said, relieved that my voice sounded smooth, unemotional.

"Whit?" Alana looked stunned.

"Boring," I repeated. "Everything about this—" my hand gestured to them all "—is boring. I'm not scared of you. I'm bored by you."

Her face flooded with color while her eyes narrowed in confusion.

"You think that trying to terrorize people makes you powerful and important?" I sneered at her, my anger desperate to fight through as I struggled to remain calm. "It doesn't. We all think you're pathetic, because we know that while high school is just a blip in time and that we'll move on and have bloody wonderful lives doing things that actually matter... you'll be stuck here. A coward and a bully who everyone looks down on. I'm not scared of you, Alana. I'm not impressed by you. I don't even think about you. Other than to pity you."

When no response was forthcoming, I turned calmly around and continued on to school. I knew once she got over her surprise there would be a retaliation, but I didn't care. I cared that I'd stood up to her...and in that moment I was willing to deal with the consequences of that because the self-respect I felt was worth it.

However, it wasn't Alana's retaliation that knocked me on my ass that day.

The bell for fourth period rang and I was walking to history, my mind on my surroundings. The sight of Jimmy coming toward me through the crowds made me want to stop and turn around, but I figured he'd just follow me. At least here there were witnesses.

I braced myself as he cut through the strolling pupils and stopped in front of me, arms out, blocking my way. I stared at him, willing someone to dump a bucket of water on him so I could watch him melt.

He smirked down at me. "Heads up—Alana's pissed about whatever ye said tae her this mornin'. Watch yer back. Ye know—" he stepped closer, the smell of cheap aftershave and psychopath making my nose wrinkle "—ye've gotten pretty tasty for a geek. I'll take ma turn soon enough. And I'll enjoy doing it," he whispered in my ear.

An awful apprehension kept me standing in the middle of the school corridor as he walked away, questioning if I'd understood what he was insinuating. How could he threaten me like that? Like it was okay. Like it was his *right*.

And no one seemed to see or care.

I stared around, checking faces through blurred vision, but everyone was just chattering among themselves, not seeing me there, which didn't seem possible because somehow I was standing in the middle of the school corridor fearful and vulnerable.

And that made me so angry I couldn't breathe.

A single tear dripped down my cheek and I brushed it aside impatiently as my rage seeped through the threat. Whether he really meant he'd assault me or whether it was said just to terrorize me, like Alana this morning, I wouldn't let him have the satisfaction of my fear.

I covered my chest with my books, holding them tight to me like a barrier, as I finally came unstuck. By the time I got to class, I was a mass of confusion and emotions. Jimmy's insidious threat echoed over and over in my head and I think I finally realized that Stevie wasn't coming back to Tobias and me.

"You look chalk white. What happened?" Vicki said in a hushed voice as I took my seat next to her in history.

Just seeing her, my ally, my friend, the tears threatened and I had to choke them back.

"Comet?" She gripped my hand, leaning in to me. "What happened?"

The whispered retelling just bubbled out of me and by the

time I was done Vicki looked ready to kill someone. "Even if he was just messing with you, he can't get away with saying that to you. Or cornering you when you're on your own. You have to tell Tobias," she insisted.

"Ladies, I'm sorry to interrupt what I'm sure is a fascinating discussion but if you could pay attention that would be wonderful." Our history teacher rolled her eyes at us.

I shot Vicki a quelling look.

But only class kept her quiet. As soon as the bell rang she said, "Maybe you should tell a teacher. Mrs. Penman or Mr. Jenkins?"

"If I tell someone, I have to tell them why Jimmy and Alana are coming after me. It'll lead back to Stevie and everything will come out. He could go to juvie, Vick."

"Why are you still protecting him?" She was no longer hiding how beyond frustrated she was with me. "If Tobias knew what just happened he would *not* protect Stevie, I can assure you."

"Don't you dare tell Tobias."

Her eyes widened. "Comet, this was serious before but now it's in serious, *serious* territory." She hissed under her breath, "Jimmy just insinuated he was going to assault you. Even if he's just trying to scare you, it's messed up!"

"Shh!" I glanced around to make sure no one was listening. "Look, what do you want me to do? It's either we put up with them until they get bored or we tell someone and Stevie gets into trouble."

"You don't have to tell them anything about the drugs."

"He'd still get into trouble."

"At school. Big deal."

"The big deal is that his life is hell, Vick. He feels betrayed."

"That doesn't mean you deserve *this*. Stop being a martyr and do something."

There was a part of me that was angry at her but only because she was speaking to the girl inside of me who wanted to fight. Yes, Stevie's life was crap right now, but how did his get any better by making my life worse? There was trying to be a friend, and then there was being a doormat. I didn't want to be the latter. Finally, I sighed. "You're right. I'll talk to Stevie."

"Not without Tobias."

I scowled at her. "Telling Tobias sort of defeats the purpose of standing up for myself."

She glowered right back at me, and we walked to the cafeteria in strained silence.

Lunch was painful. Vicki kept throwing me pointed glares that silently told me to tell Tobias what Jimmy had said, and Tobias kept staring at us in suspicion. He grew steadily more frustrated when I denied that anything was the matter. My plan had been to get through the rest of the day and then find Stevie and unearth the courage to tell him to back off.

Thanks to Vicki, I didn't have time to execute my lame plan.

School was over and I walked out of the building alone, feeling unnerved, full of trepidation, wondering what would come of my confrontation. To my shock, *I* was confronted. And by my boyfriend.

He hurried out of the school toward me. "You weren't going to tell me," he seethed, his tone incongruous to his actions as he pulled me into him for a hug. "I am so done with this. We're talking to Stevie together."

I gripped him tight. "Vicki told you."

"Yes. And Jimmy is lucky I was in class when she did, because it gave me time to calm down. He still gets a threatening warning, though."

"Tobias, don't."

His grip on me tightened, his gaze fierce. "Jimmy likes to act big but he's a bug, a tiny, repulsive little bug, and I need him to know that if he touches you I'll squash him for good."

"I wish you wouldn't talk like that," I grumbled, pulling out of his hold.

"Yeah, well I wish bullies could be fought with rainbows and unicorn shit, but they can't," he snapped at me.

I threw my head back and let out a yell through gritted teeth.

He cupped the nape of my neck, massaging it gently. I closed my eyes at the feel of his lips on my temple. "I love you, you know that, right?" he murmured, nuzzling me.

Leaning back into him, I sighed. "I love you, too. I just… can't believe what a day it's been. And it's not over. Please… please don't get into it with Jimmy. Promise?"

"Hey, I think that I have done impressively well up to this point." Tobias defended himself. "But threatening you like that crossed a line. Don't pretend it didn't."

"So let's go talk to the ringleader and end this once and for all."

Determination hardened his features. "He could be at the park where they get high sometimes."

"What if they're all there?" I said.

"If we see them all there, we'll leave and find another time to get Stevie on his own."

As it turned out, they weren't all there.

But Stevie and Jimmy were there in the graffiti-covered,

run-down old playpark that was strewn with old battered soda cans, empty crisp packets and stubbed-out cigarettes.

Stevie was sitting on a rusted swing smoking a roll up while Jimmy leaned against the metal frame laughing at something his friend had said. Neither of them were dressed for winter, wearing only hoodies and tracksuit bottoms. It hadn't escaped my notice that Stevie had stopped wearing the hat, scarf and gloves I'd gifted to him. It wouldn't have surprised me to discover that he had burned them.

The thought didn't have much time to hang around, however, because as soon as Tobias saw Jimmy he forgot all about staying calm. One minute he'd been at my side and then the next he was sprinting toward Jimmy like a bull at a red flag. Stevie jumped off the swing, eyes round with surprise. Jimmy turned to follow his friend's gaze and tensed at the sight of Tobias. It was too late, though. Tobias kept running at him and as soon as he neared him he threw a right hook that hit Jimmy with such force it knocked him off his feet.

"Tobias!" I yelled, my feet finally coming unstuck. I ran toward them, watching as Jimmy cupped his nose and groaned on the asphalt of the playpark.

To my relief, Tobias just stood over him, not making another move to attack. "You come near her again and I'll kill you. You think 'cos I've stayed quiet, let you assholes taunt us, that I'm soft? You have no idea what I'm capable of."

"What the hell is goin' on?" Stevie said, looking down at his friend, his mouth slack with shock.

As I drew to a stop by Tobias I gaped at how painfully thin Stevie had gotten. It was more than drug abuse. He obviously wasn't eating much at all, and I wondered why. Was all the money he was supposedly making doing drug deals going back into his own drug habit, and his mum didn't know because she was so sick? What about his little brother? Was someone feeding Kieran? My old friend stood and faced us in nothing but a hoodie and jeans, and he trembled. But there was something...twitchy about it. Like it wasn't from the cold... but from an irritation, an impatience for something. "Whit? Whit dae ye want?"

Tobias got straight to the point. "When is this going to stop, man? After Jimmy tries to rape Comet?"

The word *rape* seemed to slap Stevie. His head jerked back and his pale skin turned even paler. He looked down at Jimmy who groaned and sat up, wiping the blood from his nose. "He wouldnae dae that."

"Jimmy's a repulsive dickhead. He cornered her on her own and pretty much threatened to do it. He does what you tell him to do, and then takes it five million times further." Tobias strode forward and gripped Stevie's shirt, causing my breath to stop. But it wasn't an aggressive move. Tobias's words became a plea. "I'm your friend, your family. What the hell are you doing?"

Stevie looked so lost and alone, staring up at Tobias, that I couldn't help but feel for him, despite everything that had happened. I wanted to help him but I didn't know how without making everything worse. He shrugged out of Tobias's hold and stumbled back, looking skinny and unwashed and neglected. He stared at the ground for a moment and then finally looked up, staring right into my eyes with his haunted ones.

"I'm sorry, Comet," he choked out. "I'm so sorry."

He spun on his heel and began to stride away.

"Stevie!" Tobias yelled.

Stevie started to run. Tobias moved as if to go after him but I grabbed his arm to stop him. "Just give him some time."

Another groan brought our heads down to Jimmy. He held up his hand as if to ward us off. "I was only jokin'! Whit did ye have tae go and break ma nose for?"

Tobias stared at him in disgust. "It's not broken. But I can change that. I will if I ever hear of you threatening a girl like you threatened Comet. It's not okay, dipshit. It's very far from okay. And I'm not joking. You won't ever get away with that again."

"Fine, fine." Jimmy nodded, looking nothing like the intimidating vile boy who had threatened me earlier. He looked small and defeated. He looked like a coward.

He *was* a coward.

As if he realized that, too, Tobias gave Jimmy his back, done with him. I held out my hand and he took it, his warm fingers curling around my cold ones. Squeezing it, I turned and started to lead him away from the park.

We didn't say anything as we walked back through town, but I knew we were both hoping that whatever had gone on in Stevie's head back at the park, it meant the end to our torment at school.

21

It's cold here but I don't care,
We're surrounded by a million lights.
The glow warms the bitter air,
Our hearts set free like fiery kites.
—CC

As a wannabe poet I looked for the beauty in everything. At least, I'd always thought I had. Since meeting Tobias, however, I'd learned that sometimes my eyes weren't wide-open when it came to different aspects of my life. The same could be said for the city I lived in. Over time I'd gotten used to it, like you get used to anything that's in your life long enough. I forgot to see the magic in Edinburgh.

That was, until I saw it through Tobias's eyes.

It was the weekend before Christmas, and we had our last week at school ahead of us. In all the time we'd spent together, Tobias and I had never ventured out of Portobello. I didn't know if it was a conscious decision or if we'd spent so much time concealing our friendship that we feared going out anywhere that we might be seen together. Whatever the reason, it no longer existed, and after a week of tentative silence from our tormentors I suggested he and I go into the city for the Christmas Markets and Fair.

I watched Tobias's face as we got off the bus early that Saturday morning. He hadn't been happy about me dragging him out of bed at the butt crack of dawn, but the market always got incredibly busy as the day wore on. As we walked passed Edinburgh Waverly train station on Princes Street the sky was still a dark violet blue, making the Christmas lights twinkle spectacularly. It was like walking into another world. White lights sparkled in the trees like Jack Frost had danced all over their branches. The Star Flyer ride, lit up in a million different lights, stood beside—and as tall—as the Scott Monument. The ride was a pole with a flat umbrella top that moved up and down and spun. Attached to that top were bucket seats on a swing. When you were in the seat you were taken right to the top of the Star Flyer and spun out like the hem of a poodle skirt. You could see all of the city from up there—a three-hundred-and-sixty-degree view.

On the other side of the monument was the massive Ferris wheel. With somewhere in the region of twenty thousand lights all over it, it looked like it was covered in sparkling jewels. The wheel was more my speed, with little sheltered carriages to sit in so you could enjoy the view of Edinburgh without feeling like you were going to be thrown out of your seat.

"What do you think?" I asked Tobias as we crossed the street to stand beneath the Star Flyer.

He gripped my hand tighter in his and smiled down at me. "Pretty cool."

I grinned back and hugged into his side as we continued to walk down the main street of the city. The center of Edinburgh was split into two historical areas. To our left and uphill the roads led to Old Town, the medieval area. Up there was the Royal Mile, where old tenement buildings towered over the wide, cobbled road. In between the buildings were narrow passageways and stairwells, leading to a "secret" underground world. The Mile stretched all the way up to Edinburgh Castle, perched upon its volcanic rock.

From down on Princes Street it felt like the castle loomed over all, majestic, proud, and as I looked at it through Tobias's eyes, awe-inspiring.

"That is pretty cool," he said as we stood at the lower end of Princes Street and stared up at the castle. At this time of the morning, warm lights placed strategically in the rock face of the volcano it sat on lit up the castle in a surreal, ethereal glow. The streets were quiet, even of cars, taxis and buses, and for a moment we just stood there, huddled together in the cold winter morning, staring at all the lights.

It felt like we were part of a wonderland. Why had I not appreciated that until I was standing with Tobias, seeing it from his perspective?

From there we walked upward on our right. Here was the other historical region of the city—New Town. It was famous for its eighteenth-century Georgian architecture. Up there, where the expensive shops, nice restaurants and luxury hotels were situated, was George Street, and my eyes widened at the sight we found.

On the west end, bejeweled in green light like something out of *Wicked* or Disney, was Edinburgh's Street of Light structure. It loomed as high as the buildings with two towers at the front and two at the back. Connecting those were arches, giving it the stunning appearance of a 3-D castle made up of stained glass. At night choirs and bands played under it, making the whole experience feel so magically Christmassy that it reminded me of how different my own Christmas experience was compared to a lot of people my age.

"Wow," Tobias said as we stared up at it.

I burrowed closer to him, not just for heat, but because I couldn't help myself from wanting to be as close to him as possible. Always.

Not long later the fair and markets opened and we strolled back down toward Princes Street Gardens. There was tons of stuff for kids in Santa Land, like Santa's Grotto, the Santa Train, Christmas Tree Maze and lots of little rides.

At the east end of the gardens were two markets—the European Market and the Scottish Market. There were glühwein stands selling the German mulled wine, and others with traditional German bratwursts. The smells were brilliantly overwhelming as we walked among crowds that were growing by the minute. Soon, after perusing the craft gift stalls, the crowds became too much as we were jostled and bumped and almost separated numerous times. So I bought pretzels for us and we walked along Princes Street and up into New Town to St. Andrews Square. There was a circular ice rink that provided a three-hundred-sixty-degree journey around the large square, plus a bar with hot drinks to heat up skaters when they came off the rink.

For a while we just stood and watched a very small minority show off their skills on the rink, while the majority struggled to stay on their feet.

We laughed at people's antics, and when we were ready we rented skates and joined in. To my surprise, Tobias—whom I'd assumed because he was athletic would be good at everything physical—was as much like Bambi on ice as I was. We slid and skidded and bumped and clasped on to each other, and all the while we laughed. We laughed so hard that my stomach hurt and I thought I might bring back up the pretzel I'd just eaten.

It was wonderful.

The entire day was the first day we didn't speak of Stevie or Jimmy or Alana. It was the first day Tobias didn't ask me if someone had bothered me at school. The answer for the past week had been no. After our confrontation with Stevie and Jimmy, things had gone eerily quiet. I'd caught only a few glimpses of the two of them at school, and they weren't in the cafeteria at lunchtime. Alana had said a few snide remarks in the corridor between classes but she, too, melted away, whether in boredom or...or had Stevie told them all to back off? We'd waited all week for one of them to give us grief, but nothing had happened. Still, we couldn't yet relax not knowing where Stevie's head was at. Or in fact where *Stevie* was at.

But here, with winter needling our cheeks until they were rosy red and our grips slipping because of our thick gloves, I squealed as I almost fell, giggling as Tobias caught me and then struggled to stay standing. We fell against the rink barriers, arms wrapped around one another, our laughter dancing together, and I felt the safest, the most content that I'd felt in a long time.

Finally, deciding ice skating was neither of our forte, we left the ice and changed back into our shoes.

"Do you want to do the Ferris wheel?" I said as we strolled hand in hand—or glove-covered hand in glove-covered hand—back to Princes Street.

"Let's leave that for night." Tobias let go of my hand to slide his arm around my shoulders. He pulled me into his side and admitted, "I haven't visited the castle yet."

Shocked by this I decided we had to rectify that immediately. It was at least a twenty-minute walk up to the castle, and we stopped at a stall to buy a hot chocolate for our journey. Up on the Mile we lingered over street art, jewelry and a sword eater whom we and a crowd encircled in fascinated horror.

Sufficiently freaked out I led Tobias up Castle Hill and onto the castle esplanade.

"Nice driveway," Tobias said as we walked toward the entrance. His gaze roamed the view of the city below.

"Just wait. It gets better up there." I pointed to the castle.

Inside, Tobias insisted on paying for my ticket, and then I led him up the cobbled path to the main thoroughfare. From there we visited the Great Hall where royal ceremonies were held; we saw the Royal Palace and the Stone of Destiny upon which centuries of kings of Scotland had been enthroned; the crown jewels; St. Margaret's Chapel, which was built around 1130, making it Edinburgh's oldest building; Mons Meg the medieval European cannon gun; and the one o'clock gun that was fired at, well, one o'clock every day, a tradition that had started back in the 1800s to allow the ships on the Firth of Forth to set their maritime clocks. Although Tobias didn't study history or enjoy it like I did, he wanted to see everything, including the regimental museums, the national war museum and the prison re-creation.

Finally, we stopped at the Half Moon Battery, the great curved wall that hosted the cannons and gave the castle its unique profile. From there we had a fantastic view over the city. I pointed out Calton Hill with its Athenian acropolis. And Arthur's Seat, an ancient volcano and the main peak of the hills that formed most of Holyrood Park.

"I haven't climbed it yet," Tobias said.

"What have you been doing since you got here?"

He smirked down at me. "Chasing after a girl."

Delighted, I tried hard not to grin back. "He says with absolutely no embarrassment or pricked male pride."

Tobias's gaze softened. "She's no ordinary girl."

I blushed and wrapped my arms around one of his, hugging in close. "We should climb Arthur's Seat. Or you should climb it with Luke and Andy." Tobias had grown closer to the sixth year and to Andy in our year, both of whom were on the rugby team. Although he hadn't wanted to leave me at lunchtime in case anyone tried to start in on us again, I knew Steph and Vicki probably wanted our girls-only time back, and I had to imagine Tobias was missing hanging out with just the guys.

"We could all climb it."

"I'll bring the girls then, too."

After a moment of silence I ventured to say, "You know you can start eating lunch with the boys from the rugby team at school now."

"Is that your way of saying you're sick of me?" he teased.

"No." I shoved him playfully. "I just think we should get back to normality. We shouldn't let Stevie and his delinquent friends mess with our heads anymore."

Tobias stared out at the city, his gaze drawn to the opulent lights of the Christmas Fair. "How about we start that after Christmas? Just to be sure."

I could give him that. "Sounds like a plan."

He turned into me, sliding his hands around my waist and drawing me close. I stared up at him expectantly but what he said next surprised me. "Now I want to visit this poetry café of yours."

"Pan?"

"Yeah, that one."

"Why?"

"Because it's part of you. It's something you enjoy. And I'm expecting you to come cheer me on at my rugby games, so I feel it's only fair I go to your thing, too."

I struggled not to laugh. "My thing?"

He narrowed his eyes. "Trying to be supportive and mature here."

"I know," I chuckled. "And it's much appreciated. But Tobias... Pan isn't really your type of thing."

"But it's yours," he reiterated. "And I want to see it."

22

His kisses feel like a calm before the storm,
Like waves crashing harder and harder to shore.
I'm pushed in deep waters, feeling myself transform,
Now just lips, body, hands searching for more.
—CC

While I'd been excited about Tobias's reaction to Princes Street at Christmastime, I was afraid to look at his face when we walked into Pan. I was afraid of his judgment since his opinion meant so much to me.

"Drink?" he asked, drawing my reluctant gaze. He wore a neutral expression.

"I'm okay."

"I'm going to get a coffee. You grab us a table."

I nodded, bemused by his lack of reaction. Well, not lack of reaction, but lack of judgment really. He just took in the tie-dyed scarfs, weird murals and smell of patchouli mixed with coffee like it was no big deal. Grabbing a table for two at the window, I took off my hat and scarf and listened to the woman onstage recite a poem that was clearly about loss. It was a busy day, Tobias and I taking the last little table left.

He returned a few minutes later with his coffee and turned in his seat so that he could watch and listen to the woman. When she was done and everyone clapped, Tobias clapped, too.

"What do you think?" I asked.

Tobias was quiet as he slipped off his beanie hat and stuck it into the pocket of his jacket. Finally, he made eye contact with me. "She was good."

"And the rest of the place?"

He grinned and stared around at the space. "Eclectic," he finally landed on.

I smirked. "Very diplomatic."

Before he could respond a young guy, perhaps a few years older than us, stood at the mic and introduced himself. And then he began to read his poem. Like the woman before him, his poem was in free verse. I studied Tobias's profile as he listened but I couldn't get a read on him. When the young guy finished and people started chattering among themselves, Tobias looked at me. Whatever he saw on my face made his eyebrows pull together. "What?"

"No one rhymes anymore. I mean…my poetry sometimes doesn't have a measurable meter, so it technically is free verse, but I rhyme."

"So?"

"My poetry seems childish in comparison."

"No it doesn't," he said immediately and vehemently. "Yours is funny and thoughtful and sometimes sad. And I get it. Just because your poetry is different to the people in here doesn't mean you don't have something to say." Tobias reached across the table and took my hand in his warm one. "After everything you've been through, Comet, you have to know you're brave. You showed your poetry to Mr. Stone. You're willing to publish it in the lit mag. The next step is that stage up there."

The thought of getting up on that stage gave me nervous

butterflies. Poetry, any piece of writing or anything a person created, was a window into their soul. When people got up on that stage, they might as well strip off their clothes and be naked. Except baring your soul was harder than baring skin. Skin was just skin. If you pierced it, you bled then you bandaged it up. It was harder to recover from an injury to the soul.

And yet, staring into Tobias's bright eyes, seeing his pride in me, seeing his *belief* in me, I thought maybe I could do it. Tobias reading my poetry had brought us together. Nothing negative had come from him reading my words. And I think that was what had given me the courage to approach Mr. Stone. The stage at Pan was a different kettle of fish.

"Someday," I eventually said, "Maybe...if you talk to your mum about how you really feel."

The light dimmed in his eyes and he pulled his hand from mine to settle back in his chair. His sullen expression probably should have warned me to back off. Instead I pressed him. "You're still so angry with her, Tobias. And with your dad. Maybe if you tell your mum why you're so angry it would help. Just put it out there."

"Oh, like you've told your parents why you're pissed at them?" he argued.

"Kyle tried to come down on me about you sleeping over after Dean's party. I told him being a parent was an all-or-nothing deal and he'd made it clear over the years that he wanted nothing to do with me. He couldn't change his mind to suit himself."

Tobias raised an eyebrow. "And?"

"And what?"

"What did he say?"

I shrugged. "I slammed the door in his face."

He studied me thoughtfully. "That sounds like an unfinished conversation."

"At least I said something."

"So you want me to yell at my mom and slam a door in her face?" He grinned. "Already got it covered."

I tried not to smile, because this was serious. My boyfriend would go through life with a giant chip on his shoulder if he didn't try to resolve his issues with his mum. "Tobias."

He sighed, drained his coffee and stood up. I stared at him, wondering if I'd pushed him too far and he was going to leave me sitting in the café all alone. If that happened, I might cry. We'd had such a wonderful day up until this point. Why did I have to push it?

However, Tobias put his beanie back on and held out his hand to me. "It's getting late. Let's go back and ride the Ferris wheel."

Relief flooded me and I grinned so hard that when he pulled me to my feet, he didn't let go. Instead he cupped my face in his hands and whispered, "Your smile kills me."

"That's good though, right?"

"It's the best thing in my life," he answered and followed it up with the sweetest kiss.

As we walked out of Pan heading back toward Princes Street, I was filled with immense gratitude that I'd found Tobias. We could have discussions and disagree and he wasn't going to hold it against me. We could just be ourselves and love each other without fear that we had to change or hold ourselves back or mute a part of our personality.

We loved each other.

This was *real love*, I decided as he hugged me close to his side. It had to be.

Because nothing had ever felt more real in my entire life.

★ ★ ★

Steph made me proud as she strutted her stuff and sang her heart out as Roxie Hart. Despite our differences, it was impossible not to feel excited for her as she took over that stage. Everyone in the cast paled in comparison to her. She had this energy and magnetism up there that she didn't have in the "every day." Acting brought her to life, and I could see big things for her in the future.

It was the last night of the school show's run that week and just a few days before Christmas Eve. We'd had our last day of classes today and the auditorium was filled with the same feeling our classes had been—giddy joy and cheer. It was a lull before the storm. We would have our fifth-year prelim exams in mid-January, just a week after returning to school from the Christmas and New Year's break.

I sat with Vicki, who was here with both her parents. There was no tense atmosphere between them, no awkwardness that I could detect, and they were getting along well enough. I had hope for Vicki. So much hope.

When the final curtain fell and my hands ached from clapping, Vicki and I grinned at each other.

"Should we tell her how good she is? I'm afraid it might create a monster," Vicki joked.

"We should tell her. She deserves to know."

"Yeah." She smiled fondly. "Our girl is going to be a superstar."

"Well, that was great," Mr. Brown said as we stood up to leave. "You two find Stephanie to congratulate her and we'll get you at the car."

Vicki and I wandered out into the corridor outside the auditorium and waited at the double doors that led backstage. "Do you think she'll change fir—"

"So tell me the truth. How was I?" Steph interrupted.

I spun around, suffused by happiness for my friend. She stood grinning at us and Vicki and I impulsively hugged her. "You were brilliant."

She laughed in my ear and the three of us hugged each other tight. When we pulled back Steph wore this triumphant look, still somehow managing to be pretty despite the harsh theater makeup she was wearing that looked good onstage but not so much up close. Plus, she was all sweaty. But no wonder! She'd danced her ass off.

"Really," I said. "Just fantastic, Steph. I'm so proud of you."

Steph beamed. "Thanks. They've already promised me a part in the summer show."

"Of course they have. They'd be idiots not to."

"You guys are the best!" she squealed in delight. "Okay. I have to go backstage and get cleaned up. Mum and Dad are taking me out for celebratory dinner. I'll call you guys later." We hugged again and then she left Vicki and me alone.

"So," I said as we made our way through the crowds toward the exit. "Your parents are here. Together."

She nodded, wearing a careful expression as if she didn't want to show she was hopeful or excited by the thought. "They're trying. Dad is moving back in tonight, and we're doing Christmas as a family. I'm a little bit worried, though."

"Don't be," I assured her. "Nobody's parents are perfect, Vick. But you've got good ones who are just trying their best."

She frowned. "I know. I'll try to remind myself of that when they're arguing over how long the turkey should be left in the oven, while Ben and I munch on all our Christmas chocolate behind their backs."

I chuckled but inside I didn't feel like laughing. Inside, I was envious of the picture she'd painted. It sounded normal. It sounded right.

Even if I couldn't have that in my life, Vicki deserved to have it, and I was happy for her. My friend had no idea just how much she meant to me. I hugged her before she could get in her parent's car, although I'd surprised her, she hugged me back, squeezing me tight. We didn't say anything, just laughed a little at ourselves.

Vicki's parents dropped me off by the Espy, and with their well-wishes for a wonderful Christmas ringing in my ears, I walked home along the cold, quiet esplanade. The sea was rough tonight, rushing ashore aggressively, and its bad mood seeped into my good mood, dimming it.

Loneliness cascaded over me.

It always did at this time of year as soon as school let out. Christmas for me wasn't what it was for most people who had parents. On Christmas Eve, Kyle and Carrie always threw a party for their friends and while the house was filled with music and laughter, it never seemed to reach me where I sat alone in my bedroom.

When I was younger my parents gave in to tradition, and I'd always wake up on Christmas morning to presents under the tree in the sitting room. The older I got, however, the fewer the presents that could be found under there until eventually there was only a single card with a red bow among the presents I'd bought for them. Inside the card were vouchers for the bookstore. A generous amount of money, yes, but always the same thing.

It wasn't all bad, though. Every Christmas morning, I'd also wake up to a Christmas stocking at the foot of my bed. It was filled with chocolates, sweets, nail polish, hair accessories, pen sets, makeup and other cute, fun things. I knew it was Kyle. Always giving me just a little of what I wanted from him. Attention. Affection. Thoughtfulness.

But always just a little.

Temporary.

Never enough.

I blinked away the tears that had clouded my vision and huddled against the battering wind howling up the beach. It was a horrible night and the house was sure to be cold, because Kyle and Carrie were out for the evening. The heavy feeling in my chest was such that I knew I had to do something about it or I'd end up crying myself to sleep.

I'd call Tobias when I got home.

He'd take my mind off it.

As if I'd conjured him from my deep need to not be alone tonight, Tobias was suddenly there as I pushed open the garden gate. Standing, arms crossed against the cold, in my doorway.

Loneliness slid off my shoulders like tar that could no longer find a grip. It lay on the pathway behind me, forgotten, as I hurried toward my boyfriend and threw myself into his arms.

"Oof." He caught me and hugged me to him immediately. "You okay?" he murmured against my ear.

I pulled back to smile at him. "I am now."

He grinned. "Yeah? You mind letting me into your house then, because I'm freezing my ass off here."

Laughing, I reluctantly let him go so I could unlock the

door. He huddled in behind me, stamping his feet and rubbing his arms. Concern washed over me. "How long have you been waiting out there?"

"About half an hour. I thought the show ended earlier."

Tobias wasn't really into the theater so I hadn't thought it was fair to force him to come see a school show. He'd told me he was hanging out with Luke tonight. "Why aren't you with the boys?"

"I was, but they got some girls around and were starting to party so…"

So he'd left. To come be with me. "I love you," I blurted out.

Tobias smiled, bemused. "Yeah, I love you, too."

"No." I shook my head, frustrated that I couldn't articulate what was on my mind. "I really love you."

Now he frowned. "You don't think I really love you?"

"No, I'm saying it wrong." Huffing at myself, I began unzipping his jacket. He chuckled as I pulled off his outerwear with all the efficiency of a mother with her toddler. "Shoes off," I said, as I took off my coat and winter accessories.

"Comet—"

"My room. Now." I grabbed his hand and led him. Thankfully, Kyle and Carrie had left the heat on, so my bedroom was nice and toasty. As soon as the door closed behind him, I locked it.

Understanding began to dawn on his face as Tobias stared at the locked bedroom door. "Oh?" His eyebrows rose as he turned back to me. His cheeks suddenly looked flushed. "You mean…you *really* love me?"

I laughed in giddy nervousness. As soon as I'd seen him waiting for me at my door I'd known what I wanted tonight. I wanted to immerse myself completely in the one person I never felt alone with. I was scared of the unknown, nervous, feeling a little sick and knock-kneed to be honest. But I wanted to be with him more than any of those feelings combined.

Fingers trembling, I began to unbutton the blouse I was wearing.

Tobias took two long strides toward me and covered my fingers, halting me. He studied me, his whole body tense, coiled tight. "Are you sure?"

I nodded. "I… I'm on the pill," I revealed. I'd started using it as soon as I'd gotten it from the pharmacy a few weeks ago during my mortifying visit there, with Vicki as my support.

His fingers curled tightly around mine. "I have… I've got protection on me."

I flushed, squirming. It was weird how I could be ready to have sex with this boy and yet still find discussing the reality of it embarrassing. As if sensing that, Tobias grinned, a smile filled with mischief.

"Imagine your reaction if I'd said the word *condom*."

I blushed from head to toe, making him throw his head back in laughter.

"You're mean," I huffed.

"You're amazing," he replied, laughter still in his voice, and then suddenly he was kissing me, his arms wrapped so tight around me that there wasn't a part of me not touching him.

We stumbled backward, lost in our kisses, and fell across my bed. The sensation of his body pressing mine into the mattress sent flashes of white-hot heat licking up my body. From Tobias's reaction, he felt the same.

From there I was lost, tumbling into a world of magic with

him the same way I did when I cracked open a good book. The outside world faded away, until all that was left were his lips, his hands, his body and his whispered words of love.

23

"Our hearts pounded like a stampede,
of horses in the wild.
Our hot blood rushed at super speed,
We're lost. Found. Utterly beguiled."

Tobias's hold on me tightened as we lay in bed together, warm skin against warm skin. "Did you just think that up?"

"Yes," I whispered, rubbing my cheek against his chest. "After what we just did I'm not going to get embarrassed over you hearing a few rough verses."

He laughed gently. "I guess not." I felt his fingers run through my hair. "Always a poet, huh?"

"I've had more to write about since you came into the picture. Love poems for miles." I snorted. "Some are terrible."

"As bad as 'Roses are red, Violets are blue, thanks for having sex with me, I love you, too'?"

I burst into laughter, quickly muffling my giggles against his chest, because we'd heard my parents arrive home about ten minutes earlier. Thankfully, they'd gone straight upstairs to bed so they had no idea Tobias was in my room, or that I'd just lost my virginity to him.

The laughter was partly because my boyfriend was funny

and also partly because I was giddy at the revelation of love-making. I couldn't imagine doing any of the things we'd done with anyone but Tobias. Although books gave differing examples of the loss of one's virginity, they all suggested the same thing—that the first time could be either painful or uncomfortable for a girl. It was uncomfortable for me, but just at first. Then it was…transcendent. I'd never felt more connected to anyone in my life than I did in that moment with Tobias.

I'd even cried, it was so beautiful, and he only made it more so by kissing away my tears. He hadn't been alarmed by the wet in my eyes. Instead he saw past that to the joy.

To the love.

And just like that I didn't know how I would ever cope in a world where I didn't get to have those moments with him. The thought of my future in Virginia loomed over me on the bed like a dark, weighty cloud ready to burst.

"I'm going to assume you think my poetry is brilliant," he said, laughter dancing in the words.

I tried to check my sudden worry and teased, "You've missed your calling. Give up the rugby and become a regular at Pan."

"They'd probably think I'm being brilliantly ironic."

"Probably." I bit my lip, wondering if I should mention the future. Then suddenly my lips parted and the words just burst out of me. "I'm applying to study at the University of Virginia after graduation."

Tobias took a moment to answer. "I know that."

I turned my head to look at him and he turned his to look at me. He caught the worry in my expression. "What is it, Com?"

"It's my dream to study there. But now you're my dream, too. What do I do?"

"Can't you have both?"

"Can I? Would you move back to the States?" God, I wanted him to just say yes so I could have my cake and eat it, too!

He sighed. Heavily. "I can't answer that just now. All I can concentrate on is getting back on track with school so that when I do figure out what I want, I'll have options. But right now I don't know what it is I want when I graduate. All I do know is that I want you." He gave me a reassuring squeeze. "So can't we just enjoy what we have right now, and worry about all that later?"

I nodded, because I knew he was right. We still had time to work all that stuff out. So I shoved those worries back down from whence they came and did my best to ignore them.

We were quiet, just soaking in the peace of lying in one another's arms. Outside my window, beyond the garden, I could hear the harsh lapping of the waves and that, plus the adrenaline rush I'd just had, caused my eyes to droop with tiredness. Exhaustion soothed my limbs like a gentle massage, making me feel fluid and more relaxed than I could remember feeling in a long time.

Tobias's next words jolted me out of it. "I want you to spend Christmas Eve with me and my mom."

What?

I pushed up off his chest so that I could see his expression. He brushed the hair off my face, seeming calm, like the idea wasn't a big deal. "You actually want to spend time with your mum? And me? Christmas Eve. With your mum?" The mum he was currently so angry with that he barely spoke to her or spent time with her?

"Yeah. You said your parents throw a big party and you end up staying in your room the whole time, so why not spend it with us instead?" Seeing my confused expression, Tobias sighed. "Look...I talked to her, okay."

My pulse started to pick up speed. "About your dad?"

"Yes."

"Because of me?"

"Because you were right, yes."

I bit back a smile, wondering if it was possible this day could get any better. "And what did you say?"

He shrugged, the gesture far more indifferent than his sad expression. His pain took the wind out of my sails. This wasn't a moment for me to crow over as a triumphant girlfriend realizing her influence over her boyfriend. This was Tobias, sharing his hurt and anger, the weight of which I wished I could shoulder for him.

"I told her I was angry at Dad for being a hypocrite and for being on my back all the time to be something it turned out he wasn't. And angry at her for living this lie and making me live it, too."

This time my heart beat hard with an ache. It was so unfair that someone so good, so true, should have to feel this way. There was no closure to be had for Tobias with his dad gone. It was just something he'd have to deal with for the rest of his life, and my chest smarted with the unfairness of it. "What did she say?"

The muscle in his jaw flexed and I felt his body tense against mine. "She said she stayed with him because she loved him, and she was scared that if she demanded his fidelity she would lose him."

I didn't know what to say to that. It reminded me so much of how Kyle was with Carrie—so blind to her faults, so in love with her, nothing else mattered. Not even how it affected their kid. Anger suffused me on Tobias's behalf, and I must have not been able to hide it, because he wrapped his hand around the back of my neck and squeezed gently. "Hey, I'm okay," he assured me. "My mom isn't proud of herself, Com. She told me she wished every day she'd been stronger. But she isn't perfect. She's just human…and as much as I felt pressured by my dad, she reminded me that I also felt loved." Tears filled his eyes. "He did everything for me. I never felt like he didn't care. He screwed up. Big-time. And I just have to get over it. Move on."

His tears automatically produced my own. His pain, my pain.

I held him. So tight.

It was a promise that, no matter what, I'd help him learn to accept his father's betrayal and above all to remember his father's love.

Finally, when his tremors subsided, I whispered, "Yes, Tobias. I'll spend Christmas Eve with you and your mum."

He held me tighter and I felt his smile against my cheek.

24

Honesty doesn't absolve you of your crime,
In fact it's more bitter than your deception.
Perhaps understanding comes with the gravity of time,
But for now there are limits to this heart's perception.
—*CC*

"What do you mean you're spending all of today at To-bias's?" Dad frowned at me over his cup of coffee. He was sitting at the kitchen counter, reading a newspaper when I'd walked in to let him know I was leaving.

"His mum invited me." I shrugged, not understanding what the problem was. "I didn't think it would be a big deal. You guys always have a party on Christmas Eve."

"Carrie doesn't feel like it this year. She was going to make her curry. I thought we could watch *It's a Wonderful Life* together."

Bemused by the idea, I said, "When have we ever done anything like that?"

"When you were a kid we used to watch Christmas movies."

"On Christmas Day. When, as you say, I was a kid."

"I just don't think you should spend Christmas Eve away from your family. I'd rather you not go. I would have thought you'd rather be at home, too, no?"

Quickly, so fast it almost gave me whiplash, anger tore

through me in a blaze of heat. How dare he? How dare he try to make me feel guilty about wanting to spend Christmas with Tobias over him? "Are you kidding?"

Eyes flashing at my tone, he held up a hand to ward me off. "I'm not looking for an argument, Comet."

"Not looking for an argument? You're giving me crap about spending the day with someone who loves me. Loves me, Kyle. *Loves me!*"

"What the hell is that supposed to mean?"

"It means where have you been my entire bloody life?" The words, the bottled rage, just popped out, pouring my vitriol all over him. "You're a coward who chooses Carrie over me every time she kicks up a stink about you giving me attention. I know what happened to her. I know… I overheard one day. And I'm sorry that happened to her, I'm really sorry, but her hating me for existing and you choosing her over me, it hurts. It hurts so bloody much. You stopped caring a long time ago whether I was even in the room, so you don't get to suddenly become my parent and demand things of me. You just don't."

Kyle looked at me, horrified. "I love her, Comet."

That was his excuse, his answer?

What about me?

"More than you love me?"

His gaze dropped but before it did I saw the guilt. And although I'd always known it was true, it broke something inside of me. Tears built in my throat, blurred my vision. "It's not supposed to work like that, Dad."

He jerked at the name.

"You're supposed to love your kid more than anyone else in

the world." A sob burst forth before I could stop it, my pain the only sound in the harshly silent kitchen.

I tried to control it, to find a way to pull back the hurt and hide it from him.

"I…" Dad stared at me, anguish written all over his face. "I know your mum better than anyone. And I knew the way she was acting when she was pregnant that she saw you as a threat to my love for her. I didn't want that to turn into something ugly, Comet. I didn't want her to become a person she'd despise, and I didn't want you to suffer that kind of abuse. I knew I'd have to leave her if that happened, and I didn't know if I'd have that kind of strength. So I… I distanced myself from you. She needed me to do that."

More tears spilled down my cheeks as I grabbed my bag with the present inside it for the boy who did care about me more than anyone else. "I… I've sat alone in that bedroom for almost seventeen years, waiting for someone to choose me. You have *no idea* how alone I've been. *I* needed you to love me."

He choked out a sob, covering his mouth, and as I walked out of the house, the sounds of my dad's crying rang in my ears.

But it didn't make me feel any better.

Tobias knew as soon as we met halfway between his house and mine that something was wrong. I felt shell-shocked after my confrontation with my dad, and I guess I looked it.

"You've been crying," he said, his hands brushing over my cheeks where clearly my tears had left tracks.

"Crap." Worry crashed over me as I rummaged through

my bag for a compact. "I can't show up at your mum's looking like I don't want to be there."

"Comet, what happened?" he asked as I checked out my reflection.

I busied myself fixing the blobs of mascara at the corners of my eyes and rubbing the tear tracks away. "I overreacted to something Kyle said."

"Overreacted how?"

I shut the compact, feeling my eyes burn with fresh tears. My lips trembled as I tried to keep it together. "They're not having a party and he suggested I should stay home. I… I don't know what happened. I just lost it. I confronted him about choosing Carrie over me all the time and never being there for me."

"Shit." My boyfriend enfolded me in his arms and I clung to him for dear life.

"He admitted he loves her more than me." I shook hard with the force of trying to stop my tears. "I knew. I *knew*. But it feels like someone just punched a hole in my chest. I can't breathe." I shuddered and shook, struggling to contain the hurt.

Tobias's arms tightened around me and then I heard him whisper in my ear, over and over, "I love you, I love you, I love you."

My anchor, he pulled me back to myself, to him, and slowly, but surely, I began to breathe again.

Tobias had offered to spend Christmas Eve with me alone, considering what had just occurred between me and Kyle. Yes, I was devastated by the brief conversation. I was also confused by my reaction, because Kyle hadn't told me anything I didn't already know. To hear him confess his own weak will when it came to Carrie, to hear from his own mouth that yes, he did love her more than me and that he'd choose her over me no matter what was painful. I didn't know if his fears about Carrie's issues were founded. Maybe. I guess I didn't know the woman who was my mother well at all. She'd never been verbally unkind to me, though. Her cruelty had always been in her indifference.

Those were my thoughts, going around and around like they were stuck on some twisted, hellish merry-go-round, when I walked into Tobias's new house.

I tried to focus on Lena. I discovered, however, as I followed her through the narrow hallway of the three-bedroom house in the more affluent area of Porty that Tobias *did* take after his father in looks. There was a photo hanging on the wall in the hallway of a younger Tobias standing in between Lena and a man I knew must have been his dad. They stood outside a huge white house that reminded me of the wealthy homes featured in John Hughes's movies. Like Tobias, his dad was extremely tall, broad-shouldered, with fair good looks.

I'd slowed down to look at the photo, and Tobias turned around to see what was keeping me.

"Your dad?"

His eyes flicked to the photo, and I hated the pain that shimmered in his gaze. He nodded and I squeezed his hand.

"Would you like something to drink, Comet?" Lena called from the kitchen. "We have water, Coke, orange juice. Or I could make us all hot chocolate."

I tugged Tobias away from the photo. There was no need for us both to be a sad, wallowing mess today. "Yes, Mrs.

King, hot chocolate sounds lovely." We wandered into the small, modern kitchen to find her waiting on us.

"I thought I told you to call me Lena."

"Of course, sorry." I gave her a smile, trying to ignore the fact that she was raking her eyes over my outfit like she had the last time I saw her.

It was Christmas, so I'd decided on a burgundy long-sleeved thermal with gold sparkles through it, matched with a short burgundy velvet skirt with a dark red tulle underskirt that stuck out rock-chick style from the skirt. I wore thick, black tights and Irregular Choice burgundy suede ankle boots in the Victorian style. They seemed simple until I turned around—they had a huge gold jacquard bow pinned to the back of the ankle.

I'd added a bunch of chunky gold bracelets up both arms so I jingled when I moved.

I'd considered toning my clothes down but this was me, and Tobias knew this was me and all that mattered was that he loved me, loud fashion sense and all. Still, I smoothed my hands down my skirt nervously until Tobias captured one of them in his own.

Glancing up at him in question, I found myself caught by the tender reassurance in his eyes. He drew my hand to his lips and pressed a kiss to it while his gaze held mine, and I felt like he was silently reminding me not to worry what she thought of me because he thought I was perfect.

The sound of a throat clearing broke our moment and we turned to find his mum staring at us wearing a huge smile. "Hot chocolate." She gestured to the mugs in front of us.

Her assessment of my appearance ceased and instead she studied my interactions with her son. In fact, she watched everything Tobias did, and she did it in a way that made me think she missed him. I knew they'd talked and he was attempting to repair the damage to their relationship, but I perceived a wariness in Lena's behavior. Like she was scared of making the wrong move—one that might cause him to shut her out again.

We'd somehow gotten on to the topic of being clumsy, and I was telling them about my most embarrassing klutzy moment. "Someone had smashed in the huge oval glass panels in the science corridor doors but I didn't know about it. They just removed the entire damaged pane, and I wasn't paying attention so I missed the warning sign on the door. Instead I was turning around, yapping away to Vicki about something and I just put my arm out to push the door open. Except my arm went right through and I was going at such a momentum that my entire upper half went through so that I ended up dangling over the insert of the door with my skirt up over my back for the whole world to see my underwear. Of course I didn't know what had happened so I just kind of dangled over it for a while, trying to work out why my nose was inches from the ground, why my butt felt chilly and why I could hear my friends and every other person in the hallway cackling with laughter."

Tobias was laughing at the story and I slapped his arm. "It wasn't funny!"

"I'm sorry." He kept laughing. "I can just picture it. Did anyone open the door while you were still hanging over it?"

My expression turned stony. "Heather."

I could see him struggling to contain his amusement, and I threw his mother an exasperated look that made her smile.

"I can tell you about the time Tobias broke his arm trying to climb the tree outside of his favorite teacher's house."

His laughter died, turning to mock horror. "No, Mom, don't."

Lena immediately flinched. "Oh. Okay."

Tobias made a face. "I didn't mean it like that. It's just embarrassing."

"So I can tell it?"

I felt unsettled by the strain between them, realizing they still had a way to go before they'd be comfortable with one another again.

"Let's just eat and put on a movie or something." Tobias shifted the conversation.

It did seem easier for them to have the buffer of having something to do rather than being faced with more real conversation but that seemed normal, I thought. Mending their relationship would take time.

The rest of the afternoon was good, and Lena seemed to warm to me. I still had my insecurities about her, but she relieved me of those when Tobias excused himself just as I was getting ready to leave.

"I like you with him," Lena said as soon as he was out of earshot.

I blushed. "Thank you."

Her gaze drifted over me but this time she smiled. "You're not at all like the girl he used to date back home, but I can see that's a good thing. You surprised me at first. But the way he is with you…" Her gaze turned introspective. "I like what I see. And although I love Stevie and he's family, he wasn't a good influence. Since Tobias started dating you, he's stopped hanging around with his cousin. He's doing his homework again, bringing home good grades, playing a sport... He seems to be finding himself again and I just... I can tell you've had a part in influencing that. Thank you."

Embarrassed by her praise but glad of it, I said, "Tobias would have found his way back to himself with or without me. I really believe that."

"Yes, maybe. But you got him there faster. I'm glad he has you."

I bit my lip to contain the massive grin that wanted to burst across my face. "Thanks. And thank you for a lovely day and dinner."

"You're welcome, sweetheart. Anytime."

The sound of Tobias thundering down the stairs quietened us and he appeared in the doorway, clutching something in his hand. "Time to go."

I said my goodbyes to his mum and Tobias helped me into my coat. Once we were both bundled up he took my hand and led me outside. We walked in companionable silence through town, passing the large Christmas tree on a square in the High Street. The only other attempt at decoration in town was by our local hardware store, which had projected a Christmas image on the building across from it.

Tonight the sea was relatively calm, just a hush in the background as it sipped at the shore. The moon was full and bright and I remembered how as a kid I would stand at my bedroom window and stare up at the sky on Christmas Eve, desperate to see the black silhouette of Santa and his sleigh passing over the moon. I longed for the days when I'd truly believed in magic, but tonight was the first Christmas Eve in years where the longing was just a pang instead of a deep ache.

When we reached my garden gate Tobias stopped us and

reached inside his jacket. "Merry Christmas." He handed me the package.

Delight bubbled up inside of me. "I put yours under your tree while you were upstairs." I'd been sneaky a few weeks ago, asking about what aftershave he wore. I'd bought him a gift set of it. The truth was I'd been unsure what to buy him. I'd never had a boyfriend before, and we hadn't discussed budget or what was expected of us. Erring on the side of caution, I'd worried since I'd bought it that the gift was too simple.

"I want you to open it now, if that's okay," he said, and if I didn't know any better I would have thought he was nervous.

That made me a little nervous. I tore open the gold Christmas paper he'd wrapped it in, and laughter immediately exploded out of me at what was in my hands.

It was my favorite perfume! Tobias had obviously snuck around in my room to find out what it was.

"Is laughter good?" he said.

"Yes!" I hugged him. "You'll understand when you see your gift."

"Okay." He grinned in relief. "I just wasn't sure what we were…"

"Budget, expectation, generic or handmade, all the questions." I nodded in understanding, making him laugh. "Seriously, you'll feel happy with your present to me when you see my present to you."

Tobias's brows drew together. "You bought me cologne, didn't you?"

I giggled until he kissed the laughter from my lips, and I suddenly wished he was staying with me all night.

25

Time to tell that star goodbye,
Too much wishing blew its spark.
So tonight I'll watch that star die,
Watch it disappear into the dark.

—CC

Tobias was reluctant to let me go, and I tried to assure him I was fine. That was quite difficult to do when it was a lie.

For the first time ever I was anxious about stepping inside my own home.

I didn't know how my confrontation with Kyle would affect us. Yes, my parents had been negligent and self-absorbed, but they'd also never been angry or mean to me. Part of me wished I'd kept my mouth shut so that we could have gone on existing peacefully with one another, like roommates happy with the basic idea of having found someone to coexist with who didn't irritate them.

When I slipped into the house that night, I felt like I had a flurry of angry moths in my stomach, I was so nervous. The sound of the television from the living room filtered out and down the L-shaped hallway toward me, and I could smell Carrie's famous chicken curry in the air. Kyle had been telling the truth. They really were just having a quiet Christmas Eve together.

Stupidly I wondered whether I shouldn't have stayed home after all and soaked up time with my parents while they wanted to spend it with me. But that seemed desperate and forgiving, and right then I was neither.

As much as Lena King's words had lifted my spirits, and as much as I was grateful to have Tobias and Vicki in my life, it wasn't enough to forget the hollowness my parents had carved into me. I had to hope that time would take care of my wounds, that eventually they would heal, and all I'd be left with was a scar that itched every now and then.

However, that time was not quite here yet.

On that thought, I didn't announce my safe arrival home. Instead I used the bathroom, brushed my teeth and shut myself inside my bedroom.

My phone binged on my bedside table as I snuggled deep into my bed. I reached over and touched the screen, and saw a message from Vicki.

It's officially Xmas! Have a Merry One, Comet! ILYSM xx PS. I opnd yr pressie early. <3ed it!! Thx xx

I grinned and replied:

Merry Christmas, Vick! ILYSM2 xx P.S. I'll open mine in the morning because I'm a good girl xx

She replied with the sticky-out tongue emoji. I was grateful to her for putting a smile on my face before I tried to drift off to sleep. Before I could, however, my phone binged again. This time it was Steph:

MryXmas! LU! Xx

For all her faults, and whether it was out of habit or because she felt like family and I had to, I loved Steph, too. She wasn't perfect, sometimes she pissed me off, and sometimes she hurt me, but she could also be sweet. And I believed that she did care about me in her own way.

Merry Christmas, Steph. Love you, too. Hope Santa is good to you. xx

In the middle of texting her my phone binged with another notification, and when I sent Steph's text, I saw that it was a new text from Tobias:

I wywh in my bed w/ me.

Somehow he had the ability to make me blush even via text. Feeling that luscious, hot wave roll gently through me at the thought of being with him, my fingers shook a little as I replied.

Me too. I miss you when you're not here. Xx

Tobias: Did ur dad tlk 2 u when u gt hme?

No. I went straight to bed xx

Tobias: Ok. Jst know I love you. Merry Christmas, baby.

A rush of overwhelming love crashed over me at his words

and endearment. I was someone's baby. Carrie and Kyle had never called me their baby or their sweetheart or their darling. Vicki was the only one. I'd been her babe for the last four years. I loved being her babe.

But truthfully it never soothed my hurt the way that being Tobias's baby soothed my hurt in that moment.

Merry Christmas. I love you, too. Xx

And it was with his voice in my head and the phantom feeling of his arms wrapped tight around me that I fell asleep on Christmas night feeling loved despite the failings of my parents.

Something seeped into my conscious, an awareness niggling at me to wake up. My heavy eyelids fluttered slowly open and my breath caught in a moment of panic at the sight of the shadowy figure at the bottom of my bed.

Moonlight through the gap in my curtains caught on the tendrils of curls, and as consciousness found its grip I realized that the shadowy figure was Carrie.

Confusion as to why she was there cleared as I remembered it was Christmas and there was a weight at my feet that suggested she was putting my stocking on my bed. Something rustled, and I lifted my head to see she was pushing little gift-wrapped parcels back into the stocking.

Wait.

Carrie was the one who left the stocking at the bottom of my bed?

"Carrie?" Her name came out in a sleepy croak.

"Comet?" she whispered back, sounding surprised and dismayed.

Reaching across my bed, I fumbled for the light switch on the bedside table lamp. Warm yellow light illuminated the room and Carrie, who stood at the foot of my bed staring at me like a deer caught in headlights.

Her curly hair was in disarray, and she was wearing a red terry cloth dressing gown with a massive hood. Kyle had bought her it years ago and although he'd offered to buy her a new one she insisted on keeping it. It used to be a rich ruby red. Now it was faded and worn and well used.

My gaze moved from her to the Santa's stocking lying across the bottom of the bed. "*You* give me the stocking?"

She stared at me and then concluded, "You thought Kyle did."

I nodded, pushing myself into a sitting position. It was still dark out and my eyes were heavy with unfinished sleep.

Carrie sighed and suddenly slumped down onto the end of my bed. "I… I overheard your argument with Kyle."

Apprehension gripped me and I froze. Was this the part where she berated me? Called me a sullen teenager?

"You said you know what happened to me as a kid, but I somehow doubt that. At least I hope you don't know." Her words were bitter. "I grew up in a very bad house, Comet."

Something in the way she said it made my heart thump hard, like without her having to say the actual words, I knew that *bad* meant something far more sinister.

"I never wanted you to be as lonely as I was growing up," she whispered, the words thick and drawn, like they were being pulled through the resistance of thick mud. "I never meant for that with you. I'm…just…this is me." She shrugged, seeming exhausted, defeated, and yes, ashamed. "I am who I am, and I probably won't ever change. If I was a stronger person I'd try, although I reckon it's too late now anyway." For the first time in my life my mother looked at me with longing. "I wish I was stronger. I wish I was different. That I could be the kind of parent you deserve. And I'm sorry I couldn't be what you needed. But I am not sorry you turned out the way you did. I know you think I don't see you, but I do. And you are so much braver, stronger and truer than I'll ever be. Be thankful for that, kid." She stood up and walked toward the door. "Be thankful that you turned out better than either of your parents."

She left, shutting the door behind her.

I stared at the closed door for a while, trying to process her words. Finally, exhausted in body but now awake in mind, I flopped onto my back and gazed up at the glow-in-the-dark stars stuck to my ceiling.

The happy ending that in my hearts of hearts I'd one day hoped to find with my parents had just been obliterated by Carrie's confession. In that happy ending I'd dreamed of my parents admitting they had been wrong to treat me so negligently and then we'd start all over again as a happy, close-knit family, where love was shared without jealousy or insecurity.

However, both of them had admitted in the last twenty-four hours that they weren't capable of that. Yet...they'd also made an admission of wrongdoing. That was something. Not everything, but it was something to hold on to.

The hope that I could have a dream relationship with them had finally died. But the more I lay there thinking it over, the more I realized that it was okay.

Sad. Painful.

But okay.

Because now I could hope for things that might really come true.

26

I'd never win a prize for orienteering,
Always wandering around, feeling lost.
Yet today I stopped disappearing,
And to be seen I'll happily pay the cost.
—*CC*

School Christmas holidays? Blink and you would have missed them.

Before we knew it we were back at Blair Lochrie High School, and without our having to say a word to one another, I knew both Tobias and I were a little anxious about the reception we'd receive. Although the situation with Stevie and his evil band of delinquents had dissolved before Christmas, we were still apprehensive. Would they start their torment again?

Tobias and I had Spanish before lunch, so we headed to the cafeteria together, meeting up with Steph and Vicki just outside the doors. My eyes automatically zeroed in on the pool table.

It was occupied by first years.

No Stevie.

No Jimmy or Forrester or any of the guys.

I looked at Tobias and saw he was staring in the same direction. Feeling my gaze, he looked at me and gave me a reassuring smile. Perhaps it was something to do with the fact that we'd had sex, but over the holidays he and I had grown so close it was like we knew what the other was thinking without having to say a word.

"I'm starving," Steph groaned, leading us toward the lunch line. "It's all this studying. My brain hurts and my stomach is grumpy."

Our exams started in one week and we'd all been cramming since the break. Tobias and I had spent a lot of time together studying, being distracted by each other's lips and other body parts, and then studying again. Sometimes we met up with Vicki and Steph for a group study, and I found we were more productive that way because we weren't allowed to be distracted with one another in company.

"Amen, sista," Vicki joked, grabbing a bottle of soda out of the fridge. "My mum won't let me drink coffee so I'm finding my caffeine fix in Irn-Bru. Lots and lots of Irn-Bru."

It didn't sound like such a bad idea, so I grabbed a bottle for myself. I didn't even bother offering one to Tobias because, to my horror, he hated the Scottish soda drink. He said it tasted like wet pennies. When I'd asked him how he knew what wet pennies tasted like, he'd responded that he'd once swallowed one when he was a toddler and his dad had almost had heart failure rushing him to the emergency room.

"King." Luke, his teammate turned around in line. "Ye ready for practice tonight?"

"Yeah, looking forward to it."

"Aye, me, too." His eyes flicked to me. "How's it goin', Comet?"

"Hi," I answered somewhat shyly, because he was Luke Macintyre. Before Tobias had arrived, Luke had been the hottest guy in school. Plus he was older than us.

His dark gaze drifted over Vicki and Steph and then *flew* back to Vicki. "Hi," he said, with undisguised interest.

Vicki gave him this cool *I don't care who you are* nod.

Luke smirked and then turned his attention back to Tobias. "The team is over there." He pointed to a table at the back of the room where four other guys, including Andy, were sitting eating and chatting. "Sit with us." His eyes flicked back to Vick. "All of ye."

"Yeah, we'll get you over there," Tobias agreed.

Luke was soon served, and he sauntered through the cafeteria with the swagger of a boy who knew himself, liked himself and knew most others liked him, too.

"God, he's hot," Steph sighed.

"He's all right." Vicki shrugged.

I snorted, and she threw me a narrow-eyed look over her shoulder.

"What?"

"Nothing. I just think he thought *you* were more than all right."

"He fancies Vicki?" Steph wrinkled her nose and then asked Tobias, "Does he fancy Vicki?"

"I would know the answer to that how?" He paid for his lunch and when I went to pay for mine, I discovered he'd paid for it, too.

"You didn't have to do that," I said.

He just grinned at me.

"I take it we're done talking about whether or not Luke fancies Vicki, then," Steph huffed.

"Yes, we are," Vicki huffed right back, paying for her food. "Anyway," she said as we walked toward the boys' table. "I have to concentrate on my portfolio for LCF. I don't have time for rugby players."

"Do you not want to sit with them?" Tobias said.

"Oh, I can be friends with them," Vicki replied. "I just can't Netflix and chill with any of them."

It was Steph's turn to snort. "As if you've ever Netflixed and chilled with anyone anyway."

"Like any of us have," Vicki argued. Although Vicki had known I was eventually planning to have sex with Tobias, I hadn't yet told her that he and I had already taken our relationship to that level.

Tobias and I shot each other a look, mine knowing, his heated, and I squirmed at the reminder of our times together. I thought we'd been discreet, but I heard a choked noise behind me and turned to see Steph and Vicki staring at me wideeyed. Steph's mouth dropped open but before she could say a word, Vicki nudged her. As for me...well my face must have been the color of a tomato by the time we got to the boys' table, knowing the girls would reenact the Spanish Inquisition as soon as they had me alone.

I willed my embarrassment away as Tobias introduced us to the three sixth years we didn't know—Michael Haddow, David Okonkwo and Mike Green. They were friendly enough, welcoming us to the table, seeming happy to have us join them.

"So you guys are in King and Andy's year?" Mike asked.

Steph nodded. "Yeah. We're the cream of the fifth year crop."

"I believe it." Michael winked at her.

My friend blossomed under the attention, taking turns flirting with all three plus Andy. Tobias joined in on the banter with the boys while I tried to overcome my boy shyness by joking back and forth with Steph. But my ears were also on Vicki and Luke's conversation. As soon as we'd approached the table, Luke had touched Vicki's wrist and gestured for her to take a seat next to him.

"Fashion design?" I heard him ask her. His eyes never left her face as she answered.

"Yeah."

"So ye could make a pair of trousers, shirt, dress, anything?"

She nodded, smiling at his seeming awe. "I made a lot of the costumes for the school show at Christmas. *Chicago*."

His eyes widened. "No way. I saw it. My wee sister was in the chorus. Ye made all those costumes, really?"

Vicki grinned harder. "Really."

"That's amazing. I couldnae even work the sewing machine in home ecies in first year. Baked an epic Victoria Sponge, but dinnae ask me to thread a sewing machine."

My friend chuckled. "Well, I can't tackle a six-foot-two guy and live to tell the tale so I guess we all have our talents."

Luke smiled, his gaze moving over her face and then her hair. He stared at it. "You have really cool hair."

"I know," she said with attitude as if to say, *I don't need you to tell me I have cool hair.*

Instead of being offended he laughed. Hard. Drawing his teammates' attention from conversation with each other.

Luke's answer to their questioning stares? "She's funny."

They nodded, throwing Vicki curious looks, and just like that she and Luke were pulled into talking with the rest of the table. It surprised me how easy it was. How comfortable. The boys were laid-back and funny without being mean-funny like so many teenage boys I'd encountered. I could see why Tobias liked them all. And it seemed they liked us, too. We laughed a lot that lunchtime, and I wondered how it was possible that the new school term could be starting out so different from the term before.

I'd been alone and mostly content with my isolation.

Now the thought of sitting in this cafeteria by myself reading a book made me feel anxious.

"Don't you have a free period next, Comet?" Steph asked, jolting me from my musings.

"Hmm?"

"Free period, next?"

"Uh yeah. I have two actually."

"Andy and I do, too. We were going to study together in the library. You'll join us, right?"

"I.e. help us?" Andy joked. And then he explained to the rest of the table, "Comet is wicked smart. She's on the road to being Dux of our year."

I blushed at the acknowledgment. Dux was Latin for leader and the title given to the student who held the highest academic ranking. To be honest there were a few of us in our year good enough to be Dux. "Maybe. Maybe not."

Michael nudged David. "Okonkwo is most definitely going to be the Dux this year."

David nodded confidently. "Probably." He smiled at me appreciatively. "No need to be embarrassed, Comet. Smart girls are hot."

While everyone chuckled, I glanced at Tobias, who turned to David and just stared at him, a detectable warning in his expression that made the guys hoot with laughter. David held up his hands in surrender. "I didn't mean anything by it, King. Cool your jets."

Tobias threw his arm around my shoulders and grinned wolfishly at David. "All good."

I rolled my eyes, blushing harder at his public claiming.

After lunch Tobias kissed me goodbye and me, Steph, Vicki and Andy walked toward the library. Vicki's home economics class was in the same direction.

Steph groaned as we walked. "Com, you are so lucky to have Tobias be so into you."

"Lucky?" Vicki huffed. "She's not a dog. He doesn't have ownership papers for her."

"Oh don't make this about feminism." Steph pulled a face. "Next you'll stop shaving under your arms and claiming equal rights for women when what you actually mean is better rights for women than what men have."

Vicki looked murderous. "It's misconceptions like that about feminism that give feminists a bad name. It's bad enough guys are making those kind of comments, Steph, we don't need girls saying them, too."

"Oh really. Well…the glass ceiling is made up." She stuck out her tongue, obviously purposely riling Vicki.

My best friend shot me a pleading look. "I'm going to kill her."

Steph and Andy laughed, and I grabbed Steph's arm, pulling her away. "Stop teasing her."

"Why, when it's so much fun?"

"You suck," Vicki threw over her shoulder as she marched away.

"Go find Luke. He'll make it better!" Andy shouted after her.

She flipped him the bird without looking back, making us laugh harder.

"So you saw that, too?" Steph asked Andy. "He seemed into her, right?"

"Oh he fancies her all right." Andy grinned.

The two of them had their heads together as we walked into the library, and I just knew I was going to have a hard time getting them to study. It turned out they were both the worst gossips ever. Of course, that meant they loved each other. In Steph's case, I could see as the afternoon wore on, that it was a platonic kind of love. As for Andy, if that glowing look in his eyes when he looked at her meant anything, I sensed unrequited love on the horizon.

As useless as my study buddies that afternoon proved to be, they were a good distraction. English was the last class of the day and it was the first time I'd see Mr. Stone since the break. I hadn't been able to drum up anyone to join the lit magazine among my friends, so I was eager to hear if he'd had more luck finding us a team. I hadn't had much time to ponder the magazine over the break, between studying and the mess that was my family. Christmas Day had been the beginning of a strange shift in the Caldwell household. My parents had clearly decided to pretend that none of the conversations/ discussions/accusations/heartwrenching revelations had occurred. They treated me as they normally would.

However, the change was between them. They barely touched each other, or even looked at one another. They shared a polite friendliness that was completely off. I'd stewed over it during the rest of break, wondering if Kyle and Carrie had argued over our situation. Had it brought up truths neither of them had wanted to face?

It was odd to see them act so distant with one another but I had decided as soon as I realized something had changed between them that I wouldn't feel guilty about it. I wouldn't put that on myself.

That didn't mean I didn't think about it, however, and that mixed with studying and falling deeper and deeper in love with my boyfriend meant I'd been distracted from the lit magazine project. That had to change. This term that magazine was going to be a priority.

Now, walking to class, my determination to put my attention and focus into the magazine was put on hold when I looked outside the first-floor window I was passing and caught sight of something that distracted me again.

It was Stevie.

He was in the schoolyard walking away from the building. A pang echoed in my chest at the sight of him in a thin sweater, tracksuit bottoms and the scarf and hat I'd bought him. He was wearing it again.

A car pulled up outside the school gate as Stevie approached and Dean Angus got out of it. He and Stevie did some kind of street handshake, and my eyes narrowed on the flash of something that passed between their hands. Had Stevie just given him money?

My stomach flip-flopped again but this time for an entirely different reason. And the feeling only worsened when Stevie got into the car with Dean and it sped off, wheels squealing on the tarmac.

Stevie had made it quite clear again and again that he was

in that life now. It didn't make it any easier to see it or take away my concern for him.

Feeling grim, I continued to English.

"You look a little pale," Tobias said as I slid into the seat beside him. His brows were creased as he brushed his thumb tenderly over my cheek.

I swear I heard someone somewhere behind us sigh loudly in envy.

That someone was Steph, by the way.

"I'm always pale," I tried to tease but my smile faltered.

"You sure you're okay?"

I didn't want to tell him my paleness was only half due to natural skin pigmentation, the other half due to my worry for Stevie's situation. Over the past few weeks any mention of Stevie made Tobias close up like a clam, so I'd stopped trying to talk about his cousin.

Mr. Stone walked into class saving me from having to make a decision about whether I should tell Tobias I'd seen Stevie cutting school for Dean. And as soon as class was finished, I told my boyfriend I'd meet him later so I could talk with Mr. Stone about the lit mag. I waited for the class to empty and before I could say anything, Mr. Stone grinned. "It's ready to go." He gestured me over to his computer and I waited impatiently for him to log on. "For now, Mrs. Penman would like us to see how popular the website proves before thinking of putting the magazine into print distribution."

After typing in a web address, our new lit mag website loaded.

A felt a little flutter of excitement in my belly. A red banner across the top of the page and in white One Trick Pony font were the words *Free Verse*. Underneath was the subtitle "Blair Lochrie High School Literary Magazine."

"Obviously it isn't live. And we can change the name if you don't like it."

"I love it." I grinned. "This is amazing. Do we have a team yet?"

"We're getting there. I've got a couple of fourth years interested, and Pamela Perry."

I tried not to blanch. Pamela was one of Heather's minions. But, I shrugged it off. If the girl wanted to be part of the magazine, I wasn't going to stop her. "She knows I'm the editor?" I asked tentatively.

"She does. Have you had any luck recruiting a team?"

I shook my head. "I'll try again." And I would. I wanted this magazine to work.

"I'm going to advertise the magazine in school and on our school social media accounts, asking people to submit their poetry and short stories. Exams will be over in a few weeks and hopefully by then we'll have enough material to get to work on launching the magazine. And of course, we'll have material from you."

I nodded, even though the thought of publishing my work created raucous flutters in my stomach. "I'll send you the poem I was thinking of kicking the magazine off with."

"Great." He straightened up from the computer. "Another thing. I was wondering perhaps if your father might like to get involved with the project. Having his name attached to the magazine would certainly bring outside interest. If the magazine proved popular, even just within the city, it would go a long way to bolstering your applications for universities."

The thought of my dad being a part of the magazine made

my toes curl in my shoes in irritation. The feeling warred with the desire to get into the college of my dreams.

"Comet?"

I nodded, slowly, a little miserably, as I realized I'd have to swallow my pride for the good of the magazine. "I'll ask him."

"Really? Wonderful. I'm sure he'll be proud to be involved when it means so much to you. *I'm* really proud of you, Comet."

I beamed, worries about my asking dad momentarily fading. "Thanks, Mr. Stone. For everything." At his pleased nod of acknowledgment I began to walk out of his classroom. He called my name, halting me at the doorway.

"I also wanted to say that I like very much what I've seen from Tobias since you two have become…friends. It's a wonderful relationship you two have."

I grinned at his approval, thanked him and left. And as I walked down the almost empty corridors I shook my head in wonder.

Never in a million years had I ever imagined finding my place in high school. I'd always accepted the fact that I'd have to wait for university and hope that I found my niche there.

However, it turned out that maybe I didn't need to wait to be found.

Finally, surprisingly, I was no longer lost here.

After school I found Dad in our kitchen, sipping coffee and reading the newspaper. He looked up as I wandered into the room with butterflies fighting in my belly. As our gazes connected, I felt a rush of all the different emotions my parents made me feel. Longing, hurt, resentment, weariness, begrudged pride. But I didn't want to feel that way anymore.

Nothing would change our relationship, but I didn't have to be bitter about it anymore. I had a chance at a wonderful life and of maybe succeeding at making my dreams come true. Would I really let bitterness stop me from reaching for what I wanted?

No.

I wouldn't.

"I have a favor to ask," I blurted out.

Dad's eyebrows rose and he sat back in his chair expectantly. "Okay."

"It's kind of important to me."

"I'm listening."

"I asked my English teacher, Mr. Stone, if I could set up a literary magazine and be the editor. It would help with my application to universities. And he said yes."

He smiled. "That sounds wonderful, kid. I'm proud of you."

I moved farther into the room, not sure how I felt about him telling me he was proud of me. So I didn't touch it and plowed forward. "Mr. Stone thinks if you put your name to the magazine, like as an honorary staff member or something, it will draw more attention to it. That you would give it a higher profile beyond the school. And he thinks the more popular it is, the more impressive it will be on my university applications. You wouldn't have to do much," I reassured him. "Just maybe contribute a bit of writing to it every few months or something, and let us put your picture on the staff member page."

"Okay." Dad shrugged.

I blinked, taken aback. "Okay? Just like that?"

"If it's important to you, why not? It won't take up much of my time and it would be nice to be involved in your school. You know if you ever needed me to come in and talk to your class about creative writing, I could do that, too."

I tried not to blush, remembering my lie to Mr. Stone. "Cool. I'll let Mr. Stone know. About talking to our class, as well." I was feeling a little shocked that he'd agreed so easily. "You're sure?"

"Absolutely."

"Right." I gave him a shaky, relieved smile. "Thanks, Kyle."

His smile was soft, almost sad. "You're welcome, Comet."

27

Today I was a bird,
The sky my vast stage.
"Free" not just a word,
As I left behind my cage.
—CC

To no one's surprise Luke asked Vicki out. To everyone's surprise but my own she told him to ask her again once the exams were over. I could tell by her smart quips toward him that she liked him. Jordan had put her on the defense at the beginning of school. I think testing Luke to see if he would still be interested in two weeks—which let's face it was like a year in teenage-boy-attention-span-time—helped her make the decision to say yes to him when he asked her out. And he not only asked her out, he waited outside the hall where her final exam was taking place and asked her as soon as she walked out the door.

We all found a rhythm together, us and the rugby boys eating lunch together every day; sometimes we'd welcome other classmates, sometimes it was just a few of us. Tobias and I even went out on a double date with Vicki and Luke.

Steph did not feel left out, because Steph was enjoying basking in the attention of *all* boys. Andy, thankfully, seemed to realize quite quickly that he wasn't going to get anywhere with Steph and he turned his attention to a girl on the Portobello girls' junior rugby team. She was taller than him. And possibly stronger. But the boy was smitten.

As for me I hadn't escaped my friends' curiosity over *the look* Tobias and I had shared in the cafeteria that day. They'd asked me outright if Tobias and I had had sex and I admitted we had. Vicki was full of curious questions while Steph seemed happy, but as always there was an undercurrent of competition there. It wouldn't surprise me if my friend decided not to remain a virgin for very long. She hated to be left behind. Vicki on the other hand could not be moved to do something she wasn't ready for. Like me she'd wait until it felt right.

Tobias and I…well we were better than great. Closer than ever and yet both excelling separately. His improvement on the rugby team really impressed his coach. To the disgruntlement of the current fly-half player, Tobias was to play the position in the next game, and if he did well he could become the team's permanent fly-half. Although Tobias had attempted to explain the game to me, I still wasn't clear what all the positions meant. I did know that the fly-half was similar to a quarterback in football, so it made sense that Tobias would be good in that position. Thankfully, he wasn't displacing any of his friends at school but someone from the private boys' school just outside Porty, so he could avoid any awkward tension it might cause.

Our friends already had their set positions on the team. David, being the tallest and broadest of all the boys, was strong so he was the team's prop. I think he basically did what the title said—he propped up his team players in the scrum. I think.

Luke was the hooker, and as funny as the title was, I gathered from how the other guys were with him that he was a pretty important player. Both Michael and Mike were wingers. Don't ask. I couldn't tell you.

And Andy was a scrum-half.

Again, who knows?

I was hoping the more games I went to the more I'd understand what was going on and what all the rugby jargon meant.

The point was that Tobias was doing well. Every day he seemed to shed a little of his grief and anger. Of course, I knew he'd never get over what had happened to his dad and the circumstances surrounding his death, but I felt like he was finally moving on.

As for me, Mr. Stone was ecstatic Dad had agreed to join the lit mag, and my English teacher and I had moved full-speed ahead with the magazine. He advertised it in class and we'd set up an email address for people to submit their poetry, short stories and essays. We'd put together a small team that included ourselves, Pamela Perry and the two fourth years Mr. Stone mentioned whom I'd never met before—two girls, Amy and Lucy. Moreover, I'd gathered the courage to ask the boys if they'd be interested in the lit mag, and Andy'd said he wanted to join us. He also brought along a boy called Thomas whom Andy knew from the football team. It was an eclectic mix of people with differing opinions. Sometimes they were frustrating and sometimes they were fun. What was really fun, however, was the fact that we got submissions from students. Actual submissions. Andy took leadership over the layout of the website and magazine, and we worked with him on the look and feel of it, while we worked out which pieces to publish first.

Some had sent in their work anonymously through private email addresses, while others were brave enough to own it, sending it from their school email account. And every time I read a piece of work that had been written by someone who wasn't afraid to admit it was their work, I felt a surge of something inside of me.

Whatever the feeling was, it was pushing me to be brave, too.

With life at school incredibly busy, it was the end of January before I knew it and the morning of my seventeenth birthday. For the first time I was truly excited for it, because I had people who cared about me and wanted to share it with me.

Tobias and Vicki had already blown my phone up with happy birthday texts and gifs.

I wasn't expecting much from my parents, who had continued to avoid each other by burying themselves in work. Every birthday was the same as Christmas. I got vouchers for the bookstore.

Lucky me, my birthday fell on a Saturday this year and I was meeting my friends for a celebratory breakfast at the Espy. Dressed in a blue velvet dress with buttons up the front, a white Peter Pan collar and puff-sleeves, I felt girly and happy. I loved velvet. The skirt hit me just above the knee, so I'd paired the dress with thick dark pink tights. It was still too cold and wet for flats, so I was wearing black wedge boots that were mostly made up of a large fur collar. Over the dress, I wore my blue winter coat and dark pink scarf, bobble hat and gloves.

Stopping in at the kitchen for a quick glass of water, I was startled by the sound of Dad's voice behind me.

"Happy birthday, Comet."

I spun around to find him standing in the doorway, wearing an expression I didn't quite understand. "Thanks."

"Seventeen." He pushed off the doorway, and my gaze snagged on the wrapped gift in his hands. Surprise held me immobile. "I can't believe it. You'll be eighteen before we know it." Words unsaid hung heavily in the air: *and then you'll be gone.*

I frowned, wondering at the melancholy in his tone, confused by it.

"Anyway, happy birthday." He handed me the present.

Staring at the book-shaped package, I didn't move to open it for a moment. I was bemused by the whole encounter. Finally, I carefully tore the wrapping and a soft gasp escaped me. The smell of real leather hit my nostrils as I smoothed my fingers over the handmade leather wrap journal he'd given me. It even had leather ties. It was thick and lush-feeling, and when I opened it to find lined paper inside, I was startled to discover a handwritten inscription on the first page.

Comet,
I have no doubt that as long as you put you into your writing people will fall in love with the beauty of your words. You're the best person I've ever known, kid.
Love always,
Dad

Tears filled my eyes and clogged my throat as the words blurred together from my emotion. They seemed surreal. Like words written for someone else in some other house on a beach thousands of miles away.

But Kyle had written them.

My dad had written them for me.

And although the gesture could never wipe away the tears of the past, I would cherish them anyway.

At the feel of his lips on my temple, a tear splashed down my cheek. I waited until I heard his footsteps fade out of the kitchen and down the hall before I looked up, wiping the tear away. I hugged the journal to my chest, already designating it as the journal only the poems I felt most strongly about would be written in.

A little melancholy clung to me as I walked down the esplanade to the pub, wishing my dad and I could somehow magically unite to rewrite our past. We couldn't. Still…his words meant a lot to me.

The lingering sadness I felt, however, was pushed to the depths of my mind as soon as I walked inside the pub to a chorus of shouts of "Happy birthday!" My gaze flew toward the table opposite the bar and right next to the bay window looking out over the beach.

Tobias, Vicki, Luke, Steph and Andy were standing at the table and Steph was waving a Happy Birthday banner back and forth. I grinned at my friends, skipping up the small set of steps to greet them. Tobias approached me first, enveloping me in his warm, strong hug—a hug that I'd become addicted to. Truly. If I didn't get a hug from Tobias at least once a day it put me in an irritable mood. If I was a better person I'd suggest he donate his hugs to charity the way puppy dogs were used in children's hospitals to cheer them up.

But I was selfish and wanted to keep his supply of hugs to myself.

"Nice outfit," Vicki praised as I shrugged out of my coat

after hugging all of them. Tobias held out my chair for me as I thanked him and Vicki at the same time. "You look great."

"So does my vintage baby doll," Steph laughed at Andy, expecting him to chuckle with her. He just raised an eyebrow, clearly sensing an undercurrent in her words but being a boy not understanding.

But I understood cattiness. And I was braver than I used to be. I grinned at her, deciding to kill her with kindness. "We get it, Steph. You hate the way I dress. It embarrasses you. I'm sorry about that, but this is me."

She looked mortified. "I didn't mean... I mean..."

"Anyhoo!" Vicki rescued us all. "Presents!"

The awkward moment dissipated as I was spoiled like I'd never been spoiled before. Vicki and Steph had gone in on a gift together, buying me five cloth-bound books from the new Penguin Classics collection that I'd been mooning over for weeks. Along with that they'd given me a box of my favorite chocolates. To my delight both Andy and Luke gave me a birthday card with vouchers for books inside it from them and the rest of the guys.

Tobias was last, handing me a small, neatly wrapped gift. "Maybe you could open it later."

I nodded, my curiosity piqued. "Of course."

"Aw, did ye get her somethin' cheesy ye don't want the rest of us to see, King?" Luke teased.

Tobias sighed. "Whatever."

"He did." Andy laughed. "Oh come on, Com, open it. Let us see."

"Nope." I tucked the gift into my bag. "For my eyes only."

Tobias smiled at me in gratitude. "So birthday girl...breakfast is on us. What do you want?"

"Do you even have to ask?"

He and Vicki exchanged a look. "Belgian waffles."

I giggled happily.

Best birthday ever.

It was only proved as such later that night when I snuck Tobias into my room. We'd spent the whole day with our friends in the city. First we'd gone to the cinema to see the latest Marvel flick, and then we'd just wandered around, checking out shops together, having a laugh.

Being with them all was great. Having them in my life was something I hadn't even realized I was missing. Yet, I was also desperate to get Tobias alone so I could open his present.

"Finally!" I threw myself on my bed and immediately dived into my bag for the gift.

I was aware of Tobias taking a seat on the armchair across from me but I was mostly focused on the present.

Caressing the paper, I was at once excited and nervous. There was always a chance of not liking a gift someone I loved gave me and I wasn't sure I was very good at lying.

"Would you open it already?"

I bit my lip at his nervous impatience. "Sorry." I tore the paper, and my heart started to pound when I realized it was a Thomas Sabo jewelry box. Inside I discovered a thin rose-gold double-banded bracelet. The metal of the bracelets was twisted to make it look like rope. Decorating the middle was a rose-gold, unopened lotus flower inside a larger opened flower. Four tiny crystals embellished the inner flower, sparkling and catching in the light. A card fell out as I picked up the delicate, beautiful bracelet, and I opened it only to suck in my breath at the words he'd scrawled on it.

Every beautiful thing I see reminds me of you so it was hard to choose just one. But I thought you'd like this one best.

Happy 17th Birthday, Comet.

I love you more each day.

Tobias

I looked up, tears shimmering in my eyes, at his expectant, wary expression. "Do you like it?"

Carefully, I placed the card and the bracelet aside and then I launched myself across the room at him. His surprised laughter was cut off by my kisses.

He temporarily broke free of my passion to say breathlessly as he carried me across the room toward my bed, "I guess you like it."

"Love it," I corrected him, laughing as we bounced across my mattress.

"Shh." He reminded me my parents were upstairs and I tried to stifle my giggles. "We better be quiet or Kyle will kick me out before I give you your other present."

At his wicked expression I muffled more laughter. "So full of yourself, King."

He grinned cockily. "With reason."

I bit my lip to stifle more laughter and then he was kissing me, stifling it for me.

Yeah.

Definitely my best birthday ever.

28

The sky fell down today
And shattered into pieces.
—CC

"It's hopeless," I bemoaned.

"What?" Vicki said, concerned.

"I'm never going to understand rugby!"

As if to illustrate my point something happened on the field and people standing on the sidelines beside us cheered. Including Tobias's mum. "What? What did I miss?"

Lena grinned. "I have no idea. I just went with the crowd. But I think Tobias's team is doing well."

I turned to my best friend. "Please tell me you know what the hell is going on."

"Not a clue." Vicki shrugged. "Luke talks to me about the game and I think I understand what he's talking about while he's talking about it but as soon as he stops it's like all that information just dribbles out of my ears."

"Get used to that, girls," Lena said. "It's called spousal memory loss."

We laughed loudly, drawing a glare from one of our team supporters, which only made us laugh harder. Once we'd calmed we turned our attention back to the game and I concentrated so hard on trying to work out what was going on that I missed the fact that Tobias had scored. Everyone started cheering, so we started cheering, too.

"Did they win?" I cried. "Did they win?"

"I think they won!" Lena grinned.

"They won!" the disgruntled man who had glared at us earlier confirmed, making us cheer with delight again.

Tobias celebrated with manly hugs and pats on the back with his team and coach, and then he and Luke started to make their way toward us. Lena's phone rang, and she frowned at the screen. "Go congratulate the boys. I have to take this." She strode away from the loud crowds as Vicki and I hurried to meet our boyfriends.

"Well done!" I cried as Tobias swung me up in his arms. His skin felt slick and hot, and he smelled of fresh sweat and heat. I kissed him in congratulations, feeling him smile against my mouth, and when I pulled back he grinned from ear to ear.

It was the first time I'd seen this side of him—his triumphant sportsman side. He seemed to vibrate with energy and joy. Being around him was heady. "Wow. I've never seen you like this."

"Like what?" he asked, squeezing my waist to keep my close.

"All jazzed and giddy."

Tobias rolled his eyes in good humor. "I'm a guy, Com. I don't do giddy."

"Well you're the man-version of giddy."

He laughed and hugged me, lifting me right off my feet and I enjoyed the moment.

I'm glad I did.

Because the next…

As my boyfriend lowered me to my feet, his gaze moved

over my shoulder. The smile on his lips died as his brows drew together. "Mom?"

I turned in his arms to find Lena standing in front of us, her mobile curled tight in her fist, her face leached of all color. The bleak expression in her eyes made me freeze in place.

"Mom?" Tobias gently eased away from me to approach her. He touched her arm. "What's wrong?"

"That was Carole," she said, her voice hushed. "Stevie... I'm sorry, son. Stevie's dead. He..." She shrugged, looking as confused and scared as I suddenly felt. "He overdosed."

No.

No!

NO!

My hands flew to my mouth as if to stop the sudden wave of nausea from vomiting out of me. The field around me blurred at the edges and wavered as I swayed on my feet. I was vaguely aware of someone putting an arm around me and asking me if I was okay, but all I could do was stare at Tobias. He stumbled back from Lena, the color drained from his cheeks, and then suddenly he bent over, his heads on his knees as he struggled to draw breath.

His shuddered as his mum put her hand on his back in comfort and his whole body shook with tearless sobs.

Somehow I came unstuck, moving through the thick fog of unreality toward him. He looked up as if he sensed me and stared at me with a wild, frightened gaze that made me halt. And then he pushed up, jerking his mother's hand off him, and he strode away.

Soon he was just a blur, walking away in the distance being

chased by another blur, and it wasn't until I felt arms around me and Vicki's voice saying she was sorry in my ear that I realized I was crying and she was comforting me.

29

He fell into Midnight's dark embrace,
While I could do nothing to stop it.
I hope Midnight leads to a better place,
A heaven lush, sweet, peaceful and sunlit.
—CC

The turnout at Stevie's funeral surprised me.

When a child died it was customary for the headteachers to arrange for the school to be closed so classmates and teachers could attend the funeral. Stevie's funeral fell on a school holiday, so there was no need to formally organize anything or even to discuss it. Stevie's closest friends were all in attendance, including Jimmy, Forrester and Alana. Where Jimmy and Alana looked uncomfortable being there, Forrester openly cried.

There were a few other classmates, but the only teacher in attendance was Vicki's dad. When I asked him why he was the only teacher to represent the school, he didn't answer me.

The cynic in me wondered if it was so the school could distance itself from the circumstances of Stevie's death. His drug overdose hadn't happened on school grounds, and as long as they kept their distance from it they could say that it was a singular case and that drugs were not a problem at Blair Lochrie. Maybe? Was his death even going to matter to them, or had it been swept under the rug to protect the school's reputation and its ranking? Was that what mattered now? Statistics and rank protected at all costs over the welfare of the kids that walked through their bloody door?

Maybe not. Maybe Stevie just hadn't made an impact on any of the other teachers.

But I was angry.

And not really at them. Because *I* should have said something. If I'd spoken up about Stevie, they might have been able to help him.

So I was angry with myself.

I was angry for the people who had been destroyed by stupid mistakes.

My gaze drifted over Carole and Kieran. Standing next to them was an older version of Stevie and very close at his side was, what I had discerned almost immediately, a plain-clothes police officer. The man had to be Stevie's father and, although he didn't cry, there was a deep pain etched into his features that made my chest shudder as I tried to breathe out.

It was unbearable even looking at Carole and Kieran. She was frail and sallow-skinned, a black scarf wrapped around her head, and she was clinging to Tobias's mum for dear life as she cried a continual flow of silent tears. Kieran clung to her hip, his face red and crumpled as he sobbed against her, watching his brother's coffin as it was lowered into the ground.

The thought that Stevie was in there, gone forever, was hard to process, and as I stared across the grave site at my boyfriend, I wondered if that was how Tobias was feeling. Because I couldn't know for sure. He wouldn't talk to me.

It was mid-February and we were on a midterm break from school for the week. Tobias had ignored my calls and texts, so I'd tried going around to his house and his mum had said he was out with the boys. I'd asked Lena how he was doing, and she'd said he wasn't good.

Still…he wouldn't talk to me.

His rejection made me want to retreat into my bedroom and hide with my books like I had done before he blew into my life on a tornado of change. Staring at his stone-like expression as he, Stevie's dad, Jimmy and Forrester helped lower the coffin into the ground, I felt a fear building in my chest. Panic.

I should have told someone about Stevie. Someone who could have done something. An adult. Teachers, his mother, police, someone! But I'd been afraid of getting Stevie in trouble…and wasn't that just the most horrific, ironic piece of crap you'd ever heard?

Tears spilled down my cheeks and I felt Vicki squeeze my hand in hers. She'd been my support this last week, letting me grieve, letting me vent my fears over Tobias.

He regretted choosing me.

The thought turned me to ice, but I couldn't stop repeating it in my head, over and over. Why else was Tobias avoiding me? He wasn't avoiding anyone else. He'd chosen me over Stevie, leaving Stevie to that world, and it had killed him.

Tobias regretted choosing me.

Could I blame him?

I thought if we could just talk about it, we'd get through it, but it was getting him to stand still long enough with me to discuss it that was the issue. Months ago I wouldn't have been brave enough to force a confrontation. I would have turned tail and locked myself in my room and found a book that made me feel better—I'd choose fantasy over reality any day. Yet,

Tobias had come along and changed that for me and, as much as my instinct was to hide, I couldn't if it meant losing him.

Hadn't we lost too much already?

God, he'd lost so much already. The image of Tobias laying his father to rest less than a year ago made me cry harder for him. Then that image was replaced with the memory of Stevie smiling at me in gratitude when I gave him his scarf, hat and gloves. That dissolved into the memory of him hugging me tight in the corridor the day Tobias hurt my feelings. And the memory of him looking at me with such pain in his eyes and telling me he was sorry.

We should have gone after him.

Now it was too late.

I'd never get the chance to make it right. Neither would he. Or Tobias.

Gone.

He was gone.

Those three words just didn't make sense. It didn't seem possible that I would never see him walk through the school halls, or wink at a pretty girl, or laugh by the pool table. He'd never get the chance to find his way out of the mess his life had become. He'd never be able to protect Kieran, who would have no one when his mum died.

The pain for them all was too much, and I shook as I tried to contain the feeling that was desperate to burst out of me. Vicki's arms banded around my chest as she held me to her. I shuddered so hard against her, she trembled trying to hold on to me.

"Shh," she whispered, sniffling, and I realized she was crying for me.

But I wasn't crying for me.

I was crying for all the days—just ordinary simple days with his family—that were lost to Stevie. Lost to them all. It sounds silly to say I was shocked by the revelation of loss, because I had read about characters dying in books, seen them die on film, heard about real people dying all the time on the news.

It was different when it was someone you had known, though. Talked to. Laughed with. Been angry at. Cursed. Hurt for. Someone who was flesh and blood and as real as myself. The reality of it was hard to wrap my mind around. My emotions warred between not feeling like it was real and feeling like it was a nightmare come to life.

Life was temporary.

That realization had never truly taken hold of me until that moment.

Life was temporary, and for most of my life I'd shied away from living it, preferring the company of fictional characters to real people.

Well, no more.

I gained control over the inner keening, breathing slowly in and out until Vicki's hold on me loosened. Looking up from the hole in the ground to Tobias's face, I felt myself tense with resolution. No more. Tobias and I would lose no more.

As if he heard my thoughts, his gaze jerked up from the grave to find me. His eyes seemed to burn into me, filled with so much turmoil I wanted to reach out to him.

And I would.

"Tobias!" I ran after him as he stalked away from the cemetery.

After the minister had laid Stevie to his final resting place, I'd watched as Stevie's dad hugged Kieran tight and said something to Carole that made her crumple against Lena. When he'd tried to reach for her she'd flinched away and Lena had guided her from the scene while the police officer had urged Stevie's dad away.

Kieran had clung to his dad, screaming, and breaking everyone's heart and I'd watched as Tobias had just stared down at the scene, at Kieran, in horror, until Lena had returned to lift the squalling boy into her arms.

Tobias had turned in the opposite direction and started to hurry away.

This time I wasn't letting him.

"Go back, Comet!" he yelled over his shoulder.

"No!" I stumbled up the hill after him. "Talk to me."

"Look!" He spun around, glaring at me with tears in his eyes. He exhaled slowly and continued more calmly, "I just need some space right now. Okay? We'll talk later. But not right now. God, Comet, just give me that."

I bit my lip, unsure what was the best thing to do. If I pushed him harder, I'd maybe push him away for good. "Okay."

Relief made his shoulders relax, and he gave me a brittle nod before he turned around and walked away.

Despite my numerous attempts to call him, Tobias didn't answer. I received one text.

Tobias: I asked 4 space.

Although it hurt I decided to let it go and let him have his space over the midterm break. Once we'd returned, however, I was determined to get him to talk to me again. I couldn't help feeling that if he hadn't pushed me away, we'd both have had an easier time dealing with Stevie's death.

I missed Tobias.

I felt like he'd been taken away, too.

The Monday of our return, Tobias didn't even look at me when he walked into Spanish first period. An ugly feeling churned in my stomach the entire class, and I tried to tell myself everything would be okay. That was, until he stayed behind to ask Señora Cooper something, and I had no choice but to leave the class without talking to him. Was that deliberate on his part? Or did he really have something to ask her?

By the time English came around for fourth period, I'd worked myself into a jittery mess. I had a strategy to break the ice between us and I really hoped it worked.

He was there before I was, staring straight ahead with this cold expression that warned people not to approach him. I shot a look at Vicki and Steph who were already seated, and they gave me sympathetic smiles. They knew I planned to use this class to get him to talk to me if I could.

"Hey," I said as I took my seat next to him.

He gave me a nod of his chin without looking at me, and I tried to batten down the anger that threatened to rise inside me.

We were twenty minutes into class when Mr. Stone left the room to collect some mock exam papers he'd forgotten in the English office. As the noise level rose around us, I slipped the bit of paper I'd been holding on to all day and placed it in front of Tobias. He frowned but opened it up to reveal a poster for Pan. They were hosting an evening event in a month's time called Youth of Today and were inviting under eighteens to recite their poetry. "What am I looking at?"

Ignoring his snappish tone, I explained, "I'm going to do it, Tobias. I'm finally going to get up on that stage and I'd really like you to be there."

In my head it had seemed like a great icebreaker. It was something he knew I was nervous and afraid of, and I thought it would make him feel good to know that he had helped me get to the point where I wanted to overcome my fears. Be brave. Moreover, the poem I had chosen to read was one I'd written specifically for him.

Yet the way his expression darkened and the cutting look he shot me made me realize Tobias didn't think this was the greatest icebreaker at all. "Are you kidding me?"

I shrugged, blushing, because I didn't understand what I'd done wrong.

"Stevie's dead and you want to talk about your freaking poetry café? Are you that self-centered? Do you not care?"

Stunned by his reaction, by his accusation, I could only stare at him, struggling to find a reply.

He squeezed his eyes closed as if he was in pain, and when he looked at me I knew what was coming before he'd even opened his mouth. "I can't do this with you right now. I need a break. I think we should break up."

30

I'm not your Juliet, you're not my Romeo,
I won't let our love end in drama and woe.

—CC

If anyone asked me how I got through the rest of that class I wouldn't be able to tell them. I had no idea.

All I felt was pain. I remember that much.

Tobias left as soon as the bell rang, while I sat there, stunned. My muscles seemed to hurt when I moved as I forced myself to get up and put my work into my bag. To put my bag over my shoulder and make my feet walk out of the door.

Then Vicki and Steph caught up with me.

"What happened?" Vicki said. "Comet, what's going on?"

My lips felt numb. I bit them, checking they were still there. They were. So I moved them. "He broke up with me."

As soon as the words were out it felt like my chest was going to cave in, like the words had been inside me, holding me up, and as soon as they were out pieces of me just started to collapse. Panic suffused me, because I did not want the added humiliation of breaking down in public.

"I have to go," I spoke over Vicki and Steph, who were surrounding me in concern. "I'm going home."

"Comet, wait—"

"I'm going home." And I just started to run.

I didn't remember the journey to the house. I just knew suddenly my front door was there and beyond it was a place to hide. As soon as I slammed inside I dived for my bedroom, but I was barely in it when I heard my dad call my name. Suddenly he was walking into my room, frowning at me.

"What are you doing home?"

And it was in front of him of all people that I finally fell to pieces, the sob bursting out of me before I could stop it.

It was followed by another and another as my knees gave out.

A strong arm encircled me. "Comet, what happened?" my dad asked, sounding scared, and I realized it was his strong arm around me and he was sitting on the floor with me.

Instead of answering I fell against him and let the shattered shards inside of me rattle with my cries. I'd never felt anything like it.

Tobias was gone from me.

He didn't want me anymore.

He didn't love me.

How could he not love me anymore?

"Comet, you're really scaring me."

I tried to find the words to explain but I was afraid of his reaction. The fear of him making this into some petty high school drama stalled me. It was more than that. Tobias and I hadn't felt like puppy love or a first crush.

He was the first person I'd ever truly loved who had loved me back without question.

Until now.

"Tobias…he broke up with me," I whispered through my tears.

My dad's arm tightened around me. "I am so sorry. I know

how much you love him. Do you want to tell me what happened?"

I shook my head. If I did that, said it all out loud, I was afraid I'd start to believe Tobias had every reason to dump me.

My dad did something cool for me and called the school to tell them I was sick.

I stayed "sick" for four more days.

Ignoring calls from Steph and Vicki, I even refused to come to the door when they turned up at the house. Just last week the thought of missing a lit mag team meeting would have made me panic. Now I couldn't bring myself to care about it.

Instead I locked myself in my bedroom and I read.

I read book after book, losing myself in the world of make-believe, where extraordinary happily ever after endings happened one after the other. Yet...

The HEAs didn't do for me what they used to. Not one of them gave me giddy butterflies the way that a kiss from Tobias did. Not one of them comforted me the way his addictive hugs did. None of them made me feel angry or sad or safe or excited the way he did. The emotions I went through when reading a good book, I discovered, were merely a muted version of what my emotions could be. I'd never known more color or been more awake than when I'd started living in the real world with Tobias.

And I resented the hell out of him for it.

I hated him!

I loathed him!

I wished he'd get on a plane and fly back to bloody North Carolina!

But I didn't.

Not really.

Because I loved him.

Curled up in bed I found myself sobbing hysterically at an ensemble flick I was watching on Netflix. Later, weeks down the line, I'd look back on that moment in horror, realizing just how low I'd been brought.

Crumpled tissues lay scattered across my duvet along with books, cookies and empty packets of crisps. I was not a pretty sight but I couldn't seem to care. Even when my dad walked into the room and stared at me in disbelief. I paused the film, wiping my nose with the back of my hand. "What is it?"

Dad's gaze traveled all over my messy room as he stepped over books and clothes, trying to put his feet on empty floor space. "I was just wondering when you were thinking about going back to school."

"Never."

He took a seat on the bed and stared at me with an expression that raised my hackles. "Are you judging me?" I whined. "Seriously?"

He made a face and gestured to the room. "This isn't really like you."

"My heart's broken. I'm wallowing."

"Yes, well, it seems to me you've gone back into hiding."

"So?"

He exhaled heavily. "I would have thought that Carrie and I were a lesson well learnt."

"What does *that* mean?"

His gaze suddenly burned, piercing through me with sadness. "That you shouldn't let yourself be so consumed by one person that you forget about yourself and the other people around you who care about you."

If he'd thrown a bucket of freezing cold water over me, it would have had the same effect. I shivered, feeling his words deep in my bones. All this time I'd feared being like my parents, and here I was…depending so deeply on another person to love me that I was losing myself.

"Shit," I blurted out without thinking.

My dad just gave me this sad smirk. "Can I take that to mean you'll be going back to school on Monday?"

I swallowed hard, not liking the mirror he'd put in front of me one bit. "Yes." Going back and facing Tobias would be difficult, but it would be easier than being someone I didn't want to be. "Thanks."

He nodded and then seemed to be on the verge of saying something else before he stopped.

"What is it?"

"Well…I don't want to pile too much on you," Dad said, "But you need to know Carrie's going to go traveling for a while. She leaves on Sunday."

Confused by the turn in conversation it took me a moment to say, "Traveling?"

Why was she traveling? And for how long? And why without Dad? What the hell had I missed?

Dad got up off the bed and walked toward the door, this time apparently not caring about the stuff in his way or too lost in his thoughts to remember any of it was there. "Things have been a bit…well…we haven't been…" He sighed and shrugged. "Your mum and I need some space from each other."

I could only stare at him.

Kyle and Carrie Caldwell were taking a break from each other? I knew things had been distant between them but since

Stevie had passed I really hadn't been paying attention to my parents or their relationship. As far as I was concerned it was none of my business. Putting the pieces of the last few months together, I realized that they hadn't been the same since my confrontations with them at Christmas.

Had what I said to Dad finally awakened him like his words had just awakened me?

"Oh. Okay." I didn't know what else to say.

He gave me another sad smile. "We'll survive without her chicken curry for a while."

"I have the pizza place on speed dial," I joked lamely.

His expression told me he appreciated it, lame or not.

My first port of call coming out of my cave was Vicki's. I apologized profusely for pushing her away, but my best friend was admirably understanding.

"I think if Luke broke up with me like that I'd feel the same," she'd said.

Having not realized she felt that deeply for her boyfriend, I wished with all my heart that he never did.

It was with my two friends by my side that I made my way back into school on Monday, trying to keep not only my nerves at bay but the constant desire to burst into tears. It was one thing to tell yourself not to be a codependent crybaby, and another thing to actually try not to be. My parents being brave enough to take a step back from one another was inspiring though, and I thought if they could do it, I could certainly try to move on from Tobias. It would have been easier for me if he'd been nicer to me. However, I discovered right away that Tobias's plan was to ignore me. I wondered if he'd even been worried about my absence from school or if I wasn't even on his radar anymore.

Hurt turned to bitterness and bitterness turned to anger.

As the week wore on with us girls now sitting at a table by ourselves while the rugby boys sat alone, I felt the need to confront Tobias building and building within me. I tried to contain it, because Vicki advised she didn't think that would do any good. Since our breakup, Vicki was kind of stuck in the middle. She'd chosen to sit with me at lunch, but I knew she missed sitting with Luke and with him graduating this year, she wanted to spend as much time with him as possible. Luke tried to be a good guy and take turns between the two tables, but he'd confessed to Vicki that he felt like he should be there for Tobias because he was still having a hard time over Stevie's death.

I hated that for him.

That didn't mean I wasn't still a brokenhearted, enraged ex-girlfriend. But I tried to put a stopper on those emotions, because I didn't want it to lead to a huge argument between Tobias and me. That would make things super awkward for Vicki and Luke, stuck between their two best friends.

I held on to the selfless thought until Thursday lunchtime arrived. Being miserable and pretending not to be miserable for the sake of your friends and for yourself is one of the most exhausting things a person can do. By Thursday I was tired, bitter and resentful. But mostly I was sad and fearing I'd never stop being sad.

It was a scary thought.

So when I walked into the cafeteria and my gaze automatically zoomed in on the rugby table like it always did and

I saw Jess Reed sitting next to Tobias, the anger took over the sadness and I gladly let it.

"Uh-oh," Steph said beside me, having seen the sixth year sitting with my ex.

"That doesn't mean anything," Vicki tried to assure me. "Tobias isn't seeing anyone. Luke would have told me."

Right. Of course he would. I snorted at the idea as my heart pounded harder and faster in my chest. "Bros before hos."

"Did you just call me a ho?"

"You know what I mean."

"Look, let's just get lunch." Steph tried to gently nudge me toward the lunch line.

I shook my head. "I'm not hungry. And I'm not staying here to watch the dipshit flirt with Jess Reed. See you in class."

"Comet!" they called after me, but I was already gone.

Hunger did nothing to abate my anger as I waited in the library for the lunch period to end. English was next, and I'd spent the entire period preparing myself to confront Tobias. I had strapped on my mental boxing gloves, and I was ready to do it because if I didn't I was going choke on my anger.

The image of him and Jess having sex tried to push its way into my head and I wanted to be sick and scream and cry in equal measure. Everyone would look at the two of them and think, "Well, yeah, that makes more sense." I hadn't really given much thought to what anyone else was thinking about our breakup, because I couldn't handle the speculation on top of everything else, but suddenly I couldn't help wondering if they were all laughing behind my back.

I charged into English class, my heart leaping in my chest at the sight of him sitting there. Everyone was chatting away, waiting for Mr. Stone, so I took my opportunity immediately.

Sliding into the seat next to him, I bent my head to his and said, "Jess Reed? Really?"

Tobias startled at the sound of my voice so close and turned to look at me, his expression carefully blank. "What are you talking about?"

I curled my lip at him, somehow loathing and loving his face in equal measure. "I'm talking about you deliberately trying to hurt me."

He sneered. "Being self-absorbed again?"

"Me?" I huffed, pushing my face into his aggressively, causing his eyes to flare. "*I'm* self-absorbed? All this time since Stevie died, all I've thought about is *you* and how *you're* feeling. But never, I bet, have you stopped to think about how *I'm* feeling. You never even noticed when I wasn't at school! I'm a ghost to you." My lips trembled and tears filled my eyes but I forced them away. "I know you blame me, but I'm not to blame for what happened to Stevie. I won't put that on myself. It's not my fault. I will always regret not trying harder with him or telling someone who could actually have done something to stop him, but I'm not to blame for the choice *he* made. Neither are you. You are not to blame, Tobias. You are not to blame for choosing me over him. And you shouldn't regret your decision to not let you or me be pulled into that messy life with him. But if you want to put some misguided blame on yourself and on me, then go ahead. Do it. Hate me and hurt me and don't even care that you do, but I won't take it on. I won't let you make me feel worthless and unlovable again." A tear escaped but I swiped it away, turning my head so I couldn't see the emotion in his eyes, raw pain that would soften me if I let it.

I needed to stay strong, because I believed I had every right to say what I just did.

"I'll walk away from you knowing I didn't do this to Stevie and I wasn't the one who turned my back on the person I loved. You're not guilty of the first, I'll never believe that, but you are guilty of the second. When I think about that, I can't imagine ever pushing you away or shutting you out like you have me… and that made me realize something. That you never really loved me. That's okay," I whispered. "It'll only make it easier for me to get over us."

"Right, class, more exam preparation today I'm afraid," Mr. Stone said walking into the room completely oblivious, as was everyone else, to me finally standing up for myself.

The chair beside me suddenly scraped back but I didn't look.

"Tobias, where are you going?" Mr. Stone demanded.

My ex didn't answer. He just stormed out of class, and I tried really hard not to care.

31

"He's looking over here. Again," Steph said, between bites of her burger.

I missed the days when all she could talk about was the school show. The summer show was *The King and I* and much to Lindsay Wright's chagrin, Steph was playing Anna. Previous evidence would suggest this was enough to keep Steph talking solely about herself for the next few months.

Yet, somehow, ever since I'd caved to their questions and confessed to my best friends what I'd said to Tobias to make him storm out of class, Steph had grown seriously invested in Tobias and me.

Too little too late, since I was determined to move on.

"That's every day this week," Vicki said, giving me this pointed look.

"What?"

"That's he's looked over here. And I keep catching him looking at you in English when he thinks you're not looking."

A flutter in my belly told me I was not immune to the idea that Tobias was looking at me again. But looking was an entirely different creature to speaking. "Look, guys, I know you think you're being helpful but I'm trying to get over him. Okay?"

My friends shared a look that said they didn't believe me.

Affronted, I dropped my burger. When I dropped food they knew I meant business. "Did I not tell you what I said to him? That was one of the most important confrontations of my life. Don't pretend like I'm not trying here."

"Are you trying, though?" Vicki tilted her head to the side like a curious bird. "Really?"

"What's that supposed to mean?"

"It's supposed to mean that tomorrow night is the Youth of Today poetry evening at Pan and a few weeks ago you told me you were going to get up on that stage and read one of your poems. Suddenly, since Tobias broke up with you, that's no longer happening."

I scowled at her. The reason it was no longer happening was because I'd been planning to do it as a grand gesture to Tobias and reading a poem aloud about him. I said as much to her.

That didn't shut her up like I thought it would. "Wait a minute. I thought this whole moving on from Tobias thing was so that you could feel like you weren't a wallowing, self-pitying, codependent Carrie-wannabe? So why are you using him as an excuse not to do something for yourself?"

"Ugh," I huffed. "I hate when you make sense." I really, really hated it.

Vicki grinned, smug. "Good. We're agreed. You're getting on that stage tomorrow night."

"I don't know what to read, though." I hadn't written any-thing uplifting in a while.

Steph shrugged. "The Tobias poem. Just because things

aren't the same between you now doesn't make the poem any less true than it was when you wrote it."

"Says she who hasn't read the poem," Vicki said.

"No, but she's right." I nodded, somewhat surprised by Steph's wise comment. "The poem is still true." Resolve coursed through me. "I'll read it."

"Good. Because he's looking again."

"Is Jess Reed sitting there?" It slipped out before I could stop it.

"No," Steph scoffed. "He's not into her. Hopefully she gets that now."

"Why is he looking?" I grumbled. I didn't need false hope!

"Maybe he wants to come over but he doesn't know what to say," Vicki suggested. "Maybe he thinks you won't want to talk to him."

"Would you want to talk to him?" Steph said.

I shrugged. "I won't know that until he actually tries to speak to me. *If.* I mean if."

"Despite what you said to him, he does love you, Comet," Steph assured me. "I'm admittedly jealous of how much that boy loves you. He's on his way back to you. For sure."

"We'll know tomorrow," Vicki said.

"Tomorrow?"

"He knows about Pan. If he cares about you he'll be there."

Steph frowned. "Unless he forgot. Let's not pin their reconciliation on tomorrow night."

My friends argued about it while my mind drifted. The skin on my neck had been prickling all lunch period, but I didn't know if that was only because the girls had made me paranoid that Tobias kept looking at me.

Giving in to the urge that had been tugging at me all during lunch, I glanced over my shoulder, trying to make it seem casual. As soon as I did my gaze collided with Tobias's. My breath left me, and I wondered how it was possible he could still affect me as much as he had when we first met.

The thought scared me and I whipped back around. "Yeah," I murmured, "let's not pin any hopes on tomorrow." Because it would crush me if he wasn't there.

"Off somewhere?" Dad wandered out of the kitchen, his gaze drifting over me as I shrugged into my coat.

I swallowed a wave of nausea and gave him a shaky smile. "A poetry reading at Pan."

"Is that the poetry café on Tollcross?"

"Uh-huh."

"I didn't know you went there." He stared at me in question.

Ever since Carrie had left to go "traveling," Dad had taken more and more of an interest in my whereabouts. And my life in general. Especially after I'd broken down on him, crying about my breakup with Tobias. He was trying. I couldn't fault him for that, but I was still afraid of being deeply hurt by my parents, and I wasn't sure I understood what was happening in their relationship.

"You've spoken to Carrie recently, right?"

If he was surprised by the abrupt question he didn't show it. "She checks in."

"What's going on there, Dad?"

This time he didn't hide his surprise. "It's complicated."

"But is this for real?" I gestured between him and me. "You being interested in my life, wanting to be a part of it? Is it real? Or does it all fall to pieces when Carrie comes home?"

Dad stared at me so long that I thought he wasn't going to answer, but he did, in a low, gruff voice thick with emotion.

"Whatever happens between Carrie and me, I won't put her before you again. Life is so damn short, Comet. I don't want to live mine knowing I caused irreparable hurt to the one person who deserved it least. I know I can't ever make up for the damage Carrie and I caused…but I can try. I can love you. I *do* love you, kid."

My eyes filled with tears. "Would you still love me if I chose to go to uni in America?"

He gave me a sad smile. "If that's what you want, you go for it. I'll still be here."

"I don't know what I want now," I whispered, confused as to whether I wanted UVA just to get as far from my parents as possible, or if it really was the college of my dreams. I wasn't sure if my dad could live up to his promises, but I also wasn't sure I was ready to traverse an ocean to get away from him, just when it seemed like we might finally have a relationship worth staying for.

Dad was right. Life was short. Stevie's death had proved that. It had also proved that relationships were more important than anything else in my life.

Sensing my fear and confusion Dad strode toward me and placed a comforting hand on my shoulder. "You've got time to think about the future, Comet."

I drew in a shaky breath and did something I would never have imagined doing a year ago. "Will you come with me to Pan? It's my first open mic. I… I'd like you to hear my poem."

His response was a huge smile. "I'd love that."

I was crushed.

Pan was crowded tonight with regular patrons and people who rarely, if ever, frequented the place. There were older people here, some obviously parents, and of course a lot of under eighteens. The café was busier than I'd ever seen it, and yet the person I most wanted there wasn't anywhere to be seen.

My dad stood with Vicki, Mr. Stone and Mrs. Cruick-shank. Steph couldn't make it because she had a date with a college boy she'd met at the swim center last week. However, my one constant—Vicki—was with me. She'd convinced me to tell Mr. Stone about the open mic night and like my dad, his response had been immediate and positive. As for Mrs. Cruickshank, my dad and I had passed her on the esplanade on our way to Pan. She'd been surprised to see us together, and Dad had encouraged me to invite her along. The way she just spun around and started walking with us in response had made me want to cry grateful tears.

I had people here who loved and supported me, and as amazing as that felt, it still hurt not to have Tobias there.

"You've gone paler than normal," Vicki said, looking concerned. "You okay?"

No, I wasn't. I was next up on the stage, and the person who made me brave wasn't here to cheer me on. I said so.

"We talked about this." Vicki squeezed my hand. "Only *you* can be brave. Tobias hasn't got that power. He's not here? Well, screw him. His loss, Comet. You—" she smiled sweetly at me "—are one of my favorite people in the whole world and if he can't see how special you are, then it's his loss. Do this for *you*, Com. For all the people who made you feel like you weren't worthy of them."

I thought of my dad, who seemed to be doing his hardest to make up for it and who'd flinched at Vicki's words, and of Carrie, whom I hadn't heard from at all since she'd left except through secondhand conversations she'd had with my dad, of my primary six teacher who'd traumatized me and made me hate school, of Heather who'd bullied me out of envy, of Stevie, Alana, Jimmy, Forrester and their group for bullying me because it made them feel in control to be the tormentors instead of the tormented for a change, and even of Tobias, who'd made me feel alone when I needed him the most.

But despite that, Tobias had changed my life for the better. *I* had changed.

"She's right," Dad said. "Do this for you, Comet."

And even though I wanted to throw up, I nodded, and heard all of their good lucks at my back as I took the steps one shaky upward movement at a time and approached the mic. I let go of a small exhale and the mic crackled. Unable to look at the faces staring up at me, I looked down at the poem in my hand instead.

"My name is Comet Caldwell," I said, wincing slightly at the way my voice echoed around the room. "I'm seventeen and…this is my poem.

"Before you
Real life was a blurred Monet,
Dripping Tuesday's pale blue
Into Wednesday's dull gray;
All color muted to a lesser hue.

It was hot chocolate gone tepid,
And a winter with no snow.
Sea air somehow turned fetid,
Favorite shoes you outgrow.

Before you,
Real life was without magic,
No acts of heroism in sight.
Just girl, not savior, not telepathic,
No fight of dark against light.

There were no wizards or warlocks,
Angels and demons didn't exist.
Its only charm was in its boardwalks,
Where sand and sea always kissed.

Before you,
I preferred the dreams I could buy;
A plethora of worlds to explore.
Lose myself in the beauty of a lie,
Have friends who never keep score.

Where there's truth in true romance,
And uncool shy girls become heroes.
Where days are filled with thrilling happenstance,
And people have answers nobody here does.

Before you,
I judged without truly knowing,
Let people slip through my hands.
Saw someone flashy and outgoing,
And determined they'd never understand.

You made me see everyone's layers,
All their secrets and fears.
Proving we're all merely players,
Who smile through our tears.

Before you,
I believed real, true, glorious living
Was in adventure, was in the extraordinary.
But I've learned that time is not so forgiving,
And the real beauty of life is in the fragile ordinary."

There was a hush in the air when I was finished and I was afraid to look up. But then someone started to clap and then someone else, until it was loud and warm and pushing up against me, forcing my eyes upward.

"Go, Comet!" I heard Mrs. Cruickshank shout, and watched as my dad and Mr. Stone beamed proudly up at me as they clapped their hands together high and hard. Vicki appeared as stunned as I felt as she clapped.

Strangers grinned and whistled and put their hands together in appreciation for me, and I was so shocked that I almost missed him in the crowd.

Tobias.

Hope flooded upward from the shuttered depths of me. All the hope I'd tried to keep buried inside, because hope had hurt me so much in the past. But I'd come to discover that hope was an uncontrollable creature, and it danced through me now, seeing Tobias here.

I stumbled off the stage, accepting praise, stunned, bewildered even, as I tried to make my way toward Tobias. Suddenly my path was blocked by the tall, rangy body of the owner of Pan. He was an older guy, perhaps in his midforties, with a strawberry blond beard and hair he wore up in a man bun. In the past he'd only ever smiled at me and made me a hot chocolate.

"Comet, right?" He held out his hand to me. "I'm Joe,

Comet. I hope you start coming around to read more of your poetry to us, rather than sitting all the way in the back with a hot chocolate."

Surprised but delighted that he knew who I was, I blushed. "Sure."

"Good. I look forward to it. I enjoyed what you had to say up there. Cool name by the way," he said before stepping aside to listen to the next person up onstage.

I stood stunned for a moment by his praise, but just as quickly as his positivity had warmed me, I remembered whose praise I really wanted. As I searched again for Tobias, the warmth leached out of me when I couldn't find him. Panic suffused me until Vicki found me. She frowned. "He stepped outside. Tobias. He's waiting for you."

The panic receded, but I wasn't so distracted that I didn't see the dismay on her face. "What's wrong? You hated my poem, didn't you?" My euphoria over the reception of my poem died. It was great to have strangers like it, but I wanted the people I cared about to like it more.

"Do I keep score?" she blurted out.

For a moment I was confused until I realized she was quoting my poem. I took her hand. "I was talking about Steph and her competitiveness. And I used to worry a lot that the two of you would want to stop hanging out with me because I didn't want to go to parties. I didn't feel very understood, but that wasn't on you, Vick. That was all me."

Seeming relieved she nodded thoughtfully and then gently pushed me away. "Okay, you can go talk to Tobias now."

I laughed but it was almost hysterical. The mic crackled behind me and realizing someone else was about to read, I quietened and tried to make my way through the crowds before the poem began.

Tobias stood outside the door, staring at the traffic, and just the sight of him made my heart start banging away in my chest even harder than it had when I stood on that stage.

I stopped in front of him, and he straightened up into attention. "Hey."

"Hey."

He scrubbed a hand over his head. "I loved your poem."

"It was about you."

Emotion glimmered in his eyes and he seemed to swallow hard. "Yeah."

"You came."

"You were right. About everything. The day you called me out, you messed me up. The idea of you thinking I didn't love you ripped me apart and I didn't know why, because I wanted to be angry with you. You didn't do anything wrong, but I wanted to be angry with you because it was so much easier than being angry with myself." He exhaled heavily and quickly, like he couldn't get enough air. "When I got home that afternoon my mom kind of went off on one. She was worried about me and she said we were moving back to the States."

My banging heart stopped.

I was sure of it.

The horrible emptiness in my chest couldn't be anything else. "You're going back to America?"

He shook his head quickly. "God no. As soon as she started talking about it, planning, I freaked out. As bad as I feel, as guilty as I feel, about walking away from Stevie when he needed me, the idea of never seeing you again scares the hell out of me, Comet. I'm sorry I made you think that I blamed you. I never blamed you. You were right about me blaming myself, though. I didn't just walk away from Stevie when things got hard with him because it was what I felt I needed to do to protect you. I did it to protect me, too. Losing my dad and learning the truth was hard enough, I didn't think I could deal with Stevie's problems, with Carole's sickness. So I walked away. Not only did I walk away, I got myself a pretty great life. A beautiful girl, a new team, great friends. And Stevie watched me get all of those things while I pretended like my friendship with him never happened. That's on me. I just didn't know how to admit that to myself, so I pretended that choosing you was where everything went wrong.

"I'm sorry, Comet. I told my mom I don't want to leave, so we're staying. And that doesn't mean you have to forgive me or even want to be with me again, and you can even be pissed at me for making such a huge decision based off the fact that I love you because I know you hate the whole co-dependency thing but—"

I cut him off midramble throwing my arms around his neck and tugging his head down to mine so I could kiss him. The feel of his warm lips moving against mine felt so utterly epic, and I poured every emotion inside of me since we broke up into that kiss. Relief and love were the foremost.

Tobias broke the kiss to wrap his arms tighter around me and hug me so hard that he lifted me off the ground. "I missed you so much," he said hoarsely, as I clung to him. "I'm so sorry."

When I was finally back on my feet, I caressed his face and said, "No more apologies."

"I'll try not to do anything where one will be necessary afterward."

"Hmm, I don't think I'm naive enough to believe that will happen," I joked.

He shook his head in wonder. "I know how lucky I am to have you, Comet. I hope you know that."

"It's nice to hear it anyway." I smiled, trying not to cry like a cheeseball.

"And I am so proud of you for getting up on that stage tonight. And doing it in front of your dad…you're amazing."

"Thank you." I studied him, seeing the weary sadness that still lingered in the back of his eyes. "What can I do to be there for you now?"

He frowned. "What do you mean?"

"Stevie."

I felt him tense against me. "I don't have a magic answer to that. I can't help how I feel about him. I should have done something more for him, and that guilt won't just go away. I have to be honest about that."

I nodded, understanding.

Stevie's death had changed Tobias. That was the truth. It had changed us both. It was different for Tobias, because he hadn't found a way to forgive himself yet. Maybe he never would. Maybe it would continue to change him or maybe not.

That was the thing about living in the now and accepting that most people weren't heroic storybook characters. They could be extraordinary, but most days they were flawed and ordinary. And ordinary people had wounds that sometimes never healed.

I loved Tobias. I would accept him, wounds and all, as I

had from the moment we met, just as he had accepted me with all of mine.

When you were in love like we were in love, there existed a temporary forever ahead of you. A knowledge that what we had was for life, but that life was only guaranteed by the second.

Which meant that every second I had a choice to make, I had to choose what would really make me happy. What most people never learned was that sometimes what would make us happy the most also scares us the most. Sometimes being happy meant being brave.

I aimed to be brave every second of every day.

★ ★ ★ ★ ★

ACKNOWLEDGMENTS

Never have I written a book with a heroine I understand as much as I understand Comet. I tapped into so much of who I was as a teenager to write Comet's story and it reminded me of the wonderful friendships from childhood that I am thankful for.

Ashleen, I am so grateful for your friendship and have been since we were twelve years old. You were the first friend I ever met who I felt truly understood me. When we sat in class together that first day of high school it was the first time I didn't feel alone at school. And now here we are twenty years later, still best friends, and you're still there for me even with an ocean between us. If your friendship wasn't enough, you handle almost everything else business-related in my life. Because of that I could give all my focus to Comet's story. You're a rock star.

Also a big thanks to Shanine. You've taught me so much about what it means to be a good person, and I've learned by listening to how passionate you are what it means to be a fantastic teacher. Whenever I write a great teacher into my story, you are my muse. As are you, Kate. You are brilliant in every way. Thank you for all your advice regarding Mr. Stone and high school English.

Moreover, thank you to Margo Lipschultz for believing in me as a writer, for seeing the potential in Comet's story and asking me to pursue it. And a massive thank you to my editor at Harlequin Teen, Natashya Wilson, not only for helping mold *The Fragile Ordinary* into the best possible version of itself, but for truly understanding Comet. It's been an absolute pleasure working on her story with you.

Furthermore a huge thank you to the art team at Harlequin Teen for producing one of my favorite covers ever. I smile every time I see it.

These acknowledgments wouldn't be complete without thanking my wonderful mum and dad. Comet and I may share many similarities but I'm glad to say I do not share her bad luck in parents. You are the best parents anyone could ask for. Thank you for dog-sitting my two little tornadoes while I hid myself away in the Highlands for a week to finish this book. I'm fortunate to know I can always count on you.

Speaking of, thank you to my agent Lauren Abramo. You always, always have my back. It means so much to me and I know I've said that a lot but it bears repeating.

And finally, as always, to you my reader: the biggest thank you of all.